MW01103777

Mr. Jones

Also by Margaret Sweatman

The Players

When Alice Lay Down with Peter

Sam & Angie

Fox

MARGARET SWEATMAN

Mr. Jones

GOOSE LANE

Edited by Bethany Gibson.
Cover and page design by Julie Scriver.
Cover image: detail from *Grand Central Station* (1950) by Harold Roth,
courtesy of Anton Alterman/Harold Roth Photography.
Printed in Canada.
10 9 8 7 6 5 4 3 2 1

Library and Archives Canada Cataloguing in Publication

Sweatman, Margaret, author
Mr. Jones / Margaret Sweatman.

Issued in print and electronic formats.
ISBN 978-0-86492-914-3 (bound). — ISBN 978-0-86492-783-5 (epub)

I. Title.

PS8587.W36M57 2014   C813'.54   C2014-900119-3
C2014-900120-7

Goose Lane Editions acknowledges the generous support of the Canada Council for the Arts,
the Government of Canada through the Canada Book Fund (CBF), and the Government of
New Brunswick through the Department of Tourism, Heritage, and Culture.

Goose Lane Editions
500 Beaverbrook Court, Suite 330
Fredericton, New Brunswick
CANADA E3B 5X4
www.gooselane.com

For my mother and father

And you say, "Oh my God
	Am I here all alone?"
— Bob Dylan, "Ballad of a Thin Man" (1965)

PART ONE

Chapter One

Blue Sea Lake, Summer 1953

Emmett Jones watched his wife, Suzanne, in evening sun so strong he couldn't make out the gold stitching on her yellow dress, though it was a detail he'd memorized. He was wishing the sun would set. He was thirty-three years old, impatient for the pleasures of the night, optimistic at dawn. Right now he felt intensely lonely.

They were entertaining the undersecretary of state at External Affairs, Bill Masters, and his wife, Ethel, on the lawn that ran down from Suzanne's cabin to the white stone at the shore of Blue Sea Lake.

Suzanne had been listening to Bill Masters talk when she'd suddenly stood up and, with visible effort to calm herself, suggested, "Let me sweeten your drink, Bill." Emmett looked at Suzanne's lightly tanned cleavage, then down to her hips, to her knees, pressed together, suggestive yet gracious, wifely. She leaned over her Cape Cod chair and stretched her hand out toward Bill.

Bill Masters held his glass out to her, its ice half melted around a slice of lemon, without interrupting his steady stream of talk. "The prime minister agrees with me," Bill said with leering, wheezy confidence. "I told him, 'Mr. St. Laurent, we're going to put Emmett Jones through the most intensive, the most exhaustive, the most thorough investigation that any man can be put through, short of skinning him alive.'"

Suzanne, her voice hardening like burnt sugar, asked Bill, "The same?"

"You're gonna look clean as a razor when we get through with you." He gave Suzanne a glance— "Yeah, please, that's fine"— and returned his attention to Emmett. "We're gonna tell Security, 'Go to it, boys, and take your time. Run him through his paces. You'll see. Mr. Jones is an open book.'"

The Joneses' baby daughter, Lenore, planted on a white blanket on the grass, watched Bill's mouth. She was drooling, a pearly flow bubbling over and soaking her undershirt.

Sleep pooled in Emmett's brain, towing him under. He stood up and held on to his chair till the dizziness passed. Suzanne came behind him, brushing her hand across his back. "I'll put dinner on," she said, her fury apparent to him alone —though perhaps also to the ears of the undersecretary's wife, Ethel; maybe Ethel's ears were tuned to female frequencies, where Bill's were not.

Ethel sat on a lawn chair with her ankles crossed, wearing a rayon paisley dress and stockings, despite the heat, and sporting beige, rubber-soled shoes with open toes, ready for the treacherous, grassy terrain by the lake. She was overheated. Thirty years in Ottawa and Ethel still dreaded being left alone with the men. She'd had a vegetable garden back in Moose Jaw when she and Bill were first married; she grew onions and garlic, radishes and rutabagas. Ethel watched helplessly as Suzanne gathered little Lenore onto her hip and stalked across the lawn toward the cottage.

Emmett Jones knew how mad his wife was because she'd

forgotten to refresh Bill's drink. He went to the butler's wagon and checked the ice.

Bill kept talking. "We're going to give those bastards down in Washington more dope than they'll know what to do with."

Emmett felt a surge of fury at the mention of Washington, at the gall of the Americans pushing External Affairs into investigating him, investigating one of their own. He turned his back to Bill and held aloft a bottle of gin. "Tonic or vermouth?"

"Let 'em into every corner of your life, Jones," Bill went on, oblivious. "Vermouth. Tell 'em everything, every bolt and screw." He leaned forward, with his elbows on his knees. "You still got your tonsils?"

"Yeah. In fact I do."

Bill clapped his hands once, like a football coach. "Attaboy."

"What would you like, Ethel?" Emmett asked, turning to her. Ethel told him, with surprising energy, that she wanted a glass of water. In his exhaustion, he wished to protect Ethel, put her in a crate and mail her back to the nineteenth century where she belonged. When he delivered her a glass of water drained from the ice bucket, she gave him a desperate smile, embarrassment and sympathy in her brown, spaniel eyes. He made two martinis, added the twist, gave one to Bill, and quickly drank the other without speaking.

"It's what we've gotta do," Bill persisted.

Emmett took in the grounds surrounding the cottage—Suzanne's cottage really, through her mother—the docks and boats and white pine that seemed to inhale the long sunlight. The place spoke of money with casual discretion, superbly beautiful. Bill had stopped talking and was holding his martini to his shapeless lips, refusing to take a sip until

Emmett had capitulated, had agreed—he only had to tell External "everything" and he'd be in the clear; External would leave him alone and let him get on with his life; the Americans would back off.

The rustle of aspen. Purple, silkily rolling waves from the white tail of a boat's wake struck the shore. The long U-shaped dock composed of symmetrical planes of greying wood was a shrine to good taste, a discreet Canadian shrine. No obvious shrine paraphernalia, other than the butler's wagon filled with gin that he'd rolled out onto the lawn at Suzanne's request. No white paper pennants on sacred rope between the Jack pines, as there would be on Mount Fuji, paper pennants linking Japanese *sugi* trees. *Sugi* wouldn't survive in this country, and he missed them, the supple Asian trees, and then he thought of his father, and his father's Japanese mistress, and the mountain behind the house in Shioya near Kobe, where he grew up, where his father's mistress had lived. He thought of the quietude of that house in Shioya, the Japanese insistence on stillness, on purity of form and intention—a pose. But here in Ontario, he thought, people pretend not so much to purity as to goodness, a family compact, an assumption of class, a birthright, a powerful, profitable delusion.

Bill Masters was waiting. "Can't say you've got any choice in the matter. Get the investigation over with, and you'll feel a whole lot better." Then he knocked back the martini.

Suzanne called from the cottage: dinner was ready or would they like another drink? Bill held up his empty martini glass for a refill. But Ethel rose and swooped, deftly scooped Bill's glass and turned so swiftly, she bumped her broad satiny hip across Bill's Presbyterian nose. Bill followed her with his eyes as she piloted the uneven lawn to the stone stairs and wooden screen

14

doors of the cottage. So there did appear to be one person on earth to whom Bill Masters was obedient. He gave Emmett a mother-is-calling grimace and heaved himself to his feet.

Suzanne had set the table in the veranda with the white china, with a white vase filled with lilacs. Lenore was installed in her high chair beside Suzanne's place at the head of the table, opposite her husband. Solemn Lenore appraised Bill Masters, her lips firmly closed around her favourite spoon, her hands freed to fool with the bits of chicken and carrot and cooled cubes of potato in her Winnie-the-Pooh bowl.

The chairs were too low for the table, putting them all at some disadvantage. Suzanne served the chicken and asparagus and passed them each their plate, close beneath their chins. Ethel received her asparagus reproachfully, forced to commit a mortal sin, permitting herself a small protest: "At sixty cents a pound?"

Thrift was not innate to Suzanne. Speaking openly about the price of anything struck her as vulgar. She may at times have been comparatively broke, but she'd certainly never been poor.

Ethel seemed to grow more plump nestled in her chair. "My daddy used to grow asparagus," she said. "We'd be sent out to find it. There were eight of us children, you know. I was the eldest of eight." She began to speak to Lenore in her high chair. "It grew like grass, and it didn't mind the drought if it had a bit of sun and a bit of shade. That was the Great Depression. I think we might have starved without our garden."

Lenore, dangling her silver spoon from her mouth, turned her grey eyes on Ethel.

The change of venue, the unfortunate chairs, his wife's disclosures, all of this seemed to have put Bill Masters off the scent. He shook his jowls, declining the wine: "No, thanks, don't care for the stuff." Emmett watched him deposit a thick slice of chicken breast behind his molars and chew; he observed the chicken go round inside Bill's cheek and unwillingly imagined Bill making love to Ethel. Bill caught his eye and said, "Whaza matter?" Then perhaps for the first time Bill noticed that there was a baby present, Lenore, giving Bill the full benefit of her gaze. "You're gonna choke on that spoon," said Bill.

Suzanne took the spoon out of Lenore's mouth and put it in her bowl. Lenore's chin and fists were glistening with drool, her cheeks were chapped and brightly red, but she never took her eyes off Bill.

Suzanne said, "I think it's terrible, what happened to the Rosenbergs." Emmett was silent. She was familiar with that particular, disapproving silence. He didn't like the topic. "But it is," she insisted. "They were murdered! That was state murder!" She looked quickly at Lenore to see if she understood —Lennie still refused to talk, but that didn't mean she didn't understand—and lowered her voice. "Executed. That poor woman." She appealed to Emmett. "The two of them, ending like that."

"But they were communist spies, my dear." Ethel was tucking into her dinner when she said this and seemed to have surprised herself by speaking. "I read it in *Time*," she explained apologetically to Bill.

"Hunh," said Bill.

Emmett's hands rested palms-down on the table. He was staring at his plate loaded with food. The Rosenbergs had been killed in the electric chair one week ago today, at eight o'clock in the evening, as a matter of fact. He shook his head; he had water in his ear from swimming, it was hard to think

16

straight. The FBI had used Ethel Rosenberg — he saw Ethel Masters stoically fold asparagus into her mouth; the sun was low behind Suzanne's back, burning the image of Suzanne and Lenore onto his retina and illuminating Ethel Masters's facial hair — they'd used Rosenberg's wife to try to crack him, psychologically break him, make him talk.

Emmett wanted to be alone with Suzanne. To hold her, to tell her, *It's come to this, my love, my life, a very bright light, a manmade uranium sun, has led us here. So don't let them break you, but be bold, be righteous and forgetful.*

He said to Bill, "I want to thank you for all you've done for my career."

Bill was eating. "Just cooperate and it'll all blow over in no time."

"No, seriously. I might not have a chance to thank you later."

"What are you talking about, Emmett?" Suzanne asked.

"I mean, I might not have a chance to say very much, while I'm under investigation." Both ears were plugged so his voice sounded in his own head. He realized that he yearned for their sympathy. He did feel self-pity, and he was angry, very angry. He said, "Do you believe the Rosenbergs gave the A-bomb to the Russians, Bill? Simple as that?"

"Sure. That's why they went to the electric chair."

"And all those people killed in Korea, we should blame the Rosenbergs for that. Right? Julius and Ethel." Confidingly to Bill's wife, "Her name was Ethel too."

Bill thought about it and agreed, "Yeah. And communists like them. You can't tell *me* the Russians would've figured out how to make an atom bomb without help from fools like Rosenberg."

"Why not?" Emmett was behaving recklessly; Suzanne wanted a drink. He went on, carelessly, stupidly, "We did."

"We most certainly did not," said Ethel. Emmett Jones appeared to be drunk. These people, they act like bohemians. And with all that money behind them. Goes to show you. Anglicans.

He tried to pour Ethel some wine, but she put her hand over her glass so he poured some for himself, drank it, and said, "I could've sworn we dropped a couple of A-bombs on *somebody*."

Ethel, coldly, crisply: "That was not our decision."

"Well," Bill said, wiping his mouth, "it was a lousy end to a lousy war." He pushed his chair away from the table. "Very nice," he told Suzanne.

Suzanne, stunned by her husband's wayward speech, roused herself. "Oh! What am I thinking?" She pried Lenore out of her high chair. "You need a bath!"

Ethel said she'd gather the dishes, and Suzanne thanked her and fled, jostling her solemn child under her arm. When Ethel took Emmett's untouched plate, she gave a little sniff and said, "Think of all those starving children in China."

With Ethel clattering in the kitchen, and Suzanne off bathing the baby, the men were left to their own devices. It was solstice, so the sun didn't seem to set but to swerve to the south, leaving the stage for the entry of an orange moon. Bill and Ethel were to stay the night and drive back to Ottawa after brunch tomorrow, a Sunday. Emmett observed vaguely, "I believe Suzanne made a pie." They sat on, stymied, until Bill finally said, "Ah, come on, Jones," and stood, put his hands in his trouser pockets, and strolled away from the table. "Pour me a real drink, will ya?"

The place was built entirely of red pine in 1878. Emmett felt compelled to tell Bill this, his voice trembling, while he poured them both brandy. The veranda wound nearly full circle, with a tall, sloping ceiling. It was furnished with comfortably sagging furniture. And of course, there was art: framed posters of Maxfield Parrish and several of Suzanne's photographs — conventional, for the most part, aside from one nude: a man's thin back, his ribs, his bones like silver forks.

"Nice place," agreed Bill, looking like he wanted to go home.

Emmett didn't light a lamp and was warily gratified that Bill didn't insist, make some wisecrack, *Pretty romantic, Jones. Ya want me to go blind?* Bill drank his brandy and appeared to be appreciating the moon on the water.

Emmett was standing behind Bill in the near dark when he asked quietly, as if bemused, "Why *doesn't* Ottawa protect me?"

Bill jumped and turned, almost angry. "That's exactly what we're doing! Jesus!"

"In a secret investigation by the RCMP."

"It's gotta be private. You want everybody to know?" Bill turned his back again; he gazed at the rippling moon on the lake with something like resentment and added, "Actually, it's in the hands of External's Security Panel. Harold Gembey's in charge. Harold's working close with the RCMP."

"Harold Gembey. Great. Just great. Thank you very fucking much." The servile bastards at External. He was acquainted with Harold Gembey in Security. Gembey was a long-time civil servant, started there in the middle of the war, and he'd turn on any man if he could make himself look cleaner than clean. He'd be obsequious with the Mounties, obsequious with the FBI.

In the dark, Bill turned again to look at him. "You've got nothing to hide, do you, Emmett?"

"Everybody's got something to hide."

"Oh, sure." Bill seemed to be trying to come up with something, some secret of his own he'd need to conceal; he shifted from one foot to the other, thinking. Finally, he leaned forward, breathing into Emmett's face, and in a low voice he said, "Look, pal. You're young. Idealistic. These guys, these RCMP fellows, you're gonna find they're decent, real Boy Scouts. The man who runs the operation is no sucker. He's navy, a vet, a young fella, like you. He's not stupid, he knows something's up with the Russians, ever since Gouzenko." Igor Gouzenko was the cipher clerk at the Soviet Embassy in Ottawa who'd defected right after the war, exposing a Canadian spy ring in the process. "We've gotta protect ourselves from the communists. Come *on*, Emmett. Frank Miller down in Washington, he thinks *you're* a commie. So? Just answer the questions and straighten him out."

Then Bill added almost in a whisper, "Thing is, somebody's put a finger on the minister."

He meant Lester Pearson, minister of external affairs. A woman, Elizabeth Bentley, had named Pearson in her testimony to the House Un-American Activities Committee. That was nearly two years ago, it was old news, Bill was trying to pretend that he had some inside info. Emmett said, "The woman who gave that testimony about Pearson is pathetic. She's insane."

"Tell me about it," said Bill.

By moonlight, Emmett could see the blue, broken blood vessels travelling over Bill's swollen nose, the heavy lids and puffy bags under the eyes, and he marvelled that this was the face of a man with nothing to hide, nothing but self-interest masked by piety; a team player.

Bill held out his brandy snifter, requesting a refill. When Emmett returned with their drinks, Bill took a big, functional gulp of brandy, heaved himself into a wicker chair, and said, "Now. Tell me about this prick Norfield. That his name? John Norfield. What's he got on you?"

Chapter Two

Toronto, Fall 1946

John Norfield had three scars in the shape of sunflower seeds pressed into the skin of his cheekbone from a childhood bout of chicken pox. It only made him more handsome, even beautiful. The women would watch the smile come and go in his narrow jaw. It wasn't good humour they saw there, not in the sense that he was sharing the joke. He was a different kind of man, but then, people *were* different when they came home from the war. John Norfield was so terribly thin, the women said, gaunt; and his clothes hung on him, just so. That night a rumour went around his smoky party that he'd been a POW in a Jap camp.

Emmett Jones, another war vet, a student at the ripe old age of twenty-six, didn't know John Norfield, his host, having been brought by some classmates from university. He wanted to introduce himself and found Norfield in the living room talking to a girl. "Well, we had to," the girl was saying. Her back was turned to Emmett, the green stuff her dress was made of rustled, revealed her white shoulders. She wore her blond hair in a roll, and he stared at the long, shapely neck. "With the war, we had to grow up fast," she told John Norfield. She was dressed for a fancier party, so she looked out of place here, square, in her ballroom gown where most of the women wore narrow skirts and thin blouses, smoking cigarettes. Emmett

22

looked over the white shoulders to see how this fellow Norfield would treat somebody like her. With smooth tolerance. A girl like that can say any kind of nonsense to a man.

When John Norfield looked past her, directly at Emmett, his eyes changed aperture; everything changed, his interest, his expectations. Something like a lynx, a seething, cool interest.

The girl wasn't so fatuous as not to be aware that she'd lost Norfield's interest, and she twisted to look up at Emmett Jones's spectacles.

Norfield leaned past the girl and stuck out his hand, "Hi. Welcome."

Emmett said hello, then hello to the girl.

"Oh," said Norfield, "sorry." He put his face close to hers. "Susan, right?"

"Suzanne." She accepted this small slight with a neutral modesty that Emmett liked and then put her hand firmly in his. Emmett guessed from the handshake, the husky voice, the costly dress, that she had family; he was already wary of her father.

John Norfield put an unlit cigarette between his lips and took her elbow. He had to speak close to her ear, over the party noise. "Let's sit down, out of the crowd." He indicated that Emmett was to follow.

Suzanne in her green dress with an eggy white lining squeezed in at the end of a long horsehair couch while somebody gave over the armchair to Norfield and Emmett took the low ottoman, folding his long legs, his knees up around his ears. Suzanne settled, then gave a little cry and squirmed a magazine out from under her. "Oh! *The New Yorker*!"

The party was loud, a lot of rye, a lot of rum, gin, beer, and marijuana, though few of the guests knew what it was, that sweet smoke. It was too loud to talk. Norfield indicated to Emmett, *Have a look*.

But Suzanne had taken possession of the magazine. She showed a proprietary thrill in finding *The New Yorker* here, away from home, and shouted over the noise, "I *adore* their cartoons!" It might have been the cigarette smoke, it might have been that she didn't have the confidence she pretended to, but she paled as she began to read, with a quick draining away of pride. She leafed through, stopping to read a bit, slowly turning a page.

Emmett saw her and he felt disturbed, persuaded by her.

There was a girl called Carmen at John Norfield's party, in his surprisingly nice one-bedroom apartment on College Street. Or at any rate, she looked like a Carmen, alert breasts in a tight red sweater, launching herself onto Norfield's lap, probably the girl who'd stay after everybody had left. She wrapped her arms around Norfield's neck and kicked her feet, smiling at Emmett, saying, "Hi ya." Then, "Oh! She's got Hiroshima!"

Suzanne's face when she raised her head from the magazine was stricken, as if she'd been caught looking at dirty pictures. There was something young about her that would probably never go away.

For a few minutes, the party chatter pounced on this particular *New Yorker*. They argued over how it was to be pronounced. Hero-*sheema*. Hear-*ah*-shima. A young man wearing the jacket of his army uniform with a red bow tie removed the magazine from Suzanne's hand, as if doing her a favour. With drunken solemnity he pronounced, "I hope they drop a handful of A-bombs on Moscow."

Suzanne didn't even raise her head to look at him but reached to retrieve the magazine and continued to read. Her eighteen-karat hair swept up in a French roll, her ankles crossed beneath her party dress, she could have been reading *A Christmas Carol*. Emmett Jones and John Norfield studied her. Emmett asked, "What is it?"

"John Hersey's thing on the A-bombs they dropped on Japan," the drunken vet answered with clipped, elaborate sobriety. "They gave the whole issue to him. No cartoons." Then, directed at Suzanne, "Hey, little girl, it'll give you scary nightmares."

Carmen took a cigarette out of a silver box sitting on the side-table and put it between her lips for John Norfield to light. "The whole thing just makes me want to give up on the human race," she said, the cigarette bobbing between her lips.

Norfield put her off his lap. He looked unwell. Carmen pressed her palm against his cheek and said, "Hey." Norfield waited for her to take her hand away.

Suzanne's lovely forehead under all that hair. Carmen caught Norfield looking at this pretty young woman in the green gown and told her, "It's not news, honey."

"Oh," said Suzanne. "I knew about it. That we dropped the Bombs. And ended the war."

"*We* didn't. *They* did," said the bow tie. "Americans. They'll do anything, crazy bastards."

Suzanne handed the magazine to Norfield. The skin of a woman's hands slipped off in "*huge, glove-like pieces*." At the park near the river in Hiroshima, the "*slimy living bodies*" were searching for their dead families. In Hiroshima, the people in their homes, on the street, at school, they were burnt alive, little babies and children, their mothers and fathers, in a few bright seconds they were charred sticks, she knew that before, didn't she. Or, surviving in fire and ash, getting sick, their skin falling off. "Thanks. My dad'll have a copy, I'll read his."

She looked like she needed air. Norfield reached for her hand and said, "Come here." He took Emmett's arm and pushed him ahead, ushered them out, and closed the door behind him, then the three of them stood in the silent hallway.

They walked down to a diner near Spadina.

"You're just going to leave your own party?" said Suzanne, nervously flattered.

The two men waited till she took a seat at the long counter and then they sat on either side of her, their legs touching her dress.

"It was winding down anyway." Norfield slapped the magazine onto the counter and shoved it toward Emmett. "Happy reading."

Emmett drew it toward himself but didn't open it. He stared at the pleasant scene on its cover, a watercolour of a summery America taking its leisure. "I grew up there," he said. "Not Hiroshima. East. In Kobe. Or near there, in a place called Shioya. In a kind of estate for foreigners."

The girl, Suzanne, said, "How exotic!" She looked lost for a second and then asked, "Do you still have family there?"

"My parents are both dead." He saw her shocked face and added, "It's all right."

"Ah," Norfield was saying, "that explains it." He wasn't paying much attention but was looking to the end of the counter where a man in a homburg hat had just sat down. Norfield's complexion was yellow, his hands shook when he lit his cigarette. Emmett thought that maybe it was true about Norfield being a POW. You don't look well after that.

They sat with "Hiroshima: A Noiseless Flash" wrapped up in its busy cover illustration. With some effort, John Norfield was dragging himself into a sociable range for the benefit of his two new friends, who, he was aware, would find it strange to have their host take them from his own party.

Norfield had a nasty, chemical taste in his mouth. One of the challenges in returning from Hong Kong was to remember that he had to appear to be kind. He'd been back in Toronto for ten months, out of a Japanese prison camp for more than a year. Not yet enough time to be reconciled to the easily won indulgences, the boredom of his fellow citizens in the Kingdom of the Golden Mean. In the camp, a Chinese couple, man and wife, starving, slipped food to him through the barbed wire. They did this two or three times. The last time, Norfield had already received their small package, concealed it under his shirt, and was walking away when they got caught, the man and his wife. It was the smell that gave them away; they'd wanted the food to be warm. They were beheaded in the prison yard while Norfield was forced to watch. That's solidarity for you. Home now, six months ago, walking down College Street, he'd lost control of his bowels. It took a second; in a surge of terror the veneer he'd carefully applied was stripped away; he remembered how things really are, and he shit himself. Now he presented to Jones and this girl, Suzanne, his cool attentiveness. He knew that he was clean; he made sure of it.

"So you grew up in Japan," he said to Emmett, who just a

27

moment before had asked him about his bookstore — Emmett had heard that Norfield ran a bookstore and dredged up a question: "So how do you like that kind of work?"

Emmett swerved to try to intercept Norfield's sudden interest. "I lived in Kobe till I was sixteen."

"What year was that?"

"Nineteen thirty-six."

"Why'd you leave?"

"I had TB."

"I had a cousin who had that," Suzanne said and froze: the cousin had died.

Norfield spoke dreamily so it was hard to reconcile what he said with how he said it. "Think the Japs might've murdered and raped more Chinese if they'd been better organized?"

"No, I don't. In fact, the opposite."

"Just got caught up in the frenzy, eh."

"That's right."

"You speak Japanese?"

Emmett said that he did.

"Think you'll ever go back there?" Norfield asked idly.

Suzanne, her breathy voice, compassionate, "Without any family?"

"Kobe got bombed pretty good, I hear," Norfield said. "Nearly wiped out."

Emmett tightened. "That's right."

In the greasy mirror behind the grill, Suzanne watched herself with the two men. It was her first year away from home, living in residence, Falconer House, which was nice. She'd never be able to go home again; even if she went back, she wouldn't really be living there, not anymore. She saw that Norfield was looking at her. She was used to that, but this time it mattered.

Norfield was looking at Suzanne, but he was talking to Emmett. "So? Ever going back?"

"I hope to, one day. I want to find someone there. She's sort of family. She'd be an old woman by now — if she survived."

"Much chance of that?" Norfield asked. "Survival?"

"I hope so," Emmett said again.

"Full of hope, are you? Well. The Americans are their pals now. Never saw a country take defeat so easy. Duck to water."

Norfield droned on about the American military occupation of Japan, his voice flat, without inflection. Emmett was beginning to wonder if he could like him, and he scolded himself: cut the guy some slack. Then Norfield said, "Hey. What about China?"

"What about it?"

"You think the communists are going to take over?" Norfield raised his voice to ask this. At the end of the counter, the homburg hat lifted, and Emmett saw the face of a man his own age; he was surprised — he'd thought that a man dressed like that would be older. Norfield and the man in the homburg looked at each other in the mirror. Norfield gave a sudden grin with a fresh cigarette in his mouth.

Suzanne said, "I should be going." She climbed down from the stool. "Oh" — she opened her handbag — "my treat," and laid down fifty cents.

"How are you getting home?" Emmett wanted to know.

Norfield said, "We're going to take you."

Suzanne was stuck. The girls she'd come with were probably still at the party. Getting back to residence alone, the dark streets, thugs, muggers, vets. "Don't you have to go back to your guests?"

Norfield shrugged. "C'mon."

Chapter Three

They escorted Suzanne McCallum to her residence, Falconer House, trotting her briskly between them. She felt their eagerness to be rid of her, and she was bewildered because she knew they were attracted—but that didn't matter; they wanted her out so they could talk about who-knows-what. The first attraction is always between the men.

Suzanne knew men by instinct. She didn't know how she'd come by this wisdom, being an only child. And what good would it do anyway? Condemn her to boredom unless she could turn to steel like her mother; it would make her a great dance partner, though she didn't know if such things would even continue to exist, after Hiroshima and all, after the death camps and the "noiseless flash." Emmett Jones and John Norfield didn't talk much on the way. She would've liked some real conversation. There was so much to talk about. But she was shut out.

They practically tossed her at the front door, gave her thin segments of their faces, Emmett with his glasses like two O's when the porch light caught them. And John, the way his teeth fit in his jaw, so thin, and then his mouth. He stood out of the light. Yet she felt his resentment.

They each saw the hem of the green dress, and they turned away.

"What time is it?" Norfield asked.

Emmett had inherited his father's watch. It was after midnight.

Norfield asked, "Want to see my bookstore?"

"Now?"

"C'mon. Want a cigarette?"

"I don't smoke." Emmett figured that Norfield must have forgotten the TB. But after they'd walked in silence for ten minutes, Norfield said, "You don't look like a consumptive."

"I'm not. Not anymore."

"That why you didn't go over?"

"I went over. Air force."

"See some action?"

Emmett answered tersely, "Yes." He pretended to be interested in the buildings they were passing. There was an element of yearning in Norfield's question.

Norfield dragged hard on his cigarette, then flicked it into the gutter. "My store's here."

They'd arrived at a narrow storefront with a green shutter and door. Once inside, Norfield turned on a small lamp. The book dust made Emmett sneeze. He was tired and wished he hadn't come.

Norfield disappeared through a curtain behind the cash register and was gone for several minutes. Emmett called out, "Is there another light out here?" Norfield's white face reappearing. Emmett sneezed several times, saying, "Can't see the books."

Norfield handed him a cup of coffee and turned on the overhead bulb. Full disclosure, shadowed eyes. "That what you want?" He turned it off. "Better?" He took the shade off the lamp and the room brightened. "You tired?"

"I think I'm going to head on home."

Norfield held out his hand. On his palm lay two pills. He took one and popped it into his mouth, offering the other to Emmett. "This'll take care of you."

Emmett tried to swallow the pill dry, as Norfield had, and then burned his tongue with coffee.

Ten minutes later it hit him like joy. His hands could read. He could inhale the meaning of the books he slipped from the shelves. One word. One sentence. So he knew Bernard Shaw, Mayakovsky, Maxim Gorky, Jack London, John Reed, D.H. Lawrence. "What's D.H. Lawrence doing here?"

"Think he's bad?" asked Norfield. He came and stood close.

"I don't know. Sort of—homo."

Norfield laughed. He seemed—if not happy—exalted. He took the novel from Jones's hands, set it down, and said, "I liked the ecstasy. I liked the beauty, when I was a boy, before the war. When I was a boy, I only believed in beauty. I was truly sublime, man."

Emmett felt Norfield's voice like a hand on his spine. It was nearly too much. He didn't want to leave, not anymore. They were standing close, beside the counter, and Norfield leaned back on his elbows. Emmett couldn't take his eyes off John's collarbone where he'd opened his shirt and loosened his tie. From every angle, John was perfectly made, and he smelled good, a fresh oniony heat. He didn't look sick anymore. Maybe the pill had taken care of it.

John said, "Before experience, everything's just speculation. Before experience, we're sleepwalkers. Deluded."

And in this way, Emmett and Norfield began a long night of talk, pacing, riffling the books. Norfield encrypted his stories, cut them up. He said he'd had three weeks of fighting in Hong Kong. Then he was a prisoner of the Japanese for the rest of the war. Four years in Japanese prison camps. "You speak Chinese too?" Norfield asked.

"Well, actually—" Emmett was tempted to tell him, yes, a little, and he hoped to learn more. He'd discovered that it was unusual, his fluency in Japanese, a rare talent in a young Canadian man, and he planned to build on that, maybe become fluent in Mandarin, to find a career in his seemingly exotic talents.

But now Norfield was going too fast to listen. He needed to tell. He was with his brother when Hong Kong fell. His brother was hurt. It was bad, but they were together. Then the Japs shipped his brother away, to Niigata, on the Sea of Japan. "I tell you this," he said, pointing his cigarette at Emmett, "because maybe you holidayed there."

Emmett looked at him blankly.

"Did you?" Norfield persisted.

"As a matter of fact—" Emmett began. He had holidayed there.

"Forget it."

Norfield's brother died at Niigata. Emmett said, "I'm sorry." Norfield waved his hand to say, Change the subject. But he himself came back to it. "It hit me," he said. "All those deaths." He shrugged. "That one really hit me." He asked Emmett, "You have a brother?"

Emmett didn't have a brother. Norfield put his arm around him. "I came back through Guam, and heard he'd died back in '43. It hit me."

"I know," said Emmett.

"Deplorable."

The word seemed funny and they laughed, their eyes on each other.

Norfield said, "The look on my mother's face when I got off the train without him."

At Canton, his first prison, Norfield had been forced to kneel on the floor of the cell and look at the wall. "The wall, all day, every day, staring at that wall. Not even allowed to scratch the fleas. A bad six months." He inhaled almost a quarter-inch of his cigarette. Norfield's jaw was clean and fine, his scent seemed to come from his throat.

"Your eyes are nerve endings," Norfield said. "You become what you see. You get infected."

Emmett understood. He began to feel that he wore Norfield's face, a replacement of his features that would persist long after the effects of the pill had faded.

Book dust, but otherwise Norfield's place looked impeccable, newspapers neatly stacked, five pens, a silver soup spoon that seemed out of place, four broken pencils, ten pennies in a row.

Except the spoon affected John Norfield's nerves and so did the lint in his pocket; so did the little girl with a skipping rope he'd passed by that afternoon. The spoon may be put into a drawer, but he'd know it was there; it could be placed in alignment with the broken pencils but it would remain, the spoon, a stray article. For Norfield, since the war anyway, all objects and every incident in time were one-offs, un-belonging, irreconcilable.

"So—air force," said Norfield. He'd been fiddling with the miscellaneous stuff near his cash register, and now he stopped and deliberately put his hands in his pocket.

"That's right."

"What. Don't tell me. You were a pilot."

"Yes."

"Where?"

"Europe." Emmett didn't want to talk about it. He wasn't going to be one of those vets who couldn't get over it. He dreamed of doing some kind of international work. Everything he'd experienced, everything that Norfield had been through, it had to mean something, there had to be progress, redemption. He had hope. He didn't want to talk about Germany.

Norfield waited a moment, and Emmett thought, If he forces the issue, I'll leave, but Norfield turned away and said, "Listen to this."

He played a record that first drove Emmett out of his mind. Saxophone. Unnatural music. "It's Bird," Norfield said.

"No bird ever sang like that," Emmett said, wanting him to take the music off.

"Listen. It's Charlie Parker," said Norfield. "The greatest musician of the twentieth century."

"Listen," Norfield said again—was it five minutes later? "That's my soul. What I am." Disorder precedes; instinct, nerves precede. Ideals—honour and glory and sacrifice—have been reversed in precedence: the incidents, one-offs, the terror of pocket lint, of pencils, the little girl hopping incessantly, discontinuous happenstance, a tarnished spoon, this indefinite chaos is called peace. He kept a tidy place, Norfield did, but the ten pennies must be lined up with the pencils, and it was terrifying.

Norfield lifted the needle from the record. An ashtray piled high with butts. "What's the hour?" asked Norfield, looking ill. "Never mind. Forget it."

Norfield put his arm around Emmett's shoulder. Emmett took a drink of Norfield's smell inside his clavicle. He liked it very much. He moved closer, caught himself, quickly moved away. "So tell me," Emmett wanted to know, but what? Just tell me something. *What do you believe in?* "What do you believe in?" he asked.

Norfield said, "I believe in a Chinese man and his wife who shared their food with me when I was in prison." Then he said, "Tell me about Germany."

Emmett said, "A city called Hamburg."

Norfield was listening to him now, like the needle.

Emmett, seeing the view from the air, confessed, "And a place called Darmstadt. And Weser. Magdeburg. Heilbronn. Some smaller sites, hydroelectric dams, missile laboratories, that kind of thing. And some medieval towns in the Baltic. Lübeck, Rostock. Old wood, you know. It burns well." Hamburg had been the greatest success, with thirty thousand dead. Darmstadt, six thousand dead. Weser, nine thousand dead. Magdeburg, twelve thousand dead. And so on, more and more dead.

The fires rose fifteen hundred feet in the air. When they let go the four-thousand-pound "cookies," his plane sank and then soared, black earth below turning crimson, then the next wave of planes dropping "breadbaskets" filled with incendiaries, instantly, a sea of fire, that's what everyone said, It's a sea of fire. Fire sucking the air out from under him, then his plane accelerating up and out of there before it inhaled him, dragged him into the dragon's mouth, flying up, dodging flak.

"Hero," said Norfield.

"Yeah. Well. Nobody wants to talk about it." Bomber Command was not a popular memory. Emmett didn't come home with a medal for heroism. Not a single man, dead or alive—and there were more than fifty-five thousand dead airmen from Bomber Command—received a medal during or

36

after the war. And no one talked about the deaths of six hundred thousand German civilians by Allied bombing. Winston Churchill failed to mention Bomber Command in his victory speech on VE Day. Emmett was one of the untouchables. "I did what I had to do," he said.

"You miss it?"

Emmett didn't know him well enough. He said, "I'd rather think about the future."

"That's what we need more of."

"A future."

Norfield said, "Hitler and Hirohito are dead, but the fascists still run the show."

Emmett didn't know what to say to that.

Norfield went on, reluctant, as if he didn't normally bother to explain what he meant. "Look," he said, "look at how far the generals were willing to go. Thirty thousand dead in Hamburg? Okay. Now let's go for a hundred-thirty, hundred-fifty thousand killed in Hiroshima. How many in Nagasaki? Eighty thousand people killed, another two hundred thousand dead from fallout, who really knows? A couple hundred thousand people exterminated with one bomb. You think the men who run this show are ever going to give up that kind of power over us?"

Emmett had never talked to anyone about this before; since coming home he'd never confessed to his actions in Germany. His pals in the air force had mostly scattered. A few of them still hung around together, but he wanted nothing to do with them. He wasn't going to be one of those vets who couldn't get over it. He heard an awful moan, and in a panic he looked at the record player, thinking the terrible sound came from there, and then he realized it was coming from his own gut. Norfield caught him as he was falling to his knees, and held him, the two men kneeling. Emmett was weeping. He hadn't seen it coming.

Norfield held him, saying nothing, just held him steadily. Emmett felt like it was almost all right. He pulled away, stood up, wiping his face. "I can't let that happen."

"Confuses people," Norfield observed.

They were okay; they smiled.

Emmett still felt the effect of the pill, a weird ecstasy. His face was taut and salty. He didn't know why he trusted Norfield with so much, but he did, he trusted him completely.

"If we don't fight fascism," Norfield was saying, "they'll come for you anytime they please." He began to fiddle with the pennies again, arranging them. "We don't defeat the boot, we don't defeat capitalist power, if we fail to do that, we will have nowhere to go, nohow to live except in slavery, there will be no inside where we can live free from the capitalists' control. The police, police everywhere, they work for the rich with their international money invested in whatever it takes to keep us powerless to fight back. They'll watch you in everything you do, you'll be exposed at all times, my friend, there will be no privacy, they will have you by the balls." He stopped himself, lit another cigarette.

"The communists save us from that?"

Norfield was taking a drag, but his hand stopped on its way to his mouth, and with a slight, what-a-smart-boy smile, he said, "Might just."

The pill turned, tide going out, the only salve to his nerves was Charlie Parker again, Norfield setting the needle onto the recording; what had been torment now was hymn. "He's good when you're coming down."

Norfield opened the green door to sunrise, Charlie Parker

escaping. Emmett, running his nerves on Parker's sound, overheard Norfield talk to somebody at the door.

"Good morning, Mr. Farce," said John Norfield.

The man in the homburg hat stood at the door, a short stocky man in an expensive trench coat; he brought a hand up to scratch his nose. A diamond set in a gold wedding band caught the light. What kind of man wears clothes, jewellery like that? The hat said, "Working late?" He saw Emmett and added, "And who might you be?"

Norfield looked back at Emmett Jones. Gave him a look. Like he'd given him a disease. Like he loved him. "The hat's a boot," said Norfield. "Excuse me," he said and politely closed the door, leaving the hat on the other side. Lifted the needle from Charlie Parker. Quickly turned off the light. Ashen dawn. He hurried to the stacks, took down an old book, frayed and thready, handed the book to Emmett, who stuffed it into the pocket of his jacket. Norfield said, "There's a door out the back," guiding Emmett through his small office, his desk and typewriter, past a tiny bathroom with a sink and toilet, to a crooked door at the back of the building.

"Who is that guy?"

Norfield spoke as if he were delivering lines from Nöel Coward. "Everything important in history happens twice, my good fellow. The first time as tragedy, the second time as farce. You have just met Mr. Farce." Norfield's face was very white. He didn't look like he had much buzz left in him. "When Mr. Farce wants to hurt you, he does it without leaving a bruise. Trick of a second-rate henchman."

Emmett watched Norfield lock the back door. When they were standing in the lane, Emmett asked, "Is that guy coming after you, John?"

Norfield's lips, smile on one side, neat. "You don't want to know who's Mr. Tragedy?"

"Sure."

"Mr. Tragedy is dead. Forget it."

They walked down the lane. Mr. Farce, quite possibly, following at a polite distance.

It took Emmett three days to fall asleep. All in one blow: Suzanne McCallum's shoulders, John Norfield's clavicle. Falling in love, loyal forever to that one glimpse of purity you see in somebody, that kind of love, he thought, is a question of instinct, a move you make before thinking, and it changes everything in a split second.

He remembered later, how he'd stammered over the jazz. Ever since Germany, he told John, he'd been lonely, yearning to go back, to belong to a greater sum, flying in a squadron, to experience power, the bliss of pure action, pure intention. *Blooded*, that's what the air marshal had called it when he sent his boys out to bomb an easy target, *you'll be well blooded*. You're immortal in action. "Experience," Emmett had said to Norfield, "cuts, it cuts into you." He had wanted to say, Experience is love. He'd wanted to be that pilot again, to live in the sky. He slipped a novel back into the shelf, and as he did so, its paper jacket sliced his thumb.

Whatever drug it was that Norfield had given Emmett made him feel exquisitely mortal; he could feel his life, he could feel *time* running through his veins like a river of light, throwing him into the future. He said, "I've got to let the past go. We all do, we have to forget or we'll go crazy, brother." It was the first time he'd said "brother."

"Selective," Norfield had said. "Believe me. You've gotta be selective about what you remember, if you want to carry on."

Chapter Four

Emmett discovered that Suzanne McCallum was in one of his classes. Funny, he hadn't been aware of her right away. After meeting her at Norfield's party two weeks ago, he wondered how he'd cross paths with her again; then there she was in Shakespeare, a golden girl. He sat at the back of the lecture hall, where he could look at her. Her straight back, a fine line of will and beauty, leaning to her book, intensely taking notes. Miranda, daughter of Prospero.

He began to watch for her everywhere. He'd spot her in a crowd, often with several men. He liked the way Suzanne walked; for all her elegance, a bit undone, taking big, uneven strides. He was moved by her gawky determination and unself-consciousness, like she'd always be a girl. Soon, he intercepted her in the hall, hovered over her, and was disappointed by how casually she agreed to go for a walk with him. How eager she was to talk about Norfield. "You have a kind, handsome face," she told him. "John Norfield is gorgeous and probably bad." She said that she had to meet some friends, and blithely departed, "See you in Shakespeare," her skirt swaying around her long legs.

He was disappointed. Not only did she obviously prefer Norfield, but she'd spoken glibly about an encounter that had seared him, left him obsessed. He couldn't stop thinking about them, Suzanne and Norfield. Even Emmett's face, with its wire-framed spectacles, the fair hair combed straight back, his forehead, nose, and chin in a golden ratio, this pleasantly honest face seemed displaced in his own mind by John Norfield's slender, sardonic good looks. The man had made *an impression* on him.

In the warm splendour of that autumn he tried to rid himself of Norfield's occupation by dropping in on him at his bookstore, meet him face to face. *To split up with him*, he thought.

Norfield's bookstore was different by day, shabbier, cramped by bigger buildings. Emmett walked right by it once, then he retraced his steps and finally saw the painted sign: *Norfield & Norfield*. There was a shining Triumph motorcycle parked on the street out front, and when he pushed open the door, there was a bell's bright peal that he hadn't heard before and the rainy light of the store's interior, the smell of paper in mouldering leather bindings.

Norfield emerged from behind the counter to greet him with obvious pleasure, embraced him, lightly slapped his cheek. "Where've you been?"

Emmett shrugged. "Hitting the books." *Nothing to report. Except that I see you so constantly in my mind's eye, I feel like I've taken on your features.* He pointed toward the window, to the sign there. "Didn't see the name of your store in the dark the other night."

Norfield scratched lightly at the side of his mouth. "My brother and me." He smiled, resolute, ironic. "It keeps him in mind."

Emmett watched Norfield's mouth. "Is that your motorcycle?"

Norfield nodded absently and then seemed struck by a new

idea. "Hey," he said, "I was talking about you with a friend of mine, just the other day."

"Yeah?"

"Yeah. Told him you're a bright guy. I told him, if you were to call him, he should definitely talk to you, you're all right."

Emmett looked for imperfections in John Norfield: not merely the small scars—they added to his beauty—imperfections of spirit, of integrity. He said, "Listen. Any chance you could close shop for a while, get some lunch or something, go for a beer?"

Norfield put his hand on Emmett's shoulder. "You listen. You should definitely talk to this guy."

"What about?"

Norfield said, "Politics," smiling as if this were joke, or a code. He reached for and then lit a cigarette before adding, "He's a Jewish fellow. A survivor. You got any problem with that?"

"Of course not."

"Hungarian Jew. Nazis picked him up in '44."

Outside in the sunlight, someone had stopped to look through the dusty window. Norfield was distracted, staring out the window through cigarette smoke, saying, "Smart cookie. Speaks perfect English." He turned his eyes on Emmett, a searing effect. "He survived a camp."

Emmett felt the chance to come close to Norfield, to actually know him and be known, slip away. His disappointment felt unworthy. He said, "Sure. Give me his number."

The curtain behind the counter was pulled aside and there stood Suzanne McCallum. "Hello, Emmett."

She wore a white cardigan clasped with a short string of pearls at her throat, a matching sweater underneath, and some amazing kind of brassiere. When she came around the counter, he saw that her feet were bare, the toenails painted red. She shook his hand, her overly firm grasp, beaming at him, possessed by her own beauty. She stood beside Norfield, letting her arm touch his sleeve. Norfield brusquely pulled away, twisting aside to reach for an ashtray. Emmett saw pain, pain passing through Suzanne, quick as a needle.

Chapter Five

Emmett knocked, the door opened a crack, and he was examined by a sad brown eye. He could smell, even from the dingy hall, socks, the rank pong of young men, and sweetish garbage, cigarettes, burnt coffee. Leonard of the sad eyes — different from Norfield in every way: burly, hairy, older, though like Norfield, Leonard embraced him and called him "man."

Leonard Fischer spoke English with a strange accent, a hybrid of Hungary and New York. He ushered Emmett into a one-room suite to introduce him with a wave of the hand to half a dozen students, some of whom Emmett recognized from his classes. There was one woman among them, lovely and dark-haired.

It looked like a smoky, offbeat university seminar. Students strewn about on the floor or the bed, in the one upholstered chair. A sink full of scummy water, an icebox, a hot plate, books stacked on the floor or piled on shelves of two-by-sixes and bricks; magazines, newspapers, clippings, a chrome hubcap that served as an ashtray, out-of-date calendars with pictures of sexy girls wearing American sailor hats, 1942. It was grubby, and indicated a sense of anti-style, detritus, broken kitsch. The one artful object was a framed pencil drawing of a Junker 88 bomber, Luftwaffe; Emmett stumbled over someone's foot, drawn toward it.

He felt Leonard's hand on his shoulders, smelled coffee on Leonard's breath as Leonard spoke into his ear, a warm current of compassion: "Sit, my friend, why don't you," the thick fingers pressing him down. He landed beside the dark-haired girl; her full upper lip, black, abundant hair curling around her shoulders, her round arms. Leonard said, "My cousin Rachel. Touch and die." Then he laughed.

Leonard had a compact body, a dense, compressed mass. He never sat, he paced, blowing his nose into a blue hand-kerchief, saying little, while the young men in the room did most of the talking, glancing at Leonard for approval. Their conversation was intense, in what seemed like a special language. Emmett felt the envy of an outsider. He heard what seemed like magic phrases — *the dictatorship of the bourgeoisie, dialectical materialism, the inevitability of communism, the workers' democracy* — and he was embarrassed at having been so narrowly preoccupied with his own small concerns, his new loves, his abstract study of Shakespeare and British history. These young men and lovely Rachel seemed to be entranced by something brutal. "The bourgeoisie is incompetent and unfit to rule," pronounced one of the earnest students; "We must create a stateless, classless society," his eyes darting to Leonard to see if he'd made an impression. Leonard wasn't listening; he didn't see or didn't care that the others needed his approval. But Emmett felt the words ricochet through him, tantalizing, challenging his most cautious instincts. *We must create a stateless, classless society.* To dare to consider this — *no state.* He was struck by the notion that here was an idea, an ideal, grand enough to help him evade the fate of the vet who can't recover from the war. To rid himself of the state that had made him its dupe, a murderer.

The window in Leonard Fischer's single room looked down at a park. Leonard slowed there and looked out, as if restlessly hungering for things outside. He called Emmett over and asked, "You know what that is?" pointing down to the park. A man wearing a white shirt without a tie strolled slowly across an expanse of grass, his muscular body full of health, his empty hands swinging at his sides. "Boredom," Leonard said. "Beautiful, peaceful boredom. The kind of boredom we can only dream of, working in the capitalists' machinery. Becoming machines." Emmett was aware of a sudden lull in the students' conversation while they strained to overhear Leonard, who was pulling Emmett's head close, his voice softly rumbling, "Boredom is the dream bird that hatches the egg of experience." He squeezed Emmett's neck. "Walter Benjamin wrote that." Emmett admitted he didn't know who Walter Benjamin was. "You speak German?" Leonard asked quite indifferently — he was obviously a good teacher; he had a way of asking questions that permitted ignorance.

Emmett admitted that no, he did not speak German. The memory of molten fire beneath his plane, flames from a burning German city, sizzled into his mind and down into his gut, a choking sensation that augured weeping. But he was okay, he was calm. He didn't know what John Norfield had told Leonard but guessed that John had relayed nothing of his breaking down that first night they'd met, and nothing about the air force. He wanted to present Leonard with something. "I speak Japanese," he said.

Leonard laughed, deep and phlegmy. "That, my friend, would put you on the far side of the planet." He gripped Emmett's head between his hands and made as if to throw it, as if his head were a football, a loving gesture. "Glad to know you."

Leonard's cousin Rachel brushed her dark hair from her eyes and gave Emmett a scornful look.

Chapter Six

Emmett Jones was reading Karl Marx, *The Eighteenth Brumaire of Louis Bonaparte*. And there, in the first chapter of the first thing he'd ever read by Marx, he discovered the source for John Norfield's mysterious and witty aphorism that night they had first met. "All great world-historic facts and personages appear twice...the first time as tragedy, the second time as farce."

Emmett was surprised to discover Herr Marx so lively and sardonic. He wondered what the old philosopher would make of him, and of the students lounging on the floor of Leonard's apartment, and imagined that Marx would burst into laughter at the comfortable Canadian communists.

He was amazed at the power of Marx's memory, his visceral grasp of history and economics, witty, caustic. Reading this stuff made him feel again the exquisite sensation of time running through him, a river of light passing, almost painful, joyful in a ruthless sort of way.

Light travels six and a half trillion miles in a year, which was a fact that had stuck in his head from his schooldays; the stars' explosions hurling light. Light from the eighteenth century, from the French Revolution, that very light is striking earth now. Late from the homesick stars. The world is belated. An uncanny homelessness resides in things: a button with a bit of white thread lying on the windowsill in the sun, abandoned in the river of time.

What did she tell him, Sachiko, his father's mistress, in her female, singsong Japanese? She said, "Mono no aware ni kizuku." Be aware of the strangeness of things. Her melodious platitude, "Mono no aware o satoru." Be light-stricken as the world is light-stricken, be time-stricken as the world is time-stricken.

This was a Japanese cliché. She might have been saying, Wake up and smell the coffee. And besides, weren't the Japanese light-stricken? Now weren't they just as stricken as they could be? A great white brutal light.

Emmett's father's constant mistress, Sachiko, a silk cocoon, was the estranged wife of a diplomat stationed in Australia, which is where she'd learned English. She had a young daughter who had stayed in Australia because she'd chosen her father over her mother when they divorced. Sachiko never apologized for living so far from her child, but even as a boy Emmett could sense her dissatisfaction, her unhappy boredom, her pessimism. Emmett was a restless kid who discovered stillness visiting her, staring at her where she reclined, like fate, he thought, pleased with his own intellect. He thought, She has the body of a woman but the soul of a man.

Sachiko wasn't old then, he knew that now, but she was older than his mother, she coated her face in rice powder. She reclined on a chaise longue in the sunroom at the back of the house in Shioya, at James-yama Estate. Not *her* house: the house Emmett's father leased on her behalf, a short walk from the house he leased for his wife and son. His father travelled between the two women, and the younger Jones travelled too. At that time in his life, young Emmett exercised disloyalty to his mother as he exercised his body—healthily, casually cruel. He loved his mother, she was his first friend, but the pain that he inflicted on her confirmed him as separate, with separate will. Anyway, his mother's weakness proved that she deserved to be betrayed, as if he could uproot his own potential for weakness by hurting her.

There was nothing to do at Sachiko's house, and Emmett never took a schoolmate there with him. But he liked to go to sit with her, straddling a footstool to be near her, lying on his stomach to drag his boy-limbs over the Chinese carpet, mesmerized by boredom. Sachiko never felt obliged to talk or to read or even to embroider. She sat like a clock.

He preferred the way his family lived, in two houses, with two very different women, and he pitied his friends' conventional arrangements, preferring his father's courtly handshakes to ordinary fathers' hugs and feint punches; the other fathers' tussles and bad jokes seemed desperate, stupid. His father was tall, as tall as Emmett was now; he was dignified and self-reliant; he was never compelled to explain himself but kept his own counsel.

When his father contracted TB, his mother tried not to let anyone know. It seemed to shame her even more than his having a mistress did — or his mother used the shame of TB as surrogate for the shame she felt over the mistress. TB was widespread in Japan, yet it was also a source of deep disgrace. When Emmett began to show symptoms, she took him out of the country so suddenly he never had a chance to say goodbye.

He was sixteen. There'd been a small incident, a rift between him and his father. Emmett had taken a job on the estate, gardening work, cleaning yards. His boss was an old retired British field marshal. One day, the old man complained to Emmett's father about Emmett's "shoddy" work. In response, his father had, coldly furious, told Emmett that he'd "failed him," he'd said that he was "disappointed" in such a son; he'd gone on at some length, declaring that because Emmett was so lazy, he was bound to fail in life. His father was a thoroughly rational man and he had a thoroughly rational way of articulating his disgust.

Emmett was bitterly hurt. His work *had* been shoddy that one time; the old Brit had been right. Emmett sulkily avoided his father for weeks. Even when he knew that his father was really ill, Emmett held out, he never entered the darkened bedroom to see him. Then Emmett's mother swept him out of the country. He'd never had a chance to make things right with the man whom he loved beyond everyone. It had been a stupid argument. He would never see his father again.

When he got out of the sanatorium in Vancouver, his mother moved with him into a house there, insisting it was too dangerous for them to return home. Emmett didn't have any money of his own, and he couldn't make contact with Japan because it was wartime; he was kept by his mother. When his father was reported dead, Emmett, guilty, angry, enlisted in the RAF. His mother suffered a fatal heart attack while he was in the war. At the time, he refused to mourn. Under the circumstances, flying night raids as he was then, grief would have tripped him up. He stored grief in his bones. Rage inspired him, sharpened his sight, his mind, setting fire to the German cities and towns. A delicious hatred of the enemy gave him courage. He was proving — to his dead father — that he would not fail.

Grief leached out of him now. As the excitement of the war receded, grief seemed to release itself in waves that washed back over him, shaking him so deeply he might fall to his knees, just as he'd done that night in Norfield's bookstore. A fit of weeping could overcome him on a streetcar, or as he bent over to tie his shoe. He wept in his sleep, awakening wet with tears. He learned that grief is a medley of rage, pity, regret, and hunger, starvation; he was starving for his father, to see him again, to hear his voice, to be forgiven.

He couldn't afford to regret what he'd done in Bomber Command, it would cost him too much. It had been blind, *well blooded*, obedient action. A luscious poison in his veins that had won the commander's praise. The bombing, all that burning was too great, much too great. Regret would destroy him. He had to redeem his life.

When he recalled his father, it was often a memory of the man angrily turning away from him; the image of his father turning his back recurred in Emmett's mind obsessively. Turning his back in disgust or, Emmett wondered now, turning his back out of his own sense of inadequacy, a man who had failed his family. Emmett began to see mortality there, in a memory of the lonely shape of the living man. Maybe his father had been uncertain, unhappy, driven by fears and desires he couldn't control. A man who'd chosen to live outside the normal family strictures, seeking a certain self-invention and finding himself trapped, failing.

Chapter Seven

Emmett thought about Suzanne McCallum almost all the time. Her skin, her blue eyes, her confident stride, her place in the world. A rich man's daughter from Forest Hill, Toronto.

Suzanne was seeing John Norfield. A poet. A communist, or so he claimed. Compelling in a way that Emmett never could be. Norfield seemed to know everything; he could remember the names of every revolutionary, every philosopher, writer, and artist who had ever lived. Emmett didn't know anyone else who knew so many names, and he was impressed. John never again spoke directly about Hong Kong; he talked about oppression, the violence of the state, and they argued over the differences between German and Japanese fascism. Emmett listened to the slightly British cadence and thought, It's Toronto aristocrat.

Of his several new friends so affected by the war, Emmett was the only one who had killed. And he had killed, or helped to kill, tens of thousands. He had seen too much. Yes, the eyes are nerve endings.

In the company of his friends, Emmett felt a weight taken from him, a lessening of anxiety and tedium, and a new radiance, an ideal. If anybody had asked him in 1946 what he believed in, he might have said communism. A grand idea, a sublime system that would eliminate war and poverty, create a true democracy, stateless, without manipulation, no Bomber Command murdering civilians. Airplanes flew over the city, carrying not bombs but passengers. He looked up at the planes' underbellies and felt starved, abandoned, thirsting.

Four years ago, the Japanese police reported that his father had jumped out of the window of the police station. Emmett doubted this was true. His father would have been very sick with TB then. The police would be happy to get rid of a foreigner infected with the disease, especially a westerner who was intimate with a Japanese woman. He must have been pushed. It was wartime, a time for killing. The police would have pushed him to his death without giving it much thought.

Passenger planes droned overhead. The city was growing; houses were going up for the returned vets having families. He hated the way the small hours of peace needed tending. "Peace is relentless," Emmett once said, realizing too late how terrible it was to say this to Leonard. Leonard, his sorrowful brown eyes filled with mockery, dryly responding, "Take arsenic, why don't you. Put yourself out of your misery."

With the war over, sex was again indexed to real estate — that's what Leonard said. "A wife," Leonard argued, "is private property, a slave to her husband. Who in turn is a slave to his banker and his boss." Somehow it all could be traced back to domesticated farm animals, according to Leonard, who said he'd learned this from Friedrich Engels, but Emmett wasn't clear how it all worked. Leonard patiently explained. "The vets are breeding like rabbits. But unlike rabbits, they must breed with only one rabbit for their whole lives, which actually sounds okay with me. That way, the male rabbit knows for sure that the baby bunnies are his when he wants to write his last will and testament. The women and children are his slaves, but he's their slave too. The war might be kaput, but the soldiers are still in service. Pretty soon, they stop thinking altogether.

Just hump and then work like crazy to feed all those kids."

Leonard was always agitated during their conversations about sex and communism. "Fucking is the original division of labour," he liked to say. Emmett understood that this obsession was partly because Leonard didn't have a lover and would obviously very much like to have one. This made their discussions unsettling, Leonard vulgar in one moment and sentimental the next.

Emmett, reading Marx's *The German Ideology*, was weary of Marx's style, that hectoring voice. Toronto wasn't ripe for revolution. He noticed that Leonard's disciples were often quoting the people whom Marx was satirizing, getting it backward. Leonard's cousin Rachel, for example, liked to rub Emmett's earlobes between her forefinger and her thumb, a perfectly sensuous and sisterly fondling, resting her satin bosom against his chest and in a milky mezzo she would drawl, "My life is a continuous process of liberation."

Emmett thought that the Toronto communists were a hip club, a costume party. But thanks to Leonard Fischer and John Norfield, he had a life again, and he was elated. "O Mensch! Gib Acht! Was spricht die tiefe Mitternacht?" Leonard said. "Ich schlief, ich schlief — aus tiefem Traum bin ich erwarcht." O Man, take heed! What says the deep midnight? I slept, I slept — from a deep dream have I awoken.

Leonard Fischer's references, like his accent, were adopted from the US — the Bomb, the military budget, the arms trade. Leonard talked a lot about racial hatred in the South, while the Holocaust could be mentioned only in terms of redemption, as proof for the necessity of "revolution." Emmett listened in silence to Leonard and Rachel name the family that had been murdered — *exterminated*. Rachel's parents had taken her with them to Canada, to Toronto, in 1933, but everyone else had been rounded up. Leonard's parents were individually murdered in gas chambers, as were his two sisters, his grandparents, another uncle and his wife, their four children, his cousins, second cousins, friends that Leonard had made in the camp. "One by one, child by child, every day there were less of us. Do you understand?" Leonard said. "Of the six million killed, one and a half million were children. Each one of them died alone.

"Lenin understood," Leonard said, "he saw it coming, the evil, the beast of anti-Semitism. Lenin knew the nature of the beast. The Germans were bankrupt. They were told to hate the Jew, so they worked overtime, making bullets to kill him. The factory owner will always get rich on fear. Harness hatred and fear, you get very rich. It's exactly what Lenin predicted. The nightmare came true."

Leonard yearned to go to Russia, utopia, a classless society. The Russians had "cleaned up" Eastern Europe. Leonard claimed that Stalin was a good friend of the Jews. Emmett didn't argue with him very much on this point because he loved Leonard and knew that Leonard needed to believe in someone, and because Emmett himself wanted a world without any kind of state at all, no Stalin, no Truman, no generals and prime ministers, no ministers of war.

For Leonard, the Communist Party was a revolutionary party. Communism suggested bliss for both of them, but for Emmett it was more diffuse, more gradual than Leonard's dream of *overthrowing the existing state of things*. Emmett admired Leonard's belief, but he had to say, "I don't see it, Leonard, I don't see a revolution happening in Toronto."

"Then I'm going to Russia," said Leonard.

Chapter Eight

On a morning of first snowfall, cars schussing past, snow clinging to the underside of wet boughs, Emmett walked to his favourite bakery. He was trying to imagine an entirely different arrangement, overthrowing the existing state of things in Toronto. The owner of the bakery was a woman in late middle age with floury hair and buttery skin, rosy as apple pie. Snow parachuted down around him on a street fragrant with warm bread. Hushed, on the sidewalk with its few people, a pretty young woman smiled at him. The day splayed north toward solstice.

Though Emmett had been speaking only English for more than ten years, his Japanese was still good enough to get him a job translating Japanese documents from the Taisho period for a professor at the University of Toronto, a scholar of Asian history. It paid well, and he could choose his own hours. He'd switched from studying British history to studying Japanese and Chinese history, becoming one of a small group of students interested in Asia. The Canadian government was paying for his education because he was a vet. An untouchable, one of Bomber Command, he would earn no medals, but he did get free tuition. Snow lit his rooms where he worked in the afternoon, fostering a deep addiction to privacy. Privacy, not solitude.

He felt incomprehensible, and so he didn't, he couldn't, begin to make himself clearly known to anyone. It happened every time, when a conversation would come around inevitably to self-definition, he'd be tongue-tied — or, rather, bored, as if by a too-difficult calculation. His life had been contrary, a series of duplications: two homes; a father who'd dominated and also abandoned him; heroic war service that was also the shame of his nation. He had no words for himself. He felt like an empty room without light, but for the borrowed light from his friends and the radiance of their ideals.

He did not want to be bourgeois, this thing Marx loathed venomously, but he liked to wear a tie. He liked to feel superior to other men, he was competitive — though he had no appetite for business, preferring quieter work; he knew he could never make a living in sales. Passenger planes flew overhead. The city shucked off its drab wartime camouflage; money was evident in the new cars, the busy restaurants and bars. He agreed with Marx that power is something inhuman, manipulative, indifferent, mocking the sacrifice he'd made, bombing civilians. He admitted to himself that he'd been duped. It would never happen again.

By now, seven months after meeting John Norfield and Leonard Fischer, Emmett was wary of the Toronto communists. But from his reading of Marx, he'd learned something key, something that would guide him. He thought that the others, Leonard and his acolytes, didn't understand this, in their doctrinaire absorption of what they thought was communism. It was almost a trick of mind, Marx's trick, whereby a man could disaffect from what Marx called "the dead generations" that weigh "like a nightmare on the brains of the living." Emmett chose to train himself to live without belonging because belonging to anything, any sort of human community, requires a certain costuming, a borrowed language that thus makes a man a caricature.

Toronto was not ripe for revolution. But Emmett Jones had set out on a discipline that was revolutionary; he would strip away self-deception—and this discipline, he knew, would take constant practice, would necessarily comprise his very being. He would always have to make himself new.

Chapter Nine

Leonard Fischer's bachelor suite. Leonard at the window, looking down at the park where the man wearing a white shirt tucked into dark trousers ambled across the grass, his big empty hands swaying at his side. Emmett and John Norfield joined Leonard at the window. A cold summer, an early fall. Curled yellow leaves drifted softly from the ash trees. No one said anything. Then Leonard grumbled, "Same asshole."

It occurred to Emmett that the man had a routine, that he got off work and walked home across the park.

Leonard turned to John Norfield. "You know who he is, John?"

Norfield waited, and then he said, "No." Everything fell into that gap, that almost kindly pause Norfield had permitted before lying to his friends. The man in the white shirt had been present all summer, not only in the park but on the street; wherever John Norfield was, so was the empty-handed man in the white shirt tucked into dark trousers. Norfield must know who he is.

The fellow in the homburg hat — that dandy with the diamond ring — they all knew about him; even the student acolytes knew about him. The Homburg Hat was hometown, he was RCMP, and his surveillance made being a Toronto communist an interesting game, a serious sort of delinquency.

But this guy in the shirt, this empty-handed man, he looked real; he didn't seem Canadian.

Leonard was wheezing, plaintive, "Who he's working for?" His lungs mewed. He rubbed his face like he'd rub it off. With one sad eye on Norfield, bitterly, tenderly, Leonard said, "How come you're so important you've got somebody always following you, John, huh? Schmuck."

"C'mon," Norfield said. "I have some money. Let's get drunk, shall we?"

"You have some money, do you," Leonard grumbled, jealous, suspicious. "Lot of money in the book business?"

"I sold a poem," said Norfield, and Leonard laughed and said, "He sold a poem."

Emmett knew that Norfield wrote poetry; he'd seen him scribble lines of verse into a black notebook, though John never offered to let him read any of it. Now he looked sideways at John's fine features and said, "People buy poems?" John gave a surprised laugh and put his arm around Emmett, as if to protect him.

They drank till after dark; they ate fish and chips, then they drank a lot more. The pub was set below the sidewalk with a view of pretty stockings hurrying past.

Leonard grew garrulous with the first four pints and then got morbid, estranged, too lucid. He looked around at the porcelain British bulldogs, their bowlegs, bowties, the red tip of a dog's tongue at the crease of its black porcelain lips. Gothic stone arches, portraits of Sir Wilson Hidebound, Sir Henry Thirdson. Leonard peered at the brass inscriptions, his pants riding low on his bum. "How can you stand it?" He lurched back to their booth, taking his handkerchief from his pants pocket. "How can you bear being hijacked, fer fugsake? The entire fug-ig country's just a booby prize for every fraud who couldn't make it in Egg-land." He glared at Emmett contemptuously. "It's one big fug-ig sed-up, this whole country." He finally blew his nose.

Emmett drank his pint.

"Prove otherwise!" Leonard shouted.

A waiter wearing a white linen napkin tied at his waist stopped at their table, a tray of beer balanced on his forearm.

Emmett said, "There is no otherwise to prove."

Leonard put his elbows on the table and glowered, "Engage in a dialectical debate, you prick."

"I'm not going to prove anything to you."

"Fake British. Fake Victoria. Fake Parliament. Fake country. This whole country's a fraud. At least the States had the guts to have a revolution."

"You're an old woman when you're drunk."

"You're an old woman when you're sober, asshole."

Norfield sighed and adjusted his shirt cuffs. The waiter finally put the beer on the table. Even the waiter felt superior, they all felt superior to one another, in a pretentious little backwater built on mutual contempt. "This is a stupid argument," Emmett said.

Leonard said, "I want a fug-ig cigarette. I haven't had a cigarette since I'm fourteen." He blew his nose again.

Emmett's finger tracked the foam running down his glass. He was tired of himself. He'd been working long hours, translating between Japanese and English, and now he'd had too much beer. He thought about how hard Japan had tried to keep the British out, to keep a purity that Canada could never know — by definition Canada could never be anything but a mimic.

"There's this Japanese painting," Emmett said. "It's old, this painting. Ancient. Very beautiful." The brush, loaded with ink, weighted by the blackest ink. "It was painted by a philosopher," he said. "A Buddhist monk. Hasegawa Tohaku." In the sixteenth century Hasegawa Tohaku raised his arm, withheld his hand with the brush, then his soul made a decision, his arm descended, he created sentient, silent pine trees in mist.

"I don't speak Japanese, remember? Hungarian, Yiddish, German, but no Jap."

"Forget it."

"Go on," said Leonard, mopping the sweat on his forehead. "I'm being a boor because I'm tired and drunk and it makes me sad. Go on, say what you must say."

"I don't know. It's pine trees." Emmett tried to stand up. "And mist." He sat down again. "It's like overhearing God or something. The pine trees are conscious."

The painting was done with a brush of bamboo, broom, with the richest black ink. He wanted to say that the artist had revealed a consciousness in mist, in pine trees, an austere presence. The finest form of purity. Emmett said, "Fleeting. Incredibly delicate. And humble, in a grand way. Majestic and grand, grandly noble, and grandly — remote."

Leonard dug at his ear.

"You'd know what I mean," Emmett said, taking up his beer and drinking, "if you could see it."

Leonard reached for him, "C'mere," tenderly gripped his head between his hands and whispered, "You're a fug-ig idealist." *Idealist* was a Toronto communist insult.

"Yeah. But it's a beautiful painting." Emmett pushed himself upright. "And now. I am going to take a piss."

"You got it up the ying-yang!" called Leonard after him. "Emmett, my friend!"

Emmett turned around.

"Don't forget Pearl Harbor." Leonard rubbed his own heart, repeating sadly, "Never forget it."

"Why would I forget it?"

"You come from there, right?"

Japan. He shrugged.

Leonard rubbed his chest so hard he popped a button on his shirt. "You make a living, that's okay, speaking Japanese. Translating. That's an honourable trade, I know."

"All I know is, I've had seven pints. Eight pints exactly."

"I know you're not Japanese, I got eyes, you're no Jap. But hey, the Japanese are dangerous. I mean it. They're dangerous." He made a noise like an airplane smashing into the table, spilling beer everywhere. "Tsk, look at me. Zayt moykhl." The way he mopped it up with his shirtsleeve, sheepishly, reminded Emmett that Leonard had had a mother, he'd had an older sister, he'd paid attention to them when he was a boy, before they were murdered. "Do whatever you want," Leonard was saying. "It's not up to me."

Emmett turned away. "I'm going to take a leak."

Leonard sadly dabbed at the beer on the table. "Anyway. America got 'em good." His mass, the way the new fat sat uncomfortably on a body starved while it was still growing, and a private darkness coming down on him, making Emmett realize again, how much effort it must take Leonard to keep going. He heard Leonard say in a low voice, "We're unforgiveable."

Emmett stopped. He returned to the damp table. "Who is 'we'?" Leonard was concentrating on the continents of beer on the table. He shook his head. "The living."

Norfield was quiet all night. When they left the pub, he ducked into an alley and threw up, holding his narrow black tie to the side and missing his shoes. He patted his lips with his handkerchief and remained perfectly groomed, seemingly sober.

They waited for him and started walking again. Leonard laid his hand on Norfield's shoulder, saying, "John, John," but Norfield shrugged it off.

"John," Leonard said again. "There's your friend in the hat."

Across the street, the short, well-built man wearing the homburg hat and a fine pearl grey raincoat that caught the light moved through the crowds of pub-crawling students. Mr. Farce. He seemed so securely secret he didn't imagine himself visible. Emmett stopped walking and stared. Norfield, with a cigarette between his lips, took his arm and said, "Walk," pulling him forward.

Four or five blocks later, they parted company. Norfield said he had work to do, and left them, calling goodnight over his shoulder.

Emmett couldn't go home—he was renting the third floor of a house off College; the widow downstairs would evict him if he came home smelling of liquor. He and Leonard walked on to Leonard's suite. Leonard was elaborately pessimistic, talking about an uncle who was in trouble in New York. He said he'd lived there with him, with his uncle and aunt, who took him in when he first left Europe after liberation, and now his uncle was in trouble. He recited a poem about a star called Antares, a long, moody, complicated poem he said he wrote when he was a kid. He said he should go see his uncle, but he couldn't because he'd be arrested, "and what use would I be to anybody then?" He said, "This place is going to kill me. It's a big fug-ig pawnshop. Look! I'm falling south! I'm falling all the way to America!"

The streets of Toronto fall south to the lake. Sleety rain fell, the wind gusting. Emmett took Leonard's arm and they ran north into the wind, Leonard wheezing and the gutters filled with rain and yellow leaves roiling down, the slick road going blue.

Chapter Ten

When Emmett woke up in the only armchair in Leonard's suite, Leonard was seated at the end of his cot studying him. Emmett had a life-threatening hangover and broke out in a sweat as soon as he opened his eyes. Looking at Leonard's droopy face didn't help. It was barely day. The room stank like always. Leonard said, "I have to leave the country."

Emmett said, "Goodbye then," and closed his eyes. He, too, thought about getting away, going nine or ten pints back into his recent history. He sweated alcohol, he would never, ever drink again. "You told me you can't cross the border. You said they'd arrest you. Please go to sleep, Leonard." He heard Leonard try to breathe through his congestion and added, "I'm sorry, man."

Leonard stood up, the smell of weariness coming off him, gamy, friendly. "You want the bed? I can't sleep. Take the bed."

Emmett could hear him dumping coffee grounds into the sewage sitting in his sink. His heart was pounding so bad he'd never get back to sleep, especially on Leonard's sweaty flannel sheets. He said, "I don't understand why you'd go to jail. If you cross the border."

"Long story."

"I've got a few minutes. I'm composing my obituary."

The coffee pot on the hot plate, the smell of electricity. "My uncle," Leonard stopped to blow his nose, "studied to be an electrical engineer. This is in Munich. Immigrates to the States when he's eighteen years old. This is 1914. Marries an American, my Aunt Miriam. Works his ass off. Loves America, *loves* America. You heard this story."

"No I haven't."

Leonard went to look out his window. He said, "In 1940, he's been in America for twenty-six years, he's already over forty. Then Congress passes this thing, this Alien Thing. Right? Everybody, Jews, Germans, everybody who's not *American* has to write a letter of *explanation* to President Roosevelt. The FBI doesn't like his letter. They watch him. They sit outside his house, they tail him when he goes to work, they open his mail, I bet they tapped his phone. They watched him like hawks all through the war. Then I show up. He finds me through the Red Cross and gets me sent to him. I'm staying with him and Aunt Miriam in New York. He tells the FBI, this boy is my nephew from Hungary, leave him alone. They don't believe him. They think I'm a German, faking it. My uncle. A very smart man who never had a chance. Breaks my heart. Still."

Leonard placed a cup of coffee on the arm of Emmett's chair; Emmett felt its heat and opened his eyes. The early daylight hadn't yet committed to sun or cloud-cover.

"Don't burn yourself with this coffee," Leonard warned. His voice sounded forced, like bad acting. He went to the window. Then he made an elaborate show of tiptoeing over to the radio, turning it up loud, then tiptoeing in his oversized shoes back to the window, where he waved Emmett to come over. Emmett pulled himself up and went to stand beside Leonard at the window.

In the null dawn, the man in a white shirt tucked into

dark trousers strolled across the park below, his empty hands swinging at his sides.

Leonard put his finger to the side of his nose. Emmett asked, "Who *is* that guy?"

Leonard had a sort of rubber face; he could make a frown like a huge smile upside down. "Fugged if I know." He tapped his nose again. "But my money's on him being Norfield's handler."

He wondered if Leonard was setting him up, playing him for a patsy. He turned the radio off and in a normal voice, he said, "What's a 'handler,' Leonard?"

Leonard took Emmett's face between his hands. Emmett braced himself for a kiss, but Leonard whispered in his ear, "Soviets." He shoved Emmett's head away, squinting to gauge his impact. Again, the warm hands either side of his head, and Leonard whispered, "Norfield's got himself in deep."

He tiptoed to the door, held it open till Emmett passed through, locked it behind them, didn't say another word for a half-hour, shushed Emmett when he tried to speak, kept him walking till they reached the rail line north of Dupont. It was a lukewarm morning, no wind or sun or rain. Emmett was confined in his alcohol-poisoned body. "I honestly have to rest." He sat on the track.

Leonard heaved himself down beside him, then scoped the area and asked, "Want me to finish the story?"

"Sure."

"My uncle, he could've talked himself into Eleanor Roosevelt's panties. More American than Henry Ford. And he told me to talk like him when they come to interview me so they can choose if they're going to let us stay in America.

Which I tried. Maybe I tried too hard. But a European Jew? They thought we were eradicated, they come looking again and again, they want to see this talking animal. They come to the house. They interview my uncle for hours. He wants me to go away, go up to Canada, but I can't, I can't leave him. The FBI go away, they come back, they interview me for six hours, it goes on like this six days."

"Why?"

"They said he was a spy."

"God, I'm sorry, Leonard."

"Don't feel sorry for me."

"I don't."

"Well don't."

"Okay."

A train was coming. Leonard stood up and brushed the dirt off his palms. He looked like a deflated tire, his grimy trousers sagging down beneath his paunch, dragging over his shoes.

They could see the train in the distance, could feel it in the tracks.

Leonard said, "My uncle was passing information to the Russians."

"What?"

"You think he was a tailor? Hey? Some kind of small-time schmuck? He was a scientist! It never occurred to you? He never stopped learning. Ever. Yes. A Jew from Munich, *that* they never let him forget. He loved America. So much he wouldn't let her destroy herself."

They stood close to the tracks while the train passed, its panicky clamour turning nostalgic in the distance. Leonard was mumbling. Emmett asked him to repeat it. Leonard shook his head and said, "Not in your sorry life."

The sky was finally going to give rain. They started to walk again. Leonard said, "Anyway, you heard me. He gave information to the Russians."

"What kind of information?"

"I don't know. He wouldn't tell me. So I had nothing to tell the FBI."

Six days of interviews with nothing to tell. "It wasn't your fault, Leonard."

"Sure."

"None of it was your fault."

"I loved my uncle. I worshipped him."

He'd always considered Leonard old. Now he realized, Leonard was younger than he was by several years.

"Ask me where my uncle is, at this present time," Leonard said.

"Okay. Where's your uncle?"

"About thirty, forty miles north of New York. A place called Sing Sing."

"Jesus. For how long is he supposed to be in there?"

"Life."

"Life? That's terrible. God, it must be terrible for your aunt."

"I've gotta go."

"To New York?"

"To Moscow."

"Moscow, Russia?"

"Moscow is in Russia, asshole." Leonard gripped Emmett's arm and spun him around. "You think I'm just an unhappy Jew. You think I'm de*pressed*, is that right? Sad old Leonard Fischer had an awful time in the war. You think what happened to us *hurt my feelings?*"

He saw that Leonard was capable of hating him, and he felt a surge of respect. Leonard needed ecstasy, they both did, they'd been made addicts, there was no other way to get over the war but to obliterate themselves in something grand, sublime. Addiction is nostalgia for lost happiness. Again Emmett said he was sorry. "But I don't understand. How are you going to get to Moscow? What would you do if you ever got there?"

"Work. I'm not saying much to you, Emmett. What you don't know won't hurt you. But I'll tell you — they've been waiting. Hoping I'd come over. Any more than that, you don't want to know. Norfield's not the only one with something to offer. I'm no spy. But I can work. And I believe." His eyes filled with tears again. "I'll miss you." He remembered that they were likely being followed and looked around hopefully. "I'll go wherever they need me. Moscow, Leningrad, maybe a farming village by the Black Sea, who knows? I see myself driving a tractor!"

They approached Leonard's suite, then Emmett would walk on. The man in the white shirt was outside Leonard's building now, standing with his hands at his side. Leonard stopped so suddenly, Emmett bumped into him. Leonard's voice trembled. "Look," he said. "Do me a favour."

"Of course."

Leonard fumbled in his pants to produce a black leather wallet and from that a key. "My spare. Take it, will you, man?"

"Why?"

"I might have to leave some stuff. My books. I can't take them, it's just too many. They're valuable."

"They're also illegal."

"My books? There's no law against them. You're thinking of Quebec. In Quebec, they'd put you in jail. Here, it's okay.

74

You think I'd put you in such jeopardy? Never, never in my life would I do anything to harm you." Leonard wiped tears from his eyes and blew his nose. "Wait a while and go get them. Will you?"

"Whatever you want."

"I'll pay rent here for another three months, ahead. You can wait. It'll be safe."

The man in the white shirt stood just across the street, waiting at the door to Leonard's apartment building. He met Emmett's eye with a blank gaze. Leonard started to walk toward him, backward, talking, "Just go in there, like in November. Nobody's going to be waiting around in November. And get my books."

"Wait a minute." He couldn't let Leonard go. "How am I going to know you're okay?"

Leonard was across the street. "Store my books someplace. Someplace they won't think of looking."

"I don't trust that guy." The man heard and didn't respond, and his stony indifference angered Emmett.

"Put them in your girlfriend's house."

"What girlfriend?" Emmett stood in the middle of street. The whole city seemed deserted. Except for a car parked down the way, the driver turning the ignition and driving slowly toward them.

Leonard said, "Take them to her house. They won't look there. When it's safe, sell them. Give the money to my cousin Rachel."

The man in the white shirt climbed the few stairs up to the front door of Leonard's apartment building and held the door open, waiting for Leonard to go in. Leonard said, "I'll get word back to you somehow. From Russia." Then he took the stairs two at a time. Emmett had never seen him move so athletically.

The car crept up to the front of the building, the driver looking toward Leonard, who turned as he was entering the building, and Emmett could see the boyish zeal, he heard the thrill in Leonard's voice when he called out, "Live a good life, Emmett," and disappeared inside.

Chapter Eleven

The man in the white shirt vanished along with Leonard. In November, when Emmett went back to Leonard's building, he met only one man, in the hallway outside Leonard's suite, a Polish fellow, a carpenter still wearing his tool belt, who explained in a loud, heavily accented voice that he always came home for lunch. They'd engaged in praise of Campbell's Tomato Soup, the man standing with his key ready to open the door to his suite, which was beside Leonard's. Emmett had never run into him before, over the months when he attended Leonard's meetings. The Polish fellow was about to go into his suite to heat his tomato soup when he asked, "You know where he's gone? Your Jewish friend."

"His aunt is sick."

"Good."

"Yes."

"A sick aunt."

They each had a key in their respective locks. Emmett opened Leonard's door and picked up the empty wooden crate he'd brought.

The fellow said, "You're taking some things from there?"

"Yes."

The bonhomie disappeared and reappeared very quickly, then he burst forth with admiration of young fellows who like to read, he himself not being much of a bookworm but good with his hands. Emmett backed into the suite, thinking, I really like Poles, his head so filled with books he didn't wonder how the carpenter knew it was indeed books he was there to remove from Leonard's apartment.

The crate was too heavy. He unpacked it and carried a loose armful to the car, climbed back upstairs, made several trips up the four flights of stairs. Suzanne sat in the driver's seat, looking straight ahead. This stillness was her camouflage. He came down with his last load, closed the trunk, and got in beside her. There were times when she seemed to him a gauzy transparency. He believed that she was pure of heart, a quality that didn't preclude her from being his very own catastrophe. Suzanne was in love with John; he could tell by the hallowed way she said his name.

A beige Chrysler turned onto Leonard's street and was making its way toward them when it pulled over to the curb and parked. The driver was a woman. But he said, "Turn around."

"What?"

"Make a U-turn."

She did, with ease, though she gave it too much gas and backed up too close to the curb and with so much weight in the trunk, she scraped the rear fender of her father's silver Bentley. "Damn," she said. "Now I'll have to make up a story."

"Tell him you were loaded with revolutionary literature and hit a curb escaping the RCMP."

She was trembling. "He'll blame John."

"Look, I'm sorry I got you involved."

"With what? With John?" It was supposed to be a joke, flirtatious teasing.

Emmett said, "Anyway, thanks for helping my friend."

She bit her lip. "These books are illegal, aren't they?"

"Not here. Only in Quebec."

She didn't look convinced but added nervously, "It's not like we're hiding a dead body." She gripped the big wheel of the Bentley till her knuckles were white. "When's he coming back? Your friend." Suzanne had never met Leonard. She wanted small talk. "Is his aunt going to die?"

"I don't know." Emmett couldn't store Leonard's books in his rented rooms on the third floor of the widow's house because she snooped; he knew she did, he could smell her talcum as soon as he opened his door. Leonard's idea was good, probably safe, hiding the books at Suzanne's father's house. The McCallum place would be vast; he imagined many forgotten recesses thick with cobwebs. He thought they'd store Leonard's contraband with the great-grandmother's wedding dress and relics from the Boer War.

They arrived at the McCallum estate in the early afternoon. Three ancient maples stood at the gate, still in leaf, a radiant gold; the pool was drained, revealing a lotus blossom made of lapis lazuli in its marble basin; the junipers were wrapped in yellow burlap.

She parked the Bentley in a stable converted into a garage. It smelled of straw and motor oil. Six English saddles sat on wood beams covering one wall. An oak cabinet with nuts and bolts, nails of differing sizes, everything labelled. He felt abruptly homesick for his childhood at the Shioya estate. He'd forgotten the persuasions of wealth. An immaculate 1937 Alfa Romeo was parked beside a new Cadillac, gleaming chrome and leather, as polished and orderly as Japan. Beautiful objects, their magic allure, exempt from mess and happenstance, perfectly maintained. There were no half-empty boxes, no discarded suitcases or shipping crates, no dirty rags, not a speck of dust, no cobwebs, on the entire estate not a fallen leaf, not a twig. An orderly mind — he assumed it was her father's — had thorough possession of the place.

The stable was chilly. Suzanne opened the Bentley's trunk and then she, too, seemed to measure the quantity of what they intended to hide against the sheer and total consciousness behind every feature of her parental home. She gave a gasp and blushed. "I don't know why I thought this would be easy." Then she slammed the trunk shut and said, "Hello, Mama."

Backlit, at the door to the garage, a woman. Her cool voice, "Why the Bentley?"

"Pardon?"

"Why the Bentley? Why not the Cadillac?"

Suzanne's flustered grace. "I guess I was showing off to Emmett. Oh! You haven't met!"

Suzanne hauled him forward to meet the grande dame, who maintained her place and her perfect posture. Mama was dressed in a camel-hair skirt and sweater set. She had great legs. He was taken with her shoes, which were long, narrow, tri-tone leather pumps, fawn, ivory, and black. She held her head high, her mouth in a small smile, thus eliminating jowls and laugh lines.

Mama put her manicured hand into his, the "how do you do" delivered in a leathery contralto that had something to do with Scotch whisky — in proportion. "We're just back from Provence," she told him and pressed the waves of her hair into place, "and still out of sorts." She had a more cultured British accent even than Norfield's. She took a step into the chilly shade and waited while her eyes adjusted before proceeding.

"What is it you *do*, Mr. Jones?" She was examining the cars, running her finger over the canvas lid on the Alfa Romeo, then coming around the grill on the Bentley, yellowed with gravel dust. It would take a Geiger counter to measure the true value of her dissatisfaction, so unimpressed was she by the world she governed.

Emmett, feeling diminished, admitted that he was still a student. "I'm studying Asian history," he added.

She raised her head. "Chinese?"

"Japan. Mostly. But yes, China. And Vietnam."

Suzanne said, "Emmett was born there."

"In China?" Mama spoke as if quoting someone else's vulgarity. There were aspects of the world beyond her ken, where they belonged. This time, the head stayed low, examining the silver paint, slowly making her way around to the Bentley's dimpled rear end.

"No," he said. "I was born in Japan. Near Kobe."

She heard him politely, mildly curious, perhaps remembering the Bomb. Then, "And what's this?"

"I had a little scrape," said Suzanne. "A bump. I was just going to confess to Dad."

"Perhaps you should confess to me, dear."

"Oh, it was nothing. I hit a curb, that's all."

Mama surprised Emmett by squatting lithely to give the Bentley's fender a forensic exam. "What *kind* of curb?"

Mama stood. As he grew more accustomed to her features, he could see a certain warmth there, a candid irony. She said, "What have you got in the trunk?"

"Books."

"Lift the latch."

Suzanne opened the trunk.

Beautiful, manicured hands moved over the dun-coloured books, lifting a cover, "Jack London? What's this?" She lifted Theodor Dreiser from the pile, *Eine Amerikanische Tragödie*. "German?" She returned it and picked up another. "*Revolution Betrayed*. What on earth? *Literature and Revolution*. Ah. *The Communist Manifesto*. This I know. What do you intend to do, Mr. Jones? Blow the place up?"

Suzanne said, "We're keeping them for a friend."

"Because?"

Suzanne looked to Emmett for clarification, then answered bravely, "Because they were too heavy for him to carry."

Mama's sterling irony. "On the run."

Emmett took Marx out of Mama's hands. "This was my mistake. I never should have asked Suzanne to bring them here. I'll take them away." He began to stack the books in his arms.

Mrs. McCallum was speaking to Suzanne as if he weren't there. "Is this the suitor I've been hearing about?"

"No, it is not. The suitor you've been hearing about is a horse's ass."

"I am not speaking of Dirk Dupont. The other one. The new one."

John Norfield. Mama put her weight back on her heels, a position that thrust her hips forward, like a gunslinger.

Suzanne realized that Emmett was leaving the stable. "Where are you going?" she asked.

He would walk to the road and hitchhike. "I'll come back for the rest. The books will be gone by nightfall."

"That's ridiculous," said Suzanne. She appealed to Mama. "We can store them here, can't we?"

"We certainly cannot. For goodness' sake, these books are illegal!"

"That's only in Quebec, Mother."

"I cannot have — paper, here," waving, "in the garage," pronounced *gá-rahj*. She was struggling; she did not like her fear to be evident. "We'll get mice."

Emmett stood out in the sun, looking into the fragrant stable, aware of Mama's pale face, the narrow nose with its pink nostrils, Mama saying, "My husband is an important man." He turned and headed for the road. Mama's voice rose, strident, "Do you want to destroy everything your father and I have fought for?"

"*Fought* for?" Suzanne hissed. "You just sit on the phone with your broker!"

Then he was out at the road. A milk delivery truck, an old Ford, picked him up at the end of drive, as if they'd timed it on purpose. The truck's cab was upholstered in spotless Jersey cowhide, unsettlingly supple and soft, a sacrifice made by a cow. "Like it?" asked the driver. "Did it myself." The driver, a man of maybe seventy years, had no teeth; he had a habit of sucking his lips over his gums in a way that must have been pleasurable. The truck was hauling steel canisters filled with milk, everything sealed and spotless, the atmosphere milky. "Name's Ed," he said and reached across his sunken chest to offer Emmett his left hand while he held on to the wheel with his right.

Ed was cross-eyed. He took a gander at the books and stiffened, appraising Emmett for a moment, then driving several miles in silence.

Emmett expected Ed to kick him out. But then he heard

a wobbling tenor, Ed rolling down his window, letting in the wind while he sang, "You will eat, by and by, in that glorious land above the sky. Work and pray, live on hay, you'll get pie in the sky when you die." That one verse, before he rolled up the window, driving on. "Yep," he said. And a few minutes later, he added, "You a vet?" Emmett said that he was. "Non-profit enterprise," Ed drawled, nodding sagely, "unless you're in the steel business. Aircraft parts, coal, that kind of thing will make a whole lot of money in a war."

They were downtown. "Just drop me off here," Emmett told him. But Ed said, "Blood profit," and insisted on taking him all the way to Leonard's yellow brick building, where he reached around to shake Emmett's hand again, saying, "They fed you a load of horse manure, gettin' you to fight their goddamn war."

Emmett got out with his armload of books. The sky had darkened, a meagre twilight, and the air had turned cold. He stood on the concrete steps and freed two fingers to pry open the heavy door to Leonard's building, hurried up the stairs to Leonard's suite, and threw all the books down in the hallway, careless of the noise he was making, then went back down to collect the several that had fallen.

When at last he entered the apartment, a speckled dusk filtered through the dirty window. It was abandoned. But for a short, square man in a hat, the pearl grey of his trench coat catching, enhancing the last light.

"Did I alarm you?" asked Mr. Farce. Then, "What have you got?"

"Who are you?"

"I'm looking for Leonard Fischer. You know where he is?"

"No."

"Hmm. Yet, you said he was visiting his sick aunt."

Mr. Farce was connected to the Polish carpenter somehow, a network of surveillance. Emmett felt the hateful confinement of being *caught*, having his words tossed back at him by such a dandy. "I don't know where Leonard is."

"He's a good friend of yours. You might say he's a fellow traveller." Mr. Farce made the expression sound sexual.

"He's not such a good friend."

"Yet you have a key to his apartment."

Emmett said, "A lot of people have a key to this place."

"Who?"

"I don't know their names. And I don't know where Leonard is."

"Why did you say that you do know, Emmett?"

Emmett looked more closely at his interrogator. In the fading light he confirmed that they were of the same age, or close to it. So power wasn't inflicted on the powerless from above, or from an older generation; power was all around him, he was hemmed in.

Mr. Farce approached. Emmett could smell his cologne when he leaned across and switched on the lamp.

"Look." Emmett made his voice sound tired. "I was doing the guy a favour. He told me he was hard up for cash, so would I sell some things for him. The only thing he had were books, so I tried for that."

"Any luck?"

"Not yet."

The man looked into Emmett's eyes, seeing something there that Emmett couldn't hide. "It must be hard," he said.

"Who are you?" Emmett asked again.

"Oh, come on." He shook his head in disgust. "Did Leonard

Fischer defect? Is he working for the Russians?" When Emmett didn't answer, he persisted. "How about John Norfield? Dawson Elliott, know him? Joseph Chambers. Fred Shaw."

"I don't know any of them. Except John Norfield." Emmett was guilty by association. Maybe the books weren't technically illegal, but this man could require that he go with him now for questioning.

Mr. Farce gave a weary sigh. "Norfield. Yeah. I know. That, I know." He rubbed his jaw, the diamond glittering on his hand. "If you're telling the truth, about selling Fischer's books, you'd've taken them to your friend Norfield."

"How do you know I didn't?"

He smiled to himself in a condescending way. "Let me ask you something. Have you ever seen Norfield sell a book?"

Emmett hadn't. He said nothing.

"Ever wonder where he gets his money?"

"He's a poet."

This caught Mr. Farce by surprise. He laughed. "Holy god."

Emmett went to the door and opened it. He expected to be restrained, maybe even attacked, and he forced himself to move slowly, listening for a sudden move from Mr. Farce, walking out to the hallway, leaving the door open behind him. He walked down the stairs and outside, feeling the man on his back, resisting the impulse to run. He didn't know why he'd been let go.

He got back to the McCallum place just at nightfall. He took a cab, and had the cabbie wait while he loaded the books into the trunk. As the cab drove past the house on the way back out to the road, he saw Suzanne's mother watching from a window at the corner of the main floor of the house. He was certain they looked each other in the eye, though she was thirty feet away. She let the drapes fall back into place and turned toward the darkness of the house without waving.

◇

That was November 1946, only sixteen months after two atomic bombs fell out of a blue sky onto two cities in Japan. Emmett removed the incendiary literature from the McCallum estate, while in the far-off land of the Soviet Union, the best scientists were preparing for World War Three, building nuclear bombs and long-range nuclear rockets. Success was in the air in America too. The United States was making some difficult decisions as to whether they should ignite a small amount of thermonuclear fuel by a large fission explosion or contrive a small fission explosion to ignite a very large mass of thermonuclear fuel (what they affectionately called the "superbomb").

Suzanne McCallum's elegant mother let the drapes fall and turned from the window as Emmett's taxi rolled past and out to the road, lurching at the end of the drive. She did not wait to see him clearly off the property and did not see the nondescript sedan pull out from under the golden maples, following the cab back to College Street, to Emmett's attic room in the home of a snoopy widow.

PART TWO

Chapter One

Blue Sea Lake, Summer, 1953

Bill Masters, undersecretary of state at External Affairs, cut an alarming figure in a bathing suit. Lake water glittered like quartz in the silver hair on his barrel chest and over his fleshy back. It was a marvel that his small feet and narrow ankles could leverage such mass. Watching him swim, Emmett was fascinated by the pretty movements of Bill's limbs propelling him through the water.

Bill appeared to bear no ill effects from the alcohol last night. He slapped his belly and filled his lungs, "Great air," pectorals jiggling, a friendly Samurai. With a happy sigh, he raised a glass of orange juice tarted up with vodka. "Great place, Emmett."

Ethel called. "Yoo-hoo! Breakfast is hot!" She hopped partway down the cottage stairs to the lawn, decked out in a variation of the rayon paisley she'd worn the previous day, with fresh stockings and another pair of strapped sandals, shielding her eyes with one hand. Bill gave her a wave, toodle-doo. She trotted back up the stairs to the cottage, gripping the hand-railing, and then at the door, she leaned back toward Bill, her hand raised in another little private yoo-hoo.

Bill grinned with pride. "Comfy beds you got here." He punched Emmett's arm. "Ethel's having a good time. She gets along real well with Suzanne." They threw towels over their shoulders and began to walk up, Emmett following Bill's amazing white feet with their purple veins and frank toes. Bill said, "Ethel doesn't get on with too many Ottawa wives." He stopped and waited till Emmett caught up to him. "Most of them are bitches. Seen from a female mind. I let Ethel stay home from a lot of functions. Better'n her being miserable. But it's nice to see her happy. Thanks. Appreciate it."

A boat cruised by. A small inboard filled with kids and their parents, trolling a couple of fishing lines and strains of Dean Martin slurring the words to "With My Eyes Wide Open I'm Dreaming." The boat was so close to shore, Emmett could make out a turntable balanced on a cooler amid the chaos of kids, life jackets, Cokes, towels, and a dog, a beagle.

Bill said, "Now, there's a guy who likes to live." He walked ahead, "I hope Ethel lets me have bacon."

Emmett wondered how to power a turntable aboard a boat. Sun on blue water made the scene Kodak, a contrivance of colour technology. The boat wasn't familiar on this part of the lake. He thought its driver must be lucky, head of an empire. He couldn't see the man's face under a sun hat.

After breakfast Bill and Ethel packed up to leave. Bill tickled Lenore under her chin, earning her mild scorn. "Okay, little baby," said Bill. "I guess you're not the laughing type."

Ethel picked up Lenore and gave her a kiss. Lennie put her finger up Ethel's nose, Ethel clucking, capturing the baby's hand and saying, "Oh, you little bug." Suzanne retrieved Lennie, "C'mon, professor." They all went down to the dock. Ethel was thoughtful, kindly wondering: she'd never met such a serious baby. Her two teenaged boys were at Upper Canada College, bless them, but would soon be out for summer holidays. Becoming strangers to her.

Emmett lowered Ethel into the boat. She looked unsuitable for transport. Bill patted Suzanne, "You did fine," and turned his back to speak more confidentially to Emmett. "I recruited you to External because you know Asia. We're holding the line in Korea, but only so long as we keep the communists scared shitless, pardon my French. I'm not saying the Americans should drop an A-bomb on anybody, but the commies sure better know it's in the equation. Now," and here Bill shuffled a little, wiped sweat from his eyes; he appeared to be struggling to remember where he was going with this. Again he said, "Now..." his eyes darting over the smooth blue water, sweat running down his face into his fat neck. Then it came back to him, he was aiming to talk about what everybody wanted to talk about. "The Ruskies," he announced, "the Ruskies and the Chinese communists are getting ready for World War Three. And it'll be the big one. Us or them. Freedom or Communism. Anybody who doesn't believe *that* is playing The Glad Game." He gripped Emmett's hand, maybe just to steady himself. "We need men like you, and we need you here, where you can untangle some of the gobbledegook we get from Southeast Asia. You're young. You're smart. And you know the Chinese."

"Japan."

"Whazat?"

"I was born in Japan."

Bill looked at him blankly.

"I'm learning some Mandarin," Emmett explained, though Bill already knew this, "but I can't say I know the Chinese."

"Good. Stick it out. You got yourself a future, Jones."

"Okay."

"I mean it."

"Right."

"Don't dick around. Tell the RCMP what they wanta know. You get the Mounties off your back, *they'll* straighten out the Americans. Then you can get on with your work. Get on with your life. No more suspicion following you around. Once and for all. Clear?"

"Yup."

"Attaboy."

They paused uncertainly until Emmett said, "I'm driving you to the landing."

Bill laughed. "Forgot." And stepped onto the hot boat cushions, Ethel warning, "Don't fall, Daddy," and Bill saying, "I'm always on Parliament Hill."

Emmett and Suzanne and Lenore were studying Bill, Emmett wondering if it was heat stroke. Bill said, "In my mind. C'mon, Jones. Start this thing," settling his backside. "Bye bye," to Lenore; then, to Ethel, "That kid doesn't like me."

Emmett jumped into the boat. Before he started the engine, he heard, faintly, Dean Martin moving over the water.

Chapter Two

A heat wave, lasting more than a week. It was so hot in the city, Suzanne kept Lennie at the lake; she and the baby stayed alone at the cottage while Emmett worked in town.

Nobody from External's Security Panel and no one from the RCMP contacted him. Days passed, then another weekend when he was with Suzanne and the baby at Blue Sea Lake, and yet another week alone in the city, and still no contact from the Mounties. He tried to convince himself that they'd decided to let him alone.

He needed a few quiet hours at his office in the East Block on Saturday morning so he told Suzanne he'd go in for a couple of hours, then drive down to the lake. He promised to take Monday off and stay with them, if he could get ahead on some reports that needed his attention.

Leaving Parliament Hill at seven o'clock Friday evening, Emmett drove home, opening the door to an empty house, the drapes drawn against the heat, the house shady but stifling. He walked through the darkened living room, making no sound on the carpet, and stood at the foot of the stairs, listening. The house was silent but for the small, yawning vibrations that houses make in summer heat. He startled at the crackling cellophane noise of a black squirrel's feet running up an oak tree out on the lawn. There were waves in the plush broadloom, made from a vacuum, and a footprint. He remembered that the cleaning lady would have come today, letting herself in with her own key to clean the house even though it never got dirty when Emmett was alone in the city.

He went to the kitchen and opened the fridge. He'd forgotten to pick up something to eat on his way home. Nothing looked like dinner. He had that automatic feeling again, of being driven ahead by the thoughtless way time pushes him, pushes everyone, just slightly ahead of itself and then sweeps overhead like a rogue wave. He felt soulless, ill at ease, he needed to hurry, hurry to soothe himself; he was inconsolable, anxious from waiting for something to happen with the investigation. Liquor helped, it helped more and more. He poured himself a stiff Scotch and soda on ice, drank some, poured more, and went upstairs.

It was hotter upstairs. He paused to look into Lennie's bedroom. The pale yellow walls could melt in the heat. Her closet door was ajar and he crossed the silent room to push it shut.

He changed his clothes, threw the white shirt he'd worn all day into the hamper, exchanged his dark blue trousers for a pair of shorts, took off his damp socks, and sat on his side of the bed while he sipped his drink.

The doorbell rang. Emmett peered down from the window that looked over the front of the house. He saw the dented lids of three hats, the padded shoulders of three men in suits standing on the stoop. He watched them, finishing his drink. The bell was rung again.

Two of the men left to walk briskly around the side of the house toward the garage, out of sight. The third man raised his head and caught Emmett looking down. Emmett knew him. It was Harold Gembey, chair of Security at External Affairs.

Harold's face was expressionless. They looked at each other for a moment. Gembey's lips moved, he was calling the other men back, his eyes on Emmett.

Emmett went down and opened the door barefoot, wearing faded madras shorts and a green golf shirt that had shrunk in the dryer, to find only Harold Gembey standing there. "Emmett," said Harold and held out his hand. "Glad to find you at home."

The other two men returned from around the back of the house, their pant legs swinging. Harold Gembey introduced them. "Sergeant Frank Partridge. And Inspector Robert Morton, RCMP."

Inspector Robert Morton removed his homburg hat. On his hand, he wore a gold ring with a diamond and he had a gold tie clip with another diamond chip. Emmett remembered the amber-coloured eyes, the short stocky frame, the compact build of a middleweight boxer. Here was Mr. Farce come to call.

Emmett said, "Bill Masters told me you'd contact me by telephone to set up an appointment." Gembey started to apologize, but Morton pushed himself between them and walked in, and Emmett said wryly, "Make yourselves at home," then followed Morton into the stuffy house. "My wife's away with our baby girl."

They sat in the living room, Harold Gembey and Frank Partridge on the couch, Robert Morton in the chair that Emmett normally occupied when he would read the newspaper after work, when Suzanne was at home. The men watched as Emmett went to open the curtains. He offered them a drink, which they declined, and then he poured himself a big one.

"Sit down, Emmett, please." Harold Gembey had greying red hair and a red moustache and wore black-framed glasses.

He leaned forward with his elbows on his knees. "Your name has come up with the Americans. And it's our job, together, to find out why."

"Why don't we ask the Americans — together?"

Morton interrupted. "How's your pal Leonard Fischer?"

"I don't know. I don't know where he is. Do you?"

"Buggered off to Russia," Morton said, but he glanced at Partridge, as if it was a private joke.

Gembey rubbed his forehead. Emmett sensed that Gembey was in competition with Morton, that there was some kind of struggle going on between them. He sensed that they disliked each other, but that didn't mean Gembey was on his side.

Gembey had a paternal attitude. Emmett knew him as one of the Oxford University trained civil servants, confident, sharp, and literate, blending in well at External Affairs — but Emmett saw a weakness in him, a failure of confidence and the consequent desire to please men whom he considered more powerful than he was. Gembey knew all the mannerisms of authority, but he lacked self-belief, he lacked goodwill.

Gembey said, "Tell us what you know about this man, John Norfield."

Emmett said, "I knew John Norfield in the past." To Morton, he added, "I've met you before too. A long time ago." It was nearly seven years ago, in 1946, when he'd met Mr. Farce in Leonard's apartment, a few months after Leonard had disappeared, apparently to Russia — to Moscow, or to drive a tractor on a collective farm by the Black Sea.

Gembey softly persisted. "Has this man Norfield been in touch with you in the last year?"

"I haven't seen John in a long time."

"Yet you were close friends, you and him," Morton observed.

"Not really." This was a complicated question, their friendship. He could say that much honestly.

Harold Gembey asked the questions after that, but he often looked at Robert Morton, as if Morton were a ventriloquist. "Remember things as accurately as you can," Gembey told Emmett.

"Can I ask *you* something?"

Gembey glanced quickly at Robert Morton before responding, "Certainly."

"Has something happened to John?"

Even the sergeant, Partridge, who'd been silent throughout, straightened.

Robert Morton spoke. "He's been arrested."

"What for?"

Morton stood up. Gembey eyed Morton uneasily as he spoke to Emmett: "MI-5 picked him up."

"John's in England," Emmett said, surprised.

Gembey scratched his head and admitted reluctantly, "Well, he was." He looked worried, maybe he was giving too much away. They all looked uneasy, embarrassed; it would be, after all, embarrassing if the Brits deported a Canadian spy. "We're keeping it out of the newspapers," Gembey said. He looked Emmett in the eye. "He got off." With a quick, contemptuous glance at Morton, he added, "Unauthorized surveillance. No case." Then slowly, as if he were trying to cipher something, protect Emmett, or protect himself, Gembey asked, "When was the last time you saw John Norfield? Think carefully."

"1949, I guess."

"Be precise."

"It was fall of 1949. He'd been ill. Look. No one was close to John."

"Except for your wife," said Robert Morton.

"Suzanne was young and naive." Then he added tightly to Gembey, "My wife has nothing to do with this."

"From 1946 to 1949," Morton said, speaking as if he were referring to notes but his hands were empty and he studied his diamond ring, "Suzanne McCallum, as she was known then, had an affair with John Norfield that he broke off. Norfield disappeared, like smoke." Morton made a sympathetic face. "She was troubled for a while. She saw a psychiatrist, from October through December. An expensive head doctor, hired by her father. Her daddy set her up in a shop, selling pictures. And then you lost your job in Tokyo, came home, and she married you."

"She's none of your business," Emmett said, then, to Gembey, "We have a child, for chrissake."

Morton smiled, amused to see Emmett rattled. Emmett put his empty glass down at his feet and sat back in his chair, taking a breath.

At eight-thirty, though it was still hot in the house, he announced that he was chilly, excused himself, and went upstairs to change his clothes. He sat down on the bed and used the phone on the bedside table. It was a poor connection. Suzanne, through the crackling line, kept asking, "What's wrong?" He told her that he'd changed his mind, he was coming down tonight. Late. He instructed her to go now, before it got too dark, tow the small outboard behind her inboard runabout and leave it for him at the landing. He told her he loved her and hung up. He'd started to change his clothes when he noticed that the bedroom door, which he was convinced that he had closed, was now open. Partridge was standing at the doorway.

"After you," Partridge said, and Emmett walked past him, back downstairs, Partridge at his back.

Robert Morton raised his eyebrows when Emmett returned still wearing shorts but made no comment.

Gembey seemed disgusted. He wanted to get this over with. He waved his hands, indicating that it was time to get down to brass tacks. "There's something we need to establish very clearly, Emmett. Are you or were you ever a member of the Communist Party?"

"No."

Gembey looked relieved and left the room. They could hear the tap running in the kitchen. Gembey was getting himself a glass of water. Emmett wanted another drink. And he was hungry. He'd had a sandwich at his desk before noon, nothing since.

Robert Morton moved to sit close to him, and in a low voice he said, "You've lied to me before." Gembey returned and Morton moved away, saying, "And your Jewish pal, Leonard Fischer, you're claiming he never contacts you?"

"No."

Morton shook his head. "You really stuck your neck out for that jerk." Now Morton seemed to be angry at Leonard, the one who got away. He said, "How about your wife? She still in touch with John Norfield?"

Gembey cut him off: "She's not our territory, Morton."

"She hasn't seen him in years," Emmett said quickly to Morton, but he knew he sounded too defensive. He had to protect Suzanne. She was innocent, naive, he had to shield her.

Morton continued, "Did she know that Norfield is a communist?"

"Everyone at the University of Toronto after the war either knew a communist or pretended to be one."

"Now that sounds like an exaggeration."

"It's true. I guess you weren't there."

Partridge finally spoke. "You seem to think this inquiry is merely a personal matter, Mr. Jones."

"Norfield was a POW in Hong Kong. That's the most important thing about him. Everything else is an after-effect."

Toward ten o'clock, the interview got general: what was Jones's attitude toward the Soviet Union? Emmett reminded them that his field was Southeast Asia. "Yes, of course," Gembey said, "we know that. What we're trying to get at is more central."

"Wait a sec," Robert Morton interrupted. "Let's follow this for a moment. 'Mao Zedong has been China's future since the Long March.' Does that ring a bell?"

Emmett said, "No."

"They're your words."

Emmett, seated in one of the Louis Quinze chairs Suzanne had inherited from her grandmother, was thinking, *Mao is China's future, Chairman Mao has been China's past, present, and future since 1943.* He said, "Turns out it's true," and then, to Gembey, "It's not treason to know this fact."

Robert Morton came and stood over him, jingling change in his pocket. "You were—disillusioned—with the Americans' support of Chiang Kai-shek." Then, in a simpering voice, "'a symptom of ignorant imperialism.'" Morton turned on his heel and leaned to speak exclusively to Partridge, "'If the kind reader will forgive a redundancy.'" Partridge smirked.

Emmett understood then, the words belonged to him, but it seemed impossible that he'd ever talked like that. *Ignorant imperialism*, yes, but *kind reader?* "I was young when I wrote that." He remembered. He'd written an opinion piece in the student newspaper, *The Varsity,* when he was studying Asia at the University of Toronto.

"Not that young," Morton said.

"Yeah. Not that young." He'd been twenty-six. Not young.

Harold Gembey said dismissively to Robert Morton, "I don't want to weigh too heavily on something he wrote in a university newspaper."

"You still a fan of Mao Zedong?" Robert Morton asked.

"I'm not a fan of anybody."

"Mass murderer, Mao," Morton quietly observed.

Gembey said impatiently, "Let's move on," and asked, "You were recalled from your job at the Canadian Liaison Mission in Japan. Why?"

Emmett guessed that the RCMP was supposed to be taking a backseat in an internal inquiry. He answered Gembey. "Bill Masters wanted me back in Ottawa."

Morton clicked his tongue. "You were close pals with the diplomat fellow, Herbert Norman. Both of you were recalled from Tokyo." He added wonderingly, "You have the strangest taste in friends." Partridge barked a laugh. Gembey let it stand, maybe glad someone else had put that on the table, Emmett Jones's association with the diplomat, Herbert Norman, recalled from Japan just prior to Emmett's recall, a man always shadowed by suspicion of being a traitor, in league with the communists.

"Yes," Emmett said. "I worked with him in Tokyo three years ago, when I was stationed there during the Korean War." He went to pour himself a third or was it his fourth drink. "Herbert Norman has been cleared," he said, pouring whisky.

A diplomat, a scholar of Japanese history, Herbert Norman was a close friend of Lester Pearson, minister of external affairs. After Herbert was cleared, it was likely Pearson who got him promoted to head the American and Far Eastern division of External. The following year, Herbert had been sent to Washington as the Canadian representative to the United Nations. Then the US Internal Security Subcommittee went after him a second time, and within six months the Americans had pushed the RCMP and External—that would be Morton and Gembey—to interrogate him on suspicion of disloyalty—to Canada, to the US. Again, he was "cleared." Now he'd been sent to New Zealand. Exile. Dry dock. His career probably ruined.

Emmett could hear Morton give a little chuckle behind his back while he drank.

When Emmett hit the road, it was nearly midnight and he was pretty drunk. He'd taken over the Alfa Romeo from Suzanne's father that summer, and now he had the top down. When he left the city lights behind him, he began to talk to himself, over the winding road to Blue Sea Lake. It was about three in the morning when he arrived and took the small outboard across. He docked the boat by starlight, made his way up the stone stairs, and discovered Suzanne sitting in the dark veranda. She remained where she was and looked up at him. "It's started, hasn't it," she said.

"Yes."

A deep groan rose from her, but she kept her eyes steadily on his. "Would it be—acceptable—to you, if I asked you to forgive me?"

Emmett didn't know what needed to be forgiven, and disliked her for assuming that this was all about her. They weren't investigating her; he would use all his strength to make sure that they would never go after her for her relationship with John Norfield. He was too tired, but he went listlessly to put his arms around her and said, "It's all right. I'll take care of it." He didn't tell her that John Norfield had been arrested in England, and that he'd been let go. Maybe tomorrow he would tell her, but now he was tired.

She pushed him out of the way, sobbing so loudly he tried to quiet her. "Shhh," thinking of Lennie, "shhh."

Suzanne kept repeating, "I'm sorry, I'm sorry." She ran outside. He could see her white bathrobe on the path down to the dock, could hear her weeping. She disappeared behind the trees and then he saw her standing on the rocks by the lake.

He went back inside, to Lenore's room. It seemed far longer than five days since he'd held his baby girl. Lennie's bedroom at the cottage was behind the kitchen. It was painted light blue and had screened windows on three sides. The leaves soughed in the wind, the shadows of their boughs moving all over. It was crazy to put her here alone in such a wildering world. She was awake, lying on her back in her crib, looking at him with those sombre grey eyes. He collected her, gathering her into his arms with a shawl around her, kissing her neck, inhaling her, "Hey, sweet baby, hey, little girl," crooning to her, but inside his head, he was talking to Gembey, to Morton, he'd never stop talking to them. "I'll be true to you," he whispered to his baby. Gembey had wanted to know, when was the last time he'd seen John Norfield. And he remembered.

Chapter Three

September 1949

Norfield had phoned and asked him to come, so he went and found John in the back room of his bookstore, seated with a black notebook in his hand. John lifted a face swollen, yellow, sweating, clammy. He'd been sick to his stomach in his little bathroom at the back and the whole place stank. John lifted a shaky hand and said, "Thank you," and put the notebook in a drawer, as if relinquishing a duty. Then he went to the back and Emmett could hear water in the sink; John was washing his hands. When he returned, he walked past Emmett, fumbled with the door to his shop, and went out. "Please lock it," John said, handing him the key, the sweat on his face slick and acrid-smelling. "I might be gone awhile."

Emmett hailed a cab and helped John into the backseat, where he lay down. Emmett got into the front beside the cabbie, who asked nervously, "What's the matter with your friend?"

John's muffled voice came from the backseat, "Nothing that will hurt you."

Emmett took him to St. Michael's Hospital, and stayed while John was admitted, waiting in the hallway all afternoon till he snagged a doctor and asked if he could see him. "Are you family?" the doctor wanted to know. Emmett said that he was his brother and was let in.

John made an effort to sit up when Emmett entered the room—a show of dignity, or self-defence.

Emmett had never witnessed John's bouts of illness, hadn't realized they could be this severe, though he knew that John still suffered from some infection, a parasite contracted in the POW camp in Japan, and that he'd sometimes retreat from his friends for a week or more, avoid even Suzanne. Emmett would learn from Suzanne that John was ill when she'd phone and ask him if he could go for a walk, for coffee, and he'd gladly keep her company, despite the pain it caused him to see her so obsessed with Norfield. Now he asked John, "Do you want me to let Suzanne know?" John wearily shook his head, no. "Not till I'm clean," he said.

Emmett spent most of the next three days at the hospital, reading the newspaper to John, or sitting with a book while John slept. He enjoyed this interlude, and John seemed grateful—he'd never known John to be so receptive.

On the fourth day, John asked him to bring a radio, and Emmett went out to buy one. When he returned to the hospital room, John was hanging up the phone, and now he regarded Emmett with that ironic grin, and Emmett knew that their relations were back to what they'd been before.

They were sitting on the bed, tuning the radio when Suzanne pushed open the door to Norfield's room. Emmett saw her cream-coloured shoes, her shapely legs, a low-cut cream-coloured dress and a cream-coloured hat of some kind, like a Sultan. She seemed embarrassed. She looked beautiful and also silly and that seemed to make her mad. He stood, trying not to look too hard. She held a tremulous pose, a cream leather handbag slung over one arm, an unlit cigarette in the other hand. Her lovely voice, "Hello, boys." Emmett thought she must be trying to look like Barbara Stanwyck or somebody like that; he found her more beautiful than Stanwyck, as beautiful as Lana Turner.

Norfield raised one knee under his bedclothes. Suzanne came to stand at the foot of his bed, biting her lip against whatever it was she wanted to say. Finally she put her cigarette into her handbag, took off the silly hat, and said bitterly, "Thanks for letting me know," throwing the purse onto the bed. "I see you two are getting along fine." And then, "God*damn* it, I was scared."

"Of what?" John said.

"You just disappeared." She calmed herself, she wouldn't dare ask much of him. "Anyway," she said, "*are* you all right?"

John said he was. Emmett thought, He actually does love her or he would never let her see him vulnerable, in a dishevelled hospital bed. Then John held up his hand: "Shhh." He turned up the radio.

They heard a tinny voice announcing, "Russia has the atom secret." Suzanne made a movement with her head, a pony yanking at the bit. Norfield's hand went up again, and she calmed. The voice was going on about "the grim vision of an atomic war that would leave complete desolation in its wake."

"It's Truman," said Norfield. "The Russians have the Bomb."

Suzanne asked, "Are they just going to blow up the world?"

Emmett was curious to see if John would celebrate the Russians' new "atomic secret."

Suzanne, too, was watching John's face. John looked closed in on himself, as if he wanted her to leave. "Well," she said, "I guess it levels the playing field."

Norfield twisted slightly, as if her opinion disappointed him, as if she made him disappointed in himself. His skin was yellow. Emmett knew it was his liver, damaged by dysentery

108

in the Japanese camp. A shabby type of war wound. John had been an active soldier for less than three weeks before being taken prisoner for nearly four years. Emmett thought that John needed to keep the battle going; the war wasn't over for him and never would be.

President Truman had finished talking, and an announcer was asking, "Will man destroy himself?"

Chapter Four

When Suzanne visited Norfield in his apartment, she didn't know that their words and sounds were being recorded. But Norfield did. He said almost nothing.

Suzanne liked John's hands and his feet, the rare smile, his shirts, his smell, his scars, his reticence. She didn't know that Robert Morton of the RCMP could hear the sighs she uttered, or the way she whispered John's name, calling him, her lips pressed to his throat, his tender, determined silence.

"Hello," she liked to whisper in a kiss, "hello." She never felt sure that she was in the same picture as he was; she felt she was experiencing something parallax, disjointed from him. She was always shocked to see him; he left an after-image of his diffident, lonely posture, his distracted way of walking, slightly pigeon-toed.

And somewhere, deeply, innately, in John's makeup, there was money. He didn't make a show of it; he lived simply, worked steadily, selling books. Many evenings she found him in his tastefully under-furnished apartment, seated at his kitchen table, writing poetry that he hid with his hand before closing the notebook. Then he'd open a good bottle of wine and cook a couple of pepper steaks. His wardrobe was limited, but it was comprised of good dress shirts and a couple of cashmere sweaters. She'd never seen a hole in his socks. His cigarette lighter was sterling silver, well polished. He never talked about money. He was always clean, he smelled of Scotch and cigarettes, raw onions, soap, and some kind of oil he liked, made of crushed seeds.

Norfield's middle- or even upper-class fingerprint made Suzanne comfortable around him, even though she expected to be chilled. She wanted to prove strong enough to sustain his disinterest. He wasn't an ardent lover, and this was modern. She believed that she lived in an age of enlightenment.

While Hong Kong might have been John Norfield's defining experience, Suzanne McCallum's was a movie she'd seen five years ago, in 1944. *Double Indemnity*, starring Barbara Stanwyck and Fred MacMurray. Though it wasn't Barbara Stanwyck who inspired the cream wardrobe, the turban that Suzanne wore to visit John Norfield while he was in the hospital with his liver; it was Lana Turner in *The Postman Always Rings Twice*. The two actresses mixed in Suzanne's mind, for sexiness, for cunning. She once said to John, "I'm rotten to the heart, baby," but he didn't laugh.

Suzanne was only seventeen when she went to see *Double Indemnity* with her father. Until the last few minutes of that movie, it would never have occurred to her that a man would enjoy the embrace of a beautiful woman and then shoot her, twice. The force of those gunshots threw Suzanne back in her seat so hard her father leaned over to comfort her, cursing himself for having brought her there.

Fred MacMurray's surprising gesture, his hand with the gun thrust into Barbara Stanwyck's silk pyjamas, became Suzanne's nearly subliminal point of reference, an image she recalled for a fraction of a second when life would disclose its underlying violence. It was her initial reaction to Fred MacMurray's sudden act during an intimate moment, her first shock, that she brought to mind, to remind herself that she had once been naive. She thought that her womanhood dated from that moment.

One sunny afternoon last August, when she was taking a streetcar down College Street, before John got sick and went to the hospital without telling her where he was, she'd seen him driving his motorcycle, shining black and chrome. He came up beside the streetcar at a red light, and she didn't wave or anything but she had a good look at him. His handsomeness, his jaw, the shape of his head, his taut, muscular arms, all of this stung her. He was self-contained; she had no idea what he was thinking. The light changed and he sped away.

She felt an icy need for him in her blood. She thought about him all the time, if you could call it "thinking." He shook her so deeply she was almost afraid of him, but he made her feel very beautiful.

She didn't pretend to agree with what she called "John's politics," which she understood to be as abstract—or as sensual, really—as those of her own father, who was a Liberal even in the way he had a Scotch and soda before dinner. She thought that men need their politics because they need to believe they're part of a greater good. She was aware, of course, that John entertained ideas about communism and revolution, and she thought of it as an intellectual hobby, even an affectation, as if he'd taken up chess or a foreign language. At least he didn't wear a beret. It was only in relation to John's "politics" that Suzanne would feel friendliness for him, a compassionate, slightly domestic forgiveness, rather than enthrallment.

In Suzanne's country, money and goodness seemed naturally to coexist. The Canada she knew could easily afford to entertain criticism without feeling any compulsion to make uncomfortable changes. She'd read some Marx and he seemed irrelevant, historical; her mind wandered. Suzanne was pre-occupied by John Norfield because she didn't understand him and could never know him. He could never give her enough.

John disappeared in January. Suzanne waited a week. She didn't call Emmett, she didn't want anyone to know that he'd really left her this time. He'd been very distant lately, watchful and unhappy, and now she knew in her gut that she had lost him. She gave it seven days, and then went to his apartment. She knocked at his door, but she already knew he was gone.

She had her own key and let herself in. The place was silent. From the street came the sound of cars rolling over fresh snow. The windows were patched-in paisleys of frost, and a bit of condensation pooled on the wooden windowsills, but otherwise the place was spotless — except for a dirty coffee cup sitting on the kitchen table; it wasn't like him to leave something like that, he was always so meticulous. She went into the bedroom, the sheets pulled army-tight, and looked on the bedside table. She remembered distinctly that she had unclipped her gold necklace and left it on the pretty saucer he kept there, a porcelain saucer painted with gold pheasants — the necklace was gone, he must have taken it.

She opened his closet door. His clothes were in his closet, his woollen socks and laundered shirts were folded in his drawers, everything in its place. The only thing he'd taken was her necklace.

She lay down on his bed, not bothering to remove her shoes. The room had no odour, as if he'd taken that too. It was cold, but she slept anyway. When she awoke, it was dark, and the phone was ringing.

Chapter Five

The phone was ringing. Suzanne stumbled to answer it. Surely it would be John. She had never been fully denied anything before and vaguely doubted that such a thing could ever occur. Then John's voice.

"Where are you?" she asked him.

"Listen. You have to leave."

"Why? Where are you?" she asked again.

"Have you got any money?"

She looked around for her purse. "I think so."

"Get a taxi. Get out of there."

"I came to find you."

She thought she heard his sadness then; she thought she heard his yearning to see her, though he said not a word. The phone clicked several times; she said, "Hello?"

Then he said, "Suzanne."

He spoke so tenderly, she answered, "What's wrong?" But he had hung up. She put down the receiver and looked behind her. Someone was with her in the apartment.

The kitchen was dark. Her purse was in there along with the key to John's apartment, on the kitchen table, beside John's coffee cup. She needed her wallet, she needed money to get a cab. The apartment prickled with silence and electric light coming through the window from the streetlamps. She heard a shoe move. Momentum, confusion, fear brought her to the doorway to the kitchen. She saw someone standing in the dark. She said, unreasonably, "John?" The dark figure moved slightly. Suzanne moaned. She stumbled to the door, fumbled with the lock, and ran out to the street.

There wasn't much snow but sheets of ice on the sidewalks and she'd left her coat behind. All was frozen, brittle and still, the street empty, except for a police car idling across the street. The police car did a fast U-turn on the road and rolled to a stop beside her, its tires crunching over the ice. A policeman got out and called her by name. "Miss McCallum." He gestured, Get in.

She sat in the passenger seat. The policeman was a balding man in his fifties, someone's father. He didn't say anything and didn't look at her. The only kind gesture the man made to Suzanne was to turn up the heat in his car. She had been living at her parents' house in Forest Hill since finishing her BA, and when she began to give the policeman her address he cut her off and said, "I know."

She rode in stunned silence for a moment, then asked, "How?"

He had an impassive face, but still he looked at her quickly, as if to see if she was serious. In what sounded like a more fatherly tone, he asked, "What do you think you're doing, hanging around with those kind of people?"

She said nothing more then. She guessed that the policeman meant John, and John's "politics," and she didn't want to make anything worse for him because she didn't understand what was going on. The policeman had been watching the building. She thought it might be safe to tell him one thing. "There was a man in my friend's apartment."

The policeman didn't respond.

The car pulled up before the house in Forest Hill and sat idling while she rang the bell; she didn't have her key. She pounded on the door. Her mother, with her impressive coiffure, her satin dressing gown, opened, and said, "What on earth," looking from her daughter and out to the police car, which was pulling quickly away, its brake lights already bobbing where the car lurched over the culvert separating the McCallum driveway from the road.

Suzanne woke up in her girlhood bedroom in her parents' house, feeling dispossessed. She had refused to say much of anything to her outraged mother last night but had come upstairs to bed.

Now she went down and joined her parents at breakfast. Mama would not look at her, and her father greeted her with mild admonishment in his eyes. Mama was rigid, nibbling dry toast between her front teeth and finally slamming down her coffee cup, demanding, "Just what the *hell* is going on, Suzanne?"

Suzanne's father gave his newspaper a dry little shake, and now Mama was angry with him too. She said, "Don't you *dare* make this out to be nothing!"

"Perish the thought," said her father.

Mama, Suzanne, Hazel the maid—taking away the remains of the scrambled eggs—registered this as uncharacteristically mean.

"I told you last night," Suzanne said. "I was waiting for John and I fell asleep."

"But why were you out in the night like that?" Mama wanted to know. "Without your coat?"

"I was sleepwalking," said Suzanne.

Mama quivered, silently beseeching her daughter to be normal, to have normal ambitions, to date nice men without a *history*.

It was an ingenious lie, Suzanne's. She had often sleepwalked as a child. The stories of her night-wanderings had been some of Suzanne's favourites; it was fascinating not to remember an event to which she was central, though her mother told the stories as cautionary tales, a wary eye on her daughter, this vain young woman who didn't know her own mind.

Mama waited for Hazel to finish taking the dishes into the kitchen, then lowered her voice and informed Suzanne, "Your father and I have hired a private investigator to look into this, this *creep* you're so keen on. This Norfield character."

"You did *what*?"

"We *must* and we *will* protect you!"

Suzanne hated everything about her mother this morning, her voice, her lips, her wrinkled throat. She and John had been watched, then, by her parents. The perverse intimacy of this, the violation, it was sick. She shouted, "You want to know about him, do you? I'll tell you everything you want to know. This is a good man! This is a man who has suffered! He writes poetry!"

Her mother laughed bitterly, and Suzanne threw down her napkin and rose to flee the room, knowing she'd blundered.

With his right hand, her father reached and caught Suzanne's wrist as she tried to pass, and he said, "I'm sure he's a good man, Suzie. Just not right for you."

Mama hissed, "That is an *under*statement!" Now *she* tossed her napkin onto her plate and pushed away from the table. At the doorway, she lifted her chin and regained some of her irony. "Your university experiments are over, Suzanne. No more *Mein Kampf*, no more *Das Kapital*."

"*Mein Kampf*?" said her father, laughing.

"Oh, you know what I mean, Theodore! You will come to your senses, young lady. You will behave in a manner appropriate to your station." Then Mama swept from the room.

Her father gave Suzanne's arm a shake and released her, amused. "She fumbled the ball, but she'll probably win the game."

"You actually hired a private detective?"

He shrugged to indicate yes. "I protect what's mine."

Suzanne liked her father, but he'd never been physically demonstrative with her, had probably never even kissed her (he would let her kiss his forehead), and they'd never talked about anything more personal than tuition fees. She found it horrifying that he now knew that she'd slept with someone. Yet he was reading his paper now, as if he didn't mind. Did her father ever think about pregnancy, or was the paternal mind itself a contraceptive? She felt woozy. And then overwhelmingly curious: what had he learned about John?

"Well," he began patiently, "as your mother had already informed me before I spent nearly a thousand dollars on a PI, John Norfield sells communist books. Now, whether or not that's against the law seems obscure."

"It's only illegal in Quebec."

He seemed pleased that his daughter knew at least that much. "Sit down, Suzie."

She did, and he said, "He was a POW in Hong Kong. It

damaged his health. You know that. It's a terrible thing to happen to a man. Some men never get over something like that. I understand how you might be drawn to the fellow. He's obviously not stupid. But he seems to court trouble. And he's had experiences that must make him seem — mysterious in your eyes. Even glamorous. Am I right?"

She shook her head. "It's not like that," but fury and embarrassment seized her again. It was like that, it was exactly like that, and her father had to hire a private investigator before he could bother to try to figure it out.

He looked at his watch and took up his paper again, adding more firmly, "Your mother might not know the difference between *Mein Kampf* and *Das Kapital*, but she has a woman's instincts. Don't wreck your life. It happens. Even to nice girls from good families."

Suzanne poured herself some coffee. It had become painfully obvious that she had to move out. This decision made it easier to sit with her father. She felt detached. Idly, she picked up the discarded front section of the newspaper and began to read. "Who is Klaus Fuchs?" she asked.

Her father put down his paper, apparently surprised to hear Suzanne make an inquiry into the bigger world. The headline read, "KLAUS FUCHS CONFESSES." There was a picture of a man with a mass of black hair and round black glasses. "A spy," said her father. "Fuchs was a physicist working on the atom bomb in the war. For our side. He was also passing information to the Russians. He's going to jail for fourteen years."

A spy. Suzanne studied the photograph. "Is he a communist?"

"He's a traitor."

She had the impression that her father didn't know whether or not Fuchs had to be a communist to be a spy; she'd never in her life heard him say, I don't know. She poured more coffee and read the newspaper report.

Fuchs had given enough information to the Russians for them to build the bomb that had upset President Truman so much last fall, when John was in the hospital — when she'd irritated John by saying, "That levels the playing field." Fuchs was supposed to be working secretly for the British and the Americans, but he gave the atomic information to the Russians. She studied his photograph. He looked like a scientist.

She thought about John Hersey's account of Hiroshima, the terrible story she'd read in *The New Yorker* magazine, that night she'd first met John. *The slimy living bodies.* Every atomic scientist is a criminal, she thought. Now everybody has the Bomb. Why were the RCMP outside John's apartment? Because he, too, is a spy? It seemed impossible. John didn't even have a university degree, he just read a lot.

Suzanne went upstairs to her bedroom and began to pack. She had to move out. She'd have to get a job. She knew what to do. She would work in a camera shop somewhere. A camera shop would be a clean place to work; it would be like a blank slate, and even her awful mother couldn't protest. Suzanne already had a Brownie camera and she'd taken some photographs of people and trees that she knew were good; she was also good at doorways and avenues. She had taken some photographs of John, when he let her — and she remembered that she'd been surprised, pleased but surprised, when he let her.

Her father had a darkroom and he'd taught her how to develop film. She would be independent; she would join the working world; she'd work in a clean space, engaged in measuring light. It was a pure plan.

She felt strangely calm, packing her camera and a change of clothes. "What was I thinking, all this time?" she muttered to herself while she packed. "I'm twenty-three years old." She was still numb from last night, and from the stark possibility that she might never see John again. She wondered, For how long had he been watched by the RCMP? Did they think he was a spy like Fuchs? The craziness of it felt like an analgesic against the pain she'd soon feel if John really had disappeared. It was almost exhilarating to have lost what she thought was "everything." John was everything.

Her father stopped her when she was going out the front door with the big leather bag she'd used for books when she was at university. "It's cold out," he observed, conciliatory. He offered her a ride.

It was her father's considered opinion that this Norfield character would turn into one of those vets who just can't move on after a war. He assumed that Suzanne would grow impatient and look elsewhere. A police car in the driveway didn't faze him in the least; that's what the force was there for. His was a family of eccentrics, had been for generations, sleepwalkers, all of them. Suzanne had the family spunk, the family brains. The beauty and eventually the money. If Norfield went after any of it, he'd — what? — kill him, one way or another, but it wouldn't come to that: his daughter's radical phase was on the wane. She was the kind of woman a man wants to marry. And she wouldn't marry a shopkeeper with night-sweats and a bad liver.

He dropped her off on Bathurst, ignoring the traffic that

had to slide to a stop behind him. "Wait a sec," he said, catching her arm, and with his mild, distracted affection offered his forehead for a kiss. He had a big, warm face. She asked him for change for the streetcar, and he topped it up with a five.

She had to go back for her purse, which she'd left on the kitchen table in John's apartment, beside his coffee cup.

She took a streetcar, found a seat, and looked out the window, trying to see everything with the eye of a photographer. She thought, I have a tool to protect me from confusion. There was cloud cover. Her father had taught her that evenly distributed light reveals the object with less distortion. She would like that, a lucid perspective. She was not on solid ground. She would retrieve her purse. If the man was in John's apartment, she'd take his picture.

Klaus Fuchs was going to prison for fourteen years, but he was a scientist, he'd given the Russians real information. What was John? A war vet, a hero, a believer.

She would go now, retrieve her purse, and photograph John's apartment. If he didn't come back, she'd have something, a memento. She hated the police for spying on John, and didn't believe for a minute that he had done anything to deserve it. He'd seen how force works, in the war. He wanted it, like light, to be evenly distributed.

A believer; she thought about that, getting down from the streetcar at the stop near John's suite. It's not the right word. A disbeliever. That's better.

Where do the believers live? In another country. There was

no place for that kind of thing in Toronto. Everyone around here was an agnostic.

How she longed for him to answer the door. But no one came when she knocked, not even the RCMP. Then she remembered, she'd left the key inside when she'd fled. She stalked down to the basement level and rang the super's bell, told him that she was John's sister and that he'd asked her to fetch some family insurance policies for their parents, got a key, climbed the stairs back up to the second floor, and went inside.

It made her ache, the stillness of the place, steam from the radiators, a complacent winter sun, and now she was aware of the smell of Norfield's soap, leather, wool. He had gone away, really absented himself. Such absence made her weep.

Weeping, she went to the kitchen. It was empty. Clean. Her purse on the table, her wallet still inside. The coffee cup. The key. She took out her Brownie and as she began to photograph these things in the even light, her sorrow evened, became quite blank. She photographed the bedroom, the bed. His closet, a pair of tanned shoes. His drawers, three leather belts rolled — that he rolled up his belts, that they were of such quality, made Suzanne again feel desperate. She considered staying here tonight, but her courage didn't go quite that far.

It was time to leave. Yet she opened the kitchen cupboards and photographed the glasses there and then the forks in the drawer. The forks were beautiful; when she brought the camera close enough they could be the span of a bridge, a fence. She was an amateur, as a woman, a lover, a photographer. So be it. She didn't wish ever to be cured of John.

She was very tired. She went back to his bedroom and this time she pulled the covers back, intending to climb in, to get warm, maybe to sleep. That was when she found his notebook. Lying on the sheet near the foot of the bed. As if he'd intended her to find it.

When it was time to leave, she locked John's door, returned the key to the superintendent (keeping her own key in her purse, a hedge; finality did not suit her) and bundled out to the street. And there was Emmett Jones, standing across the street, looking at her.

Suzanne's nerves were frayed, and she warmed to Emmett's solitary vigil. Emmett belonged, she felt, among safe, reasonable people. It was snowing heavily now and milder; big flakes were falling, the cars mumbling congenially over deep tracks of snow, the red light where she waited to cross to join him refracted through moist air.

Emmett didn't move, though he twisted his body slightly to watch her approach. When she got to him, he looked down at her — they were both tall people, Emmett and Suzanne, but Emmett was six-foot-two — neutral and intent. He let her come right up to him without speaking. He had snow in his hair. She said, "He's not there," and waved at the apartment building across the street.

Two men in a beige Chrysler parked at the corner turned to look.

A man in a hat tucked his newspaper under his arm and hailed a cab driven by an ordinary fellow in his fifties.

Suzanne shifted her bag to the other shoulder, conscious of John's notebook tucked in among her few things. "Do you know where he is?" Then she regretted that she'd asked.

Something leaked out; some reserve fantasy of her own stoicism. She shook her head. "Never mind. Forget it." She smiled sadly at Emmett. "I always knew this would happen."

She started to walk, assuming that Emmett would accompany her, which he did. Suzanne felt pain spooling from her solar plexus, like fishing line. She said, "Can I ask you something?"

Emmett nodded.

"Why were you standing there?"

"I got a phone call. From John. He asked me to come. To see if anybody was around."

"And was anyone there? Besides me?"

"I don't know. I don't know how to look for those things."

Suzanne didn't really know either. But she would learn. *Looking* had become her domain. She had nowhere else to live.

Chapter Seven

Suzanne did become a photographer but not in a shop; her father put an end to that. Her father said, "Start at the top and take it from there," and paid the rent for Suzanne to have her own studio at the front of a low, single-storey building on Avenue Road, with her own suite in the back, looking out onto a small, overgrown garden. She hung out a sign: "McCallum Photographs." She was finally pretty independent.

She felt she was strong because she was broken. Not merely broken-hearted; she'd broken faith with life. Until she'd seen John Norfield's face, witnessed his loneliness, his sexy and cursed loneliness as it found expression in the way he smoked a cigarette, till she'd been so affected by his cool elegance, his vice, Suzanne might have anticipated a future as smooth as a golf green: a marriage to someone a little older and a little wiser, a few children, annulated maturity by means of Christmas turkey, Easter ham, the dinner rituals of the Christian calendar, the cadence of the beautiful and the good. But now she appeared to be rejecting her own tribe.

After John's disappearance, she was initially in a state of shock, under a spell, an interdiction. She felt she'd driven him away by wanting too much of him. In the myth of Cupid and Psyche, Cupid — a male creature of terrible beauty — forbade Psyche to look at him, and made love to her only in complete darkness. And when Psyche lit the forbidden lamp to look at her beautiful lover, he punished her by vanishing. Suzanne had only the photographs she'd taken of John. She became obsessed with the darkroom, she could control her fate by making his image rise, make it rise again and again to the surface.

She was skinny in those days and drank brandy at dawn. Word got out about her studio, and people started to drop by to see her work; even a few strangers came to buy her photographs. The "art photos" made her parents' social circle feel sorry for the McCallums; they thanked god that their own daughters were interested in the newly minted lawyers or men starting out in the financial sector, solid young men working for banks and accounting firms or in upper management in manufacturing and sales. Friends of her mother's said that Suzanne had been ruined by education. They predicted that she would end up an anxious little spinster, after the family money ran out.

Suzanne's was a Toronto of unhappy childish images. A wedding veil on a naked mannequin through a smashed window and the inevitable bald dolls. But her work improved. A chipped china bowl overflowing with a bushy coleus — even her mother's friends thought it beautiful, but one asked the other while Suzanne pretended not to hear, "She shows the roots and not the flowers? Those are robins' eggshells?" "They are potato peelings. With orange peel, and mould. It's not coleus, it's red cabbage." "So much colour in a black-and-white picture, I'm amazed." "I'm reminded of Wyeth." "Oh, go on, Wyeth is an artist who makes art." "It's a still life, isn't it? And death *lurking* under us, in*form*ing our lives. I surprise you. You forget, I've had some training." "Oh you're deep all right, as far as it goes, but she's just a sex maniac having a nervous breakdown."

Her father sat for a portrait of himself posing in a guberna-torial chair before a black velvet drop, well and proper. "The girl could make a decent living, taking portraits of our best people. Like Karsh." "Sure. But she thinks she's some big *eccentric*." It was only lonely, balding Miss O'Brien, the Catholic spinster who used to teach piano, who could possibly be pleased with Suzanne's portrait of her in the Irishman's butcher shop beside the bloody shank of lamb.

Half-price Suzanne McCallum. "Don't you dare feel an ounce of pity for her. She could have married Dirk Dupont and had all the money in the world."

Chapter Eight

At the time of John Norfield's disappearance in January 1950, Emmett was supporting himself by translating Japanese documents from the Russo-Japanese War for a professor at the university. The Russo-Japanese War was initiated by Japan in a Pearl Harbor–style attack on the Russian navy at Port Arthur, Manchuria, in 1904, and it was like a rehearsal for World War One, fought hand to hand in the mud with bayonets, with anywhere between one hundred and thirty thousand to more than two hundred thousand soldiers killed in a year and a half—no one bothered to keep an exact count of the dead. Emmett was translating love letters written by a high-ranking Japanese officer to his mistress, letters filled with explicit, erotic descriptions of blood and guts, erotic carnage. Perhaps it was the love language of the Japanese officer that led to Emmett's nightmares.

He worked at home, and didn't speak with anyone for days on end, drinking countless pots of tea during the hours he sat writing, and after dark he would walk for miles until he thought he could sleep.

This work paid him enough to live on. But he needed a career. Several professors at the university, seeing Jones flounder, had suggested that his language skills could get him a job in the civil service, with External Affairs if he wanted it.

The vets were still being celebrated, but nobody talked

about Bomber Command; he would be a source of shame to his professors, if they'd known that he'd bombed German civilians. Bomber Command violated the ideal that permeated peacetime versions of the war; he'd been one of those who had behaved like the fascists who'd bombed London.

So when his bearded professors suggested that he "try External" for a career, when they said that his internationalism combined with his (no doubt) heroic deeds in the war would make him a prime candidate for a role with the Canadian civil service, he would go silent in their book-lined offices. Privately, he did not believe there was such a thing as a *civil* government. He was unmoored. He read Marx's essay called "The Perversion of Human Needs."

"Alienation," Marx wrote, "is apparent not only in the fact that my means of life belong to someone else, that my desires are the unattainable possession of someone else, but that everything is something different from itself, that my activity is something else, and finally, that an inhuman power rules over everything."

Someone had described Emmett's condition. Everything is different from itself. An inhuman power rules over everything.

He was bored in an ugly way. Bored by surfeit, bored by indecision, a buzzing hovering boredom that would not land. He missed the action of the war and hated himself for it. He had liked the chemistry of skill and fear in his blood when he was a pilot, and now he had to discover whatever would replace it. He missed John, he missed Leonard, he didn't think he could love anyone but Suzanne. John's disappearance had made Suzanne almost into a haunted widow. No word came from Leonard; maybe he'd actually made it to Russia, his communist paradise.

Emmett wrote, drank tea because he couldn't afford liquor, walked, and slept. He dreamed about Germany. He dreamed of the burnt people, dreamed that they had gladly given themselves to the fires that destroyed them — their minds, their faces above their charred bodies were coherent and ordinary, and they spoke to him casually, even cheerfully, though he couldn't understand their language.

His duty was to sample their flesh. In his dream he could taste the meat beneath the oily, roasted crust. He ate the flesh of one big man, his chest, the fat around the middle, then the thighs. He tasted the meat, which he found gamy, like venison, and he thought, I don't like wild meat. The next burnt body offered to him was of a woman, and when he tore the crust with his teeth and bit into the roasted flesh, she tasted dark — rich and very dark, like wild fowl. He had only taken one dutiful bite when he decided he really couldn't stomach anymore; he did not like the flavour. But there was the problem of the bite taken from her chest. He covered her with green leaves because he couldn't bear to think that he'd spoiled her for the next man who might enjoy her.

He awoke and dressed and made tea and toast and began to work. The taste of wild game persisted and he felt sick. Downstairs, he heard the chime of his landlady's grandfather clock, and then the doorbell; he heard her open the front door, and the old house shook a little when she slammed it shut again. He thought she must have gone out. But a moment later, there came a knock at his door.

A voice whispered urgently from the landing, "Emmett! Open!" He opened the door and there was Rachel, Leonard's cousin. His landlady shrilled below, "Mr. Jones! Really!" He looked over the banister to where the landlady stood with her hands on her hips. She cried, "Disgraceful!"

"She's my cousin," he said. Even from three flights up he could see the disgust on his landlady's face.

Rachel was puffing furiously. "A harridan," she said. Then, loudly, so the landlady could hear, "An anti-Semite!"

Emmett ushered Rachel into his attic suite. She was dressed in grey wool with a white blouse buttoned high at her throat and a black hat with a band of red satin. She unpinned the hat and her hair fell around her shoulders. She'd become even more beautiful. He squeezed her arm and offered the chair at his kitchen table, moving aside his papers.

"The old sow didn't want to let me in."

"I'm not supposed to have women here." He liked the sound of that. As if he sometimes "had" women anyway.

"Is that what she meant by 'your kind'? 'I don't want any of *your kind* in my home.' She meant Jew."

He realized this was true. "I'll move out." Ashamed. He should have been aware.

Rachel smiled at him and put the cool palm of her hand to the side of his face. "Still the innocent." She surveyed his small quarters, took in the documents stacked on the table, her square fingers stroking a page of Japanese script. "So learned, Emmett. I'm in awe."

He offered tea and put the kettle on, feeling neither innocent nor learned. "It's good to see you," he said. He'd been solitary too long and didn't have anything to say, but he was glad to see her, he was afraid his loneliness would show. He asked her if she'd heard from Leonard.

Rachel pursed her lips. "Yes, in a manner of speaking, I

have heard from Leonard, the most incomprehensible palaver. Honestly. I don't know if he's happy or miserable, starving in the desert or working happily in the People's Eden."

"You got a letter from him?"

"It was his handwriting for certain. But I couldn't hear his voice in the words he wrote, and he wrote the strangest things. "

"Where is he, Rachel?"

"Russia, I'm almost certain. Though the stamp was from Holland. That didn't stop the police from opening the letter. They didn't even pretend it hadn't been opened before it got to me."

"Is he in Moscow?"

"I don't know. I worry, Emmett. His words went around and around, but I don't know what he's doing or if he's really all right." She watched him pour the tea. "One thing, I came to discuss. In his letter Leonard wrote 'thank you for watering the plants.'" She watched Emmett's face and, though he didn't say anything, she nodded, "I know. When did Leonard ever have any plants? I turn it over in my mind, and I wonder, what would be the same as a plant in Leonard's life? Then, lightning strikes. His friends. His friends. And his books. Those are the plants he's asking me to care for. You know him. Friendship and books matter more to him than anything—more than the Communist Party, if truth be known. He is at heart a lonely soul, betrayed, hungry for hope, starving for ideas, starving for friends to share his ideas. Tsk. So much trouble men will go to because they won't admit they're lonely."

She put her hand over his, where it lay on the table between them. "Oh, Emmett. Thine eyes are upon me, and I am not." She sighed tremulously. He didn't know what she was talking about.

She went on. "I didn't come here to trouble you. I know

that Leonard asked you to take his books from his apartment. He told me he was going to ask you to do that. Did he?"

Emmett felt seared by embarrassment. Leonard had told him to sell the books if he didn't return, to give the money from the sale to Rachel. He'd forgotten this entirely. He indicated the several crates side-by-side in a corner beside his bed, serving as a table, nailed shut against his landlady's incursions, and admitted, "I forgot they were there. What do you want me to do with them?"

"The police watch me, you know."

He thought this sounded incredible.

"They're probably watching you too, Emmett."

He turned his back, looked out through the frost on the window. "They wouldn't be interested in me."

"I don't want you to suffer for Leonard's sake. And Leonard would sooner die than be the cause of harm to you. A friend is coming to take the books away. With your permission."

It was such a gloomy morning the streetlights were still on. There were two cars parked across the street; only one of them had snow on its roof. "What about the risk to you?" he asked.

She sighed. "It makes me sick to be a dumb handmaiden to the Revolution. I must be useful. Can you imagine how hard it is? To accept a government that allowed the Holocaust to happen? What was the Canadian government doing to help us, while Hitler carried out his plan? Emmett? What did our government do while we were being—exterminated?"

He turned again to look at her. Her face was beautiful, serious, her mouth drawn down, her heavy eyes lowered, he could not match her sorrowful weight, he'd avoided weight, he'd been trained since birth to avoid weight. His nightmare came back to him, the taste of wild meat in his mouth.

She looked up at him trustingly and continued, as if he'd agreed, as if he would especially appreciate her view: "It wasn't enough. It was the wrong kind of help and it wasn't enough. I'm finished with compromise. I'll go to prison if I have to. Now," she patted Emmett's hand in rhythm, "may I take Leonard's books?"

He said yes, of course, and she took up her hat with its red satin band, went to his window, opened it, and waved the hat in the cold air, then she closed the window and returned to sit, drumming a drill pattern with her fingers on the table.

They heard the doorbell and the squawking protests of the landlady and the thud of boots on the stairs. Rachel opened the door and let in a burly man whom Emmett had never seen before.

Rachel introduced him as Max. Max sat on the edge of his chair. Emmett guessed that Max dreaded a delay in action, dreaded polite conversation with the irrelevant man who stored Leonard's books. Max's eyes wandered over the papers on the table, the Japanese script, then looked back up at Emmett with brown-eyed suspicion.

Max resembled the man in his nightmare, the one whose body Emmett had eaten. The table wobbled when Max leaned on it with his elbow; Emmett's translation of a Japanese military sensualist rippled in dry air from the radiators. Rachel was talking and he understood that she was telling Max that Emmett was wonderful, her flattery prickling like hives in his skin, self-contempt hauling him down. He felt old, he would soon be thirty. His body understood sin even if his mind didn't. He'd been tricked into killing German families while they slept. Now he was translating fascist eroticism for academic fascination, for rent money.

He heard what Rachel was saying, she was talking about the international hope in communism, she was mixing what he thought might be her Jewish version of Sunday school because she was talking about Egypt, Exodus, the ransoming of slaves. He was nervous that she was being too passionate in her speech; he'd been trained through his childhood in restraint, in ironic understatement, and he thought that what Rachel was saying might be lovely nonsense, but he was afraid that she was ultimately reasonable and that he would be called to act on her reasonable persuasion. Then he thought, I must give my life to something that will ransom my slavery, I must either redeem my life or kill myself.

Finally, Max asked Rachel in low voice, "Where are these boxes you want me to take to the car?"

Rachel indicated the three crates of books, and Max seized one and departed. On the third trip, he hoisted the last impossibly heavy crate onto his chest, nodded to Emmett, and left.

Rachel put on her coat. She stretched her arms above her head and somehow the thick rope of hair disappeared under the hat. She kissed Emmett on his lips. "Now you will have to make good on your promise to move out."

He went to the landing to watch her descend the stairs, passing the landlady at the door. "Family documents of murdered relatives," Rachel told her sternly and stepped out into the snow on the front porch.

Emmett tossed out the remaining tea, rinsed the cups, put his papers with his Japanese scrawl before him, and sat for a long time doing nothing. Patches of snow from his visitors' boots melted on the oak floor. Rachel will risk everything for the Communist Party, to protest the failure of the Canadian government to protect Jews from the Holocaust. The landlady's clock struck the hour. He remembered meeting Rachel in Leonard's smoky apartment several years ago, hearing the earnest students talk about *a stateless, classless society*; he recalled the joy he'd felt at that moment, when he realized that he might free himself from the government that had fooled him into piloting for Bomber Command. Could he redeem his life, did he have the stamina, is there an ideal that could actually lift him physically from his solitude into action, into bliss?

Then he had an idea so contrary, so paradoxical, he laughed out loud.

He began to pack his few belongings.

Two weeks later, Emmett Jones wrote the entrance exam for the Department of External Affairs. He was interviewed, twice. And was accepted.

In April 1950, Emmett was preparing to move away from Toronto, to Ottawa, where he'd take up his position as a policy analyst with a special interest in the American occupation of Japan. He hadn't seen Suzanne since John Norfield's disappearance. She didn't phone him anymore, and he was giving up on her. Moving away to Ottawa would put an end to his fixation. But he couldn't leave without seeing her; he had to say goodbye.

Near the streetcar stop at St. Clair, he met a boy sitting on the yellow grass and on sudden impulse he gave the boy three dollars for the bicycle that lay beside him. The freckled, redheaded boy gladly took the money. Emmett had already ridden away before it occurred to him that the redheaded boy didn't own the bike in the first place.

He cycled up to the McCallum property in Forest Hill. Mrs. McCallum, Suzanne's mama, was standing on the white gravel drive between the stable and the house, talking to an old woman with a very crooked back. In the heat, the bent old woman wore a wool suit with a grey mink collar and grey kidskin gloves. She had abundant white hair arranged on her head, which sat at an acute angle, spools of hair wisping around her ancient face.

Emmett's bicycle made a chewing sound over the gravel; white dust rose up and coated his shoes. He dismounted and sneezed.

Mrs. McCallum greeted him: "It's Mr. Emmett Jones." She turned to the old woman and more loudly said, "It's Mr. Emmett Jones, Mother. An acquaintance of Suzanne's. From her university days." He realized that she thought he had a double name; *Jones* would be beyond her ken.

The old woman lifted her head like a tortoise to look at him with tortoise eyes. She was something out of Lewis Carroll, beautifully grotesque with age, privately amused. He felt himself liked, and he instantly liked her. She reminded him of his boyhood, when he was liked simply for being lanky, when people were pleasant and wealthy and offhand about their wealth. She offered him a kidskin hand to hold, a soft little nest of bones, gave a light, vigorous shake, and said, "How do you do, Mr. Emmett Jones."

He said he was pleased to meet her, and the old woman announced, "You'll have to come to tea."

Suzanne's mama sized Emmett up, regarding him with cool warmth. "You're not carrying any books," she observed.

"I was wondering if Suzanne is at home." He realized that he might have phoned first; he'd been impatient.

Mama's eyes widened. "She's not here," she said with some surprise. "She has a 'studio' on Avenue Road. She camps out in her 'studio.'" She took in Emmett's disappointment. "You didn't know."

He looked down his dusty shoes. "We've been out of touch."

"It's on Avenue Road," said the old woman decidedly. He guessed that the grandmother did not disapprove of Suzanne's "studio." Then she added, "Have you seen her photographs? They're pretty good."

Mama gave directions to Suzanne's "studio," and the two

women silently watched him remount the bicycle and waver on the gravel drive out to the street. When he reached the pavement, he stole a look in their direction and saw them deep in discussion.

Suzanne had been drawn from her darkroom to the front window to stare out at the street, and there was Emmett. She felt a pang of jealousy for his boyish handling of the bike, the long leg swung over the seat while it was still moving, Emmett letting it drop on the frowsy margin of weed, then rapping at the door as if he didn't really care if he didn't find her there. She opened the door at once.

She was in the midst of a project and had taken down the exterior sign that read "McCallum Photographs" because she didn't want anybody to interrupt while she was at work on this new stuff. She was in a large room with lots of wall space and three clotheslines strung from wall to wall to dry the prints.

She'd had been up since five that morning and had kept herself going with brandy and coffee, as was her routine: to sleep from one until five or six, work in the darkroom till ten and then have a bath, go to bed for another couple of hours, rise, and go out and take photographs. She liked afternoon light. Today, she'd strayed from routine, skipped the bath and morning sleep, kept up the spiked coffee in the darkroom, not necessarily because she was making great advances with the work but because she couldn't stop.

It was eleven o'clock when Emmett made his surprise visit. She'd emerged from the darkroom a few moments earlier, her heart pounding. Her vision was as she imagined a fly's vision must be—stills flashing at three frames per second. When she saw him swing his leg off his bike like a boy, she envied his healthy unconsciousness.

Emmett noticed the purple shadows under her eyes. The room smelled of burnt coffee and booze and a chemical reek that he'd soon learn came from her darkroom. Her puppet-like movement unnerved him. When she embraced him stiffly, he could feel her ribs raking out from her spine. He said he was sorry to drop by so suddenly, and she said, "No!" and waved for him to come inside.

As he walked between the lines of photographs, he could sense her holding her breath.

In every print there was a figure walking away over an expanse of concrete or lawn, a man or a woman, sometimes a dog, always images of their departure, their private intentions. He was struck by the geometry of streetscape and her skilful use of film, the depth of field, detail and focus, the pocked texture of cement, veins of creosote in a telephone pole, a brick storefront, rusty trash cans. Somehow the colour of rust was suggested in the black-and-white film, just as the blades of grass crisscrossed by afternoon shadow suggested green. A formal presentation of the banal, her stark attention to emptiness. And he thought, She's still grieving for Norfield.

When he told her the photographs were "good," she laughed sharply and said, "No no."

He asked her, Could they go out for something to eat? She said that would be nice, but she wasn't fit to be seen so why didn't he come through here? They walked through her curtained darkroom and into her suite at the back of the building.

She told him to have a seat at a rickety white table while she took a knife and sawed at a loaf of bread that had been left there. She was skinny but crazily beautiful.

"There," she said, smiling and throwing down slices of the stale bread, sitting, then jumping up again, "I've got butter!" But her fridge was empty except for a jug of water.

"Can't you sit down?" he asked.

She sat, tapping her foot.

"I met your grandmother," he told her.

For a moment, Suzanne's face relaxed and fell open. "Did you?" She was so rapt it cost her further effort to think this through. "You were at the house?" She darkened. "You saw Mother?"

"That's how I knew where to find you."

She nodded, Emmett, watching her, thinking of her as a pearl in a string of pearls. When he told her he was going away, she gave him a stricken look. Then she asked, "Are you going to find the old woman?"

He was amazed. This was a story he'd told her years ago when they'd first met; a not-entirely-true story about his childhood in Japan, a story about the "old woman," Sachiko, his father's mistress. Suzanne had turned his life into a fairy tale. He told her that he didn't know if he would find Sachiko. Maybe she's dead.

But Suzanne yawned and with one finger tipped a dry piece of crust, letting it fall back onto the plate. "Well," she said, "we'll miss you."

"We." Did she mean her mother and her? She was fractured, multiplied by the loss of John Norfield. It was hopeless. Anger pressed his jaw tight. She was oblivious, caught in a light, mesmerized, he'd been wasting his time.

What was it about Norfield that had captured her? Emmett would exceed Norfield, he'd better him, he'd prove to be the better man. He'd cut free of both of them. He said he had to go and finish packing.

She saw him out distractedly. He imagined that she was embarrassed. She was astute about men; she'd long understood that he was attracted to her, and she was uncomfortable. Let her have her ghost, Emmett thought, the mysterious Norfield who has vanished liked smoke. Let her live on smoke.

They didn't embrace. She held her front door open while she watched him pick up his bike and when he was ready to go, she said, "Well. Goodbye."

From the street he turned to look back at her over his shoulder just as she was swinging her door closed and their eyes met. Only a few minutes ago he might have been encouraged by the confusion he saw there. But he was through with that. He rode quickly down the falling slope of the city.

Chapter Ten

Emmett moved to Ottawa and began his career as a policy analyst, dealing with reports coming out of Tokyo where the Canadian government had a Liaison Mission whose main job was to explain in bureaucratic lingo the American occupation of Japan in the wake the bombing. He taught himself shorthand and typing so he wouldn't always be dependent on a secretary. His modest salary with External was twice what he'd been making as a translator.

His anger toward Suzanne cooled and hardened. He counted the years since he'd got "tangled up" with her and with Norfield as lost years. His relations with them now seemed quite corrupt—as if he'd been their pet, their audience.

He threw himself into his new job at External Affairs. He was thirty years old; he had catching up to do.

In his capacity as analyst, he soon became fascinated by reports written by a man by the name of Herbert Norman who was working out of Occupied Japan. Herbert Norman described the circumstances of the current American military occupation there in a style that Emmett would try to emulate: lucid tracts, with cultural allusions dating back far before the Meiji era.

He studied Herbert Norman's writing and researched his sources. He sought out other publications by the man, editorials in *Amerasia* composed in the 1930s in the midst of the Depression; this was youthful work, provocative, pretending to apologize while the writer admitted he was "stepping on the toes of economic, political and national vested interests."

Emmett worked hard, stayed late into the night or smuggled files home for his private hours, sipping Scotch while he worked, letting his mind play. But it wasn't enough to be reading. He needed to have real influence. He couldn't sleep and there was never enough work—not enough to make him feel substantial. He needed a sense of glory that certainly wasn't available to him in the well-mannered offices of External Affairs.

He pushed his superiors at External to give him a posting in Japan. He cultivated the mentorship of a senior civil servant by the name of Bill Masters, a professional bureaucrat who liked to see himself as a key player in the careers of young men. Bill was convinced that Jones was his very own creation, a delusion that Emmett encouraged.

He was always there by the time Bill Masters arrived at eight a.m. When Bill saw Emmett at his desk, he'd stop for a minute and happily observe, "At it again, Jones? Don't burn yourself out."

Emmett kept Bill aware of his restlessness and ambitions. He let Bill know that he was testing External, that he wasn't sure if it was the right career for him. Bill had boasted to the prime minister that he'd made a talented new recruit. Prime Minister St. Laurent didn't like a department with a lot of coming and going. It was important to retain talent, to foster a stable civil service that would keep the Liberal Party in power.

It paid off quickly. Bill Masters arranged for Emmett to be posted to Tokyo for six months on probation, with an extended contract if he worked out, at the Canadian Liaison Mission to Occupied Japan. He was to start work there early July 1950.

On June 25, North Korea attacked South Korea. The UN Security Council voted to go to war against communist North Korea. The Russians, North Korea's allies, boycotted the United Nations that day, so the vote in favour of war was unanimous — though no one was permitted to call it a war: it was called "a police action." The execution of the war in Korea would be in the hands of US General Douglas MacArthur, who was also running the American occupation of Japan from his offices in Tokyo.

Emmett told himself that he was going "home" to Japan. He was also returning to war.

◇

June 30, Bill Masters, Emmett's newly acquired mentor, took him to the airport. Bill got a real kick out of launching his protégé on his first foreign assignment, and he talked at Emmett right up to the departure gate, giving him the lowdown on his own successes ("and that's just the *half* of it"), his stories pivoting around the countless times he'd been pursued by inferior associates. "So I told them, 'Look'" — with one stubby finger Bill tapped at his wristwatch — "'I don't have time to dick around. When you fellas finally figure out the difference between your ass and a hole in the ground — get back to me.'"

It came time for Emmett to board the plane, and Bill's voice rose in pitch as he talked faster. They were calling the flight when Bill began to recount an incident in 1945, just before the end of the war, involving *Amerasia* magazine and J. Edgar Hoover. A complicated story involving thousands of stolen classified documents from British and American Intelligence that Hoover's FBI discovered in *Amerasia*'s New York editorial offices. Bill kept saying, "You understand? This is the FBI we're talking about here. Herbert Norman was writing for *Amerasia*. That makes Herbert Norman hot, in the eyes of J. Edgar Hoover. You're going to meet Herbert Norman in Tokyo. Comprendez?" But there wasn't time for the whole story, the plane was waiting, its engines drowning out Bill's voice, and Bill said, "Do I have to spell it out?" He embraced Emmett, his eyes filling with tears, and said, "Choose your friends like you choose your enemies and you'll do fine, son."

Emmett walked across the tarmac, the sun on his back, his shadow stretching ahead. Bill shouted something, but a weedy wind was blowing, an orange sun bulleted off the belly of the airplane, a North Star. He passed a rippling red flag, climbed the stairs to the plane, was greeted by a pretty blond, and took his seat. Peripherally, he could see Bill, looking diminished, standing where he'd left him. Emmett was troubled by Bill's loyal witness to his solitary departure and the whisper of small, inflated significance. Bill's warning against Herbert Norman had actually enlivened his hope that the man would work with him. He needed to feel the edge of conflict. Being a Canadian civil servant, he had already learned, could be like living in a padded cell. He had to have access to something radiant, something much bigger than himself.

The North Star stormed into the air. The aircraft was unpressurized; it was like being inside a steel drum in a hailstorm—the noise was deafening, it was cold, the constant vibration drilled into him. The plane was a pig compared with the Lancaster he'd piloted. But he was flying to Japan. He comforted himself through the long flight by conjuring memories of the home he would soon see again.

Chapter Eleven

Tokyo was hot, and everywhere there were beautiful Japanese women in western dress, hundreds, thousands of beautiful women, unaccompanied, cool, and apparently untroubled. Japanese blossoms wearing Betty Grable shoes picked their way through the rubble of bomb craters, delicately stepping over the amputees begging on the streets, the homeless and the orphans who lived in the railway stations.

Emmett was shocked to see so much of the city still in ruins from the American firebombing, and he asked himself if he really had been living in solitary confinement for the last five years—he should have anticipated this much devastation. A million and a half people had lived in the wood-and-paper city firebombed by B-29s in 1945. No one knew how many had been killed; their ashes lingered in the scorched city.

Overhead remained the shell of a brick office building with its windows blown out. Emmett walked in its shade, then turned a corner and was blasted by sun. An entire block on the western side of the street was a bomb crater filled with rubble even now, more than five years later, being pulverized under the treads of a yellow Caterpillar. The city had an ersatz frontier feel, like a movie set, with American jeeps and Cadillacs driven by steel-jawed chauffeurs transporting American army uniforms and the black suits of the non-Asian financiers.

He made his way through the ruins toward the Canadian

Liaison Mission, sickened by the soot on his clothes, oily grime that collected on his socks and pant legs. The journey to Tokyo had taken five days, the North Star landing to refuel on five airstrips en route, and in that time he'd barely eaten or slept. He'd comforted himself with nostalgia on that long journey, imagined arriving to his lost past, to a pre-war Tokyo of grilled mackerel, salty miso, black cherries, the taste of the sea and blossom, the special occasions for a little boy who would come to this city with his mother and father, to take holiday pleasures, to eat in restaurants and go to museums.

Emmett picked up a newspaper and sat with it on a park bench while he tried to get his bearings. He fell asleep every time he blinked. He felt unwell, he had that taste in his mouth again, the taste of wild meat, and he finally went into the bushes that circled the park and vomited. When he returned to the bench he lay down and fell asleep. And dreamed of burning cities, saw the flames from the cockpit of his airplane, felt turbulence, dreamed of fighting his way up and out of a firestorm and being sucked into the fires he'd lit himself. When a Japanese man in a clean black uniform poked him awake, Emmett realized he'd been shouting. A small Japanese boy wearing an oversized New York Giants baseball shirt was watching him thoughtfully with his fingers in his mouth.

An hour later, he was at the Canadian Liaison Mission, in an inconspicuous building with an ultra-modern reception room furnished in teak and presided over by a sleek woman wearing a black shift and a string of white beads. He gave her his name, and she pinched a file between blood-red nails, scrolled a list, gave him a nod, her smile curt and quick as if she'd typed it, tipped her head toward the corridor while tucking yet another file under her shapely white arm.

"I just came to check in," he said. He was a mess, he smelled sour and unclean. "I've been travelling," he told her.

The receptionist marched forward, indicating he was to follow, her black heels tapping on the parquet. Coming to a halt at a closed door, she leaned her bare shoulder against it and swung into a square box, her hand on the doorknob. Then she waved, swanlike, Enter.

There were two desks with chairs, an empty bookcase, an empty filing cabinet with its drawers open. The receptionist finally spoke. "Looks like you'll be all on your lonesome here, honey."

He was disappointed by her voice, which was reedy, tourist-town Ontario. She perched on a desk, "Take a load off, might as well," and indicated that Emmett was to occupy the other desk beneath a map of Japan and the Korean peninsula. She sighed with peevish boredom. "I guess they only hired the one of yous."

"I just came to check in," he said again. "I'll be back in the morning."

She gave a little burp. "That's the Pepsi talking back."

"I have to find a place I can lease for six months."

"Yeah, get yourself settled. Well, any-who." He wasn't her type. She started out to the hallway, then turned, "Be a doll and do me a favour? Take a file over to Dai-Ichi?"

She thought he was hesitating so she patiently explained, "His nibs' office? The general? It's a secret report and he's gotta give his royal assent."

Dai-Ichi, the headquarters for General Douglas MacArthur, Supreme Commander of the American Occupation, SCAP. Emmett agreed, he'd deliver the report to his nibs.

"Swell," she said. "See? I'm putting your name on it. Jones, Emmett, Canada. That way, he'll make your acquaintance."

Chapter Twelve

Dai-Ichi was a six-storey building that had housed an insurance company before the war, near the moat surrounding the emperor's estate, a solid building somehow spared, though bombs had struck the imperial palace. Emmett showed his new papers identifying him as a member of the Canadian staff. A starched MP shouldered a rifle and escorted him to the sixth floor, to a warren populated by uniforms running from one desk to another. He followed the rifle to a large office and saw through its open door a well-built man in khaki appear then disappear, a long-stemmed pipe gripped between his teeth while he paced, apparently dictating.

The MP stopped at the door, and Emmett entered, bringing the oratory to a halt. "General MacArthur, sir," he said. "I've come from the Canadian Liaison Mission." He offered the file marked "Top Secret."

With graceful discourtesy, General Douglas MacArthur turned his back on him and said, "Put it on the desk."

Emmett took a look around the room. An ugly onyx clock stood on the mantle. To one side was a worn leather divan and a gentleman seated there. This gentleman, too, had a pipe between his teeth, but he removed it and warmly observed, "I'll bet you're Emmett Jones."

Emmett admitted that he was.

"I'm Herbert Norman," said the man and stood to offer his hand. "I've been expecting you." He was as tall as Emmett and was perhaps only ten or fifteen years older, but he demonstrated the debonair formality of another generation. It was the analyst who wrote for *Amerasia*, the man whose reports from Japan had so filled Emmett with admiration, the man whom Bill Masters had warned him against because he'd attracted the attention of the FBI.

General MacArthur waved a patrician hand, taking in Emmett's rumpled clothing. "You may as well stay, now you've interrupted," resuming his monologue.

Emmett was flattered for the first ten minutes and then, gradually, horrified. After twenty minutes, he glanced at Herbert Norman seated beside him on the divan. Herbert met his eye with a look that managed to convey, It is amazing but do not *be* amazed.

"Lucius Aemilius Paulus," the general was saying. "Abraham Lincoln. George Washington. These are my advisers. I look into their lives, and there I find almost all the answers. They are my source, my lodestone." He evoked Napoleon Bonaparte too and named each famous battle. Friedland, Jena, Eylau, Ulm, Marengo, and Bassano. But he qualified his admiration of Bonaparte, adding that his first inspiration in manoeuvres against the enemy's flanks was Genghis Khan.

Several fighter jets flew over, low, rattling the windows, but MacArthur went on, his granitic face entirely unfazed, effortlessly raising his voice. Emmett could see the tightening muscles under the khaki shirt. General Douglas MacArthur was not insane by wartime standards. Even President Truman, at this juncture, was satisfied, even happy with the general's abilities in occupying Japan.

From war, MacArthur moved to economics. Emmett guessed that he was practising a speech, in his strange broad accent, oratory that he intended to deploy in more significant arenas but that was all out of proportion for an audience of Canadians. "The best men in America," he intoned, "our great nation's key industrialists, will be *stultified*, will grow *inert* under the burden of socialism." Another squadron, or the same one returning to salute on its way to Korea, zoomed overhead, closer, louder. MacArthur fumed steadily, implacable. The bombers flew off, the clacking of desk officers resumed.

"A Marxist philosophy of financing the defence of other nations will lead directly to the path of communistic slavery." The general finally stopped to light his pipe.

In this respite, Herbert Norman idly commented, "Japan excepted."

"I beg your pardon?"

"The United States is financing Japan," Herbert observed.

MacArthur didn't miss a beat. "We do as God instructs us to do. When Japanese guns were silenced, it was my sacred duty to carry to the land of the vanquished foe, solace, hope, and faith." In a low voice, he added, "I am not come to destroy but to fulfil."

Emmett choked. A loud bark, a startled, horrified laugh erupted from his gut.

The general strode close and gazed down on Emmett Jones, as if from afar. His pose, shaken but indomitable, was contrived to suggest a statesman's sorrow over the vulgarity of the common man; he was sad but not for himself. Emmett saw shyness even in the general's imperial attitude — shyness and megalomania. MacArthur was embarrassed, and this increased Emmett's dread because it indicated how invincible the man believed himself to be; his pride was fragile and titanic. MacArthur swung back toward his desk, where he lifted and weighed the top-secret report that Emmett had delivered, but now he was evidently self-conscious, acting.

"Well," Herbert Norman said softly, "I believe we'll leave you to your work, General." Emmett followed Herbert's cue and stood to leave.

MacArthur was studying the report and he gave a dramatic are-you-still-here wince. By the time they were at the door, the general appeared to have regained his composure. Emmett heard him speak — privately memorizing — "Jones. Emmett. Canada."

Chapter Thirteen

The road to the James-yama Estate in Shioya was steeper than the one in Emmett's memory, its surface more broken, riven by mud flushed out by the rains. Shioya hadn't been firebombed as completely as nearby Kobe had been, but still, he didn't recognize the few houses he passed.

The sky cleared and Emmett remembered that mink smell, that fecund stink in the summer wind blowing from the Inland Sea. A fresher east wind kicked up; the sunlight seemed stained, saturated with the red leaves of the sumac that grew beside the mountain road where he climbed. When the road curved north, the wind failed. In the shady forest, holly fern grew beneath the maples and red pine. He turned his back on the mountain to look down at the distant, silent sea.

From a blind curve, an army jeep hurtled toward him. Emmett heard it, and felt the gravel scattered by its front tires, before he flung himself off the road. The jeep passed so close he saw the sun flicker on the driver's brush-cut as the vehicle raced away. An American army uniform. Emmett stood carefully and spit on his hands to remove the dirt embedded in his skin. He caught his breath and resumed his climb when the birds began to sing again.

Around the next curve the road ascended more steeply. The wind blew once more, and then he saw the granite lion that

157

marked the entrance to the estate. The sight was so familiar it was as if he were seeing himself. Here he used to play with his friends after school. The lion's stone mane furled down its chest, its jaws opened in a grimace big enough for a boy's head.

His parents had sent him to a private school called Canadian Academy, with kids from the US, Europe, and Australia. Japanese children from Kobe went there too. A pretty teacher would take them all down to the seashore, the boys in short pants, the little girls in printed kilts that they held above the waves. He'd been compelled by the decisive, delicate way his Japanese friends moved, like a habit of flight. Now most of those schoolmates were dead. Five years ago, in 1945, more than eight thousand people were incinerated in Kobe, in twenty-three thousand tonnes of magnesium thermite. All the supplies of napalm had been used up on Tokyo. Emmett knew it to be true. He had searched out this information within days of his arrival in Japan.

He had searched through the names of the dead. He had found Sachiko. She must have been evacuated out of the estate, to Kobe, where she'd been killed in the firebombing.

Thinking now about Sachiko's death, Emmett felt a rush of high-voltage fear in his body. As if he didn't exist but was a play of light, a staged illusion. From the cockpit of a Lancaster, in the name of glory, he'd rained fire, just like the airmen who'd dropped the firebombs on Japan. The terror remained in him and he tried to calm down, but he felt like he was evaporating, sizzling into nothingness. He was not loved, he hadn't been touched in too long, he needed more than sex, he needed someone to gather him in.

He came to the withered row of plum trees that hedged the lawn surrounding Sachiko's long, low clapboard house with its bronze roof. The peaty soil had washed away, exposing the trees' tough ochre roots. The lawn was overcome by weeds, but the house seemed in fair shape; its plaster needed whitewash, the cypress shutters needed oil, but it was intact, unscathed.

The shutters were open, but he couldn't tell if anyone was living there now. If Sachiko hadn't been evacuated, she might still have been living in this house; the place quite accidentally would have turned out to be his father's parting gift, a refuge for the woman who destroyed his family. Emmett rephrased that. The woman who defined his family.

He stood at the plum trees to watch the house for signs of life while he walked his mind through its rooms; the entrance with its umbrella stand (his father's hat on the umbrella stand, a telling clue for him as a boy as to whether his father was here); the elegant dining room with its portraits of English gentlemen; the sunroom where Sachiko sat and where Emmett's father would sit with her while he had a whisky and soda.

There might have been some time, months, maybe even years, when Emmett and his mother didn't know of Sachiko's existence. It was eventual as dawn, his father's lies giving way, not to truth but to a double world where he could let his wife and son know with a nod, with wincing disapproval as if at their bad manners, what was to be acknowledged and what was to be ignored, until Sachiko became an aspect of his father, a necessity, in such a way as to make Emmett and his mother feel complicit, almost responsible, being inadequate to capture his father's full attention. Gradually, imperceptibly, Emmett's mother acknowledged Sachiko, though never face to face; his mother had behaved helplessly, with pathetic righteousness. Emmett loved her resentfully, despising her weakness, angry that it might reflect his own.

For about three years, mother and son, father and mistress, had formed a louche club. During this interlude, Emmett grew tall, grew at least four inches every year. He was a wiry kid in tennis sneakers, wearing a white sweater over his shoulders, knotting its sleeves at his chest.

Now he stood beneath the plum trees and watched the house, wondering how he should approach when he heard a man call out in a loud voice. "You looking for the girl?"

A westerner, his enormous size exaggerated by a blue kimono, was striding toward him from a footpath that Emmett remembered having taken as a shortcut through the estate. "The girl," the man repeated, approaching, "you looking for Aoi?" He had a mid-west American drawl.

Emmett couldn't immediately frame what he'd come looking for. (My father loved a Japanese woman who sat in the sunroom that looks toward the mountain.)

The American brought all of his own horsepower to a standstill; Emmett could hear the machinery of that body seize and tick. He had a thick, sunburned face and neck, the red flesh scored by white seams, and he bore the attitude of a man who considered himself of great good nature that nobody should take for granted. He waited for a reply, his firm mouth opened a little, lightly panting. The kimono must have been specially made: no Japanese kimono would have fit him, and the blue was too artificial for Japanese taste.

"I used to live here, in a house nearby."

"Where'd you spend the war, friend?" the American asked with abrupt suspicion.

"Air force. England. Germany."

"You a Canadian fella?"

When Emmett said that he was, the man didn't try to hide his disappointment but looked up at the house, seeming to weigh the worthiness of a Canadian against whoever lived there now. He scratched a sunburned cheek, giving off a sagey male scent. Some kind of darkness rushed over him, and he shrugged it off and walked away, his blue kimono billowing in his wake.

A moment later Emmett was ringing the bell, hearing the door chimes inside play "Waltzing Matilda," a detail he'd forgotten.

The young Japanese woman who answered wore baggy wartime trousers and a man's white dress shirt. She looked like a southerner, solidly built with a big face that barely accommodated a mouthful of oversized teeth that she showed in a confident smile. He was drawn to the way her lips parted, and to her eyes, which seemed capable of genuine surprise. She pressed the open door between her breasts. In English, "Yes?"

He told her his name. He said he used to live here at the estate, he said that this house, too, had once been leased to his father, for his father's friend. "I was curious to see it again." He peered around her, as if Sachiko would appear. "My father's friend was killed in the war."

The young woman seemed bemused. So he had lost a house, a friend. War took nearly everything. "The Americans gave the house to me," she said with pride. She was in her early twenties, maybe a little older. She surveyed him, taking in the pressed pants, the polished shoes, and said, "Would you like to see?"

Inside, he saw an unsubstantial smattering of cheap furniture; only a few pieces of the heavy Edwardian stuff remained. The umbrella stand was still there, as was the sideboard, and Emmett remembered that at either end of the sideboard was a drawer: one that had contained silver cutlery displayed in crinolines of black velvet, the other containing liquor. His father would come in, remove his hat and place it on the umbrella stand, take off his coat and hand it to the Japanese butler, then pour himself a drink.

The sideboard stood in a dining room with lead-paned windows too high up to permit a view. The dining room table was gone, as was the Indian rug that he used to lay on, tracing the mandala. Somebody had covered the cypress floor with linoleum. It looked like a boarding house.

She saw his face and suggested, "You may come this way," leading him through the kitchen — it had remained the same, the same high cabinets, the yellowed icebox, the stone floor — and through the swinging doors to what had been the library, emptied of books, pale spaces like day-moons on the sooty blue wall above the fireplace where the portraits had once hung, and through to the sunroom.

This was where Sachiko had sat, always elegant, sometimes traditionally and sometimes wearing western dress. She would let Emmett spend an afternoon with her here, while she sat doing nothing, yet with an attitude of sufficiency. Her chaise remained, as did the petite point ottoman that he would sprawl on, dangling his arms and legs onto the rattan matting. He stared at where Sachiko had sat, where he'd lingered in her neutral presence.

French doors opened to a garden where there was a small pond that had once held goldfish and a lawn bordered with the naked stems of azaleas and the reddish-purple, almost black glow of late chrysanthemums. Here was where eventually he'd come to hide from his father. The heat remained then too, and the zing of cicadas. His father was really sick, hidden from sight at the other house, where his mother could watch him slowly deteriorate in a bedroom that Emmett never entered, observing the quarantine necessary for patients with tuberculosis. At home, he was keenly aware of his father's unseen suffering, and so he spent his time at Sachiko's house. Sometimes he pretended that he was his father. He mimicked his mannerisms. It compensated for never being able to tell the man how he yearned for him.

Her name was Aoi. She was an unusual-looking young woman who believed herself beautiful and thus became so. He'd begun by speaking to her in Japanese, but she always responded in English. The room where they sat had been Sachiko's room, and now he moved slowly, staring, remembering, nostalgia a sweet syrup in his veins. Everything appeared to be coated in a greasy film; he thought it was from the candles they'd used for light during the war.

He asked her where she'd learned to speak English. In Australia, she told him, she'd gone to school there. Her father had died, she didn't say how. She said that when she returned to Japan after the surrender, the Americans gave her this house to live in. "Mr. James wants me out," she said, but she made it sound like this, too, was a special benediction. Everything she said sounded like that—her victory over English partly made it seem that way; she had a victorious accent, and her Japanese decorum was like that of a clown, a geisha in baggy trousers, a strangely beautiful woman.

When Emmett was a boy, the James-yama Estate was comprised of fifty-five houses, plus Ernest W. James's own mansion and a clubhouse with a gym that had once employed an Italian trainer who ran exercise classes to music. Earnest W. James was buying up yet more of the mountain when he was imprisoned by Japanese police, July 1940, along with another fourteen British residents of Kobe, including Emmett's father, who was so ill with TB. A Reuters correspondent by the name of Cox had written a letter that found its way to the house in Vancouver where Emmett lived with his mother after he'd got out of the sanatorium with a clean bill of health. The letter informed them that his father had died while being interrogated. The official story was that he had jumped out a window.

Earnest W. James fled the Shiyoa estate, fled the country, and the Japanese government froze his assets. His mansion then served as a recreational hall for the Imperial Japanese Navy, while Germans, Italians, French, and Japanese citizens lived in his fifty-five houses.

"You knew this house before the war," Aoi said.

"My father leased it, yes, and another house for us, my mother and me. But he lost both houses when he was put in prison."

"Two houses!" said Aoi, ignoring the fate of his father.

"His mistress lived here." He yielded to the temptation of playing the prince. He liked that he could please her.

She smiled her toothy smile and jumped up. She had a great figure. He was beginning to find her quite magnificent. She said that she was terrible not to have offered him something to drink. "Wait," she said and left the room. Even in the baggy clothes, she was voluptuous.

He went to the doors that led to the garden and pulled them open—the sound of them opening was not as he remembered —such a small thing for a body to remember—so he looked closely and saw the miniature mountains of sawdust on the mat, and then he saw the white ants.

The house sat on timber that had soaked up rain delivered by the spring typhoons; the wet wood had invited termites. He went outside. The sun had set behind the mountain. The road would be dark on his descent. He walked the perimeter of the house. Everything returned to him, every window frame, every inch of clapboard, but it was being eaten away by the white ants. In the dusk, he saw them moving in the wood; the house, its stasis seemed to depend on their agitation. So this is the way, this is the way the material world will reveal its secret, destructive aspect.

He re-entered through the French doors to find Aoi seated on the floor. She had changed into a white kimono and she held a lute on her knees, a *biwa*. Her black hair was cut so it exaggerated the broadness of her face and formed two black triangles on each cheek, then gathered in a long ponytail snaking down her back. The *biwa,* the kimono, her posture, all indicated tradition, but the smile she gave him was self-mocking.

She took a fan-shaped pick, a plectrum, from the folds of her kimono and struck the strings, drawing a wave of sound, a metallic, exciting music, her hand forcefully striking. She began to sing. Her voice had a muscled lower register, a masculine, glottal voicing of the Japanese.

It was a long, ancient song about the fall of the Heike. Emmett had heard performances of it at least twice before, but never a performance by such a woman. Her hand with the plectrum striking and gliding like a knife-sharpener against the steely voice of the instrument, her muscular voice thickening on the consonants, then thinning eerily.

When the song was finished, Aoi bowed, stood, bowed again, and shuffled from the room, carrying the *biwa* by grasping the instrument at its neck. The plectrum had disappeared somewhere. She was wearing white gym socks. He thought of Charlie Chaplin.

When she returned, she carried a tray with a glass and a bottle of bourbon. The kimono was of padded white silk and made her seem unapproachable. He had come to seek a trace of Sachiko, his secret mother, and instead he'd found this extraordinary woman. He wanted her so badly he was touching her sleeve when he spoke to her, touching her knee.

He began to drink bourbon. No matter how much he drank he felt sober. Aoi offered to cook dinner and took him to the kitchen. But when he saw the tiny portion of rice she found in the kitchen cupboard and generously offered to him, he said that he wasn't hungry.

When he undressed her, he was shaken by her beauty. She was of such grand scale she was almost intimidating. He held her breasts in his hands, kneading them in a way that he knew hurt her a little. She smelled of rice powder, a smell that made him ache. He had never inflicted lust on a woman this way, heedless of hurting her, with her long legs around his neck, rising over her while she laughed, catching her breath.

In the early morning they went down to the seashore and watched a boy and a girl, likely a brother and sister, on the pier. The little girl studied her brother as he let a net into the water, then raised it and searched through the kelp, laying the net on the dock. It was windy, sunny, but suddenly cold. From the beach, families flew kites that darted like swallows in the wind. He watched the keenly coloured kites, and then again searched out the two children on the pier. The brother brought his net out of the water, laid it down, then picked up something whitely blue and fleshy, and held it up to show his admiring sister. The thing changed shape in his hands and dangled its many legs. The little sister clapped her hands.

Chapter Fourteen

Herbert Norman asked Emmett to have lunch with him. They didn't exactly work together; as envoy, Herbert had higher status than Emmett did—but Herbert had maintained a kindly interest in Emmett's progress as policy analyst with the Liaison Mission. It was October now, and Emmet was finding his way on the job.

They were sitting at a long counter in a noodle joint. Herbert bent toward the bowl of ramen and let the steam wash over his face. "General MacArthur believes that the Chinese communists won't get involved in Korea." When Herbert raised his head, his glasses were fogged and he removed them. "He says the American forces will 'strike awe in the Chinese heart.'" Herbert did a pretty good imitation of MacArthur. He smiled sadly. "The general believes that the Orientals will 'bow down before America's supreme power.' Chinese soldiers are little men, see? All three hundred thousand of them."

Herbert Norman had been working around the general since 1945. "Our views are 'divergent,'" he said, bending again toward his soup. "In MacArthur's terms, 'divergent' means barbarian." Then he burst out bitterly, "Why the *hell* would they investigate me."

Emmett asked him what he meant. "Investigate you? Who?"

"Never mind. I'll spoil your lunch."

Emmett waited till Herbert reluctantly explained, "Someone named me in his testimony before the US Senate Security Subcommittee."

Emmett said that this sounded far-fetched, Herbert's name coming up like that. How could such a thing happen? He was remembering Bill Masters warning him to be cautious of Herbert Norman.

"I take it you've heard of Senator Joe McCarthy," Herbert said.

"Sure. But how could McCarthy touch you?"

"He can't. But I'm unnerved, I admit."

"It's crazy, isn't it?"

"Crazy. Yes."

"You've got nothing to worry about. Surely. It's outrageous." But Emmett knew it probably wasn't outrageous. Herbert had been flagged by the FBI by writing for *Amerasia* — the New York-based magazine that had been discovered with stolen high-level secret documents in its offices. He wondered what else had brought Herbert to the attention of the American Security bloodhounds.

"The minister assures me I'm protected," Herbert was saying wanly. "Pearson is a friend of mine. I'm a Canadian citizen. Still — one's name — " he broke off and put his spoon down. He saw Emmett's face. "I don't think it's gone so far as to affect those around me."

"I'm not worried about that."

"You should be."

At Herbert's right, a Japanese man had finished eating, but rather than leaving right away, as everyone else did, he stayed, eavesdropping. Herbert said, "How about we take a walk?"

It was a warm fall day. They made their way to the moat surrounding the emperor's palace. Emmett reached to touch the twisted branches of the cherry trees lining the path. The broad moat and brick wall surrounding the palace grounds were on a grand scale. He'd been scrutinizing detailed maps and aerial photographs of tiny Korean villages, of mountain roads and hidden valleys, he was under-slept from working long hours and then taking a train back out to see Aoi for one night on the weekends, and now he stumbled and gripped the iron railing to prevent himself from falling down the steep slope into the water with the swans and lily pads and the rifles trained on him from the emperor's gardens.

Herbert noticed Emmett's unsteady step. "Are you okay?"

"I think I've been working too hard." Emmett took off his jacket. "Ottawa wants a report about women's book clubs in suburban Tokyo."

"That's knocking you out?"

"Spurious inaction takes a lot of energy."

Herbert said vaguely, "This war that is not a war."

Emmett told him that he intended to do some research into the relationship between the Japanese mafia, the Yakuza, and the government since the surrender. "I've been ordered to avoid anything hot. I'm told to stay away from the subject of the war in Korea. I wonder if General MacArthur has complained about me. I don't think he likes me very much."

"You laughed at him. Big mistake. Don't be blinded by his melodrama. The Japanese love him. He's truer than true." Herbert hesitated. "MacArthur is going use his popularity to lure the Pentagon into giving him more rope. Then he'll provoke the Chinese communists into full-scale war."

"Where are the Chinese troops now?" Emmett asked this abruptly, as if the question had just popped into his head. Herbert jumped a little and answered, "In China, for all I know."

Emmett shrugged, "Does anyone have any real information? Does MacArthur have any intelligence? Is he all shadow play?"

"I don't know," Herbert said with more emphasis. Then, "Look. I'm leaving Tokyo."

Emmett asked him where he was going.

"Ottawa. Pearson believes it'll go better for me if I'm there while the RCMP do their investigation."

"I see," Emmett said. "Ottawa wants you to lie low for a while. For show. To appease the Americans." Herbert Norman's face revealed some relief at this assessment. Emmett continued, "You'll go to Ottawa, you'll clear things up, you'll return to Japan, and get on with your work. Good."

"Think so?"

"You have to face down this kind of speculation in person." Herbert turned his back, and Emmett could feel his loneliness. "Easy for me to say," he added.

Without looking at Emmett, Herbert said, "I want to give you some advice. When you've used my name on any of your reports, you should redact it, don't name me anywhere."

"I won't erase your name, Herbert."

Herbert shook his head. "You don't understand. A man thinks he's defending his own freedom, he thinks there's no reason for him to tell, say, the FBI what he's doing, he thinks it's none of their business. Turns out, it's always their business. Protect yourself. Redact my name and never mention me again."

Herbert Norman quietly left Tokyo a week later, mid-October 1950. Emmett didn't redact Herbert's name from his files and correspondence. He fobbed off the report on ladies' book clubs to a female researcher who was glad to get out of the office while he went ahead with his own investigation into the connections between the CIA, the post-war Japanese government, and the Yakuza. The report was received cautiously in Ottawa, considered risqué, overly confident: Canadian civil servants were expected to be euphemistic, uncritical — but he wasn't formally censored. Bill Masters sent a fatherly, personal note urging him to take a stronger interest in what the Japanese ladies were reading. "We're looking for soft information," Bill wrote, "the stuff you can get only from civilians. Something credible."

Emmett wasn't supposed to board an airplane with a group of American journalists he'd befriended and fly into North Korea. So he didn't tell anyone; he took a sick day, claiming to have the flu. The sleek receptionist answering his early morning phone call told him to take two aspirin and drink plenty of Pepsi. "How sick are you?" she asked. He told her that he thought a day in bed would get him back on his feet; he'd be in tomorrow.

He took a taxi from his suite to the airport in the company of the American pressmen, pulling his hat low over his eyes and telling the journalists that his government wasn't too keen on field trips. That appealed to them, and at the military airport they told the pilot that he was a reporter from Michigan. They said he had the nondescript good looks of somebody from Kalamazoo.

The clipper carrying the pressmen was on the trail of the air force plane carrying General MacArthur, who wanted to see the Yalu River, to gloat over the apparent retreat of the Chinese People's Liberation Army. They were flying very low, at about six thousand feet, deep into the war zone, but the ancient mountains were peaceful. There was a village on the north side of the winding black river. Emmett heard the newsmen nervously speculate over whether there were anti-aircraft guns in the area.

In the seat beside Emmett was a journalist named Wilson, an American in his late forties who'd been in the Far East for well over a decade. Wilson stood up and leaned over him to see out the window. Against a startling blue sky, a heavy grey American bomber, a B-29, was approaching from the south. The plane carrying the general suddenly veered, and the plane with the journalists followed in a steep curve that threw Wilson into Emmett. They untangled, Wilson apologized, and when Emmett looked out again, the bomber was visible about five hundred feet below. Emmett took a leather pouch not much bigger than a cigarette lighter from his jacket pocket and from it he slipped a silver object, a miniature camera, into his hand. The bomber was circling back toward the river. Then it dropped its load.

The bombs struck the village, igniting a fire that spilled out in orange blooms and black smoke. Emmett photographed the roiling flames and what he believed were the tiny figures of the peasants scattering. There were no trees; even from this altitude the gunner had a clear view. Dirt rose in yellowish puffs from the dry earth around the burning village. No one from the ground was firing back.

The air force plane flew on, following the river, and the journalists' plane trailed after them. Behind them the sun shone on smoke that rose into columns of pink marble.

"I'll be damned," said Wilson shakily. "That was some show. I bet we weren't supposed to see that." He took out his notebook.

The plane was filled with shouting men. What did you see? What do you know about that? Somebody said, "We laced into them, didn't we! Son of a bitch!" Whether in anger, disgust, or valorous excitement, Emmett didn't know. He watched the mountains for signs of Chinese troops, his camera held ready.

Wilson was making notes in shorthand. He glanced over and said, "That's a really small camera."

Emmett shrugged. "A hobby of mine." Then he said, "Those were breadbaskets, each carrying seventy-two incendiary bombs filled with napalm."

Wilson gave him a look and returned his attention to his notebook. Emmett read Wilson's shorthand. Day, time, location, number of bombs, estimated size of kill by bombing, by fire, by machine gun, estimated number of enemy. He said to Wilson, "There aren't any soldiers here."

"They're hiding."

"I don't think so." There'd be no sense for soldiers to hide here. The village isn't close enough to the railway line, and it's too exposed. Who would the soldiers attack, anyway? The only danger came from the air.

There weren't any anti-aircraft guns. Wilson could figure

this out for himself. But Emmett asked Wilson, "If you write that nobody shot back — that there probably weren't any soldiers anywhere near the village the USAF just bombed — would your newspaper print it?"

Wilson angrily muttered, "Sure." He took a flask from his jacket pocket, offered it to Emmett, who gladly accepted. "But I'm not going to report it that way." Wilson saw Emmett's disappointment, and he added, "How do I know where the soldiers are? We're nearly two miles in the air." Wilson drank, muttering, "Goddamn fucking bastards."

Emmett guessed that Wilson meant the Chinese communists. His eyes searched the mountains for signs of Chinese troops but saw no one. They were flying over a rail line broken by bombs, but he saw no people anywhere.

Wilson went on writing and drinking. He noticed Emmett's intense white face and he observed, "You're in a funny spot."

"Think so?"

"You came out here just because you were curious?"

"That's right."

"Got more than you bargained for."

"I'm glad I know what I know."

"Sure, but what can you do about it? You can't even report it to your government. You're not even here."

"I'm glad I know," Emmett said again, looking toward the Korean mountains, their summits filled with snow. He believed that the air force had bombed that village to give the general an exciting show.

"More stupidity," Wilson said, "more gratuitous cruelty. Mean, blunt force. You're glad to know?" Wilson had had quite a bit to drink, but he appeared to be sober. He had an unmemorable face, his features obscured by capillary veins across his sagging cheeks, his green eyes moist and heavy-lidded. His first assignment as Far East correspondent for *LIFE*, he'd told Emmett, was to cover the Nanking Massacre. "Yeah," Wilson said, "it's better to know."

Wilson continued, "It makes it hard to enjoy life, to feel good about being a human being, knowing what people are happy to do to each other. So" — he took a drink — "I don't intend to live very long. But I won't live my life like a bat in the dark. I'll look at it full in the face."

Emmett stared into the mountain sky. "These kinds of things," he said, "evil things, they can make a man turn. Make him nihilistic. A man's got to find something to hope for. He'll go crazy if he can't imagine something better. He'll start to hate himself. And hate others." He turned toward Wilson.

The way Wilson shook his head indicated he'd already, long ago, considered that. "It's a commitment, understand? Knowing how bad it can get and not looking away. It's like deciding to love someone. Love the bastards who blow the place up."

"What if you hate the bastards?"

Wilson shrugged and handed him the flask. "Then you've let them kill you too."

Emmett took a drink.

Wilson said, "I believe in the margin of error. I will forgive human fallibility till I finally get run over by an army jeep."

Their plane was heading back to Tokyo. Ahead of them was the air force plane carrying General MacArthur. Wilson was saying, "A buddy of mine, a reporter, was in the Philippines with MacArthur when we dropped the atom bomb on Hiroshima. He said that MacArthur was all cut up about it. My friend told me he walked into MacArthur's quarters in Manila, and MacArthur could hardly talk he was so sad — he was all quiet for a change. MacArthur asks my friend, 'Do you know what this means?' My friend says, 'What does it mean, General?' MacArthur says, 'It means there'll be no more wars.' He says, 'It means I'm obsolete. The scientists are going to run things now.' MacArthur was as sad as sad could be, over the atom bomb." Wilson shook his head. "No more war. He wept."

Chapter Sixteen

In October 1950, MacArthur believed he would win the war in Korea by Christmas. By October 20, his forces had overtaken North Korea's capital Pyongyang, and General MacArthur had told President Truman, "If the Chinese try to get down to Pyongyang, there'll be a great slaughter."

Unless the Chinese gained air protection. And only the Russians had the power to provide air protection to the People's Liberation Army.

The Chinese had Russian air support by the first of November. Then the Chinese People's Volunteer Army infiltrated the UN lines, cut them off and circled their flanks, drove them out of Pyongyang into the snow-covered mountains in small, disparate groups of wounded men. Anyone too injured to walk froze to death or was captured.

November 27, thirty below zero, one hundred and fifty thousand Chinese soldiers marched through the snow of Manchuria undetected and came out of the night to encircle the Americans at the Chosin Reservoir in the northeast of North Korea. MacArthur began to try to orchestrate a massive retreat. He wouldn't permit anyone, however, to call it that, a retreat. Reporters were instructed to write that the American troops had "moved back to new prepared positions."

———

On a sleeting day in December, Emmett was working from his office at the Canadian Liaison Office in Tokyo when the receptionist popped in and told him he had a visitor.

"Who is it?"

"Beats me." Following Emmett down the corridor, she added, "He looks like the nervous type."

A man in his mid-forties wearing a wrinkled black suit with a white shirt and a skinny black tie, unmistakably jet-lagged and harried, sat smoking in one of the Bauhaus chairs. He wore black glasses, had an oblong face, and he looked unhappy.

He stood and offered his hand. "Miller. George Miller. US State Department. How are we today, Mr. Jones?"

The interview took place there, in the reception area, while staff came and went, and the receptionist sat at her desk reading a Sears Roebuck catalogue. George Miller told Emmett that he was with the Policy Planning Staff, a Washington-based "think tank." He announced that he was going to lay his cards on the table. "I hear you speak Japanese," he said, adding with strange emphasis, "must be handy with the girls."

Emmett said nothing.

"Talking the talk, right?" Miller prompted. "It gets you a head start with the ladies."

"Not really."

"Poor little Japanese butterflies," said Miller.

Emmett thought, He's talking about Aoi. He had been to see Aoi just that weekend. He could still smell her on his clothes.

Miller put out his cigarette and leaned forward with his elbows on his knees. "We're glad Canada has men like you working here. Top-notch."

"Thanks."

"We just want to make sure we're on the same page."

"Of?"

"What's that?"

"Same page of what?"

Miller gave him a dirty look, running a finger over his lips. "You speak Chinese too, that right?"

"My field is strictly Japan."

"You sure?" Miller made enough of a smile to suggest that it was okay if Emmett laughed. Then he said, "I hear you're a great fan of Mao."

"I wouldn't say that. It's not baseball."

"What's that?" Miller cocked his ear.

"I'm not a fan of anybody."

Miller sat back. "Good."

Emmett said nothing.

"You've got friends in Ottawa."

"Oh?"

"A real rising star." Miller began to scratch irritably at the back of his head. "I keep telling Washington, the Canadians aren't stupid. But you know what? Sometimes they don't believe me."

Miller went on, "I'm being direct with you. Why? Because I respect you. Sure I do. We keep working with you. Why?" He polished his glasses, deliberating, Emmett supposed, an alternative. "We work for a common goal. What's that? Freedom! We're going to wipe the communists from the face of the earth.

"Listen, pal" — Miller leaned toward Emmett — "you want to wear a — what," he motioned, "sign around your neck tells everybody who you are? Huh? Don't be a patsy. It's like the

Middle Ages over there in China. Soviet Union? Same damn thing. There's no *equality*," Miller scoffed, as if Emmett had been arguing with him. "They tell you, Emmett, you go work in this, what, rice paddy. I don't care who you are or how many goddamn languages you speak, how many college degrees you got or who you know. The thing is this. The communists have the A-bomb, and millions, *millions* of innocent people are going to die. Rosenbergs, you heard of them, you know them?"

"Sure I've heard of them."

Miller paused. "You ever meet them?"

"Of course not."

"Course not. How would that happen? Forget it. I'm talking in my sleep."

"Mr. Miller," Emmett said. "Can I call you George? What do you want?" He told himself to stay calm.

Miller gave a savvy, sideways look and jumped out of his chair to speak into Emmett's ear. "Who knew the Chinese were going to get involved over there?" Miller pulled back and jerked his head to the left, aiming west, to Korea. Then he came so close again, Emmett could smell the urinary fragrance of airplane in Miller's hair. "Somebody knew. How about your boss?"

"I've got many bosses."

Miller said, "Aw," sour and self-pitying; this must be a chore, a time-consuming errand, going after a junior analyst. "The diplomat who's under suspicion."

"I can't speak for Mr. Norman."

"You can't speak for Mr. Norman. How about yourself? Can you speak for yourself?"

"Yup."

"So?"

"The Chinese are crammed between a rock and a hard place."

"Okay. Send them a sympathy card." Miller sat down again, jittering his knees.

"I don't know why your government keeps propping up the Nationalists. It seems almost stupid. Arrogant but also stupid. Your pal Chiang Kai-shek is a lame duck." Miller jumped a little, hearing this, and Emmett could feel anger like a welcome drug in his veins; he spoke in a low voice, fury rippling through him. "A *corrupt* duck. He and his soldiers, his bankers, they're all on the take. You guys are being taken for a ride."

Miller smiled as if he'd hit the jackpot. He spoke more loudly, apparently so the receptionist could hear him from her desk, as if he would impress her with his wit. "We're a bunch of ignorant imperialists. That's how you put it? Ha ha."

The expression sounded sophomoric. Emmett leaned forward as if he might punch Miller's condescending face.

"Go on," Miller said.

"Of *course* Mao Zedong's going to get involved in Korea," Emmett said. "He gets military support from the Russians. And the Russians have wanted to take over Korea for years."

"Your pal Herbert Norman tell you that?"

"Everybody knows it. Except you. You guys cut Mao off, so he goes to the Russians for support. What else can he do? You pretty well set up the People's Republic of China."

Miller looked at him in disbelief. "You know what you're saying?"

"I'm not saying anything new. Everybody knows about it but the US of A." He hated Miller now, hated him for assuming he had power over him.

Miller stood up, ran his finger over the starch burn on his neck. "It's interesting. How these ideas get around. Circulate." He put his fingers under his nose and sniffed them.

"It's common knowledge among us thinking folk."

"Yeah. Sure. Let's hope there's no cause for any further divergence, Mr. Jones." Miller surveyed the room. "You might want to consider your future. You like Tokyo. Must be a real homecoming. Be too bad to be sent back. Kind of a disgrace." He smiled. His Adam's apple bobbed up and down.

"Nobody's sending me back, Mr. Miller. In fact, if I weren't a gentleman and a Canadian civil servant, I'd suggest you go fuck yourself right about now. And that would be rude."

Chapter Seventeen

He went back to his office, shaken. Miller had threatened to have him "sent back," and while the American official should theoretically have no influence over his career, he'd let himself be cornered, he'd said too much, and though he'd smiled while he told Miller to fuck himself, he'd made a mistake, snagged an enemy.

"Glad we met," Miller had said generously, and he shook Emmett's hand rather slowly, looking into his face with paternal pity. Poor bastard, Mr. Miller implied in his handshake.

Emmett wrote a report for Bill Masters; revised it, drinking, revising till he'd achieved a politely detached position outlining the fatal ignorance of George Miller from Washington.

Bill Masters responded with a scolding memorandum, giving Jones "a little history lesson."

"You ought to know," wrote Bill, "the US policy, keeping the Russians and the Chinese from the vast industrial potential we forecast in Japan and the rest of Asia, is crucial. Take a minute and consider the repercussions of a world takeover by the Chinese and Russian communists. We support the Americans or we lose <u>everything</u>. <u>That's</u> our policy. Pearson made that clear in '48."

"By the way," Bill wrote as a postscript, "your friend Herbert Norman has been cleared."

———

Emmett wasn't the only person to wonder this: If there was really no evidence that Norman was a communist and a threat to security, how could the US Senate Committee have persuaded Ottawa to recall him to investigate? There must have been a grain of sand, a seed, a Herbert Norman who might actually exist. Herbert Norman had been right to grieve over his lost reputation. His life would never be the same.

A week passed, then Emmett got another dispatch from Bill Masters. "I had a personal visit from George Miller, your friend with the State Department. What kind of socialist flummery came out of your mouth, Jones? You're a fan of Chairman Mao, are you? I'm reminding you — you're on probation."

Emmett paced, furious, despising his own shoebox career. He packed a few things, took the train south to Kobe and then a bus to Shioya, and climbed the snowy road to see Aoi.

He arrived late Friday night. The lanes of Shioya were sparsely lit with lanterns. He hadn't realized that it was nearly Christmas till he got to James-yama, where the American armed forces personnel who still occupied several of the houses of the estate and the British subjects who were returning in their wake had strung coloured lights and hung cedar with red bows. Approaching the house, he heard the thrilling clatter of a *biwa*. The player reached the end of a phrase and began it again.

There were big footprints from a man's boots in the snow leading to Sachiko's front door, where there was nailed a Sakaki branch, bare of ornament, a relic.

Emmett rang "Waltzing Matilda." Something made him look back at the road. In the blue light he saw a man passing from view behind the plum trees, the deeper blue flag of his kimono billowing in his wake. Emmett carried his duffle bag containing his shaving kit, a change of underwear, clean socks, and condoms. He realized he might have warned Aoi that he was coming. She'd finished practising, had begun to play with her customary gusto, and didn't break off to answer the door. But the latch was open, he discovered. He left his bag in the hall and went through the empty house to the sunroom, where he found Aoi engaged in an epic recitation of the Satsuma rebellion; she didn't stop but leaned forward as if he were some kind of elemental force she must press against.

He took to the chaise and waited for her to finish. She wore the white kimono. He sensed that it was going to be a rocky night.

When at last the Satsuma rebellion came to its mournful end, Aoi stood and ceremoniously swept the sleeves of her kimono from her arms to carry the *biwa* to its case before turning to him and bowing.

"It's late," she said. "And you didn't call."

He apologized.

Aoi ushered him to a room he didn't know existed; it must have been off limits when he was a boy. It was more traditional than the rest of the house; its tatami mats were in good shape. She was flustered. "I have things I must do," she said. He apologized again for showing up unannounced. She said, "Well, you're here now," and bowed and left him there.

The hibachi was already lit, the room was warm, the bedding had been unrolled, and a clean towel lay beside water in a basin. Dimly he marvelled that she was so well prepared for him. The heated room made him sleepy so he lay down on the futon to wait for her and fell asleep.

He awoke to the presence of someone in the room and saw her figure against the glowing embers in the stove. "Aoi?"

She came to kneel beside his bed.

"I'm not good," she said.

"Yes you are. You're very good. You're beautiful."

She made love the way she talked, he decided later, with the same laconic self-absorption and pride. In the darkness, his bed was a raft at sea, with no direction. The walls of the room melted away in waves of pleasure.

When he awoke, Aoi was gone. It was not yet dawn. Embers glowed in the hibachi. The room was chilly. He got dressed and put on his coat and boots and left the house.

He was on his way up the mountain as the sky lightened, following a path lit by snow. The ascent was vigorous enough to warm him, the path cleared of fallen trees; even the pine needles had been raked and swept.

He'd often thought that he preferred the country of his birth over the country of his nationhood; preferred its cultivated grace to the wild waste of tree and rock. In Canada, he'd yearned for Japan, homesick for a land so ancient as to be an extension of human thoughtfulness; all the countryside a shrine. Now, ascending the mountain pursued, in his mind, by a Washington think tank, the countryside made him feel claustrophobic, it felt like a binding contract. He wanted wilderness.

He climbed until the path levelled out and spread through the trees. A stone fireplace had been built among the cypress and *sugi*, and rope decorated with white pennants linked the trees. A Shinto shrine. He looked to the low mountains in the distance, the neat brown and blue arrangement of forest. The *Kami*, the spirits of this place, were silent. Mist drifted in to obscure the pine trees, winding itself around the branches of the pines. Emmett had walked this mountain before, with his father, years ago. Now he felt that his father remained hidden in the mist, in the silence of the *Kami*. The pines were visible, then invisible, while the mist shifted, leaving its wet trace. His father is dead. His father's lover, Sachiko, is dead. His mother is dead and gone. Nothing remains of the dead, but the damage they've done.

There was nothing to do but walk back down. Snowy, morning light reminded him of Ontario. The path returned him to the garden at the back of the house, under a layer of snow patterned by birds' feet, covering the stones right to the edge of the black water of the fishpond. Green grass thrust raggedly through the snow. He'd gotten cold, his boots were wet, he'd snagged brittle twigs from the persimmon tree in his hair. He approached the house and tapped on the glass of the French door.

Aoi stood inches away, separated from him by a pane of glass. She was huge, wearing a cloak, a weave of black and ochre, and her face was coated in heavy white makeup with an aureole of rouge beneath her eyes. Her thick black hair had been lacquered so it rose high from her forehead, adding several inches to her considerable height. Her shining hair was again shaped strangely into jet-black triangles at her cheekbones.

She didn't blink. He swayed his body far to the left then far to the right, and her red-rimmed eyes followed him, the whites of her eyes, her nearly black irises tracking his movement, but she was unsmiling. Like a bat unfolding its wings, Aoi spread the wide sleeves of the cloak, revealing her muscular forearms, and opened the door. Heat pulled him to itself and he fell inside. His feet began to needle and thaw.

He shook the twigs from his hair onto the mat and tried to remove his boots, but the laces were frozen. Finally he pried them off and peeled off his wet socks. When he looked up to address Aoi, she put her finger to her painted lips, "Shhh." She waved, Follow.

Aoi returned him to the tatami room. The curtains were drawn against the morning light. He fell onto the *futon* with a childish moan of contentment and then stood up quickly: his clothes were damp and not very clean. Aoi shuffled in her white socks to stand before him and take his musty tweed jacket, folding it and placing it near the stove. She returned and put her cold hands under his sweater and lifted it over his head. He laughed but she shushed him.

Her cloak had silk buttons, one looping over the other. He reached curiously to touch her hair, but she gripped his right wrist while she undid the silk clasps. Then she let him go and stepped toward him. As she did so the cloak fell away, revealing the naked body below her painted face, the creamy whitewash that ended at her collarbone.

He travelled his fingers over her breasts and rounded her stomach, then ran along the strong shoulders, pushing her backward till she was lying down. The rouge around her eyes made them look huge and animal. He moved so his body covered hers and pinned her arms back. He felt the delirious surge of freedom, an existence without restraint; his life lifted from him, a fleeting sliver of childhood, pure greed, destructive and pleasing to himself. This time he cried out.

Aoi put her hand over his mouth and forced him back until he kneeled between her legs while she sat up. The careful arrangement of her hair had become a tangle of rich black braid. There was the dense scent of her rice powder smeared on his chest.

She walked to the window and pulled aside the curtain.

Emmett followed, gathering up the cloak to drape it over her shoulders. With a tone of defiance, Aoi told him that the cloak had belonged to her grandmother. "It is from Manchuria," she said.

He began to get dressed. Even the sparse furnishings seemed disappointed. He wondered why he felt as if they'd just had an argument. He asked her if she was all right.

Aoi, cloaked and pallid, shook her mane and arranged the garment around her feet. She might have been preparing to greet His Imperial Majesty. In a low voice she asked him, "Why do you never ask me about my father?"

Emmett was struggling with his pants. He wondered, indeed, why he'd never asked her about her father. She'd said he'd died. And the Americans had let her stay in the house. He apologized; he was sorry that he'd spoken to her so little; he was always distracted by her unusual looks, her uncommon beauty. "Tell me," he said.

She shook her head.

Emmett put on his shirt.

"He was a hero," she said.

Her voice had a shrill register he'd never heard before from her. He continued to get dressed. He wanted to be prepared for what came next.

"He was a *hero*," she repeated. "A Japanese hero." Then she laughed in the way that he liked, in her estranged, solitary victory over the meaningless defeat of her country. She abruptly saddened. "Ah," she said, "poor Father."

Aoi looked from the window down onto the snowy lawn and the road beyond. She spoke softly in singsong English. "When the dead are listening, what do we tell them?" In the eggy light, her broad face was a moon, even in its irregular shape. She lifted her face to him, tears flowing over the white surface of her face. She opened her mouth, but no sound came out. The moon was crying. She lay down on the floor with her face buried in her arms and raised her head to look at him. Her tears had washed the rouge into two V's under her eyes. The remains of lipstick were smeared to the corners of her mouth.

She rolled over onto her back, wrapping the Manchurian cloak around her body, but for her right breast — and it did look like a lotus blossom — and the dissimilitude of her large form, its continent of Manchurian ochre and shades of black, and its floating breast in misalliance with her gorgeous clown-face, all made him keenly glad he'd come here after all.

She stared up at the ceiling, coiling her hair round her finger. "My father died to redeem his purity."

This was a Japanese expression. Emmett guessed that she meant that her father had died by suicide. A redemptive, purifying suicide. There must have been shame. It would be indelicate of him to question her on this. So he said nothing.

A half-hour later, she walked down with him to where he could catch his bus. It was cold and she covered her ears with mittened hands. Once, he turned to find her kneeling several feet back, rocking herself, inwardly, intensely focused. She held up her hands filled with fresh new snow and showed him this.

He looked hard to see what she wanted him to see. Snow. And all around, trees, which were very good trees, in the way Japan was good, and which were good in ways quite unlike the good trees of Canada.

Aoi stood up in the freezing wind, regarding him from behind her ruined makeup, her hair wildly dishevelled, like a giant and sexually knowledgeable child.

"I can't leave my country," she said.

"I'll see you in two weeks," he promised. She didn't respond; she didn't believe him. Women have a way of doing that, he thought; they make you feel bad and then refuse to tell you what you did.

He succumbed to the temptation to be at a loss for words and left her on the road below the plum trees. He was some distance away when he heard her calling out. "Emmett Jones!" He stopped and listened. I have taken something from you! Aoi's voice winging overhead, her tone of victory with a desperate edge.

Chapter Eighteen

Emmett walked to a low row of artisans' shops in Kobe, to a warm wooden room where a handsome, middle-aged woman sat at a drafting table drawing maps. The walls were covered with similar hand-drawn maps and below them twenty or thirty cubbyholes were filled with scrolls. There were hangers draped in sea charts. Land surveys hung from the rafters, swaying in the heat coiling up from the hibachi. The place smelled of sandalwood. The woman looked at him from under the papery folds of her eyelids, laid her pen in a dish, opened a drawer, and removed the train schedule to Tokyo. The cartographer's office served as an information centre. She said in English, "So much coming and leaving."

With her smooth, greying head, she looked like a piece of soapstone. While she prepared his ticket, she asked, "Where is your home in the United States?"

He told her he'd been born in Japan but that he was actually Canadian. She uttered a cry of delight and called out in Japanese. A Japanese man wearing a *hakama*, a fellow in his mid-twenties with a shining, merry face, unmistakeably of the same family, appeared from behind a screen. She introduced him. "My brother," she said. "Dr. Kimura." She said the name as if it were a light joke.

"Canadian," said the woman, pointing at Emmett. "Canadian," she repeated, pointing at her brother.

Dr. Kimura bowed. In neat consonants, he said it was wonderful to meet a fellow Canadian.

"I was born here," said Emmett.

Dr. Kimura burst out laughing. He had a boy's voice. "I was born in Ottawa."

His sister smiled wanly, with a tremor of disapproval.

Dr. Kimura said, "I'm going to Tokyo tonight, to board a ship and go home." He put stubborn emphasis on the word *home*.

Dr. Kimura's sister remarked that she had found him a companion for his journey to Tokyo, for she happened to know that Mr. Jones was catching the same train, and they both must hurry or they'll miss it. "Ah!" said Dr. Kimura. "I'll be glad to have a chat with you!"

The night journey to Tokyo was intensely pleasurable. Kimura loved to talk, but he was also a curious listener, and Emmett trusted him with harmless, almost gossipy details of his life.

Several times Emmett brought the conversation round to Aoi, to the difficulties of her relations with a *gaijin*. He tried to imply that she confused him, intending to portray himself as a man willing respectfully to submit to women's irrationalities. Kimura listened with a look of subdued merriment on his face.

They arrived in Tokyo at nine that night and found a bar doing brisk business in the rooms upstairs, catering to Japanese sailors and the new Japanese police wearing shabby, hand-me-down American uniforms. Emmett ordered sake from the very pretty, very young girl.

Kimura wasn't yet a doctor; he was still a student. The war and an internment camp in Guelph, Ontario, Kimura pointed out, had slowed his progress. Kimura called himself

"a relativist"—a Nisei, he insisted, being a man of two exist-
ences. His father had remarried as soon as his first wife died,
and he'd left his daughter, Kimura's elder sister, sixteen years
old at that time, behind in Japan while he journeyed to Canada
in search of—what?

"Freedom!" said Kimura, laughing. "Crazy, eh?"

Kimura was born within a year of their immigrating. They
couldn't go back. Japan had closed herself off again, to purge
all enemies of the *kokutai*. It was hard for Kimura's sister, left
behind, but things got much worse for her in the war years
when the thought police, the Kempeitai, watched those with
even the slightest connection to the United States. Anyone
who gave her employment was suspected of harbouring a spy,
a decadent infesting Japan with the foreign ideology of indi-
vidualism. She'd nearly starved.

"But you aren't American."

Kimura laughed and put his arm around Emmett's neck,
kissing his cheek.

Kimura was tough on his race, but if Emmett gave way to
any criticism of the Japanese, Kimura would flip to the other
side in passionate defence. "The manner of a man's death will
determine the value of his life," he said and added, lugubrious
with drink, "We can't expect someone like you, Emmett Jones,
Christian, to understand our noble tradition of *seppuku*. An
act of honour, a demonstration of free will." Here, he shrugged
and winced. "But to suicide for the emperor?" He made a light
sound with his mouth: "Pfft."

Kimura was *we* as a Japanese and *I* as a Canadian. "I am
not convinced," he went on, "that every one of the tens of
thousands of suicides in the last ten years adds up to nobility.
Maybe it's impossible to do anything nobly anymore. Nobility

has been diluted among too much population on the planet." Kimura smiled like one of the Gods of Good Fortune and called out for the pretty little girl to bring them Scotch whisky.

The sailors and police in their shabby uniforms put down their beers and turned to look at them. Kimura cheerfully raised his cup and said in English, "Goodbye, Buddha-Heads! Goodbye, everlasting shame! Goodbye, kokutai! Tomorrow I go home to Canada!"

Without a word, four sailors pushed back their chairs and approached like men called to perform manual labour, casually fitting brass knuckles onto their hands. The man who reached Emmett first took a swing, but he was so drunk Emmett dodged the first blow, and he heard the brass knuckles clatter to the floor. The sailor staggered back and hit him barehanded, this time punching his face hard enough to break his glasses. Emmett's mouth filled with blood. He hit the man under the jaw, snapping his head back till his body leered toward the floor and he fell.

Two sailors were holding Kimura so another could hit him square in the gut. Emmett caught one of the sailors by the arm, turned him around, and hit him with his left fist, knocking him to the floor. He knew immediately he'd broken his hand. The policemen abandoned their beer to join the fight. Emmett grabbed the brass knuckles from the floor, then wrapped his arms around Kimura, twisted him out of their reach, and hurled him toward the door. With the brass knuckles in his right hand, he swung his arm full length and caught a Japanese policeman in the throat, axing across his larynx with his whole swing. Blood spurted from the man's mouth and nose and he buckled suddenly, bleeding so much Emmett could smell it.

Emmett dragged Kimura, limping, out to the street, where they flagged down an American SCAP vehicle.

The car was driven by a fellow from SCAP whom Emmett recognized from meetings at Dai-Ichi. The fellow turned around and looked at Emmett's bleeding face. Emmett said, "Bar fight."

Kimura said, "Damn! I think I've torn my meniscus cartilage!" Kimura and Emmett began to laugh too hard. Kimura's merriment had been changed, as if his cheerful transparency had become opaque. His laughter was harsh, despairing.

The American took them to the dockyards, dropped them off on an oily dock, and drove away without comment.

Kimura and Emmett hid behind a stack of wooden crates. It was a cold night and they huddled together for warmth. Soon Kimura limped off and returned with a wet cloth to wash the blood from Emmett's face. "You've broken your nose," he said, and then gripped Emmett's nose with the heels of his hands and gave a firm push sideways. Emmett heard a crunch.

At six o'clock the following morning, Kimura boarded the ship that would take him away from Japan. Emmett couldn't see well without his glasses. He stood on the dock and waved goodbye to Kimura, a vague figure standing at the ship's railing. During the night, they had agreed neither of them could afford to be caught in the brawl. Kimura would never escape Japan; Emmett would face criminal charges and lose his job.

"That man I hit might be dead," Emmett had said to Kimura.

Kimura calmly responded, "We would have been beaten to death."

Emmett was dimly surprised to discover such a steel edge in the young doctor, but he thought about what Kimura's sister had endured. And Emmett knew how brutal the Japanese police could be—it was Japanese police who had killed his father.

Emmett had black eyes and a swollen left hand; he'd have to explain to the people at the Liaison offices how this had happened. He and Kimura agreed: Emmett would report an incident that had taken place that night. He would report that he'd been accompanying a Japanese man from the Tokyo train station when they were jumped. He would even give the name, Kimura. Kimura is a very common Japanese name. Emmett had been struck in the face and had broken his hand with a clumsy punch, but there were no other injuries. This man Kimura had gone his own way once they'd assured each other that they were all right. Emmett hadn't called the police because the muggers had vanished; assaults were common on the streets of Tokyo, and the police would have nothing to go on, tracking down homeless men.

Emmett would always wonder what the SCAP official who'd picked them up off the street thought had happened. He never learned the man's name, and he never heard from him, even when the dailies reported that a policeman had been killed by "a thug" in the Minato district in the early hours of Monday morning.

The Japanese police didn't report publically that one of their own had lost his life in a bar fight with a white man, no doubt an American. They did not antagonize their occupiers. They bent, supple. Emmett was relieved of any consequence of the fight.

Chapter Nineteen

The receptionist tapped her nails at his office door while Emmett was on the phone with an optometrist. His new glasses would be ready to pick up that afternoon. He'd bandaged his hand, and he fumbled as he put the receiver down. She poked her head inside and said, "It's his nibs. He wants to see you."

"I have an appointment."

She looked at him while she waited for him to understand that he had no choice, and then she retreated, leaving his door open, her high heels tapping, calling out in a singsong, "Better run, sweetie pie. The general said 'now.'"

At Dai-Ichi, making his way into MacArthur's office, Emmett had to step aside to permit a flurry of reporters who were on their way out. Somebody said, "Hey, Jones. Who won? Her husband?" Their faces were blurry, but he didn't think that his friend Wilson was among them; Wilson had said he was going to Pusan, to observe the chaotic retreat of MacArthur's Eighth Army.

It was a few days after Christmas and the UN forces were getting shot in the back. MacArthur had just fed the press the news that his forces had managed to wipe out thirty or forty thousand Chinese and North Koreans during the "withdrawal." Nobody talked about the hundreds of thousands of Korean civilians being killed. The reporters chatted happily as they filed past. They'd been under a UN-imposed censorship, so it was gratifying to get the lowdown from the general.

General MacArthur was seated at his desk when Emmett arrived. He made a slight grimace when he took in Emmett's black eyes and told him to close the door. The din out in the hallway faded away and then the room got so quiet, Emmett could hear the ticking of the onyx clock. He must have waited ten minutes while MacArthur sat with his manicured hands spread upon a green felt desk blotter, absorbed in thought until, in due time, he took up a pen and several sheets of paper and wrote a lengthy note, unhurried, without hesitation or erasure. That done, he lit his pipe.

Finally, MacArthur spoke. "Mr. Jones. How many communists are in North Korea?"

Emmett began to say that he didn't know when MacArthur interrupted: "I think you do. But I will clarify. There are nearly three hundred thousand Chinese communists soldiers in North Korea. There are one hundred and sixty-seven thousand North Koreans, soldiers, and guerrillas. Add to that six hundred and fifty thousand Chinese communist soldiers in Manchuria and another quarter of a million communists on their way to the thirty-eighth parallel. As we speak. More than a million communist soldiers, Mr. Jones, well armed with Russian matériel. And I lost fewer than thirteen thousand men."

"Yes. I heard," said Emmett, wondering what MacArthur had meant by "I think you do." He added blandly, "It's remarkable, sir."

MacArthur stood. "Then why isn't that knowledge reflected in the irresponsible statements emanating from your government?"

"My government, sir?"

"Your man Pearson." MacArthur began to pace so quickly he stirred the papers on his desk. "That fool Atlee. Nehru. And your man Pearson."

Emmett said that he would communicate the general's dissatisfaction to the minister.

"Do," MacArthur said. "Tell Mr. Pearson that he's damaging the morale of my troops. Ask him, Mr. Jones, kindly to restrain himself from sabotaging my war. Tell him to confine his commentary to the superior manner by which I've executed our tactical withdrawal. That is, if he is capable of behaving in a way suitable to a foreign official, and not like some small-town gossip."

MacArthur returned to his chair. "When I flew over the Yalu," he said softly, "I could see all the way to the Siberian border. All that spread before me was an endless expanse of utterly barren countryside, and the black waters of the river. It was a dismal, bleak, utterly empty landscape. And it was blanketed in snow."

MacArthur fell silent. Emmett wondered if the general actually had gone mad. There was snow only high in the mountains when they'd flown over the Yalu. MacArthur of course didn't know that Emmett had been there, in the plane with the newspapermen.

MacArthur whispered, "Snow. A massive deployment of hostiles, a phantom army moving only at night, absolutely camouflaged during the day, blending into the land. Their tracks covered by snow. They moved by stealth at night. And by day, they simply folded themselves away."

MacArthur's tone changed. "But that wasn't their sole

advantage, was it? There was something else, something your man Pearson and his ilk don't acknowledge in their easy perversions of truth. Do you want to tell me what that was?"

"Pardon me?"

"I asked you, Do you wish to conjecture, what was the communists' third weapon?"

"That's beyond my scope, general."

"Beyond your 'scope,' is it? Then let me help you. The communists' third weapon is a traitor in our midst. The Reds won the first rout because they have a spy. Correction. They have spies. They're being 'tipped off.'"

Emmett let nothing show on his face.

MacArthur was warming up. "There is a leak in intelligence. It's in Washington. It's in London. Why not in Canada? You seem to want a 'moral persuasion' on the world stage, with your holier-than-thou pulpit diplomacy. It's blatantly evident that my operations are known to the enemy in advance. My strategic movements are being conveyed to Lin Piao. The Chinese knew that Truman restrained me from moving against them at the Sui-Ho dam. That's why they could infiltrate and fragment my units. There is a leak in Washington, Mr. Jones. And now, tell me, why shouldn't I believe there's a leak in Ottawa too? I have a hunch it doesn't stop with your friend Mr. Norman."

The general put his pipe between his teeth before politely inquiring, "And why are you not laughing now, Mr. Jones?"

Chapter Twenty

Spring broached, and no one had connected Emmett with the death of the policeman in the port district. It looked like the SCAP official wasn't going to make any trouble. No word came from Dr. Kimura, and Emmett figured that he had returned to Ottawa, had taken up his medical practice, and would prefer to forget an unfortunate manslaughter in a Tokyo bar.

No word came from External Affairs either, nothing that would indicate that Bill Masters or anyone in External knew about the general's theory, his phantom Canadian spy leaking information about his troops' movements. Emmett had dutifully written to External to report the encounter with General MacArthur in self-mocking terms, as a humorous episode while he was temporarily handicapped by a painful hand and the loss of his spectacles, injuries he'd sustained while defending a stranger from a gang of homeless men living in the streets of Tokyo.

Then, abruptly in early April 1951, General MacArthur was fired.

It was the end of May, and sunny, when Emmett awoke in his suite, a few blocks away from the Liaison offices. He'd been dreaming about John Norfield; he could smell John's scent of cigarettes and Scotch.

John had been asleep in thick moss of the kind that grows on granite. Moss, emerald green, wet from recent rain. It must have been summer; it was warm in the untrustworthy Canadian way. Pain emanated from John, who slept inside Emmett's sleep, one nightmare after another all night long in an exhausting rosary that must be worked and worked.

Emmett lay in bed and watched strips of blue sky through the blinds in his apartment. He'd been telling himself that he'd soon go to see Aoi. But as the weeks passed, the silence between them grew almost tangible and he began to feel stubborn toward her. He admired her, but he didn't understand her. She made him lonely; it was like being in love with a mountain range.

Someone knocked at the door.

He was wearing his pyjama bottoms and an undershirt. A Sunday. He got out of bed, pulled a cardigan over his undershirt, and opened the door to a tall Japanese man wearing a black uniform with gold braid epaulets and matching cap. It couldn't be the Japanese police; the uniform was too new. Anyway, a uniform on a Japanese man could signify a general attitude rather than a particular rank in a particular force. As it turned out, the gentleman was a taxi driver. The taxi driver held a letter in his spotless white gloves, offered it to him, bowed deeply, and departed.

Emmett kicked the door shut with his bare heel, tearing open the envelope. The letter was from External Affairs, requiring his presence in Ottawa. He had been recalled.

Monday morning, hungover, Emmett stood at the teak desk of the sleek receptionist. The receptionist was on the phone and swivelled her chair to face the wall. *The New York Times*, dated May 30, lay on her desk. He picked it up and read the headline.

Two top diplomats in the British Foreign Office, one stationed in London, the other in Washington, had defected to the Soviet Union.

He took the newspaper to his office to read it.

Their names were Guy Burgess and Donald Maclean. Burgess was a high-ranking secretary in the British Embassy in Washington. Maclean was head of the American Department at the Foreign Office in London.

The British Commonwealth brigade was fighting in Korea, so messages passing between the Pentagon and Dai-Ichi would have been copied to the Attlee government through the British Embassy in Washington and the American Department in Whitehall, both domains of Burgess and Maclean. The two Brits would have had access to information passing between the Pentagon and the headquarters in Japan, and they could have easily forwarded it to the Soviet Union. All of MacArthur's plans for fighting the war in Korea could have been flowing into the hands of the communists through the British Foreign Office, through Burgess and Maclean.

Thirst drove Emmett down to the staff cafeteria, where the talk was all about the two spies and the damage they must have done. No one there appeared to know about Emmett's recall; they moved their chairs over to give him room without interrupting their flow of talk. It was unlikely that they knew about his situation and didn't care; this kind of instability in the Liaison offices made everyone uneasy, and the staff was still shaken by the loss of Herbert Norman. Emmett sat stiffly with his former colleagues, young men who were not hungover, who were not under a cloud, who seemed stupid and uninformed but enviable nonetheless.

The language specialists, policy analysts, secretaries, and assistant secretaries, all the men and women in the cafeteria agreed: there are communists everywhere, hiding. That's how the Reds work. To infiltrate, to sap our strength and weaken us from within. One of the women, a pretty little redhead, confessed that she was scared, her eyes tearing up. "It's hard," she said, "to keep my Christian faith *constantly* on guard against so much evil!" The young men murmured encouragement, but she went on, "No, honestly! It's not just the communists! It's — it's the fairies! The *queers*!" In some confusion the men moved their chairs a fraction apart. Several of the young men laughed, not unkindly, and one of them said with a hint of irony, "You've just gotta be vigilant, Mary," and another said more seriously, "The fact is — it's up to all of us to be vigilant."

Someone began to hold forth about President Harry Truman. Truman had suddenly relieved General MacArthur of his command in April, charging him with insubordination over the fiasco with the Chinese in North Korea. "The spy scandal spells the end of President Truman," the fellow said. "They should impeach Truman and elect MacArthur."

"MacArthur for president?" The conversation moved on to MacArthur's recall, and all the controversy surrounding the war with the Chinese. The blond young man seated beside Emmett insisted that they should've dropped a nuclear bomb on the Reds at the Yalu. "Would've saved a lot of lives," he solemnly asserted.

One by one they went back to their desks. Emmett sat alone at a table strewn with overflowing ashtrays and torn matches. He pulled the letter from his back pocket, smoothed it, and reread it. It was a toneless instruction to return to Ottawa "at his earliest convenience," to report to External and receive further instructions, signed by a man he'd met only once, in the Far Eastern Division. It was marked "For Your Eyes Only." So no one at the Liaison Mission knew.

But when he returned to his office, the few belongings he'd kept there were in a small cardboard box. He opened his filing cabinet. It was empty, as were all the drawers in his desk. There was a paperclip on the carpet; otherwise the room was cleaned out. When he was gone, it would be without a trace.

The phone on his empty desk began to ring and he answered. It was the receptionist, her voice for the first time indicating some interest in him. "I've got a call for you," she said mockingly but impressed. "Long distance collect. She wants to know if you'll accept the charges." The receptionist gave one of her little Pepsi burps and added, "You got yourself a girlfriend, mystery man?"

It was Aoi. He said that he'd pay for the call. The receptionist said, "Okay, honey, here she is," and put Aoi through.

He had never before spoken to Aoi on the telephone. She sounded vulnerable. He asked her if she was all right, and she said that she was. Then she said nothing. He told her, "I'm tied up at the moment. I'll come out to see you—the day after tomorrow. Is that okay with you?" She said that it was okay, but she sounded diminished, and a sense of dread rose in him when he said goodbye.

He picked up the cardboard box and walked. On his way out he left some money with the receptionist to pay for Aoi's call. The receptionist gave him a knowing look and said, "Good luck, eh?"

Emmett began to make arrangements for the long journey back to Canada. He hesitated to say goodbye to Aoi, telling himself that it would be needlessly painful, that he might jeopardize her claim to the house on the estate. He thought that the American in the blue kimono must have been watching him come and go from her house, and he considered the possibility that the blue kimono was connected to Mr. Miller, who in turn had connected him with the British spies. He felt he was the subject of conversations everywhere.

The UN forces and the Chinese were bombing North Korea to pulp, killing each other and tens of thousands of civilians. There were more than one hundred and thirty thousand POWs — Chinese and North Korean — crammed into a UN concentration camp on an island off the coast of South Korea, in conditions that had nothing to do with the Geneva Convention. All night Emmett walked the streets of Tokyo, stopping for a drink in a bar, then walking again. Very early morning he awoke on a park bench. Young Japanese boys were playing baseball a few yards away. They were in spotless white uniforms, but, he noticed, their white socks and sneakers were blackened. The cherry trees had burned when Tokyo was bombed; saplings were growing up around the burnt skeletons of the trees, but the soil was still sooty. He didn't want to go to his apartment, so he walked all morning. Even before noon, the delicate Japanese girls were tripping over the rubble of freshly cleared bombsites, holding hands with American soldiers and smoking Lucky Strikes. The Japanese, encouraged by the profits the banks were making off the Korean War, were practising *demokurashii*.

He spoke to no one but bartenders for four days. Before he finally started the grasshopper route back to Canada, he typed up a letter to Aoi, telling her that he had to leave the country and he didn't know if, much less when, he'd be back. He gave her the Ottawa address for External Affairs and asked her to write to him there. He told her that he would miss her very much. He thought for a minute and then, because his left hand was still in a cast, he signed it clumsily with his right hand, "Love, Emmett."

Chapter Twenty-One

At quarter to nine on the third Monday of June 1951, Emmett was on his way to see Bill Masters. Beside him, climbing the stairs to Bill's office in the East Block on Parliament Hill, was a balding man wearing a brown suit, anywhere between forty and fifty years old, patchily shaved, his green face leached by alcohol, carrying a paper lunch bag smelling of egg.

Emmett had anticipated that his appointment at the Liaison Mission in Tokyo would be extended for three years, yet he'd been recalled after only ten months. He intended to remind Bill that his work had been good, better than good. In his brief time there, he'd assessed the Japanese constitution, he'd written what he knew to be lucid analyses of General Douglas MacArthur's relationships with the Tokyo press, and he'd been able to unravel some of the horrors of the Korean War. He'd written several profiles of Tokyo gangsters. He'd even overseen insightful research into ladies' book clubs! He'd mastered a certain congenial, authoritative tone in his reporting on American influence in East Asia. He already had analysts working under him, men who'd been there longer than he had. This is the speech he'd prepared for Bill.

In one of the last reports that Emmett had written — before his unnerving meeting with General MacArthur — he told the story of Herbert Norman and John Emmerson, who was with the State Department, taking an army jeep to a prison camp just outside Tokyo in 1945, to pick up two Japanese prisoners, Shiga Yoshio and Tokuda Kyuichi, communist leaders who had been incarcerated since 1928. The prisoners were interrogated by American officials, returned briefly to prison, and then released.

It was General MacArthur who had ordered the release of the two communist leaders, believing that it would let off steam, moderate the antagonisms between the old Right and old Left. Emmett had written that MacArthur intended to "geld" the two men, brand them as impotent old-timers no longer a threat to national security.

Emmett had paused for a moment before writing about communists. The flu-like symptoms of the Red scare made it contagious even to say the word *communist*. But he believed that he was demonstrating that he had nothing to hide.

Then the British spies defected. And now there were going to be communist conspiracies around every corner, in every closet, under every bed. Here he was, stuck in Ottawa. His usefulness in Japan was wasted.

At the gloomy landing to the third floor, the man with the egg-salad sandwich let out a tidy fart just as a good-looking woman briskly stepped ahead of them onto the stairs. The woman in her trim tweed skirt and high heels, a brunette with her hair swept up from the nape of her neck, surged ahead and the egg salad wearily dropped behind. When Emmett was still following her into the corridor to the left where Bill Masters had his office, she looked back, appraised him, and gave him a smile. He said, "I'm not trailing you." And she said, "Too bad."

So he was feeling better when he passed by Bill's secretary, Agnes—who'd been there for decades—and entered Bill's office.

Bill reached across his desk to shake Emmett's hand. "Glad you made it," Bill said. "You all in one piece?"

"Yup. Same as always." Emmett took a chair.

Seated opposite, Bill looked like a part of his desk. He'd been in that same office or one very much like it since the end of the war, and Emmett had the impression that everything in it was not merely an expression of Bill but actually *was* Bill. The light was always bad in the East Block, and Bill wouldn't get rid of the thunderously heavy velvet swag drapes that darkened the room. Beside the inevitable leather sofa, there was a credenza decorated with golf trophies and a tray with rye and glasses, and it, too, was Bill.

Bill saw Emmett eyeing the liquor and said hopefully, "A bit early, isn't it?"

On the desk between them lay the report that Emmett had written shortly before his departure from the Tokyo Mission, the one about the two Japanese Communist Party officials released from prison.

"What's up, Bill?"

Bill grimaced. He patted the report. "Nice work."

"Yeah. So?"

"I don't know why—" Bill began.

"I was doing good work in Tokyo. How do you expect me to get anywhere if you don't leave me alone and let me do what I have to do?"

"Wait a minute."

"Just tell me why I'm here, so I'll know how to get out again."

"Since when did you get to be such a hothead?"

Emmett got up and poured himself two fingers of rye, no

ice, and when he turned and met Bill's surprised gaze, he said, "I'm on Tokyo time."

"Look," said Bill. "We're just trying to make the most of our resources. Meaning you. And guys like you. We can make better use of you here."

"Doing what? Translating the Tokyo newspapers?"

"That and other things."

"Are you serious?" Emmett thought about the man with the egg salad sandwiches coming to the office every day, probably speaks five languages but lives a life so boring his wife is glad he drinks so much, she's hoping for cirrhosis, a widow's pension.

Bill didn't look friendly right now. "Remember George Miller?"

"The Washington 'think tank.' So what?"

"So what? Who's running the show in Japan, huh? How are we going to get anywhere if we alienate the Americans?"

"I don't give a shit about the Americans."

"Then you're stupid." Bill picked up the Liaison file and slapped it on his desk. "Why'd you go and stick your neck out? After I *told* you they were none too pleased with your talk about the Chinese. And this—" indicating the file, he made a show of calming himself down.

"I'm reporting facts."

"There's no such thing as facts. MacArthur wanted to *geld* a couple of old communists? What the bejeezus are you talking about?"

"I don't trust MacArthur," Emmett said. "But that was an intelligent decision. Surprises me, in fact. It seems too reasonable."

"Be that as it may, MacArthur is yesterday's man."

"Not to the Japanese." But Emmett didn't want further conversation about MacArthur. He'd written that material before MacArthur had insinuated that he was leaking information about his troops' movements in Korea.

Bill pointed at Emmett. "Let me give you some friendly advice. Not that you deserve it." He gazed longingly at the glass in Emmett's hand. "Always look at the bigger picture."

"That's what I'm doing."

"Of human affairs, Jones, of the real political situation in real human terms. Not some perfect world where men are angels."

"You bring me here to tell me this? This is a fucking house of mirrors." He drained his glass and was going to pour himself another when Bill told him coldly to sit down.

"Here," said Bill, and he poked his stubby finger into his desk, "right here in Ottawa, or in Tokyo, what the Christ, Manila, Seoul, anywhere there are Americans, we work with them. You don't think I know my ass from a hole in the ground? What we're doing here is selective, you know that. We're not winning any elections, we're here to support the men who do. And that means we smooth the way, we avoid controversy. We don't sell our souls to the devil, but we do get along with the Americans. Anything short of that is for the pulpit. You want to think you're changing the world, get a job in a university, become a preacher. You want to have a real effect on real events, Jones—Emmett." Bill was winding down. "Look"—he almost said "son" but stopped himself—"I'm talking about the long run, a career in the service. You want to be another flash in the pan?"

"It's for my own good, is it, Bill?"

Bill's hazel eyes regarded him from under swollen eyelids. "You might view it that way. In time."

Emmett stood up to leave.

"Did it ever occur to you —" He wanted Emmett to thank him for his support; it would have been a bleating appeal for gratitude, but Bill reined himself in and brusquely placed the last Tokyo report in his OUT pile, then plucked another file from his IN pile and picked up his pen. "Tell Agnes to bring me coffee," he said. When Emmett opened the door to go out, Bill added, "Come for dinner sometime. Meet my wife."

So Emmett did say thanks and left, cursing.

Chapter Twenty-Two

He had to get resettled in Ottawa and then report to somebody in the Far East Division. But he went to Toronto instead.

After Japan, even in ruins, in its forceful repair, the ugliness of the Canadian cities weighed on him. Ottawa was craven and stale, eager to imitate whatever the citizens guessed might be sophistication. The squat concrete and limestone buildings had no history; it was a bland, cringing, bloodless colony. He was angry all the time. He got drunk the first night back in town and then again the second and third nights. He wanted to get into a fight with a stranger in a bar; he was bursting apart, he had to be held, he had to be reassembled in the arms of another, he needed a woman. But he was thinking, This is Canada, this is McCallum land, he wanted only Suzanne McCallum of Forest Hill, and he was sick of pretending that he didn't.

He bought a car, a three-year-old Plymouth coupe, and drove it down to Toronto. He thought he'd drop in on her, just drop by. She was probably seeing someone; maybe she was even married. A woman like that. He'd drop by and probably find her married to someone, and then he'd finally let her go and get on with his life.

He drove through a suffocating hot afternoon and got into town under towering storm clouds, in air gone yellow and electric. A dog, a yellow mutt, lay in the centre of St. Clair Avenue. He thought it must have been hit and killed, but it lifted its head when his car came to a stop a few feet away, hauled itself up by its front legs, and slouched off to one side to let him pass. In his rear-view, he could see the animal amble back to the centre line to lie down again.

The broad hot avenue with its broad hot sidewalk was nearly abandoned except for the Greek men sitting out on cane chairs drinking little glasses of wine as if they were in their own living rooms. A streetcar rumbled toward him, and he thought it was louder than it should be when he realized it was thunder he was hearing. He didn't have time to roll up the window on the passenger side before the sky opened.

The rain sluiced down, flooding the street, rising up to the curbs. He thought Suzanne's place was several blocks north of St. Clair, he couldn't remember how many, but he could barely see through his windshield and he was in the wrong lane to turn onto Avenue Road.

He saw a woman standing at the corner. She was empty-handed, not even carrying a purse, which seemed unusual, as was her thinness, and the way she let herself get soaking wet. She wore a blue dress, or maybe it was green, and it clung to her legs. Her feet, in flat shoes, were in an inch of rainwater. What struck him hardest was that she was so calm and uncaring about the scandal of rain pouring down on her in her nice clothes. He pulled up at the curb where she stood. A delivery van had been following and it lurched to a stop and the driver leaned on his horn. The woman bent down to peer in at his open passenger window, taking in the rainwater pooling in its upholstery. Her eyes were filled with light, sky blue. She smiled at him as if they were fools to have made such an irresponsible arrangement. Emmett thought, Oh god, I want to marry you, Suzanne McCallum.

———

It was the same studio that Suzanne had set up before he took his leave for Japan. But it was altered, had been made more upscale and less — "less broken," she'd said when she saw him appraise the curtains on the windows, a fairly new settee to one side. Patrons could extinguish their cigarettes in a standing bronze ashtray with a bare-breasted Athena. There was a small fridge in one corner, where, when she opened it to fetch cream for his coffee, he saw a bottle of gin and three lemons. He would have liked a drink of gin for his nerves, but he was holding his breath, waiting to learn that she was seeing someone, a good-looking lawyer selected for her by her father.

She sat down on the couch and crossed her bare legs. She'd disappeared awhile to change out of her wet clothes. Now she had on a soft green dress that was like a shirt, with buttons all the way down, belted, and he was imagining unbuckling, unbuttoning. She said, "I think I was a bit — oh, I don't know — a bit of egg shell last time we saw each other."

"Better now?"

She nodded "Uh-huh," and smiled at him peacefully.

The rain wasn't letting up. He hoped it wouldn't. Her blond hair was drying into waves and the daylight grew dusky. He walked around looking at the photographs on the walls. She offered to turn on a lamp and he said no, he could see fine. "What makes them shine like that?" he wanted to know.

She told him it was a method in the darkroom she'd been learning. "I'm becoming a bit of a cliché. But I love the way it looks, the silver."

"Luminous."

She laughed, flattered. He remembered that about her, an easy modesty; something he liked very much. But just then she stretched, as if she was bored, and looked out the window, and he thought for sure she had to be somewhere or she was expecting someone, the eldest son of a Liberal MP. She pushed her hair into place, a gesture he'd seen her mother make, caught him looking and laughed uncomfortably. "I didn't expect to ever see you again."

"No. I should get going."

"I have a date tonight." She said this with some anguish, blushing. "I *never* have dates! I think it's the first one I've ever had!"

He doubted this was true but sort of knew what she meant. He looked at her curiously, feeling his nerves ride down his arms and into his fingers. "It's all right, it's normal."

"It doesn't feel normal. It feels stupid."

"Suzanne."

"I guess I got a bit lonely. A bit bored."

"Do you ever see Norfield?" He felt he could ask this now, though he'd been wondering forever.

She indicated no with a small shake of her head. He'd pried. She didn't want to talk about it. She wilfully regained her composure and sat up straighter.

He said, "You look as if you're doing okay. As a photographer."

"I do sell some," she said. "I might have a book!" And then that candid modesty again, "I also get an allowance from my family." She liked to laugh at herself, dismissing the importance of her successes and maybe diminishing the significance of her failings.

Emmett stood to leave and she walked him to the door. She was running her hands down her sides, pressing the wrinkles from her dress with her hands on her thighs. She grumbled,

"I wish I didn't have to. I don't like dates. I don't know what I was thinking. I never want to do anything I'm supposed to do." She looked up at him. Her blue, blue eyes had a rim of black around them.

"Then don't," he said.

PART THREE

Chapter One

September 1953

The RCMP and the Security Panel of External Affairs began questioning Emmett Jones at his home in the summer of 1953. They always came late at night or early in the morning. Emmett was sleeping very little, either from being too angry afterward or from being anxious that they'd show up before he'd had a chance to shower in the morning. All these weeks, Suzanne had stayed at Blue Sea Lake with Lennie. But summer was past, it was suddenly fall, Suzanne said she wanted to come home.

He wanted her home. Each morning of her absence he remembered her bare shoulder where she would lie sleeping beside him, her hair spread across the pillow, and how he would put his lips to her warm skin to feel her voice when she'd lazily murmur good morning. It was better that she stay away until Gembey, Morton, and his sidekick, Partridge, all with their invisible apparatus, were left behind like dogs chasing a car.

The investigation was a grinding, repetitive test of his memory and his endurance. They reviewed Emmett's activities since the war again and again, forcing him to reproduce the same answers. When they came to his home, Gembey, head of Security at External, was always present. But after a couple of weeks, the RCMP requested that Emmett come to their offices downtown, where Morton would question him without Gembey present, without the feigned goodwill of the Canadian government.

Tonight Emmett was alone downtown with Morton, and with Partridge, whose surliness, Emmett had come to realize, was intended to mask real stupidity. Morton was no fool, though, and Emmett guessed that Morton kept Partridge around mostly for show, to fudge the fact that he really didn't work with anybody.

Morton's questions were jolting, doubling back to review Emmett's earlier statements. Emmett knew that this was another of their strategies, to pretend they had him. "Who's in charge?" Morton asked, leaning back to view him across the table.

Emmett asked what that meant, and Partridge, standing with his back to them, answered, as if digging at Jones was the most tedious aspect of an otherwise interesting career. "He's asking who's your case officer." He turned to look at him. "Who's running you?"

"I still don't know what that means. I work at External. You know that. I don't have a case officer. We don't work that way."

"Who's 'we'?"

He tried to tell them about the kind of work he was doing at External, translating, mostly.

"Chinese," Partridge asked.

"Japanese. I speak very little Mandarin and no Cantonese. I told you this already."

Partridge was distracted by something going on behind Emmett's head. Emmett turned around and thought he saw an after-image of a red light. Morton and Partridge left the room without saying anything, leaving him alone. There was nothing but the table and two chairs. He wanted to walk to the window but felt too constrained to move. It was late. He was tired.

This time, Robert Morton hadn't asked him if he was a Soviet agent; he'd asked, "How long have you been working for the Soviets, Emmett?" When he told Morton that he'd never worked for the Soviets, Morton smiled that tired disgusted smile and then, as if only now remembering, "Hey, we got news of your pal, the Jewish guy who defected, Leonard Fischer. They say he isn't doing too well."

Morton stretched out his legs, studying his shiny shoes and the diamond ring on his hand as he liked to do, as if reading it. Emmett knew this was one of Morton's tricks, to make him want something from his interrogator, and he resisted for a few minutes. They sat in silence, but he finally had to ask, What news did Morton have of Leonard Fischer?

Morton shrugged. "What do I know about that jerk? He's not doing too well." He removed his jacket, revealing a gun in a leather holster, snug against his chest. "Russian food is bad for his health. Says he needs medical treatment, so he wants to come home. Only, he isn't a Canadian citizen. Who wants him?"

"Dumb Polack," said Partridge.

"Hungarian," Morton corrected Partridge with a satisfied wince, his superior intelligence confirmed yet again. Morton suddenly leaned forward toward Jones. "Say. This new hydrogen bomb the Russians set off a few weeks ago, a real big one. You pretty happy about that?" Then quickly, angrily, Morton switched focus to another close friend, John Norfield.

This was a sore subject. John Norfield had been apprehended by MI-5 on Morton's recommendation and then got off; the charges wouldn't stick because of "unauthorized surveillance"; Morton's mistake, an embarrassing error, and frustrating, to be kept on a leash when he was so close to nailing Norfield as a spy, just a courier, sure, but a traitor, a commie. "You two were close," he observed. "John and Emmett, fellow travellers. But maybe he was closer to your wife. Or was it all three of you? Very close friends."

Emmett told them they were friends. He tried to say "friends" in a redemptive tone; he tried for dignity and sounded like a prude. He heard Morton sigh tiredly. "John Norfield, Leonard Fischer, Herbert Norman," Morton said. "You sure know how to pick 'em."

Herbert Norman had by then endured not one but two investigations by the RCMP and External — by these very men — and had been cleared yet again. But it appeared to have ruined his career: Ottawa had exiled Herbert Norman to a diplomatic posting in New Zealand.

Morton had never discovered any hard evidence of Herbert Norman spying. But it didn't matter; Herbert's career was permanently damaged. Now Morton brought the interview back around to probe Emmett's friendship with Herbert when they were working together in Tokyo. Emmett reiterated, he admired Herbert Norman's intellect. "Hmm," said Morton, "intellect." He made the word sound weirdly sexual. Then Morton sat up a little, as if with a fresh connection. "Why don't you tell us about your Japanese girlfriend?"

He meant Aoi. This was a new subject in their interviews. Emmett didn't successfully hide his shock that Morton knew of his private life in Tokyo. Morton saw his confusion and pressed forward. "You kind of left her in the lurch when you lost your job there."

Emmett recovered enough to respond calmly. "You want to know about a girl I dated? You're really scraping the bottom of the barrel, Morton."

Morton said, "The Japanese police thought it was interesting."

Japan's police were the underpaid men in their cast-off American uniforms who'd been drinking in the port district of Tokyo on the night that Emmett and Dr. Kimura had got into a brawl, December 1950. The night when Emmett had picked brass knuckles up off the floor of a bar and swung backhand across a policeman's throat.

"I'm not really that interesting," Emmett said. He'd let Morton see vulnerability, and now he hoped that Morton would figure it had something to do with Aoi, a false scent.

But Morton went on. "You got into a street fight shortly before leaving Tokyo."

"Yes."

"Well?" Morton could sense something.

Emmett looked at his watch. "I was mugged. I was walking with a friend when we were attacked."

"Who was the friend?"

Emmett didn't hesitate. "Well, not quite a friend. A man I'd met on the train."

The boorish Partridge guffawed at this.

Morton said, "What's your friend's name?"

"Kimura." Emmett had reported the "mugging" to the Canadian Liaison Mission, where he worked, and he'd named Kimura, a common Japanese name. He couldn't make a report to the police and had asked the Canadian Mission to just let the matter drop, offering the rationale that there were countless homeless people in post-war Tokyo; the men who'd assaulted him and even this man Kimura were untraceable. Emmett had added that he was partly at fault for being in the wrong place at the wrong time. He had to bet on the chance that the only report on his activities in Japan came from the Liaison offices.

"Where's your friend Kimura now?" Morton asked.

Emmett shrugged. "No idea. We travelled together by train and arrived in Tokyo that night. We got roughed up by some street thugs, we got away, and I never saw him again." He pretended to be distracted, studied his nails, suppressed a yawn, and added, "I was in better shape then. Anyway. It's late."

Morton was making notes and didn't look up when he said, "Partridge. Drive him home."

Emmett found Kimura's name in the phone book. Kimura had a medical practice in Ottawa. Emmett made an appointment to see him.

He'd often imagined getting in touch with Kimura, he didn't know why; it seemed like a better idea to let the incident in Tokyo be forgotten, but he had liked the young doctor, he felt a bond with him. And now he felt compelled to take control of the situation, to make sure that he could trust a man whom he'd only known for a few hours.

He'd made a mistake when he'd reported the incident to the Liaison office; he'd been shaken up from the fight, perhaps even had a mild concussion, and wasn't thinking straight—he'd given the name of his companion, the ubiquitous Japanese name Kimura, but he'd added an unnecessary detail: he'd said that his companion was leaving for Canada. At the time, in his fuddled state, it had seemed reassuring to have his accomplice out of reach. Now it was possible that Morton would see this single detail and have one of his many underlings spend a few afternoons looking for a man named Kimura who had entered Canada in December 1950, or maybe January 1951. Emmett needed to be sure that, if Kimura had learned anything of the death of the policeman, it would continue to be kept between them.

Chapter Two

Kimura's round face lit up when Emmett walked in. "I saw the name and hoped. Now here you are!" He seized his hand, pumping it, then suddenly relaxed his grip. "How's the hand? All better?"

"It's fine," Emmett said. "Anyway, it was my left."

Kimura smiled cheerfully, as if from a happy memory, and said, "Sit down, Emmett. I'm glad to see you." He first made a show of examining the alignment of Emmett's nose — "Pretty good" — then leaned against his examining table, crossed his arms, and said, "What can I do for you?"

Emmett told him that he was suffering from insomnia.

Kimura prescribed secobarbital — in fact, he gave him two tablets then and there — though he recommended liquor as a first resort. "Unless you are alone. I don't recommend that you drink alone." He seemed surprised to learn that Emmett was married. Emmett remembered their conversation on that train ride from Kobe to Tokyo, remembered his complaints to Kimura about Aoi's moodiness, and felt a pang of remorse when he realized that he'd rarely given Aoi a thought since leaving Japan three years ago.

Emmett had his medication, it was time for him to leave. He looked into Kimura's cheerful eyes, saw the transparency of an untroubled soul, and didn't wish to disturb him. He thanked Kimura and stood up.

But Kimura observed that Emmett was his last patient of the day, and he suggested they have dinner together; he knew a steak house where the martinis "are built like pleasure domes," he said. "Since your wife is away," he added. "We bachelors are always looking for husbands on the loose."

They had a couple of martinis with dinner and reviewed their working lives. Kimura said that he'd been working so intensely he'd forgotten to get married, but he seemed content to listen to Emmett speak about Suzanne, and he expressed envy for his new fatherhood.

Emmett wanted him to meet Suzanne; it was the quickest way to make Kimura understand how he could marry so quickly. Seeing Kimura again made him more acutely aware that he'd treated Aoi unfairly, that he'd used her when he was lonely and then had almost forgotten her. It wasn't in his character to do that; he thought of himself as a loyal man.

Kimura was curious about small things—a quality of mind that Emmett normally associated with women. He began by asking about Suzanne's interests, and he listened generously while Emmett told him how bright, almost uncannily bright, was his baby girl, Lenore. He brought the conversation around to Emmett's discomfort, his inability to sleep when his family wasn't in town. "Why are they not with you at home?" he asked.

Kimura waited with mild, neutral curiosity while Emmett drank the dregs of his second martini.

"I've had some trouble," Emmett began—though he deflected; he began with Herbert Norman, putting Herbert's story before his, concealing himself behind the other man. He defined Herbert as his "superior," an intellectual, flawed by naivety in his association with a magazine that had run into trouble with the FBI. "Ever since Gouzenko," Emmett said, "Canada's been as paranoid as the US."

Kimura waved to a waiter and ordered another martini for Emmett. And while Emmett drank it, he confessed to Kimura that he, too, was being investigated. He described the gruelling sessions with Robert Morton and Harold Gembey. "They come to my house. The house where my wife and daughter live. They want me to tell them that I'm a communist. So everything I say is wrong, it's the wrong answer."

"They don't believe you?"

"No. But they can't find any evidence that I would have betrayed my country."

"Of course not," Kimura murmured. He was staring at the glittering cutlery scattered on their table, the watery look of silver on white linen. Emmett described the interrogations while Kimura listened intensely without comment and without looking at him.

"How senior is this Harold Gembey?" Kimura wanted to know, his eyes on the dancing candlelight reflected in silver. "What's his background?" His questions were quirky, personal, probing the mind-set of External Affairs through the person of Harold Gembey. "You're a hazard to Mr. Gembey," Kimura eventually declared. "If this RCMP fellow is right, and you're a communist," he went on, not smiling, "then everyone in the civil service will be open to suspicion. He's as nervous as you are."

"But I'm not a communist," Emmett said.

"No, no," said Kimura. Then he seemed to awaken, as if from a trance, and beamed at Emmett. "You're a nice man."

Emmett realized, as Kimura's interest soaked into him with the gin, how lonely he'd been. "I shouldn't be telling you any of this," he said. "I need you to promise not to speak about it with anyone else. I realize that's unfair, to ask you to swear to secrecy."

"You and I, we have a bond," Kimura said. "A friendship. Our origins are in secrecy." The light merriment in Kimura's eyes darkened and closed again, and Emmett remembered the steely will, unexpected in such a generous, gossipy man. Kimura shook his head almost imperceptibly. "We don't need to talk about that night in Tokyo either," he said. "Better to let sleeping dogs lie."

Chapter Three

The investigation into Emmett Jones by the Security Panel and the RCMP had been going on for three months, and then quite suddenly, just before Thanksgiving, it was over. Emmett was told that he'd been cleared. The news came to him in a phone call from a stiffly courteous Harold Gembey, who named the investigation a "review." "We've completed the review," Harold Gembey said and paused.

"So? What now?" Emmett had to ask.

Gembey sounded mildly surprised by the question. "Oh. Just carry on." He blandly added, "I imagine it'll be easier to concentrate on your work with this monkey off your back."

If the interrogation had made Emmett feel rigid and apprehensive, its vague conclusion left him adrift. A space had opened around him. In telling and retelling his version of events to Gembey and Morton as they probed into his life, his friendships, his beliefs, he'd incidentally manufactured a fiction. And now his life consisted in how it might be told rather than lived.

There were a few outward signs of support, a faint sense of rehabilitation. The minister wrote an uncommonly stern letter to the US Senate Foreign Relations Committee telling them that the investigation had been thorough, and it was complete: they'd uncovered no evidence that would indicate disloyalty.

What the minister didn't say was that Emmett Jones was not and never had been a communist. Such a disclaimer should be unnecessary; it should be an implication of the acquittal. But there was no parade: the questioning had been conducted in secret and its conclusion was discreet.

Emmett felt as if he'd participated in a sordid social experiment. When Suzanne was away, he searched the house, running his hands over every inch of the walls of every room. He pulled the mattress from their bed, overturned the couches and chairs, he took apart the telephone, dismantled the lamps, and he could find nothing, no bugs. But he had no privacy; they'd tapped him, planted a bug in his mind. He felt quarantined, hyper-aware of his own speech. For far too long he'd no contact with what he thought of as the "outside world." He felt no persuasion, no reassuring guidance; there were no meetings, no interesting requests for his talents. He remembered himself as a man with an ideal — and he believed that an ideal is itself a talent, it's the light he needed to live by, a sense of being inspired by motivations superior to the motivations of other men. An ideal, a talent, a private radiance in his life — all of this had abandoned him. He wondered if his existence had become that small bare room where Robert Morton had interrogated him.

At External, no one outside Harold Gembey's tight circle on the Security Panel and the team run by Robert Morton at the RCMP — nobody outside this small circle, other than Bill Masters and the minister — knew that Jones had been under investigation. After the fourth interview, Emmett had told Harold Gembey that he would resign if word got out. He reminded Gembey that he'd stuck with External even after being recalled from Tokyo, he'd been steady in his work on the East Asia desk. He said, "I didn't join External to be a liability. If there's any publicity about this, I'll resign."

Gembey carefully stacked the pages of transcript, put them in a drawer, calmly sat back in his chair, and lifted his chin to view Emmett more squarely. He had clear eyes, Gembey, not possible in someone who likes a drink. Emmett was reminded of the missionaries back in his childhood home in Japan, the ones who'd quietly left the church to acquire a local business. Smarter than most men, they made certain they were irreproachable, living a balanced life. Ruthlessly suitable men.

Emmett planned to take Dr. Kimura to the cottage and introduce him to Suzanne. He thought they'd have Thanksgiving weekend together and try to celebrate the end of his ordeal. But before this could happen, on Friday, Bill Masters asked to have lunch with him.

It was a warm day. Bill wanted to pick up hot dogs at a food stand and sit outside on a bench to eat them, so that's what they did. Bill had two, devoured them, then crumpled up the wax paper and wiped his mouth with it. "I've got something to tell you," he said, swallowing. "And I don't want you to get mad."

Emmett looked at the pink end of his hot dog, at the neatly scorched grid from the grill.

"We've kept this thing quiet," Bill said. "And that ain't easy in Ottawa." Bill's face was beaded in sweat. "The FBI is so goddamn pushy when it comes to Reds."

Emmett shoved his uneaten hot dog into its wrapper and crushed it, then he stood up and chucked the mess three feet into a trashcan, waiting, refusing to help Bill, who was squirming, explaining wheezily, "You know what they're like, Emmett. The Americans have been after us ever since your name surfaced at the hearings at their Foreign Relations Committee. And I want you to know—External didn't fold, it did not fold, I swear. I want you to know that."

"Did somebody fold, Bill?" He came and stood over Bill.

"Thing is," Bill said again, "the FBI's been going real hard on the department to forward everything we've got on you."

"You didn't send my file, though. Right?"

Bill looked up him beseechingly. "We delayed and delayed and delayed. Now that the investigation is over..."

A car passed by slow and close, and Emmett turned and caught sight of his own reflection in its passenger window, a tall, bewildered man.

"Thing is," Bill went on, "Harold Gembey held them off for nearly a month."

"Gembey sent my file south."

"What else could he do? He couldn't keep the stuff from the FBI any longer."

"You should've stopped him."

"No. No. That's not the way to deal with these guys. I'm always telling you, you gotta be straight."

"Fuck."

"Think about it!" Bill went on, labouring under the hot sun. "We have to cooperate with the State Department. We've got no alternative. It's the only way to clear you."

"By giving my file to another country?"

"Another country? It's the US of A, for chrissake. Don't go off all haywire now. It went directly to the FBI. It was the only way to keep it quiet. You don't want bad publicity from those guys. Do you? You want J. Edgar Hoover telling bad stories about you? Emmett? Listen, listen to what I'm telling you! Do you want that? Bad stories that aren't true?"

"Who else knows about this?"

"Well, the minister, of course he knows."

"Why doesn't he talk to me directly? Is he going to talk to me?"

"Sure. Sure he'll talk to you."

"When?"

"You gotta know, the minister feels bad. He objected at first, till he had time to think about it. And it was explained to him, it's inadvisable. It's clearly inadvisable not to cooperate with the FBI and the State Department. At this point in time."

Bill became resentful that it was taking so much effort to calm Jones down; Jones was being egotistical in all this, a small incident in the broader scheme of things. "You know," Bill said, his gurgling voice still blurred by the two hot dogs easing their way down his digestive tract, "bigger things than you are on the table right now. The DEW Line, just for instance, early radar. Now the Ruskies've set off another thermonuclear, we've gotta let American Air into the Arctic. You think we've got wiggle room on that? Think again. You think the Russians care about the difference between an American and a Canadian when they're dropping an A-bomb on the city of Windsor? Eh?

"Aw," Bill went on, "don't worry so much. This is good news. You're clear. You handled it with real guts, real gumption. It's over and done. No evidence of disloyalty, that's what our file says. Worst thing Security said about you is, you're naive."

"I'm cured of that, Bill."

Bill mopped the sweat from his neck. "Bejeezus warm day. Come on, let's take a walk."

Emmett declined. He didn't want to walk with Bill. It was evident now, Harold Gembey was taking his orders from the FBI. And the FBI never let go. They'd come after him again, just like they went after Herbert Norman again; the FBI would make External and the RCMP resume the interrogation any time they chose. External Affairs had no intention of protecting Emmett Jones. He was on his own.

Chapter Four

Thanksgiving weekend of 1953 was a glory. Calm, golden, the lake a mirror. Suzanne was surprised at Emmett wanting to bring a friend down to spend it with them. She was getting into her car Friday morning with Lenore. "I just want a day to putter," she said. "All the stuff that needs doing before winter." Emmett told her he'd pick up Dr. Kimura after work and they'd drive down together. She gave him a funny look.

All summer, while the investigation into Emmett's loyalty grinded on, Suzanne had watched the changes work on him: the softening of his voice, a myopic hesitancy about the eyes. He was being sweet to her, so considerate her teeth hurt. They needed to have a fight to clear the air but couldn't risk it: too much might be said, so they weren't talking much.

All summer long and then into September, Suzanne had waited at the cottage. She would put Lennie on the dock wearing nothing but a hat, in a porcelain basin filled with lake water, to sit beside her on the warm grey wood. She told Lennie about the investigation, the story animal-coded. The RCMP are bandit raccoons digging into garbage. She mimicked Pearson's lisp, talking like Elmer Fudd, and Lennie rewarded her with a skeptical smile.

Lenore was only seventeen months old. But sometimes Lennie looked at her mother with such remote consciousness.

Suzanne thought it should be sort of *unconscious*, this mother-daughter thing. Yet it seemed that the baby was keeping her mother at a polite distance, as if she was actually *uncomfortable* around her.

There were many reasons to be glad that summer was over. She cleaned the cottage, every drawer and cupboard, moving the furniture to clean behind and under. It was warm in that turned, distilled, autumn way, without the sticky pollen of summer. She held Lennie on the dock and climbed down the ladder with her into the lake, naked, their breath taken by the cold, cold water.

Suzanne had no one to talk to so she chattered at Lenore while she cut celery and onions for a stuffing and Lennie banged away with the pots scattered over the kitchen floor. "I should be happy. It's over. There's no American Subcommittee, no Subsubsubcommittee going after him now, no sirree bob." She muttered while she minced the onion into tinier pieces. "No Foreign Relations Subcommittee, no FBI, no Veterans of Shitty Foreign Wars, no National Bloody Rifle Association will ever spy on us again. 'Cause you're our boy, aren't ya, sonnyboy, you're our very own sonnyboy." The onions made her weep. It was her fault that Emmett had gone through this. She knew it, nothing would change it, even if Emmett said it wasn't so. But it wasn't fair, it was unjust.

The Mounties pried into her life. It wasn't something she'd been raised to expect. She imagined men wearing hats in their offices, their glossy black shoes up on their desks, idly leafing through the transcripts of Emmett's testimony and laughing at what a patsy she'd made of him. He had protected her, she didn't know how but she knew why, and his loyalty scared her, made her feel ashamed, and she tried to match his loyalty now. She didn't know why they had investigated him. Except to get at her. She was the guilty one. She was the one who'd been so obsessed with John. The memory of John's cool beauty disturbed her. His so-called communism had seemed to her an aspect of his style — rebellious, wounded. Now the government, the Mounties, the Americans, and their un-American committees had gone after poor Emmett because of her, because she'd fallen in love with John. Because everyone is insane, filled with hatred and fear of the Russians, setting off atom bombs in the desert, for what? Because they love power, they love the fear they can instil in people.

She'd hidden at the cottage all those terrible weeks; it wasn't for Lennie, it was for herself. She caught herself dressing more modestly even when they were alone. She walked differently now because someone was judging her, somebody was watching her who considered her immoral. Emmett had been too worn out to want to make love these past weeks, and she was glad because she couldn't shake the feeling that they were watched, overheard, that someone was always listening. The young woman she'd once been with John Norfield, that vain young woman who'd laughed at the phone tap on John's phone years ago, that silly delinquent still haunted her just as John haunted her. But this was her marriage, this was her motherhood, the only life she'd ever have, she wanted to be a good woman, she had to be, there was Lennie, she had to be a good wife and mother, so she cleaned the cottage, she talked to Lennie.

She told herself that they are, she and Emmett, first-class people. Her father had threatened to kill somebody, he'd been so indignant and furious, but he'd never, not for an instant, taken the charges seriously. "A witch hunt," her father called it. "The Americans are a bunch of Puritans. Ottawa should have better sense."

Her mother had surprised Suzanne by responding philosophically. Mama had quite a soft spot for Emmett, whom she described as "a dreamer." "It's about the books, isn't it," she asserted. In a way, it was about the books; it was guilt by association. Mama had leaned toward her son-in-law, putting her hand on his arm, and in her whisky contralto murmured reassuringly, "You were simply an idealistic student mixed up with the wrong crowd."

Suzanne understood that her mother liked Emmett so much because he was a healthy contrast to John Norfield. Mama thought that Emmett had "saved" Suzanne. The two of them, Emmett and Suzanne, were "birds of a feather," tempted by all that radical claptrap in their university days. But they'd grown up. And Emmett had proved himself with External Affairs. She liked to tell her friends, "My son-in-law is with Ottawa. We're originally Ottawa people."

"It's simply absurd," Mama said. "Who on earth would believe a good-looking man like you would be tied up with those awful communists?"

Who would? Suzanne didn't have any close friends, there was no one she could confide in. She told herself, Emmett is my best friend, she imagined herself telling people, My husband is my best friend. She was a good wife, wasn't she? She overlooked how much he was drinking, she deeply sympathized with the pressure he was under.

It was over, and surely no one would find out that Emmett —that she and Emmett—had been *compromised*, the word came to her. Emmett had been under suspicion of disloyalty because she, Suzanne, had been involved with a communist. That was how it worked. Guilt by association. But their government would protect them. No one would come after Emmett ever again. External Affairs told the Americans, the RCMP told the FBI — there was no evidence of disloyalty. No evidence. The FBI would leave them alone now.

They're Canadian citizens, and the Canadian government protects people like Emmett and Emmett's good wife. "Doesn't it?" Suzanne said to Lennie. "Of course it does. Why am I crying?"

At a quarter to seven, she went to meet Emmett and his new friend at the landing in her boat, an impeccable twenty-two-foot Shepherd runabout. Lennie in her sleepers looked baffled, doubtful, with her mother putting her in the boat in the dusk.

Suzanne had been navigating back and forth to the landing since she was a young girl. But Emmett's friend appeared to find it exotic; he kept exclaiming over the white wake shining "like silver coins" illuminated by the boat's stern light. It was dark now. "How do you know where you're going?" he wanted to know. It was appealing, a lark, to experience the familiar through unfamiliar eyes. Dr. Kimura looked at her, and she knew he found her beautiful. She felt rakish. It was, she realized, perfect to have someone with them. She was glad she didn't have to play the cheerleader, with Emmett in such a black mood.

All weekend, Dr. Kimura carried Lennie around with him. The moment he saw the baby in the boat, he picked her up as if she'd long been his, and Lennie seemed immediately to love him. Suzanne felt a bit jealous, Lennie didn't like *her* to dandle her like that, but it was nice to have her hands free. On Saturday she took some photographs. Kimura asked many questions about her camera, her methods of developing film. He asked to see her prints.

"Most of them are in the city," she told him.

Emmett was all keyed up. Without a word now, he went and dragged a shoebox out from under their bed. "Suzanne's the photographer in this family." He tossed the shoebox on the bed and opened it. "I can barely use a Polaroid."

Some of the photographs in the box were old, pictures of Suzanne as a child, probably taken by her father, who'd once been in love with the camera too. Then there was a package tied in yarn. Suzanne bit her lip, seeing it in Emmett's hands as he untied it. Dr. Kimura sensed her anxiety and said, "We don't have to look at these now." But Emmett had already loosened the bundle and spread the photographs on the bed.

"It was my avenues and doors period," she said ruefully and began to collect them.

But Emmett moved her hands aside. He laid out the photographs like a game of solitaire. Among the avenues and doors, there was one strange sequence, exhibiting Suzanne's skill with focus and light. The banality of the composition jarred with an attention to detail, knives and forks in a kitchen drawer becoming strange by virtue of her fastidious work in the darkroom; men's shirts in a chest of drawers, leather belts coiled like snakes, a pillow on a tidy bed, the shape of someone's head still visible in the creases on the pillowcase.

Emmett stood aside in bitter silence. Kimura mildly observed, "You have a fondness for still life, I see. But you have also taken some handsome portraits."

"How do you know that?" Suzanne asked, looking nervously at Emmett.

"I saw them at your house. We stopped by on our way out of town so your husband could change his clothes," Kimura said. "The portrait of your father. You could compete with Karsh."

She blushed. "That's an awful picture."

Kimura smiled, acknowledging that yes, it's quite bad. "But the print in the veranda. Here, at your cottage," he added, "of a man's spine? It's very good."

"Oh," she said.

"A thin man," he continued. "And several portraits of him at your lovely home in the city. He's the same man, no?"

But Suzanne had left the room. Emmett wordlessly stacked the photographs and retied the string.

She put her hand on Kimura's arm. "We have been lonely," she told him. "We've had almost no — wait — we haven't had *any* visitors this summer. Not since Bill and Ethel Masters. And that was in June."

"Did you invite some and they wouldn't come?" Kimura asked her this with neutral curiosity; it appeared that it wouldn't have affected his own pleasure at being here if they had indeed been shunned by everyone in Ottawa.

"I guess not." She laughed sadly. "But nobody called, once the, the thing got underway."

"The investigation. But, of course, no one knew. This was a coincidence."

She shrugged to indicate, It's a mystery. Kimura had rocked Lenore till she'd blessedly fallen asleep. He'd cheered up Emmett too; Emmett had emerged from his bad mood to carry Lennie to bed. It was after midnight, moonlit and still not very cold, so Suzanne was sitting down on the dock with Dr. Kimura. "I haven't even seen any bear since mid-July," she said. "No deer since the beginning of August. There used to be a strange little fox that would show up if I roasted a chicken, but he's gone. No turkey vultures."

"Where'd everybody go?"

"I don't know, Kim. Nobody likes a communist, I guess." She could sense Kimura perk up, pleased. She wanted him to like her. Emmett had never brought to her someone, a man, whom he obviously liked. Emmett wasn't a man's man. "Anyway, I'm glad you're here. And I know it's good for my husband."

Emmett joined them. Suzanne said that it was amazing that Kimura had been able to get Lennie to sleep. "She never sleeps."

"I am soporific with females young and old," Kimura said.

"You're magic, that's what you are. I'll go to bed while I can." Suzanne said goodnight and went up, leaving the men on the dock.

She could hear them talking, an hour or more later when she got up, thinking she'd heard Lenore awaken. The baby slept, and the men were out in the canoe. She could see their silhouettes against the mica scales of the lake. They weren't paddling but drifting, Emmett idly guiding the canoe. Kimura had turned from the bow to face him. The water carried their voices, but she couldn't hear what they were saying.

She searched for, and found, her tenderness for Emmett—it occurred often when he didn't know that he was being observed; the shape of his head, the way he held his shoulders. She hadn't fallen in love with him "at first sight." Now their lives were braided. To what degree this was because they loved

247

a child together, she couldn't tell. She thought, by its very nature, marriage is decent; a family is defined by *a certain quality of goodness*; she wanted it to make her good, she hoped one day to feel it.

Emmett was happy to be with Kimura, though he certainly wouldn't have been happy to be with her tonight. The investigation was over, and she sensed that he was blaming her, though he said he wasn't, blaming her for getting them tied up with John. She knew that Emmett was in love with her and always had been, but that didn't mean he didn't also resent her, blame her, hate her, in a way.

She thought that Emmett and Kimura were "falling in love." What funny words. She could never say that to them; in fact, it would probably wreck it. In the morning, she didn't mention that she'd seen them talking so late. It must have been the most beautiful night of the year.

Emmett heard nothing from the FBI, a silence he likened to the whisper of a bow being drawn back, taking aim.

He saw the strain on Suzanne. Her loyalty surprised and moved him. Even her parents had been steadfast through this. The McCallum clan were the worst possible target of scandal: hypersensitive about the family reputation, proud of their public faces, and defensive of their privacy. Yet they'd proved loyal to him. He wouldn't risk letting Suzanne or her parents know that the FBI now possessed transcripts of the interviews, the notes from surveillance.

For now, the FBI was quiet about whatever they owned on him. He had no way of knowing the full contents of the Jones file. He'd kept his responses repetitive in the interviews with the RCMP and External Affairs, answering their questions with reiterations of the same information over and over. But he could never know what other information they had on him — the stuff that Morton had abruptly revealed, for example, the stuff about Emmett's time in Tokyo, his relationship with Aoi. This preyed on him: the bleeding of the investigation into his time in Japan and the proximity to the incident in the port district. Morton must have been bluffing when he claimed that he'd seen a report from the Japanese police; there is no such report, Emmett had to believe this, the dead policeman would not come back to haunt him. But what else did the RCMP know about him? Was there a stray photograph or observation, an unconnected dot in the composite of Mr. Jones?

Winter resumed, a cold blossom, cellular, isolating. He made his way to work early every morning through snowdrifts two, three, four feet high, though there wasn't enough for him to do there. It was agreed among his superiors at External that it would be prudent to remove him indefinitely from contact with American officials "till things blow over." The Americans didn't appear to trust anyone who knew anything about Far Eastern affairs. Gembey's summary report exonerated Emmett Jones of suspicion of disloyalty. But Gembey privately to the minister and to Bill Masters questioned whether Jones could ever again be an "effective" foreign service officer.

Bill said, "You're damn right he can be."

Snow descended at a leisurely pace without wind for thirty-six hours, then let up for a few days and descended again. The city slowed, nearly stopped. Emmett asked Bill Masters what he might expect in the way of meaningful work; he told him he needed to dig his teeth into something challenging. He tried to persuade Bill to let him play a role in South Korea, and maybe in the French War, in Indochina.

"I could be an observer for Korea and Vietnam," he told Bill. "I've got some Mandarin. I could pick up French pretty quickly. You could use me in Southeast Asia. I'm wasted here."

Bill stalled. "I'll talk to the minister."

"When?"

Bill told him to slow down, reminding him that the investigation hadn't been over for more than a few weeks. "Let it cool, will you?" said Bill. "I'm working on something for you."

After the New Year, Bill finally came up with something for Jones to do. "It's nothing to do with Indochina," he told him. "It's not exactly a posting." Emmett groaned, and Bill persisted, "It's too soon for another foreign posting. In your heart of hearts, you know that."

Emmett pushed. "Who said it's too soon? Who's in charge of the Department? J. Edgar Hoover?"

"Relax. You tick like a time bomb sometimes, do you know that?"

"I can't waste my life, Bill."

Affection softened Bill's features. He was looking more like a frog every day. "You're a hothead, Jones. But I like your ambition." He patted Emmett's shoulder. "Tell me something. What do you know about strip mining bauxite?"

"Nothing at all."

"It's something to grow into," said Bill.

Chapter Six

Emmett's next assignment did have a lot to do with the wars in Asia, where new American military technology had given rise to a huge demand for alumina bauxite. One of the major sources of bauxite was in the West Indies, in Jamaica. There was a rush on this deal, Bill Masters said, because the Russians didn't have any bauxite and they were going to make a move on Jamaica and Cuba like they were already moving in on India. "We've got to go quick on this, Jones. It's up to you to keep the Russkies outta the Caribbean."

"It's up to me, is it?" Emmett said. But he agreed: Mr. Jones would join a trade mission to Jamaica, with a visit to Cuba tagged on for no specific reason.

There was no Canadian consul in Jamaica as there was in Cuba, where the Canadian Embassy's only real job was, and had been for a couple of hundred years, to smooth the trade of Atlantic salt cod for Cuban sugar. The Americans had a monopoly over Cuban oil, but otherwise Cuba was one place on the planet where Canadian trade relations had some reputed independence from the US and Britain.

Canadian banks and mining companies intended to make a lot of money by getting bauxite out of Jamaica—while saving the world from communism. Emmett would have several days with the fellows from the Royal Bank, meeting them in Manchester, Jamaica, and then he'd go to Cuba as a guest of the Canadian Embassy. "You're gonna like Havana," Bill said. "Maybe you'll meet Hemingway."

He asked Bill if the failed revolution in Cuba last summer was affecting international business there. "Are you kidding?" said Bill. "It's better than ever. Batista's open for business."

"Did you run this by Harold Gembey?"

Bill nervously scratched at the back of his balding head, squirming, and then admitted, "Actually, it was his idea."

Emmett was intrigued, and troubled. He knew that Gembey would normally be wary of sending him anywhere that the Americans might consider him a security risk. Cuba was politically hot. The revolt against Batista had failed, but Cuba wasn't the backwater posting that Emmett had dreaded—he'd pushed for Asia but had expected something even less consequential than New Zealand, which had been Herbert Norman's fate. He suspected that a jaunt to Cuba was a set-up, and wondered if Gembey—or whomever Gembey was trying to please— wanted to put him into a hot situation just to see what he'd do. He said, "I don't know, Bill. I'm a language guy. But Spanish is Greek to me."

"I know that. You think I don't know what you know? Listen. In Jamaica, you'll be with some smart jokers from the Royal Bank doing business with bright young guys from Toronto, got themselves a mining company, built some kind of strip mine up in the mountains. Young buggers are building their own roads and their own dockyards. We're talking big dough here. *Jee*-sus, what? You can't enjoy smoothing a huge deal in resources, hot and exotic? Then you go to Cuba for pretty well a holiday. Do a little gambling. Bring me home some rum. "

The alumina deal in Jamaica would have a real effect on the American military power, Emmett figured that much was true. He continued to muse over Bill's little coda, a stopover in Cuba on the way home. Batista still managed to reign over his peasants by means of the mafia, Standard Oil, and American arms, but he'd barely avoided a revolution. It was a strange place to send a man so recently under suspicion of being a communist, and he decided that he was being played. "I'd like to meet Hemingway," he said, watching Bill's face.

Bill, at his desk, his great rosewood lily pad, looked gratified, as if he'd swallowed a fly. "Attaboy," he said. "Cigars," he added, "cigars and rum."

Emmett helped lever a deal for Can-BauX Alumina to buy a thousand acres of mountainous land, the ferns and palm and the leaves of giant Miranda trees at two thousand feet above sea level, inland from the Caribbean Sea near Royal Flat, Parish of Manchester, Jamaica. With the Can-BauX men, he walked the low mountains, red dust on his shoes and on the pant legs of his new white suit. Beyond the green glade rose green hills, and beyond the hills rose cool ridges of green mountain. A creek glistened behind shacks built on stilts. In the rainy season, the creek would flood with run-off from the mountains.

One day, with his help, the red dust that bound root with rock would be extracted from the stripped soil, loaded onto trucks on red roads running down to the sea, where it would be loaded onto ships and taken away to make American weapons to kill farmers and villagers, Emmett thought, with the inevitable defeat of the French, in Vietnam.

He worked on the "win-win deal" of commodity export out of Jamaica. (By virtue of Canadian know-how, impeccable Canadian integrity, and clean Canadian money, thousands of Jamaicans will find employment — and be saved from communism — Can-BauX told the Royal Bank, who told the Canadian government, who told Mr. Jones to make it good.)

He finished the deal and flew to Cuba, where he did a little gambling, demonstrating to embassy staff that he was a regular guy, though he declined the teenaged prostitute delivered to his hotel room by an unknown benefactor. At the embassy, he asked polite questions about the stability of the Batista regime, aware that anyone he was speaking to could be reporting on him to Gembey in Ottawa. He drank with the urbane diplomats and was noncommittal when they told him candidly that the regime was too corrupt not to fail. He was careful when he went out on his own, mostly avoiding situations where he might be perceived as seeking information beyond the interests of a tourist. The sensation of being observed was very strong.

Now that Gembey had betrayed him and sent his file to the US, Mr. Jones didn't really belong to a country. He believed that as a civil servant he was employed by a company of merchants trading salt cod for sugar; he was at the service of the "Canadian honest brokers" making millions selling alumina to US arms manufacturers. Once, recklessly, he asked a Cuban cab driver, "What does that sign mean?" It was graffiti. Emmett knew what it said — it said, *Viva El 26 Julio*. What he was really asking was, what does that mean to you?

The cab driver shrivelled under his cotton shirt and mumbled, "No sé."

The 26th of July Movement was Fidel Castro's movement, a revolt spreading from a prison cell on the Isle of Pines to the streets of Havana. Emmett got out of the cab and walked like a stick man toward his hotel, where he put on his pyjamas, brushed his teeth, and climbed between the cool sheets. When the prostitute knocked on his door a couple of hours later, he gave her some money and sent her away.

On his return to Ottawa, External Affairs and Trade and Commerce reported contentment with Jones's work in the commerce end of things. Bill Masters seemed truly happy with the cigars and poured them both a rum and Coke, Bill flushed, delighted and talkative. Emmett told Bill that if he met Hemingway next time, he'd try to go out fishing with him, implying that he'd be glad to be sent back. He commended himself for concealing his anger so well. He used the secobarbital to sleep. There was no place in the land of the golden mean where he could express his humiliation and his unease.

Chapter Seven

Suzanne's prints, on white cotton rag paper, were "beautiful," the newspaper said. She had a successful show that made her starved for more time in her darkroom. She hired a nanny for Lenore a few days a week, went down to her basement darkroom and stayed there pretty well all day, coming up to make dinner and going back down again after putting Lennie to bed. She told Emmett that she hadn't felt so much like herself since before Lennie was born. She was desperate for that moment when the forms of light rose to the surface in the developing solution.

The people on the streets of ByWard Market were strangers, yet she believed she loved them. She laughed when she told Emmett about her new obsession with photographing strangers, and he saw that she was happy. He knew about this obsessive quality in Suzanne's character; it was how he'd first known her, in her compulsive fascination with John Norfield. Here is something, photography, Emmett thought, that will finally replace John. He believed she needed something to be obsessive about, to get her out of her own head, to focus her energies. A house, a child, a husband, this was not enough for her. He ordered expensive Hahnemühle paper as a gift, had it mailed by special order, beautiful cotton rag paper.

She rapidly built up a series of portraits of strangers at the market, people in the streets. The prints were good. She slid them into a portfolio, took them to the little gallery downtown, and arranged the show. Emmett liked that she was driven, that she was exceeding herself. She tried to demonstrate that she was a devoted wife and mother; he believed that this role wasn't enough to keep her. And he wanted to keep her.

On a freezing winter Sunday, she went out alone to meet the gallery owner to talk about a catalogue. The gallery was closed, and when the meeting was over at the end of an hour, Suzanne stayed behind for a while, telling Hughie, the gallery owner, that she wanted to "think." Hughie gave Suzanne an "Oh the mystic artist" look and showed her how to close the door so it would lock behind her.

At four o'clock, the place wore a pleasant evening gloom. Suzanne's silver halide portraits glowed and pulsed in their swank frames. She hadn't had a chance to be alone with them since the opening nearly a week ago, when she'd worn her black sheath and a string of pearls. She'd had plenty of white wine on that occasion, had gone home and made lustful love with Emmett, wakening miraculously without a hangover and with her head full of nothing. This nothingness had, over three days, filled her to overflowing.

The series wasn't a documentary, wasn't telling a story. The show was not, as some people said it was, the work of a dilettante playing at social justice. They were *photographs*, they didn't *do* anything. She named her subjects as they wished to be named: "Jack McLeod," "William from Lake Mistassini," "Dolorous King." She didn't think about the people themselves very much; how could she possibly pretend to know them?

Sunlight struck their complicated faces, revealed them in their aloneness.

She'd returned to the market several times, carrying her prints, but she'd found only a few of her subjects. One man, a very poor man, when she delivered his photograph into his hand, had politely handed it back. Only three people from the market came to see the show — not the opening, but later, Hughie had told her.

The show received a pleasant review in the newspaper and the prints were already selling. But there wasn't much to say about beautiful photographs of street people taken by a pretty blond woman. The photos were superbly chromatic and classical. Her show's signature portrait was of a reflection in a hat shop window: Suzanne's blond face partially obscured by the camera, and beside her, the watery reflection of a ruined old woman, her head wrapped in a babushka against the cold.

Suzanne was lonely over the exhibit, partly because of what was hidden: an argument with Emmett at the opening. Emmett had begun the evening with blandishments that became excessive while he drank until he suddenly turned on her and said he hated her self-portrait with the old woman.

"You hate it?" she asked, stung. "Actual hate?"

"Am I supposed to like all your work? I'm not allowed to have an opinion?"

"What don't you like about it?"

His lips curled as if he felt revolted. She wondered if he couldn't stand to see her present herself. He'd been gung-ho about her getting back to photography, but he probably hadn't thought it through and now here was his backlash. He said, "It's egotistical."

"Shut up," she said quickly and snatched another glass of white wine from the passing waitress. It was one of her favourite prints. She liked the way the glass window distorted her face so she merged with the face of the old woman. "It's the opposite of egotistical."

He looked coldly around the room. "Your slum photo period."

She thought, he's got the same tight resentment against art as the women at the tennis club, he's just a narrow-minded bureaucrat. In a low voice she said, "You know nothing about what I do, and you know shit-all about slums."

He looked victorious, her venom seemed to please him. He reared back, she realized how drunk he was, and she was aware of his physical power. "It's funny," she hissed at him, "it's very funny how the Mounties never asked you about your brotherhood with the poor, if they thought you were such a big-time communist."

"How do you know they didn't?"

"Because they didn't. You don't give a shit about poverty."

He put his icy hand on her throat and tugged at her string of pearls as if he'd break it. Suzanne wasn't quite angry enough to miss the signs, however: that he yearned for her, that he was being mean because he was scared that she might leave him for her "art." She said, "I love you."

She needed to be alone; on a snowy Sunday afternoon in Ottawa, the gallery owner blushingly bid adieu and backed out into a white day, showing her how to lock the door behind her and leaving her to "think." Suzanne heard a catfight in the alley out back, she wondered if Lenore loved Emmett more than her, she stared at the mink pelt she'd worn, discarded over a white Plexiglas table, while her "work" shone in solstice dusk. The mink is actually quite red, thought Suzanne. She decided to give the money she was making from the prints to a local charity. She ran her hand over her smooth legs in their silk stockings. Then she wondered if Hughie had any booze in the place.

Somebody rapped loudly on the gallery window, and came and rattled at the door, finally pushing it open and stamping his feet at the entry.

She cried out, "They're closed!"

"Then I am double-lucky," said Dr. Kimura.

"Kim! What are you doing here?"

"There's nothing to do in Protestant Canada on a Sunday!"

Suzanne went to take his wet wool coat, feeling suddenly savage. Dr. Kimura would expect her to play hostess at her own show. She was sick of performing for men. She hadn't quite metabolized the fight with Emmett at the show's opening, her resentment still snarled in her gut.

Kimura put his hands behind his back, the gallery patron's pose, literally disarming. He always looked amused so she wasn't uneasy over that. Anyway, she didn't give a damn. He'd interrupted. Let him take his fill and get out. If he left within the quarter-hour she still had maybe forty-five minutes before she really had to check on Lenore and Emmett, damn them all.

Kimura took his time, closely visiting each photograph. When he'd done the rounds, he startled Suzanne by coming to stand close to her knees in their silk stockings where she sat with her mink. He'd lost his bemusement or any expression at all, which made him appear angry in the way she most dreaded: masculine, as if masculinity made his anger perfect. "Why did you take these photographs?" he demanded.

"I was just asking that of myself, Kim, when you arrived. I don't want to be rude, but I need time to myself right now. I hope you understand?" Her hands were shaking when she reached for his coat and held it open behind him.

Kimura let her help him into his coat. "Are you only now asking yourself this important question?"

"Sure. Nothing complicated ever crosses my pretty little head. Now." She made as if to walk him to the door. "I'll see you out."

He wouldn't move. "Do you not feel responsible for the harm this brings to your husband?"

"To my husband?"

"Do you playact the communist now? The police watch everything! Don't kid yourself. Once the authorities are suspicious, they never let go. You know that it's serious. You're ashamed, you feel sorry for yourself. Then you display this — this *socialism*!" He waved at the street people. "Even housewives are watched. The police will come to Emmett's door again. Only this time, it will because of his wayward wife!"

"They're photographs, Kim."

"They're poor!" He stamped his foot. "They're lonely and ill! You don't know how it is for them! How dare you pretend it is only aesthetic! I am Japanese! I know where aesthetics can lead! You cannot pretend that beauty is so nice, a flower!"

Suzanne laughed, but she was also crying. It was always like that; male anger always made her cry, even if her conscious mind despised men's histrionics.

Kimura didn't soften or try to comfort her. His voice grew quieter but more guttural, more—Japanese. "A woman who cares about her husband's reputation does not draw attention to herself."

She had too many things to say to this and so was silenced, choking on her indignation. Kimura was only baldly stating what everyone said behind her back. She was being pretentious, selfish. She should make Emmett's life smooth, she should be beautiful and demure, she should serve on the Women's Committee raising money for the symphony orchestra.

Kimura said, "The suspicion surrounding your husband will linger for the rest of his life." He shook his head. "You know his history. You, too, have a history."

And Suzanne thought, He knows about John Norfield. What had Emmett told him? It hadn't occurred to her that the two men shared secrets, as women might do. She said, "There are many parts of Emmett's life that I don't know, I don't share. Even after we met. His time in Japan."

He nodded. "He made mistakes."

"Maybe there's no such thing as a mistake."

"That's disgusting. Only a spoiled rich girl could say such a thing."

"We might have to do certain things, to prove ourselves." Falling in love with John had not been a mistake. It had broken her. She was glad.

"Ah," said Kimura, "it's too difficult to behave wisely, so why not pretend that a life of error is inevitable. It's stupid. It's cynical."

Kimura went on. "Emmett must be discreet. His wife must be discreet!" Kimura did up the buttons of his coat, grumbling,

"Now things have gone beyond his control. Is *that* innocence?"

Suzanne had to ask him what he meant.

"The FBI will run with this new information."

"But the FBI are finished with us," she said. "The minister wrote a letter—" Then she asked, "What information?"

Kimura was muttering, "The child complicates matters."

"What child?"

"Why don't you understand? You must be like water! Invisible!" he cried.

She grabbed his lapel. "What child? Are you talking about Lenore?"

He tried to pull from her grasp. "You have to speak with your husband."

She gripped his coat and wouldn't let go. "I said," through gritted teeth, "what child?"

"It's unsuitable for us to speak of this."

"Of course we will speak of this!"

Kimura forcefully put Suzanne aside and headed for the door. "Don't you dare—" She dragged on his coat sleeve. Kimura shook her off, but she came at him again and he struck her arms away. Suzanne saw that he was horrified but guessed that it was at the lack of decorum. His coldness brought her up short. She had wanted to be certain that he wasn't talking about Lenore. Now she wasn't so sure. He was right. She had to talk to Emmett. "I'm"—she would *not* say sorry—"I'm staying here." She opened the door and let him out, Kimura passing her warily, as if *she* were the horror.

Chapter Eight

1957

Four years—a long time—after Dr. Kimura had spilled the beans, Suzanne and Emmett could speak about Aoi's child almost naturally, wearing helpful, positive faces with tight smiles.

Suzanne wasn't very shocked by Emmett having had a child "out of wedlock." What she couldn't reconcile was the two months that had passed between Kimura's bringing Emmett the news and Suzanne's quite accidental discovery.

"Would you have told me?" She wanted to know—then and forever, she'd wonder, "Would you ever have told me?"

"I didn't tell Kimura not to tell you," he said, pretending that that's what she'd asked.

The little boy would be six years old now. Lennie would soon turn five.

Suzanne believed that Emmett was pleased that he'd fathered a son. She didn't like to be jealous, she wanted to be fair and aboveboard, and went through the rigmarole of telling Lennie that she had "a big brother in Japan." Lennie wanted to meet him, she wanted to go to Japan and bring him home.

Suzanne heard herself saying, "But he *has* a home." Lennie gave her that grey-eyed look and asked how she, Suzanne, could be happy when her little boy wasn't with her. Suzanne would say, "He isn't *my* little boy; he's Daddy's." And so on.

"Do you love James?" (For that's what Aoi had called her and Emmett's son, James.) "Do you love James like you love me?"

Emmett had begun to send money to help support James as soon as he learned of his existence. Aoi wasn't married; maybe no one would have her now, though Emmett, remembering her unusual beauty, thought this unlikely. Suzanne encouraged him to bump it up and offered to supplement it from her own money — Emmett declined. In a show of impartiality too earnest to be true, she invited a financial adviser to their home, a Nisei recommended by Dr. Kimura for having a good understanding of Japanese banking. "My husband's child," she said, "my husband's son, James, will require money for his education."

The financial adviser looked nervous. He was a broad-minded man, but he didn't like the breezy way Suzanne said, "My husband's child." In his heart, he knew that she and the husband were deviant; maybe they weren't even married. They sure had some weird art.

Kimura might have been indiscreet in letting Suzanne know about Aoi's child, but she was quite sure that the information wouldn't go any further. Nobody else in Ottawa would know, as long he didn't tell, and Suzanne believed that he wouldn't. There was a bond between the two men that she envied a little.

Emmett had first met Kimura in Japan, she knew that. The encounter must have mattered to Emmett because later, here in Ottawa, he'd purposefully looked Kimura up. She didn't think there were any other men with whom Emmett was close, though he always spoke of Herbert Norman with reverence that was compounded by their shared difficulties with the RCMP. When Emmett liked a man — as she knew he'd liked John — he was intensely loyal.

After her rage at Kimura had subsided, their tussle in the art gallery on that winter afternoon strengthened her friendship with him—or it did from Suzanne's perspective; she felt she'd revealed something of herself to him. She had never before fought physically with a man. Combat can be like sex, she thought, intimately instructive. She apologized to Kimura, "Sorry I hit you." He didn't say, "That's okay, I deserved it." But he behaved with greater gallantry thereafter. "You have a bit of red in your hair," he observed. There developed a tender quality between Kimura and Suzanne, a shy afterglow.

Suzanne didn't have any close women friends. Unless you could count Ethel Masters, who kept talking about Tommy Douglas. She'd made some inroads at the tennis club, until at the end of a doubles match she'd wiped the sweat from her throat and said, "I don't want to bother showering now; I'm going right to my studio anyway."

She could tell by the looks on the ladies' faces: they didn't like the word *studio*.

She'd built a certain reputation as "a woman photographer" and had installed a very good darkroom in the basement, but she also rented a studio in Vanier for the staged photos that increasingly compelled her. Her life seemed fixed; her status a product of her money, her family. Privately she felt fraudulent, and she was getting bored.

She lived with Emmett more graciously than she would have if they had to rely on his civil servant's salary; her money kept them nearly at the same status she'd enjoyed growing up, which seemed natural to her. As for Emmett, he didn't really think about money, as excess or as a deficiency. He accepted the house, the good food and liquor as if, by not looking directly at the wealth that she'd brought to the marriage, it could be neutralized. His mind was elsewhere. He talked about the future, how he needed to have "an impact." "On what?" she wanted to know.

He badly wanted a posting abroad. He was so irritable when he returned from trade junkets to the Caribbean. He wanted to go back to Japan, to Tokyo; he said there should be something with the International Control Commission that had been set up after the defeat of France in Vietnam; he told her he could contribute to a settlement in Indochina. When he raised the subject of Japan in the presence of Kimura, Kimura was quiet; Suzanne guessed it was because of Emmett's indiscretion, his Japanese son.

Emmett wanted her and Lennie to go with him, he wanted them all to go and live in Tokyo. This would put him in proximity to Aoi and his son, James. He'd really have it all, if he had a posting in Japan.

Despite her jealousy — shameful, it was shameful, her jealousy — Suzanne began to believe that she wanted to go. She was thirty-six years old. If she didn't get away from home, she'd get old here. "I must be crazy," she told him. "It's like I want to meet your other wife."

"She's not my wife," he said, touching Suzanne's hair. But he was distracted, thoughtful, as if he truly had another life, if not another wife. She liked that he was, in some ways, a mystery to her.

Chapter Nine

Emmett knew something of what it had been like in 1945 when the Japanese were forced to pull out of Vietnam, so he wrote some background material that Bill Masters forwarded to the minister, who then circulated it to his advisers. It was unusual for the top brass to read what was considered academic stuff about a current complexity, and External Affairs was mostly distracted by the crisis in Suez, but this time Jones's quirky information proved valuable when the minister and his entourage travelled to Saigon. Jones's was just the right kind of "soft" material so useful at receptions and dinners when a diplomat could casually draw analogies between the Viet Minh guerrilla movement after the withdrawal by the occupying Japanese forces back in 1945 and the tactics of the current communist insurgency.

Tokyo was going to happen, Emmett was convinced. He was filled with energy and began to stay at the office till nearly midnight. The higher-ups knew he'd be a useful member of the Canadian team on the International Control Commission, the ICC; he was too valuable to overlook.

In April 1957, he was trying to put through the arrangements with External to make the move. This was more complicated than it had been seven years before when he didn't have a family; the ICC had a policy of rejecting married men. There was some difficulty over his salary, but Bill was strong-arming Finance on his behalf. When he got a message that Bill Masters wanted to see him right away, he figured it was about the contract.

It was six in the evening and the East Block was mostly abandoned. He went to Bill's office and found Bill seated, typically, at his redwood desk in his old leather chair. Bill looked up at him with watery eyes. His thick, fleshy throat convulsed as he tried to speak. Emmett could smell the rye. He asked Bill what was wrong.

"Herbert Norman is dead," Bill said.

Emmett slowly answered, "I see."

Bill swung the words harshly: "He killed himself."

"No, he didn't. That must be wrong."

"He was on the Suez business."

Emmett knew that. Herbert had been released from a diplomatic holding tank after three years in New Zealand. Pearson had him appointed ambassador to Egypt because he needed his help with the dangerous situation at Suez. "What happened?"

"He's dead."

"He was killed?"

"I told you already. He killed himself."

"I don't believe it. That's wrong information. Herbert's not the kind of man to kill himself."

"Well, that's what happened," Bill said angrily, as if his own credibility was in question. "He killed himself in Cairo." Bill put his head in his hands. "The Senate subcommittee was after him again, down in Washington. They just wouldn't let him alone. He was overtired, Mike Pearson said he was exhausted with all the work, getting the UN peacekeepers into Egypt. And he just — cracked." Bill wiped his eyes. "I don't know why it hits me so hard. Seeing a man hunted till he does something crazy." Bill looked pleadingly at Emmett. "He grew up in Japan, just like you. Is that why he did it?" Then, "Want a drink, Emmett?"

Emmett left Bill's office. He went to the washroom at the end of the hall and splashed water on his face, then took the stairs and went into his secretary's office to search for a cable, for a confirmation of what Bill had told him, but there was nothing. He left the building and went to the tavern on Elgin and had a few drinks. Then he drove home.

It was raining. Cold splats of rain on his windshield, nearly sleet, his view of the street approaching the driveway to his house obscured by rain thick as oil paint. From a block away, he thought he saw a familiar car backing out of his driveway and driving off.

He got soaked just getting to his front door. From the darkened entrance he could see down the hall to where light fell from the kitchen. There was the rich smell of the bourguignon Suzanne liked to make. He thought of his mother. When he was a very little boy, she had been his best friend. He wanted to go to her and put his head in her lap. She would put her hand on his forehead to feel for fever. Her benediction, *You're hot, darling, why don't you go put your head down?*

He went eagerly to the kitchen. Suzanne was at the sink filled with a big bunch of carrots, their lacy green tops, the bright orange; she was looking out the window above the sink. It was raining so hard the sound was orchestral. Her hands were on the edge of the counter, one foot was bent backward, the pale leather sole of her shoe.

He approached and touched her arm. She cried out and jumped away, putting her hand over her heart. "My god,

Emmett, you scared me." In her initial fear, she'd looked grotesque. "I didn't hear you come in," she said.

"Herbert Norman is dead."

"Emmett," she said, watching his face. This was what she
did when she had to discover what things meant to the men
she loved. "Are you all right?"

"Bill says he killed himself."

"Yes. I know." She gestured toward the front of the house.
"Kim was here. You just missed him."

"Kimura? I saw his car. Why didn't he wait?" She was
studying him, gauging his distress. He pressed her, "He told
you Herbert's dead? How did he know?"

She shrugged, "I guess he must've heard it on the radio."

"The radio?"

"How else?"

"What did he say?"

"He wondered if you're going to be okay." She touched his
wet hair. "He dropped in out of the blue. When you weren't
here, he left. He said he was going to look for you at your
office. *Are* you okay?"

He shivered. The sun was going down and the house was
cold. He went upstairs to change out of his wet clothes.

Suzanne appeared at the doorway to their bedroom. Into
the hallway behind her shone lamplight from Lennie's room,
where Lennie was lying on her stomach on the floor, colouring
with crayons. Emmett hadn't even noticed her there. Suzanne
felt irritated with him, contagion from the depression that
emanated from him, a bad radiation.

She knew that Herbert Norman was a man whom Emmett
had admired. From his Tokyo days. She associated the name

272

with Aoi, knowing that this wasn't a rational association. Herbert Norman was from that portion of Emmett's past that made him unknowable to her. His private life, the portion of him that compelled her. "Why don't you lie down awhile? I'll feed Lennie, and you and I can have dinner later."

He sat on the bed in his socks and underwear, his hands dangling between his knees. Long face. Self-pity around the mouth. She could tell that he'd been drinking. Fury burned its way into her veins, the sort of chemical anger that would take hours to extinguish, and she knew she wouldn't sleep tonight and certainly wouldn't sleep with Emmett.

But she made one more try, went to sit beside him on their bed and put her hand on his back. "He killed himself in Cairo," she said.

That's what Bill had said. People liked to say that. He killed himself in Cairo. "That's a stupid thing to say. He fucking well didn't kill himself."

She took her hand away. He had no right to speak to her like that; she never interfered with his precious memories of Tokyo. "How did he die then?"

"Sounds like you know more than me."

She stood up. "Kim said he jumped. Out of a window or — off a building or something." Then she felt an access of generosity. "Oh darling, I'm so sorry."

"I'm going to lie down." He got under the covers and put his arm over his eyes.

Suzanne closed the door behind her.

But he came downstairs soon after, went into the living room, and she heard him pour himself a drink and dial the phone.

Lennie came down and stood in the hallway, looking at her father reproachfully, with a child's antenna, sensing him out, as if he emitted a poison, some kind of evil.

He made phone calls. Suzanne heard that much while she fed Lennie at the kitchen table. Afterward she bathed Lennie and got her into her pyjamas. All the while, Emmett sat in the living room, on the phone or making notes on a notepad on the arm of his chair, his legs crossed, wearing navy blue trousers and a pinstriped shirt as if dressed for the office, except for the tie. Suzanne disliked his note-taking, the self-importance, the indulgence of a crisis.

She read to Lennie and left her in bed while she went to take a hot bath, dreading any further conversation with Emmett and knowing that any release from the anger in her blood was out of the question; she'd need to drink it off.

She wasn't being fair to him, not at all. Warmed from the bath, in her silk bathrobe, barefoot, she took a bottle of wine and two glasses into the living room. "Did you learn more?"

He shrugged, looking helpless. "Kimura says he heard about it from friends in Tokyo."

"Herbert Norman had been troubled for some time," she offered tentatively.

Emmett removed his glasses and rubbed the bridge of his nose. His face now looked featureless without them. "They were going to investigate again. Why would they go after him like that?"

"Who?"

"Same as me. Same as me."

"The RCMP?"

"They wouldn't leave him alone."

She asked again, "The RCMP?"

"Yes! You know that. Kimura told you."

He seemed to be angry that Kimura had told her first, as if the news should all belong to Emmett.

Kimura had told her that Herbert Norman was suspected of being a traitor to the country. And possibly a homosexual. Homosexual behaviour made him an easy mark for blackmail. The Russians would use that. With the Suez being such a powder keg, it was the kind of information that could derail the negotiations, set off some real trouble. Kimura had drawn a portrait of a man pushed to the limit, who saw a way out, who jumped.

"I don't believe it," Emmett said. He was picturing the man, the leap, the lonely decision to fall.

"Did he have children?" she asked.

"No."

"That's good."

This struck him anew: it was beyond despair when it was good that one didn't have any children. "He was pushed," he said.

"Oh! How terrible. How do they—who did?"

"Everyone."

"Oh."

After some time, chilly, listening for Lennie, she began, "Emmett? Tell me. Was he?"

"A communist?"

"A homosexual."

"What?"

"It's just that—it would make it that much harder for a man."

"No, Suzanne. He was not a homosexual. He was not a traitor. We are the traitors."

"Speak for yourself." She got up. Her feet were freezing. Her heart was hard against him. "I'm going to bed."

He sat on alone awhile and then went back to the tavern on Elgin Street.

Chapter Ten

Harold Gembey spoke to Emmett about his friendship with Herbert Norman during the time when they'd both been posted to Tokyo. Emmett had already told Gembey everything worth saying, and in the retelling, he couldn't help feeling false.

"Were you two at all—intimate?" Gembey focused on his own hands while he spoke, then glanced up quickly, almost generous in leaving his real question unspoken.

Emmett pretended not to understand. "We had a very fine professional relationship," he said. Gembey looked relieved.

The newspapers were filled with news, speculation, and righteous indignation over Herbert Norman. The liberal commentary was outraged over his "persecution" and blamed the Americans for his suicide. It became common knowledge that at the time of his death, Herbert Norman was facing his third investigation by the RCMP, instigated by a US Security committee.

But people wondered: if Herbert Norman was innocent, why should he fear an investigation? If the man wasn't a communist, did he possess other, unsavoury qualities? He was married, sure, but he had no children. The reporters began to dig deeper.

Then the *Ottawa Citizen* ran a photo of Herbert Norman, a handsome headshot of Herbert smoking a pipe, and beside it, a photograph of Emmett Jones getting into an Alpha Romeo from his parking spot near Parliament Hill. This photograph looked furtive if only because Emmett was ducking his head as he stooped to get into the low-slung car. Its proximity to the photograph of Herbert Norman paired them intimately.

The story beneath the photographs was polite and nearly accurate: Emmett Jones was identified as a civil servant who had shared a posting with Herbert Norman in Tokyo in 1950; it stated that Herbert Norman had suddenly been recalled from that posting because his name had been raised before the US Senate Foreign Relations Committee investigating disloyalty in government offices.

The journalists got excited about the story.

Within two days, it was revealed that Emmett Jones had also been recalled by Ottawa on suspicion of disloyalty.

The newspapers dutifully reported the additional information that Emmett Jones, like Herbert Norman, had been fully cleared. The minister made a statement expressing his grief over Herbert Norman's death and his furious disgust with the unwarranted attacks on the integrity of Canadian civil servants.

Everyone was talking about Emmett Jones. Conversations stopped when Emmett entered a room. External Affairs gave him a leave of absence he hadn't asked for. Suzanne couldn't go to the grocery store without raising a flutter of gossip around her.

Not everyone shunned them; there was a contingent of men and their wives who paused at receptions to wish them well. But certainly nothing more was said about the elusive contract with the International Control Commission that would take him back to Asia. People's suspicions of him had a palpable sexual quality. Jones's wife and daughter, his knowledge, his work, his entire life, seemed like a failed disguise.

Chapter Eleven

To avoid Ottawa, Emmett and his family went to Blue Sea Lake. They invited Dr. Kimura on the weekends; he was given a standing invitation — the guest bedroom came to be considered his, at the back of the cottage, beside Lenore's.

Kimura did his best to reassure them that the public's suspicions would subside. He said there were many people who believed that Emmett had been unfairly targeted, just like Herbert Norman. Kimura asserted that those who slandered him would be ashamed of themselves one day.

Lennie would not sleep. It wasn't only an effect of the palpable tension, the anxious pall over the family since the investigation had been made public. In her infant years, her wakefulness had exhausted Suzanne; she and Emmett had spent many hours talking about how they might change their little girl's behaviour. Now, at five years of age, Lennie still seemed to be awake all the time.

Suzanne asked Dr. Kimura about Lenore's sleeplessness. Kimura was casual about it and noncommittal about a prognosis. "Who knows?" he said. "Maybe she'll sleep all the time when she's a teenager. Then you can worry about that."

"But what keeps her from sleeping?" Suzanne worried that it was something in her innocent daughter's psyche, a child's intuition that there was something wrong with the adult world.

"Is she fussy when she's not asleep?" Kimura asked, knowing the answer, for he had never heard Lenore cry.

Lenore wasn't fussy at night; she was never fussy at all. Suzanne would gently open the door to Lennie's bedroom and find the child awake, but calm, not seeming to need anything.

Suzanne thought about how eerie it was to find her daughter lying in the dark with her eyes open. Sometimes she would discover Lennie sitting up, quietly chatting with her assembly of stuffed animals and dolls. Lennie didn't want a nightlight, didn't want them to leave a lamp lit for her. When she was an infant, it was the light that would make her fuss; as soon as they turned it off, she calmed down, satisfied, peaceful — thoughtful.

"She talks to her dolls, of course, every little girl does that."

"She is a wonderful storyteller," Dr. Kimura agreed.

Lenore told stories at other times too, not only when she was alone, not only at night. She might stop the adult conversation with a yarn seemingly inspired by something they were discussing. She could be sententious; her listeners might feel they'd been reprimanded without being able to say exactly what for.

"You are a master of the fable," Kimura told Lennie. He was scrambling two eggs for her. It was a hot day in June, and Suzanne and Emmett had gone down to the dock to have a swim while he gave her some lunch.

Lennie levelled her grey eyes at Kimura. She was patient with grown-ups. Her nose was running. Kimura used his handkerchief to wipe her nose and then brought the scrambled eggs and sat down beside her at the table. "Do you know what a fable is?" he asked.

She had the most impersonal gaze. Kimura felt foolish. She was really plugged up, breathing through her mouth. "It is a tale about animals," he said.

"Like a bat."

"Yes." He wanted to point out that bats are indeed the only mammals that can fly, but he restrained himself, knowing that she'd find him pompous.

"You killed it," she said.

"The bat. Yes, I know. I was here at the lake when that happened." He and Emmett had trapped a bat in a closet, using a broom and a roll of toilet paper, laughing drunkenly.

"It had a face," she observed with some emphasis.

"It did."

"It wasn't a bat."

"Oh?"

"That's okay," she said charitably and poked at her scrambled eggs.

"What was it then?"

"It changed."

Kimura wondered if they were talking about death. He felt he might have something to contribute in this instance. He was particularly fond of the subject. "Yes. Things change when they die."

She granted him that. "Things change when they die," she repeated with sad wisdom and added, "They become the next thing."

He hesitantly agreed, then had to ask, "And what might that be?"

"Oh," she sighed, "what other animal made it die."

"So, the bat would—be—me?"

She scrutinized his face. "Kinda." She laughed. Lenore laughed so seldom and it was such a lovely sound, Kimura sat back in awe. Then he, too, laughed, with tears leaking down his round face. She touched the tears with her pliable little fingers. He begged her, tell him everything. He was beginning to understand. "If a cat kills a mouse, the mouse is going to become a cat, is that right? One day? Or, when?" he asked.

"When it gets born, silly."

"So, if a fox catches a bird, the bird gets born a fox?"

She gently pushed her fingers into Kimura's cheek.

Hesitantly, Kimura asked, "And is the fox reborn as a bird?"

She nodded, yes.

Encouraged, he continued. "And if a bear catches a fish, the fish will be born a bear, and the bear will be a fish. Is that how it works?"

She climbed down from her chair and up into his lap, her hands on either side of his face with a compassion that unnerved and thrilled him. "I don't want my lunch."

"But I am such a good cook."

"I know." She wiped her nose with her bare arm, smearing her face. He felt her forehead; she was slightly feverish. He asked her if she would like a dip in the lake. Lenore loved the water. She said she'd like to but didn't climb down; she continued to study him. "Kim," she said, "you eat lots of fish."

He agreed, he did like fish, and he liked to go out in the boat to catch them.

"You hit the fishes on the head," Lennie observed patiently. "Lots of you get born," she explained, "every time you do that, Kim."

Suzanne came in, her blond hair wet from swimming, a blue towel around her yellow bathing suit. "Everything all right?"

Kimura said, "I'm being trained in Lennie's cosmology."

Suzanne touched Lennie's forehead. "She's hot." Then, to Lennie, "You didn't eat the nice lunch Kim made you."

"She doesn't want to be a chicken," said Kimura.

Suzanne folded her towel and sat down on it. She was tanned and lithe from swimming. She had given over entirely to being pleasant in these weeks of Emmett's "leave of absence," to making pleasant meals and conversation, playing Fish with Lennie, and drinking rather a lot every night.

Kimura wasn't finished with Lennie's lesson; there were nuances yet to be discussed. The egg, for example: it's not exactly murder, is it? He would broach the subject carefully. Lenore said, "The chicken didn't give the egg-people the egg. They took it from him."

"Her," Suzanne said distractedly. She was waiting for Emmett to come up from swimming. "The chicken is a hen, a her." Suzanne went to the end of the veranda from where she could view the dock.

Many things turned over in Lenore's mind. She slipped from Kimura's lap and stood at the table, just tall enough to place her arms there; she stared at the pale yolk on her plate. She had a way of staring, absorbing and being absorbed by the smallest things.

Kimura put his hand on her thin shoulder, saying, "Maybe the chicken wanted you to have the egg. It was a gift."

Lennie looked at him scornfully, then followed her mother to the end of the veranda. "I want to go to bed now."

"Now?" Suzanne said, surprised. "Don't you want a swim?" Then, "All right," picking her up, Lennie wrapping herself around her mother, being taken away, giving Kimura her owl stare when he wished her a pleasant nap. Suzanne stopped and said to him, "Will you go down? He's so unhappy."

Kimura sat alone for a moment rubbing his sore knee before beginning the painful walk down the stone stairs in search of Emmett.

Chapter Twelve

Kimura found Emmett sitting where the rocks were hot and flat and fell sharply into the water. Emmett's hands were under his thighs, he dangled his feet into the lake, disturbing the pine needles blown in last night's storm. Kimura eased down to sit beside him.

"I have been engaged in dialogue with Lenore," Kimura began. "Her Socratic method grows more dictatorial with every passing year."

Emmett smiled wanly.

"She is concerned for the chickens," Kimura said.

"I'll bet she wouldn't eat her lunch."

"No. Sorry. I used parsley. That was stupid."

"We're having trouble getting her to eat anything." The sun's rays dove and angled into the lake. The algae hadn't yet bloomed. "She thinks it's cruel."

"It's more than that," Kimura said. "She's afraid she'll become whatever she eats. In the next life."

Emmett said, "Well, she might be right about that."

"She'll have to take her chances."

"She's just a little girl." A pair of mallards flew low over the water, chortling, and disappeared behind an island. Emmett watched them as if he'd like to go with them. Lennie was his to protect, and he was afraid that he couldn't do that. His love for her was a raw nerve. He didn't trust himself with such love.

"The diplomat's death has made people afraid," Kimura was saying. "When people are afraid, they're stupid. It's easier for them to believe that Herbert Norman was a homosexual than to consider that he was murdered. Who would murder him?" Kimura put up his hand to indicate that he didn't want to talk about a conspiracy; Emmett had gone on about it, his theory that Herbert had been murdered, maybe even by someone in Canadian or American intelligence. The potential was too great for a European war as a result of the crisis in Suez, Emmett argued. He believed that someone had perceived Herbert as an obstacle to the process and therefore killed him.

Kimura continued, "Besides, we see much sympathy over his death. There are reasonable people in the world as well as crazies." He waited a moment and added, "You're grieving. It'll pass. All the excitement will pass and people will forget."

Kimura could sense Emmett's torment, but he couldn't feel it. He loved this family, yet he didn't want one of his own. Something in his own history—the war, possibly; the betrayal of the internment camp where he and his parents had been made prisoners of war in their own country; his medical practice, all of this had made him dispassionate. He admired the passions he witnessed in Emmett and even in his uneasy wife; he thought he would be terrified to live that way, it would be terrible to be so vulnerable in love.

It was hot where they were sitting, fully in the sun, and Dr. Kimura was wearing trousers. He grunted and heaved himself to his feet by pushing up with his hand on Emmett's head. "I'm going to swim." He took off all his clothes and dove into the water. Kimura didn't look athletic with his clothes on, but naked, he was perfect. He swam out fifty yards and returned, swimming over to the dock. He could swim as long as he kept his sore knee straight, but it hurt getting out of the water.

Kimura was naked when the boat went by. It slowed so quickly the motor jacked up with a loud wallowing noise and the boat drifted for a minute or two. Somebody laughed. They gunned it and went on. Kimura cursed himself and went to the dockhouse. He found an inflatable yellow tube shaped like a duck that he could hang about his waist, but he opted for an old towel smelling of gas, and with this wrapped around him, he went up to the cottage. He had an inspiration.

A half-hour later, dressed in his *hakama*, Kimura quietly pushed open the door to Lennie's bedroom and peered in. She was sitting up in her bed, looking out the window. Her stillness, her isolated consciousness, startled him, but he gave her his most cheerful smile and barged in. "I have been thinking!" he announced, sitting on her bed, missing the days when he could sit cross-legged, as Lennie was. The boy never leaves the man. And this, in a way, was another aspect of what he had come to convey. He looked at her expectantly, as if he'd already delivered his good news. Lennie had a sort of peek-a-boo game where she seemed to believe that if she suppressed a smile, no one could see it. It always delighted Kimura. "Well?" he said. "Aren't you going to ask me?"

"Ask you what?"

"What I have been thinking!"

She refused, her face torqued with the effort of hiding her smile.

"Then I won't tell you."

Her hand darted to his sleeve, the quickest entreaty. Kimura thought, This child breaks my heart. He forgot his meniscus cartilage for a second and tried to sit as he wished and was brought short by the pain.

"Ah," he said with exaggerated sorrow, "I am a hundred years old."

Lennie was astonished and obviously believed him.

"So you must listen carefully because these are the words of a very old man." Lennie listened with every nerve and fibre. Kimura always loved an audience, but this was most superb.

"Take the duck," he began, "or, say, the fly. Yes, the fly who becomes the spider. And the fish who becomes the bear. Or, in this case, the fish who becomes the doctor. And the bat, the bat who also becomes the doctor. Ah. Be that as it may. This, I have come, oh wise one, to discuss with you."

Lennie wriggled with the importance of it all, waiting for the rest.

Now he didn't quite know how to express his idea. It was too great. The full-leafed summer sun pressed forward. He had come to tell Lenore about the totem, the synchronicity between things; that the fish didn't get caught — it yielded. One form for another and another. That what drives life is not appetite or the will to conquer but something entirely benevolent and joyful. "I have come," he began again, "to remind you of something. Because, Lenore Jones, Lennie the Penny, Princess of Jones, Lennie loon, loosey goose of the McCallum Tribe, this is something every creature and every blade of grass — everything in the whole wide world is born knowing. But sometimes we forget. So as your friend and doctor — "

Lenore was on her knees, imploring, pulling at the sheets and shouting, "Tell! Tell!" and he could hear Suzanne approaching, calling from the kitchen, "What's all that racket? Lennie?" He was out of time, he'd let his golden tongue get the best of him. He said, "The fish loves the bear, and the bear loves the fish. As I love the fish. It's love, Lenore. Everything in the world is made of love."

And then Suzanne was in the room, and the sweet air, the sweet piney air was green, green with blue shade, the red floor of the forest beyond Lennie's bedroom windows zinging in the heat. Kimura felt like Cupid, he had shot his pretty bow, he'd found the mark, a direct hit to the heart.

Lennie fell back on her bed as if she truly had been struck. She put her bare feet up, pressed the tender young soles of her feet to the window screen, the sun speckled in the delicate pattern of the screen on the child's skin.

Her mother stood uneasily at the side of the bed. "Everything all right?" she asked brightly.

Dr. Kimura searched Lennie's face for a signal that his words might have made her happy. Lennie was rapt, focused on the leaves of the white poplar clapping lightly or on the silvery shimmer of the screen. Kimura wondered what he had just told her; he wondered what he meant by love. He was no longer confident that he had any right to use the word. The beauty he saw everywhere was terrible, terrible beauty.

PART FOUR

Chapter One

Ottawa, 1959

Emmett lay beside Suzanne in early sunlight. She was awake, turned away from him, he could hear her swallow, could feel her thinking. Crossways at the foot of their bed with its white cotton sheets lay Lenore. Skinny, tanned Lenore, wearing light white cotton pyjamas, lifted one narrow foot to scratch a mosquito bite on her ankle, then replaced the foot so she was lying straight, assembled, taut as a sapling.

He remembered a lunch hour in a coffee shop many years ago in Japan, watching, fascinated by a young office worker who sat bolt upright with a full cup of cold coffee clutched in his hand, sound asleep. Buses, trains, park benches were always occupied by Japanese men in white shirts and black suits, briefcases on their laps, upright, sleeping deeply, and women in housedresses with shopping bags, not dozing — sleeping, soundly sleeping. The Japanese are superb at sleeping in public, their jaws closed, chins raised, no drooling. Beneficiary of the dream.

But Lennie would not sleep; something in her refused it. Emmett thought of this as an economy: like a ledger, it balanced — someone else must have all the dreaming because she had none. And again he remembered, today is Lenore's seventh birthday. How many hours had Lennie now been awake? He did some math in his head.

Lennie had been awake for 58,400 hours and she was only seven years old.

East-facing bedroom, sunrise. The three of them on a sunny cloud. "Happy Birthday, Lennie," he said. He could hear her receive this, heard her tip her head back against the sheets so her throat was exposed, her narrow chest raised by her wing-like shoulder blades, her immeasurable quivering, a fine filament. Suzanne rolled over and sat up, golden hair tumbling. She reached and stroked Lennie's skinny arm. "Happy birthday, baby," she said.

Lennie smiled without showing her teeth. Something of a young monk, he thought. A Buddhist smile of patient suffering, though he didn't think that she was in any physical pain. She likely hadn't closed her eyes all night.

Late last night, on a street near home, Emmett had been out walking under the streetlights, the fragrant leafy trees, hearing only the quiet mallet of his own footsteps. He rounded the corner and saw his house, the table lamps lighting his living room. His legs ached. Exhaustion made him feel shy; he just wanted to go to bed.

His front door was unlocked. The entrance and hallway, the stairway, all were in darkness but for light cast from the living room. He heard Suzanne speaking quietly and seriously, one sentence levelled after another. Her seriousness, the adult, sober containment of a situation, it was dry and sexless and made him feel separate, critical of her. He entered the living room in expectation of some difficulty he'd have to dispatch without losing his temper.

He was physically surprised when he saw her. As if his body had forgotten her. Her legs were curled beneath her skirt. She saw him and stopped speaking; she put her hand down on the cushion and leaned toward him. She was pale, without lipstick.

A man was seated in the armchair partially hidden by the entrance from the hall where Emmett now stood. Emmett saw the crossed legs, a pair of fine umber leather loafers; he noticed the socks, the expensive summer wool of the trousers, saw the man's wrists on the arm of the chair, the hands framed by white shirt cuffs with bloodstone cufflinks, and he entered the room.

John Norfield lifted his face, a half-smile, the wide mouth and finely defined jaw. "Hello, Emmett. It's been far too long." Emmett took John's hand and pulled him up into an embrace, saying his name.

They held each other, and when they pulled apart, Emmett said, "My god, it's good to see you," and, shaken, turned to sit beside Suzanne. The drapes weren't fully drawn and the black window reflected back their shapes. John might have been followed. Emmett returned to close the curtains. Lowering his voice, he said, "Our daughter's a light sleeper," and indicated the dark stairway leading to the second floor.

John lit a cigarette. There was a butt in the ashtray beside his chair. He'd been here long enough to smoke one cigarette. He looked older — not as an aged, declining man, but more defined, the narrowing destination of oneself. He wore his hair differently, slicked back behind his ears, parted in a clean line — he must use a comb to make such a definite part in his hair — and the tendons on his neck showed like wires sustaining his handsome head. His face was longer, a longer space between his nose and his lips. He held the cigarette close to his palm so his hand masked his mouth when he drew smoke. "It's been ten years," he said.

For some reason, he said this as if it were a lie, though Emmett knew that was correct, it had been ten years — or close enough, nine and a half. Winter of 1950. It was now June 1959. You'd think a man like Norfield would lie easily, but he didn't and he never had, in Emmett's knowledge of him. There was always something voluptuous about the way John spoke a falsehood. Emmett heard the lush tone and glanced at Suzanne to see what she would make of it. Suzanne was focused on John, reading him eagerly. Emmett asked him if he'd like a drink. "No thanks." Coffee?

John crushed his cigarette out in his ashtray, no. "I was held up with some business tonight, here in town. I meant to drop by earlier. Now it's late, isn't it." He spoke loudly, despite the light sleeper up the darkened stairs.

"What business?" Emmett murmured. Then he announced, "I'm going to have a drink." On his way to the liquor cabinet in the dining room, "Change your mind?" Now he was forgetting to keep his voice down. He poured himself whisky and drank it, poured more, then returned, glass in hand. "I want to ask you where you've been."

"Sure." Then John said nothing. That familiar insincerity.

Suzanne gave a slight gasp and a giggle. She began to trace figure eights on her bare calf, her skirt pulled aside for this purpose.

To John's right, on the narrow wall beside his chair, was one of the stylish photographs that Suzanne had taken of him: Norfield wearing a dark suit, seated in a chrome chair, cigarette smoke obscuring his unsmiling face, jazz cool. John twisted his neck to see it, quickly turned away. The difference the years had made. He had less confidence, or less hope. Emmett would never then have described John Norfield as hopeful; only in retrospect did he seem once to have been so.

Emmett tried again, tentatively, "Of course you'll understand, we wonder where you've been."

"Not wise."

"That's all right," Suzanne said soothingly, "you don't have to say."

The way John looked at her — as if tantalized by an offer he couldn't accept. He confessed dryly, without self-pity, "They looked after me quite well, considering that I was just a courier, a go-between."

Suzanne, almost in a whisper: "The Russians?"

John winced. Emmett had seen him wince that way before; John disliked melodrama, even coming from Suzanne. He lit another cigarette, speaking with the cigarette in his mouth, "Is it quite safe to talk here?"

Emmett said, "Sure."

"Not bugged?"

Emmett loosened his black necktie and said, "No."

"You sure?" John smiled. "I haven't had a candid conversation in a quiet room for — well, for a long time."

"Of course," Suzanne said.

"You seem well, Emmett," John observed with just a trace of resentment. "The investigation didn't put you off your game?"

"You know about the investigation?"

Suzanne made a small choking sound, her confession.

"Things going well?" John meant in the aftermath.

"Yes," Suzanne answered on his behalf, "very well."

"I'm in the trade end of things, if that's what you mean," said Emmett. "Bauxite alumina, for one thing."

"In Jamaica," Suzanne added with renewed or remembered loyalty. "And cod in Cuba."

John stared hard at Emmett, a quick take, and said, "Not anymore, to Cuba, I would imagine."

"Not at the moment."

"Still," John said, speculating, "must be interesting to get close to a real revolution."

"The Caribbean isn't exactly what I had in mind when I joined External."

John let cigarette smoke drift across his face. "What did you have in mind," he asked languidly, "when you joined External?"

"Asia." Emmett went to refill his glass. "Do you have any news of Leonard Fischer?"

"I believe he's been sent northeast, to a village there. He tried to leave Russia, you know. He doesn't have a passport, no papers. Not even Hungarian. Everything burned in the war, of course. It's made him unpopular everywhere."

Emmett, in his exhaustion, imagined that he himself had set fire to Leonard's passport by dropping the bombs that spilled the fire. He took a drink and asked, "Is Leonard safe?"

John gave a nearly imperceptible shake of the head. "His lungs trouble him very much. Alas." And there it was—the University of Toronto accent, fake Brit. "Russia isn't so friendly to Jews, as it turns out."

John was very ill, Emmett saw that clearly now, and the love he felt for this man tasted bitter, returning like an addiction he thought he'd overcome. John fumbled to put his cigarettes inside his suit jacket, standing shakily in a suit shinier, shabbier than at first sight. He looked feeble and uncertain; his eyes were continually drawn toward the darkened stairs.

Suzanne asked, "Do you need a place to stay tonight?"

Emmett would never know how John might have responded to this proposal because now John was staring hard toward the staircase. He turned, and there was Lenore, seated on the bottom step in her white pyjamas, looking much longer than a child only seven years old, her bare feet on the cold floor.

John's slurred liar's voice. "Oh, hello," he said.

"Hello." Lenore mimicked him, matching John's mild insolence.

Suzanne rushed forward so all three adults, smelling of cigarettes and liquor and Suzanne's tired Chanel, stood casting their shadows into the hall and onto Lennie in her white pyjamas.

Suzanne nervously said, "Hello, darling."

Emmett made a move toward Lennie, but John beat him to it, going down on one knee before her. Lennie received him, neutral, but also interested and flattered, as if by her first suitor. "Do you know who I am?" John asked her.

Lennie nodded yes.

"Really. You're a very bright little girl."

"You're the man in the photographs."

"That's right."

When Lennie stood, she was almost at John's shoulder. He leaned toward her. Perhaps resisting the impulse to embrace her, his hands hovered, withdrew. She walked, waif-like, with him following in her wake, and surveyed the few portraits in their discrete positions through the main floor of the house. At each stop, John stood close to her. They made the rounds in silence so complete, Emmett could hear the ticking of the kitchen clock.

Suzanne finally protested, "Lennie, it's late. You must go back to bed. Tomorrow's your birthday."

Lennie solemnly reiterated for John's sake, "Tomorrow is my birthday. Are you going to come?" She laid it down as a regal duty.

"Ah. No. I regret that I cannot."

She frowned and levelled at him her serious appraisal. "When, then?"

"Mr. Norfield is just visiting," Emmett said. Lennie shot daggers at him. Really, she was carrying the Princess in the Tower thing too far. "Lennie, baby, Mr. Norfield has to go home now, and you must go to bed, it's very late for a little girl."

She ignored this and asked John, "Where do you live?"

"In a suitcase," said John.

"Go to bed!" Emmett shouted.

Lennie shot him another killing glance and then, absurdly, indicated to John that he must again kneel. When he had obeyed, she said, "Is it true?"

John betrayed his own fatigue and bewilderment by looking up uncertainly at Emmett before responding limply, "Is what true?"

"About the Russians taking care of you."

"I think you'd better listen to your father and go to bed."

"Have you got it?" she persisted in a whisper. "Did you bring it?"

"Did I bring what?" John said, alarmed.

"The secret atom."

John was getting to his feet. "Really, you should go to bed."

Suzanne seemed frozen where she stood. "What did she say?"

Lennie pulled on John's arm. "Give it to me."

"Mr. Norfield is leaving," Emmett said.

"I promise I'll keep it safe. Cross my heart and hope to die."

"But I haven't got it," said John. He even searched his pockets anxiously as if in proof.

"If you don't give it to me right now, it might get out."

"It won't." John calmed himself, bent close to Lennie's face and tenderly added, "It won't get out."

Lenore shook her head. She backed away, took the first few steps backward slowly. With one last dire, disappointed dismissal — "I don't trust you" — she went up the stairs.

Emmett followed her into her bedroom and sat beside her on the bed while she arranged her limbs, as was her habit. He could hear their voices, John and Suzanne's, downstairs. He patted Lennie in a vague attempt at comfort. "What was all that about?" he asked. She didn't answer but laid herself neatly. It could be from television, he thought; she probably imagines all kinds of things, and the TV is all about the atom bomb right now, the Russians and the Bomb. She'd heard the word *Russia* on the news countless times, she'd heard it tonight, eavesdropping from the balcony. She was an imaginative child and shared her mother's taste for melodrama. He asked, "Can you sleep?"

"No."

"Well. Try." He was impatient to get back downstairs. He kissed her, patted her leg under the light blanket, "Night-night," and left her there, turning at the door to say, "I'll be back up in a little while."

"It doesn't matter," she said.

"Sleep."

When he returned to the living room, he found it empty. So was the kitchen, and the sunroom, the backyard. He went down to the basement, to Suzanne's darkroom. The door was shut, he tapped softly and went in. Her red lamp was burning. She must have been here; she never left it on. The drawers where she stored her prints were closed. He knelt and opened the bottom drawer, looked inside, and then closed it again.

The basement was chilly. The sweater she always wore when she was working in here had fallen off the stool and lay on the concrete floor. Evidence of a life that did not need him. The Scotch was wearing thin, and reliable fond love had turned, like the worm, into grievance. He turned off her lamp, went back up to the living room, and switched off the lamps there too, then sat on the couch in a path of light from the street.

She came home long after midnight. She didn't see Emmett waiting in the living room but went to the foot of the stairs and stood with her hand on the banister, looking up. Her arms were bare. He shifted in his chair to let her know that he was there. She startled, "Oh! Emmett, it's you."

"Where have you been?"

When she came closer, he could smell cigarette smoke on her clothing. "He's dying," she said. "That's why he came back."

"Eleventh-hour conversion?"

"I think he still feels the same. I mean, about Russia."

"He doesn't look well."

"He just came to —" She waved toward the chair that John had occupied, as if he were still there, faintly receding. With greater resolve, defiantly, she continued, "He came for his notebook."

"What's that?"

"The black book he always had about him—you know how he used to write in it all the time."

"Yes."

"Well, anyway, he wanted it." She was wearing a gold necklace he didn't think he'd seen before, twisting it around her finger.

He thought of her darkroom, the empty bottom drawer. "And you'd kept his notebook for him, all these years?"

She nodded yes. "And he wanted to see Lenore."

"Why?"

She began to run her hand up and down, up and down her bare arm.

"Why would he want to see Lenore?"

She didn't look ugly—she never could—but her face was abandoned, especially the eyes, which regarded him with all the neutrality of water. She made the slightest movement, barely a shrug.

He reached to touch her hand to make her stop stroking herself.

"Is she sleeping?" she asked.

"I hope so."

Then her face seemed to come to life for him again. She called to him softly, "Emmett. Let's go to bed."

They passed Lenore's bedroom on their way to their own and saw her lying wide-eyed. Suzanne gave a low moan and would go in. "Come," he whispered to her.

He closed their door behind them. Suzanne was stiff, distant, and then he began to feel her stir and respond. He was almost dreaming, he shut his eyes while he caressed her.

He'd pulled her under him, when the door opened. Suzanne slipped out from beneath him, sitting up and with a shaky voice was asking Lennie, "Are you all right?"

Lennie stood at their bed. Suzanne took one of her pillows and put it down, and Lennie laid herself crossways at their feet. Then the customary arrangement of her limbs. Suzanne asked her if she needed the mohair throw and she shook her head—Emmett could hear her hair scratch at the pillow, No.

The sheets were white and fresh. He curled on his side and tucked his hands between his knees. When he woke up in the night, aware that he needed to be careful not to disturb Lennie at the end of the bed, he could hear her, could hear her wakefulness. "I don't trust you," she had said. Maybe she was too intelligent, over capacity. Too wary. How easily she had adopted John's cool accent. Today she was seven years old. How many hours had Lennie been awake? He did the math.

Chapter Two

The little man standing on the front stoop peered from under a hat that was too big for him, as was his grey flannel suit. He had papery white skin and teary pink eyes that blinked furiously in the midday sun. He looked like a white rabbit.

Lennie's birthday had dawned warm and quickly grew hot. She followed her father to the door, and when she saw the little fellow in the oversized grey suit standing there, she climbed up into Emmett's arms, her feet dangling almost to his knees. "Yes?" he asked.

"You are Mr. Jones."

He agreed, he was Mr. Jones. He thought he was speaking to a Fuller Brush salesman. Lennie laid her head on his chest and wound her legs around him. She was expecting that the arrival of the rabbit had something to do with her birthday.

"Would you come with me?" Rabbit demanded.

Emmett heard Suzanne clatter with the pans in the kitchen, preparing lunch, and he turned uncertainly toward the interior of his house, Lennie twisting so she could keep an eye on Rabbit. Emmett returned his attention to the little man and asked, "Who are you?"

Rabbit looked from under the brim of his hat, blinking painfully in the sun. Despite the absurdity of his appearance, he assumed absolute authority. "Lieutenant Morton sends for you." He stepped back to let Emmett pass.

With some difficulty Emmett unwound Lennie and set her down. He made a move to indicate that he would go back inside to say goodbye to his wife, but Rabbit, by dint of a small impatient gesture, let him know that there no time, he was to come forthwith.

He left Lennie standing at the open front door. "Tell your mother I'll be right back," he said. A black Buick was parked on the street. Rabbit ushered him into its backseat and shut the door, jumped in behind the wheel, and the car started to roll.

A Mountie in khakis stood at the gate marking the entrance to wooded grounds surrounded by a stone wall covered in ivy. The Mountie casually saluted when the car pulled up before the gate and moved aside so the groundskeeper, rake in hand, could let them through. The car was now on a private road surrounded by birch stands mixed with dogwood. The floor of the forest was cleared and raked. Emmett felt naked without his wallet, his jacket and hat.

They pulled up before a stone house with small windows. He tried to get out of the car, but there was no handle. Rabbit leapt out and around and opened the door for him, his eyes leaking, his white face with its pink eyes shrivelled against the hated sun. He piloted Emmett into the house through a massive oak door.

Inside stood Robert Morton, stockier, rather better-looking than he was even a few years ago, in a dark suit with narrow lapels and unusually narrow trousers. He greeted Emmett politely, "Glad you could make it. I'd like you come this way, if you please."

The rabbit stepped up so close to Emmett's back he could feel the gun in its holster inside the absurd grey suit.

Morton interrupted sharply, "That'll be fine, Grey. Wait in the car."

Grey, Rabbit, chewed something between his front teeth and looked as malevolent as his size would permit. Emmett was glad to walk away from his hot little body.

They went through a large old kitchen and outside to the backyard. Morton took a path set in flagstone. On either side the grass was wet, recently watered. The place reminded him of the house his father had kept for Sachiko, and then he was reminded of Aoi, and of his son, James, in Japan. The memory heartened him because it was his alone.

At the back of the yard, fifty feet away from the main house, was a small cottage in the Tudor fashion, white plaster with timber braces. "Go ahead," Morton said and watched while Emmett stooped under the low doorway before coming in after him and shutting them inside.

They were in a pleasant space furnished in an old-fashioned Victorian way. Two men seated before an empty fireplace stood when Morton entered. They were dressed in plainclothes with black leather jackets. One of them said, "Good afternoon, Mr. Jones." Emmett wondered where Morton's stupid sidekick Partridge had gone to.

Morton indicated where Emmett was to sit, and when they were all four settled, he said, "First of all, I have a present for you." A leather legal briefcase sat beside Morton's chair. He bent down, opened it, and removed three accordion file folders. "Here you go." Without fully standing up, he took a step forward and placed the folders in Emmett's hands. The plainclothes officers looked on with bland goodwill.

Emmett propped the files upright and read the labels on each one.

Robert Morton said, "The Jones Files. One, Two, and Three. 1949–1959. Of course, we don't have the FBI's stuff on you."

Jones 1949–1959. Emmett had been under surveillance for the last ten years, under surveillance long after he'd been "cleared" in the investigation of 1953. He suspected this, yes, but their spying on him was so professionally accomplished that he hadn't seen it, had warned himself against becoming paranoid. He thought he'd been cured of any naive belief that his country would not purposefully set itself against him, when the RCMP had given their files on him to the US. But a residue of faith had remained despite his wariness; he'd fallen yet again for the myth of goodness. What a fool. He was unable to conceal his shock. He looked up into Morton's smug face.

He placed the files on the floor at his feet and then picked up one with shaking hands. It was in chronological order. His editorials published in the university newspaper, *The Varsity*. Copies of reports he'd filed in Ottawa in 1950. Memos he'd sent to Bill Masters as a policy analyst in Tokyo. A letter from George Miller of the Washington think tank, memos to Harold Gembey of the Security Panel. Transcripts of the interviews when he was formally under investigation.

"It's not everybody gets to see their file," Morton mildly observed.

And there were photographs. Emmett with Leonard Fischer and John Norfield walking down Avenue Road at night, Leonard's arm around Emmett's shoulder. One of Aoi wearing her Manchurian cloak. She is kneeling in the snow and Emmett is walking away from her, toward the camera. He hadn't seen anyone taking these pictures.

Suzanne crossing College Street. She's young. Carrying what looks like a school satchel. How young they were. There's an attitude of self-satisfaction in Suzanne that is no longer there.

"It adds up," Morton observed. "I mean, in sheer bulk."

The two plainclothes smirked, but Emmett had the impression that they rarely expected to understand Morton and didn't care whether they did or didn't.

On a table beside Morton lay a black notebook. He opened it, leafing through pages of handwritten script. In a low voice, as if to himself, "Out-of-date phone listings and a bunch of poems." He tossed it to Emmett.

"Facts," Morton continued, "are simple enough, I suppose. So-and-so left the house at such-and-such an hour in the company of so-and-so's wife. That kind of thing. Simple. What's hard, what takes skill, is in the assembly. Shifting, rearranging. Try it one way, move the pieces, try it another way. Making a picture. Right?"

Emmett began to look through each file more carefully. His instinct was to feel shy at being observed while looking at himself. They weren't loving photographs, not family photos, these. The mechanism of the telephoto lens. How furtive they seem, he and his beloveds. And how deluded. He tried to handle the material as if he had a right to it and wasn't revealing a weakness for the regard of others.

Morton added, "That's most of what we've got."

There's more. Emmett started to review Jones File One. Here is Leonard Fischer. The private density of Leonard's body,

309

the intense impact of the evil he'd endured. One and half million children murdered, Leonard's sisters among them, only fourteen years ago, so many millions killed. He recalled Leonard's phlegmy laugh. *Ich schlief, ich schlief—From a deep dream have I awoken.*

He riffled through Jones File Two. He needed to see whether they'd ever photographed Suzanne with Norfield.

Morton spun his chair and straddled it backward, tipping it eagerly toward him. "You enjoyed a reunion with an old friend last night."

Emmett deposited Jones File Two on the floor and picked up Jones File Three, sorting through it while he answered Morton, "Yes, John Norfield was at my home last night."

And suddenly it was in his hand: his son, a photograph of a little boy, the shock of love and recognition, his son, he's looking almost directly into the lens, his wondering face clear, innocent, beautiful, and the skirt of a woman behind him, likely Aoi.

Emmett was aware of a tightening apprehension in Morton's attitude as Morton observed the effect of this remarkable disclosure, this revelation. Aoi had never sent any pictures; Emmett had never before seen his son, yet he knew with every fibre that it was he.

Emmett clumsily shuffled the photos, finally sliding the photograph of the boy back into the deck. He forced himself to speak as if continuing the conversation. "Norfield came by our house. Unexpectedly." He looked up and met Morton's gleeful eyes but made himself continue, "He visited for a little while. Then he left."

"Accompanied by your wife."

Emmett slid the photographs into the briefcase. He had to keep talking, his voice was constricting. He had seen his son. He would not let Morton know his feelings. He said, "I've told you many times. Norfield was a friend in university."

"Now, that's not entirely accurate, is it."

"My wife was a student then. Naive. We were all naive. You're spying on school friends. You must get tired of it."

"Not at all."

Indeed, Morton didn't look weary; he was tanned, fit, enviably clear. He watched Emmett, waiting for him to explode. "If we're all finished here," Emmett said, "I'd like to go home."

"There's one more thing. Before we release you to the wild." Morton stood, carefully replacing the chair at the kitchen table. "Our mutual interest — that is, the elusive Mr. Norfield — is at an end."

Emmett had to ask what "at an end" meant.

"He's come in."

"He's very ill."

"That's probably why."

"He has decided to return?"

"So he says."

If that were true, John would spend the rest of his life being followed, interrogated by Morton and his "intelligence." Surely he was intending to slip out of the country again somehow.

"At any rate," Morton continued with mild impatience, signalling Emmett's dismissal, "he's done you a favour."

"Has he."

"We made a deal. A bargain. We leave you and your wife alone, and he gives us his full cooperation."

The plainclothes stood. Morton picked up the briefcase

and was handing it to Emmett when he stopped, put his hand inside, and removed a white cardboard box. Emmett recognized it as a box for audiotape. Morton laid the white box on the table and then offered again to put the briefcase into Emmett's hands. "We've kept you long enough. "

Emmett didn't move. "I don't need another man to bargain for me. I've got nothing to hide. You've proven that."

"Grey will drive you home."

"Yes. But not because you made a deal with Norfield."

"I'm sorry to have disturbed your lunch."

"I'm going to talk to John."

"That would be stupid. And irresponsible. You're a family man."

This was apparently funny; the plainclothes grinned.

"Take the path around," Morton told him, "you don't need to go through the house again." He went to the door and opened it. "You'll find the car waiting for you out front." He looked at his watch to indicate that he had more important things to do.

Emmett took the briefcase. He passed Morton so close he saw the spindles of amber in his eyes, as if the sun had got into him and made him invincible. He said, "I'm not part of your ridiculous bargain, Morton. I've got nothing to do with you. I'm not even part of your fantasy."

"Ah." Morton smiled sadly. "And here I've been feeling so close."

Chapter Three

Blue Sea Lake

The ryegrass on the lawn by the lake prickled Lennie's legs and shoulders and neck, but she focused hard on *infinity*, which rose farther than the feathery clouds and travelled deeply past the sky.

Summer was a time to recover from Grade One, to let the giants of Classroom 1-B shrivel and wane. She and her mother "got away" the minute school ended, at twelve noon June 28, the car packed to the roof, somewhere in all that stuff a new bathing suit for Lenore.

Grade One was behind her. And good riddance. She hadn't been the most popular girl in 1-B, not by a long shot. Peter Robinson in the desk behind her had called her "a hairy fink" when she wasn't there to hear him. That nice boy Adam had informed her of this. And face it (a phrase Lennie liked, "face it," or "let's face it"), her two best friends, Sarah Martin and Jenny Walker, weren't her best friends anymore.

Sarah and Jenny would be going to a different school in another neighbourhood for Grade Two, for something called "Acceleration." The teachers said they were "above average" and chose those two morons to take a bus to another school. Anyway, Grade Two was in September. Far away, far as Mars.

Sarah and Jennie might have been smarter, but Lennie

was more *intelligent*. Her Grade One teacher, Mrs. Duncan, called Lennie "a dreamer." Lennie had felt *the holy ghost* swell through her blood when she heard this; she'd thought it was a compliment. But Mrs. Duncan has betrayed her. Things happen in patterns. Lennie understands that she will be betrayed often in her whole entire life.

An airplane cut the sky, a hurting, carving sound. Up there, her father told her, it's always today; he said that if you go up out of the sky, *past the blue ocean of air,* if you travel up and out of here fast enough, time no longer happens. What we have is *gravity* pinning us down, forcing us into seconds, minutes, hours, days, weeks, months, years, decades, centuries.

This is a great loop of thinking that Lennie tried once to explain to Sarah and Jenny. Sarah and Jenny fell backward together onto the couch in Jenny's den, which is a room of windows above the garage, the two of them rolling their eyes and saying, "Really, Reilly, you're a riot," whatever that means. It was their new saying. They put on an English accent when they said this.

Lennie remembered how sick of herself she was that day, just standing there like a *clown* in her red stretch pants that bagged at the knees. She tried to tell them that if you go way up into outer space fast enough you don't get any older, you're always just how old you are now. Seven. Forever. She drew her hands over her head to illustrate what she called "the great domain of life." Sarah and Jenny said, "Really, Reilly, you're a riot," and broke open a box of Ritz crackers, intending to eat the whole thing. Gravity and time pressed on Lennie so hard she went home. She hadn't seen either of them since, and wouldn't see them all summer because they went to Anglican

Summer Camp. Lenore would never go to Anglican Summer Camp. She'd *die* there.

The lake shushed at the shore. Seagulls floated on the hot wind above where she sprawled on the grass and sent herself into space. Faster than light, Dad said, means faster than time.

When it rains after an atom bomb, the rain burns holes in people's faces. They start to throw up. When they look in the mirror, they're melting, their skin falls off in globs of pus. They run outside and die in the middle of the street with everybody watching from their picture windows.

The secret atom got out. The man in her mother's photographs took it to Russia. Lennie had wanted him to like her and think she's pretty. She's ashamed of this. She might grow up to be a murderer or a thief. The great domain of life hurts inside her chest. The man in her mother's photographs came to her house and liked her. The photographs are her.

Except for Kim and except for Dad and President Kennedy, men smell bad. They make cigarette burns on the tables in the living room. One man stepped on her toe at a cocktail party and didn't even notice. Cocktail parties are *revolting*. Jenny's parents have them and they boil lobsters alive.

But the hardest of all is knowing Dad is a spy. A spy and a communist. Adam told her way back in Grade One, he told her nicely. There are hardly any nice boys, but he's one. He told her when they were at the sandy end of the schoolyard where the stinkweeds get tall and nobody else could hear, and he told her like it was something he felt she should know and he felt sorry to have to be the messenger. He has a nice voice, Adam. Lenore saw he felt sorry for her. Shame is hot as pee.

Lennie knows her father loves her. He still picks her up like she's a baby and talks to her at night when she can't sleep. He's handsome. He's very intelligent. He has a boy called James who lives in Japan. And he is a communist spy. Often the work of forgiving him makes her eyes sting with tears.

Lenore's friends' dads give them nicknames: "Muffin," "Doll-face." When they were in Grade One, Sarah's father spanked her and Jenny and Sarah for running through the living room after Sarah's mother had waxed the floor, so Lenore never went back there; they always had to play at Jenny or Lennie's houses. He made her bend over and then he whacked her bum. The shame is on him. Jenny's dad tells knock-knock jokes and sits on the floor beside the hi-fi he got her; he also bought Jenny a Harry Belafonte record. These fathers aren't communist spies. But they're simpletons.

Sometimes she envies simpletons, but she wouldn't want one for a father. Simpletons send their moron children to Anglican Summer Camp. She raises her legs and waves her feet in the air.

Suzanne threw their bags into their rooms, collected the saucers of mouse seed from the corners of the veranda, put the food away, and went to her darkroom — what used to be a pantry between the kitchen and Lenore's bedroom at the back of the cottage. She closed the door behind her, and without turning on the light she breathed in the sour stench.

She would have a show opening in the fall, her work along with the work of several other "women photographers." A journalist from the newspaper was coming to the cottage soon, this afternoon, to interview her "in her native habitat." She and Lenore had to take the boat back to the landing for three o'clock to collect the journalist. Too soon. She'd barely arrived.

She'd been interviewed before. But she was anxious about it. The rush to get away from Ottawa as soon as Lenore was released from school, all the packing and watering the garden and the blinds drawn and Emmett tied up till tonight; she couldn't stop this automatic rush forward, and her nerves were crisp, prickling across her face.

Suzanne stood in the pitch-dark. She'd let go of the door handle, and in the small, familiar space she had the sensation that she didn't know where she was, that she could be hanging upside down or one step away from a deep pit. Outside in the bright world, white poplar and aspen clapped in the sun, the gulls cried over the lake. She was still—what—shiny, glinting from her encounter with John. How like him to show up that way, mysterious, bitterly unromantic and very, very romantic too. He was bad for her. She had escaped him. But seeing him again had made her feel seared, singed inside, nervy yet beautiful.

Now John was gone, gone for good, to live in Russia where the streets are wide and the winters cold. He'd told her, Leningrad looks like Ottawa. Imagine. Broad streets that look like Wellington Avenue, John said, but the buildings there are pink and yellow, drab from war. He might be back in Russia by now. She will never see him again. Eventually, slowly, this pain will subside, she'll no longer feel this way, like the strings on an instrument, stretched, pitched, played by him, awful, grotesque, almost unmanageable; she'd scolded herself, driving here, she was afraid she'd get in an accident so distracted was she, listening to his silence as if for a code. But she has Lenore now. There is Lenore. There is Emmett. She'll recover again, and there will be Emmett.

She felt a surge of hope. She had a good life. She loved her family. Here in this space, she intended to do good work all summer. She shuffled a step backward, then again and again before she felt the cool pine door at her back, the door handle jabbing her, she opened the door to the heat, to colour, and went to find Lennie.

There were the pale blue shorts, the matching jersey, stretched out on the lawn. Lennie's bare arms rose and twined like thin white snakes. Suzanne couldn't hear her, but she guessed that Lennie was talking to herself.

Lenore's loneliness in this past school year, the patient way she took it, filled Suzanne with fearful admiration. It reminded her of when Lennie first learned to swim, the moment of letting go, seeing her buttery baby pedalling through the water, no strings attached. Now, Lennie's narrow chest like a birdcage, her aloof sideways approach, her reserve, and Suzanne yearning to gather the kindling of elbows and knees. She let the screen door bang shut and walked across the lawn. "Hi."

"Hi." Lennie gave one of her lucid glances and resumed her study of the sky, sunlight through her fingers as they formed a cat's cradle, or a pentaprism; maybe Lenore, the grey-eyed observer, will become a photographer.

"Whatcha doin'?"

"Nothin'."

Suzanne sat beside her and began to finger through the grass, searching for a four-leaf clover. Green is complicated by blue and yellow and red. Colour was making Suzanne anxious. She didn't know if her unease with colour photography was the result of good taste or a complete lack of talent. Her colour photographs often failed—they were pictures *of* things, unless she manipulated the filters till the subject morphed in a hallucinatory way. That flinty little critic Walmsley was probably right: her voodoo on film is pretentious.

Part of the show in August would be another series of staged images with lamps and gobos and filters on her lenses. She'd hired an actor and photographed him in a trench coat, against paintings, a diorama of an alley or a highway, climbing a rise to a crossroads with a watercolour sky ahead of him, away from her, his face hidden. It was important to her that he be an actor.

Of course these are photographs of John. Emmett has figured that out, she knows, and she feels rather awed at the largesse of Emmett's love.

In a subseries for the show, the actor's face is revealed, heavily made up with a thick layer of white powder and the high, startled eyebrows of the geisha. In other portraits the actor wears more conventionally glamorous makeup, slanting eyeliner and false eyelashes and so on, his lips painted a red that looks black in the photograph. Who are these people, who are they meant to be? No one. A proliferation of empty wishes.

She'd like to develop more natural portraits of Lennie, but Lennie said she'd take her *soul*. Lennie permitted Emmett to take her picture; she'd even sit still for him. But if Suzanne went anywhere near her daughter with a camera in her hand, Lennie vanished like a little animal down a hole. Suzanne didn't want the blundering power that she held over her daughter; her maternal force was like an overdeveloped muscle, like a Charley horse.

She knew she'd spoiled Lennie's fantasizing. Even the westward clouds lose fluidity, do they? When a mother comes around? "Want some lunch before we go to the landing?"

Lenore gave her a look that said, Must you bother me with lowly matters?

"Cucumber sand-wishes." Her little girl's word for *sandwich* and, judging by the disdainful response, out of date. Suzanne ran a hand down Lennie's shin to her ankle. "How about a swim first. It's hot."

"A swim?"

"See if your new bathing suit works."

A temptation. Lennie rewarded her mother with a smile for an okay try at a joke. She took a last look at outer space. Angel-time being over, she had to get back to the land of the living. She got up, dizzy, and said, "I like it when I can see the whole planet."

Suzanne didn't know what Lennie meant, but her heart leapt. Lennie let her kiss the sunny top of her head.

Chapter Four

Now that Emmett knew that the surveillance had been ongoing for ten years, he could never trust his privacy again. And knowing now that his son James was under surveillance, he needed to get to Japan, as if seeing the boy was the same as protecting him, a sort of magic thinking.

From his window, across his darkened lawn when he went down to turn off the lights at night, he'd think he'd seen someone, a shadow crossing the driveway, dodging behind the garage, a small figure, impossible even to tell if it was a man or a woman. Perhaps a mirage. If he went outside, of course the shadow disappeared, absorbed into the leafy back lane.

Norfield's reappearance had been unsettling, reawakening a friendship, or love. Emmett hadn't told Suzanne about the deal John had made with the RCMP, the exchange of his freedom for theirs. She's upset. Better that she thinks that Norfield is in Russia. She's high-strung. She can't handle it, thinking John has harmed himself for their sake, thinking he's accessible, that he might show up again, surprise them. It was time — not to let go of their past but to let it change meaning; let the past become foreign.

Emmett was thirty-nine years old. The world he'd gone to war for, and the post-war world he'd once been convinced he understood better than most men, was both banal and insane. The Russians had recently tested the world's first intercontinental ballistic missiles, preparing for long-range nuclear rocket strikes, playing a game of catch-up with the Americans in a race to blow up the planet.

A Conservative, John Diefenbaker, was now prime minister, elected with a strong majority last winter, and Diefenbaker's band of earnest oddballs was running things in Ottawa. Diefenbaker was incoherent on the arms race. Emmett wondered if he was crazy. He'd met crazy leaders before — General MacArthur came to mind — though Diefenbaker was Canadian-crazy, un-heroic crazy, tormented by fear and envy of President Kennedy.

Emmett tried to talk to Bill Masters about Prime Minister Diefenbaker. "These Bomarc missiles," he said to Bill over lunch. "You know that Dief is prepared to arm them with nuclear warheads?"

Bill was eating a hamburger. He nodded, sure he knew that.

"Paid for by the Americans," Emmett continued, "who are instructing us to store them here, where we'll be targets for a first strike by the Russians."

Bill took a slug of Orange Crush. It was noon, he wasn't having a drink, doctor's orders. "We need defence," said Bill. "We're gonna need a hell of a lot more than the Bomarc missiles if there's a nuclear war."

There were more than Bomarc missiles. Diefenbaker was making verbal commitments to store American nuclear missiles in Labrador and Newfoundland. The US pressed Diefenbaker to agree to store atomic bombs along with anti-submarine nuclear warheads. Canada would be the battlefield of a nuclear World War Three, a quick bright battlefield in a war that everyone on earth would lose in a matter of minutes. The world would burn to ash, nothing would survive, neither root nor branch, this was a fact of every Canadian's strangely dull existence in 1959.

Chapter Five

At 4:25 on a summery Friday afternoon, Emmett's secretary asked to be let go early; her husband was picking her up so they could go to Kingston for the long weekend. Emmett told her to go, and she sweetly wished him a good holiday next week, telling him she'd "hold the fort." He could hear the voices of people well-wishing as they fled the building, a peaceful, glad evacuation, and he stood at the window watching them rush out into summer.

With everyone gone, the offices were provocatively quiet, waxy and gleaming, and he felt excited to find himself quite alone in the citadel. He didn't have to hurry; Suzanne had said she'd keep Lennie up late for the boat ride to the landing to pick him up. He took a key from his trouser pocket and unlocked his desk drawer where he kept his lovely little Minox in its leather wallet, small enough to fit in the palm of his hand. He stroked its cool surface and slipped it into his pocket.

He was agitated and decided to go for a fast walk downstairs and run back up again before finishing the paperwork on his desk. He was on his way down when he encountered Prime Minister Diefenbaker on his way up.

"Good day."

"Oh. Hello, sir."

The stairwell was empty. The prime minister pivoted, one foot on the upper stair, and said, "Say."

"Sir?"

"I read your memo."

"Thank you —"

Diefenbaker raised his hand to indicate, No need. It was almost unbelievable that this particular prime minister would read a memo by staff. Diefenbaker distrusted the civil service. But he said, "This Vietnamese character — President Diem —"

"Yes, sir."

"The Vietnamese aren't happy with him."

"Nobody is, Mr. Prime Minister."

"So you say, so you say —"

He had read it. Emmett waited.

Finally, Diefenbaker said, "The Americans are backing the wrong horse!" He chuckled.

"That might well be the case in this instance, sir."

Then Diefenbaker added in a confiding, conspiratorial tone, "I'm thinking of inviting Khrushchev for a visit."

Emmett held his pose, thinking that he must surely be joking.

But Diefenbaker continued, "It'll show that son of a bitch Kennedy, we're not some crushed satellite he can kick around."

Emmett blinked, trying to reconcile this with Diefenbaker's recent eagerness to store the Americans' nuclear warheads at Goose Bay.

"You like the idea, young fellow?" Emmett was casting about for an answer when Diefenbaker suddenly asked, "How is your wife?"

"My wife? She's well. Thank you."

Diefenbaker turned his back and began to climb the stairs. "Give her our kind regards, will you?"

Our kind regards. His and his wife Olive's kind regards.

324

There was not a snowball's chance in hell Diefenbaker even knew Suzanne's name. Pearson did. The McCallum tribe was Liberal. Emmett slowly descended the stairs. He felt lightheaded; he lived in a place without any atmosphere. A man has to fight hard to find purchase in this country. He was floating aimlessly through space, turning and turning in the zero gravity of his quiescent land.

Lennie and Suzanne were sitting in the boat at the landing when he drove up and parked. He kissed his wife, apologizing for being late, but he could see that she was so distracted as to not really be here. He kissed Lenore, who was sitting on the engine cover wearing her pyjamas and a white canvas life jacket. A still night. Mars shivering in the black water.

She piloted them to the cottage, a faint mist rising as the lake cooled, the throaty rumble of the engine giving them an excuse not to talk. They docked and tied up, and Suzanne carried his duffle bag so he could carry Lennie, and still they didn't speak.

Suzanne made hot chocolate. Emmett put a bit of rum in hers and a lot of rum in his. They took it to the veranda, Lennie amazed at being out of bed at this hour, breaking the silence. "I'm going to be ten someday," she announced defensively, "and thirteen. When I'm a grown-up, I can do whatever I want."

"You've never been as old as you are this second," he said.

Lennie's grey eyes widened. "It's because of all the light hitting us." She looked out the black window. "How can I get older when it's night out?" Suzanne gave a giddy laugh. Lennie went on, answering herself. "Because I've got light inside."

Now that it was possible to speak, he told Suzanne that he'd had a conversation with the prime minister a few hours ago, adding that Diefenbaker had sent his and Olive's kind regards. She said, "That's nice," and she nestled into her wicker settee.

He drank his rummy chocolate. Suzanne had assumed the prime minister would know her. He said, "It wasn't entirely nice."

"Why?"

He tried to resist the urge to hurt her feelings. He was tired, tired of being Sisyphus, pushing the stone uphill, performing incremental work. She was at home, she'd never known anything but home. He'd let her have everything she wanted, and tonight he felt tired and resentful and frightened and sick of it. Frightened of the possibility of nuclear war, very frightened that he couldn't protect them, frightened that whatever he had done to redeem the value of his life, to make his existence extraordinary, it wouldn't matter, his courage and ambitions were an inconvenience to her, she needed him to do nothing more than be the banal facilitator of her pleasant life, the one she got instead of John Norfield. He was a servant. He realized that he was scalding mad.

"What did the prime minister actually *say*?" Suzanne asked.

"He read my memo."

"No," she said, "I mean about us?"

Lennie got out of her chair and stood on one leg, her cup of hot chocolate in her two hands. She was beginning to bristle, starting up her almost invisible fibrillation.

"I could do — I could," he waved his cup, then drained it, "do some good work."

"You could do some good work how?" Abruptly alert, she added, "Where?"

"Oh, I don't know, how about Asia? Not that it's my specialty."

"No married men. That's the policy. You're going to have to divorce me."

Lennie put both feet on the floor.

He said, "No." Then to Lennie, "I won't."

Lennie was visibly trembling now. Suzanne told her to go brush her teeth and she'd come to tuck her in. "Go," she repeated. When she was gone, Suzanne said, "You want to see Aoi. You want to see your other family. You fret about your son. Don't think I don't know how you feel."

"Let's drop it for tonight," he said.

She repeated her question, what exactly did the prime minister say?

"He thought you might want to help me host a state visit from Khrushchev."

"Me?"

"Why not? Cook him a fancy dinner. Show his wife around Parliament Hill."

Suzanne threw her head back, exposing her throat. "Oh my god, that's so crazy."

She'd started to laugh, but she'd also started to cry. It surprised him, his anger toppled and subsided. He went to sit beside her and put his thumb to the corner of her eye to feel her tears.

"Are you serious?" she asked. "Diefenbaker wants to invite Khrushchev and we'd have to entertain?" She was sobbing with laughter.

He laughed too, his tired eyes stinging, and he said, "We're the perfect couple." He stroked her hair.

"Everybody would be so happy to believe we're communists," she said, weeping and laughing. "They'd finally understand us."

"Do you want everyone to understand us?" he asked. "What do you want?"

She jumped a little, a guilty, involuntary, wall-eyed shying from him. "Nothing. I want" — she waved at the room — "this. You."

"I could be useful," he said quietly. "I can see things clearly." She looked startled, he thought, as if threatened. In the memo that Diefenbaker had actually read, he'd written that President Diem was a disaster and couldn't hold out much longer. He'd written that the Vietcong were a national movement in Vietnam and that they'd win from inside the South. Now he said to Suzanne almost lazily, feeling the rum sweeten his fatigue, "The South Vietnamese support the Vietcong communists. There's going to be a coup in Vietnam."

He watched her face fall. "A coup," she repeated. "Did you tell the prime minister there's going to be a coup?"

"Everybody knows it."

"Emmett," Suzanne said slowly, "will he think that you got this information from some kind of inside source?"

"A spy?" He whispered, "I got it from *The Globe and Mail*."

"You did not."

"I read between the lines."

"Tell me. How do you know what's going on with the communists in Vietnam?"

"It's my *job*, it's what I do."

"Who do you talk to?"

"I have lunch every day with a mysterious representative of the International Ladies Garment Workers."

"I'm serious."

"So is she." He put his hand where her shirt opened at the collar, pulled at the strap of her bra, and felt a rush of desire. "Hanoi is taking over the insurgency from the southern communists. It's war. China's involved, Russia's involved. The Americans will be bombing the place one day soon."

Warily she asked, "Where'd you hear that?"

"In an American tabloid."

"Where did you get it?"

"I subscribe."

"At the Department?"

"I told the prime minister that any attempt at military victory over the communists in Vietnam is going to fail."

"You told the prime minister that the communists are going to take Vietnam."

"They will."

"He'll fire you."

He liked that she understood that much; it was strangely true in Canada, in mimicry of the situation in the US, that any man reckless enough to contemplate the possibility of a victory for communism anywhere on earth was considered disloyal. But Diefenbaker couldn't fire a civil servant. He tugged at her bra strap. "He can't," he told her. "I'm non-partisan."

She laughed again more calmly and began to fool with his hair, one of her habits, trying to make it curl around her finger. "Tell me really. How do you know all this stuff?"

He said, "I'm not all by myself in my great wisdom."

"Emmett, baby," she breathed, "are you happy?"

He took her cup to put it on the floor, she leaned forward to run her hand down his spine and then up around his neck. He was thinking that he'd have one more drink and then he would make love to his wife, he'd make love, he'd make sex, he murmured into her hair, "I'd like to take you to bed," and looked toward the lamplight reflected in the window where he saw Lenore, so it was at first unclear to him whether she was inside or outside looking in.

Lenore, pale, puppet-straight, shot him her dire stare.

He heard Suzanne's lips pluck apart. Lennie's attention dropped to the floor for a second, then back to his face. It was enough, this fracture, this momentary show of self-consciousness, to release in him a hot surge of contempt. He bellowed, "Don't sneak around!"

Lennie was out of the room before he finished the sentence, Suzanne rushing after her, hissing, "Asshole!"

Alone he went to the kitchen and poured rum into Suzanne's cup, drinking where her lipstick remained. There was nowhere to go in his wife's cottage. He was too drunk to go swimming. Out on the water, he heard the chittering love talk of a pair of otters, *a party*, he and Suzanne had once said, watching them twine each other in moonlight one summer long past. An innocent desire that eluded him, lowly consort to the Ice Queen.

He drained the cup, poured more rum, returned to the veranda, and poked under a rain-stained wicker table with drawers filled with poker chips, playing cards and matches, a cribbage board, stray Scrabble pieces. Beneath the table was a pile of dusty magazines where he found a copy of *Chatelaine* 1953. A time of bliss, till solstice, that June when he'd learned that he would be investigated by the RCMP. But he had survived.

He lived alone among men and alone among his loved ones. He had known this was his fate even as a boy, in the parody his father had made of his family, his father opening the stage to self-consciousness by introducing his other love, Sachiko. In the war, he'd fallen for the delusion of belonging to Bomber Command. That had been an ecstatic well-blooded belonging, cynically devised by the generals. He'd awoken from that delusion to the pain of knowing that he'd been manipulated. Yet he fell in love again, with John Norfield, with Leonard Fischer, with their rejection of ordinary ambition, their communism, a totally paradoxical belonging that would always counter its own definitions. *Ich schlief, ich schlief—From a deep dream have I awoken.*

Norfield and Leonard's communism required homelessness and the courage to live in that condition. Tonight, aloneness was painful because he was tired and he'd had too much to drink. Aloneness was his source of strength, his pride. Tonight it led to a sense of despair; tomorrow it might yield its private radiance. He could see things clearly only when he made himself awaken from the perpetual lure of belonging. Of longing to belong.

He'd fallen in love with Suzanne knowing that she loved him in return only as a rational, hopeful, compensatory method of surviving the passion she felt for John. Emmett thought, Yes, I'm a fool. Being alive is foolish. I awaken from one dream only to fall into another. The constant in his series of errors and delusions was his abiding love for Suzanne and Lenore.

He was looking at an article that he wouldn't remember tomorrow. It was called, "The Pill That Could Change the World." Then Lennie arrived smelling of lake water and slipped under his arm to lay her head on his chest and in her boy's voice to ask him, "What are you reading?" She didn't expect or wish him to answer, she didn't give a damn what he was reading, she was giving him *attention*. He experienced the melting joy of a rehabilitated criminal.

Lennie sprawled with elaborate kindness across his lap. She had a quick gag reflex, and her father smelled of man. It was her duty to touch him with her wings.

He tossed aside *Chatelaine* to stroke his daughter's cool bare arm.

Chapter Six

Emmett awoke the next day to a perfectly windless Saturday morning and discovered Suzanne gone from their rumpled bed. A white-throated sparrow sang its six notes. He had a hangover. Again. It wasn't such a severe hangover that it wouldn't be expelled by a swim. Outside in bright sunlight, his body was white in his swimming trunks, his bare feet on the cool stone stairs looked fungal, the skin puffy and premature.

Lenore and Suzanne were sitting on the dock wearing big and small versions of the same hat, straw with silk roses, their skin golden, their eyes as clear as the lake reflecting granite and pine boughs that rippled with the morning sun. He passed them and dived.

He was a foreigner here, a city creature, but his girls were lulled, he could see, creatures of Lethe mesmerized by pleasure, by peaceful boredom, rolling aside to let father-fish flop onto their towel stiff from drying in the sun. Suzanne put her finger into the beads of water on his freckling shoulder and murmured, "You'll burn."

She was relaxed, she wasn't thinking about John, she was his again. He couldn't sit or settle so he prepared a big breakfast that she and Lennie consumed as if this were simply a phase of their own photosynthesis.

Lennie still avoided eggs but put away a bushel of berries and a half loaf of bread. Chewing, she reached to put her palm to his chin and rubbed at the shadow there. "You're priggly." Her nose was plugged; it husked her voice.

"What if you get born a raspberry?" Emmett asked.

Lennie wouldn't answer a question that was negligently aimed at her cosmology. Saucily, she sighed and asked him, "What if you get born a robin? What if you get born a dragonfly? What if you get born a ladybug, what if you get born a bee, what if you get born an ant?"

Rising with the plates, he asked her, "What were you *before* you were born?" The look of dread on her face made him hurriedly clear the table, sorry.

Suzanne's stomach was taut; he could see the muscle through her bathing suit. She'd put on one of his tattered white shirts to come to breakfast and now she let it fall open as she leaned back in her chair and pushed her plate toward him, crossing her tanned legs. "That was good." Unfazed. Her blue eyes full of light. Then while he was filling the sink, she came behind him and wrapped her warm body around his back. "Why don't you take a break," she offered and nudged him out of the way.

They'd had a storm that had ripped some shingle off the boathouse. He looked among the debris stored under the cottage to find a package of spare shingles and began to set himself up to make the repair. He thought about his son, James, and the life he was leading without his father. He wondered what it would be like to have a boy about the place, and whether the money was getting to Aoi, who never wrote back.

He discovered that a joist had rotted, which led to another search to discover some dry lumber stacked on a canoe rack and wrapped in a canvas tarp. Caterpillars had sewn white sacs to the canvas, it smelled sweet with mildew, he pulled the pliable silk cocoons off with his hands. Wild rose grew here, under the deck, in the parallel lines of sun shining through, they scratched his bare legs with their thorns.

He hauled a four-by-six from under the cottage and then found the handsaw and carried it all down to the dock. The saw was dull, the job took forever, and he had to stop for a beer when he was halfway through, partly from thirst and partly to put out the fire that burned in his head.

It was nearly time for lunch, but he got the paint-splattered stepladder from the shed and carried it inside the boathouse to position it beside the boat slips where Suzanne's runabout and the nine-horse were moored. The gulping sound of the boats when waves rolled in. Sweet golden shade rippling. With his dull saw, he began to cut away the rotted wood.

The lumber was soggy but nice to touch, fibres coming loose in his hands, splinters of ruddy blond wood softened by the rains. It smelled good in there. Jerry cans of gas and tins of outboard motor oil. At his left ear poised a leathery black spider the size of a small mouse. The portion of rotten wood fell into his hands.

"Whatcha doin'?" Lennie stood at the doorway to the boathouse, peering in.

"Fixing the roof." He looked down where she stood in a hot slab of sunlight, her T-shirt a sweet pink against the bleached wood of the dock and the blue water behind her. He was enchanted by her lucidity, her remotely attuned attention; she was a tuning fork.

She inhaled the rich fumy shade. "How come you're fixing the roof if you're standing inside?" She sighed patiently. "Anyways, Mum says it's lunch."

He leaned from his stepladder and handed Lennie the soggy

piece of pine, which she accepted without flinching. "What am I supposed to do with this?"

"Put it under your pillow."

They went up to the cottage for lunch. Lennie pondered his suggestion. She didn't like to ask for clarification. He worried that this was something that might cause her trouble later in life, a competitive streak that could make her reject her teachers. She still carried the rotten wood; it was smearing her T-shirt. He took it from her. "Here," he said, "I'll throw it on the wood pile."

"You were kidding about putting it under my pillow, right?"

"Yup."

"I knew you were."

They had lunch in the veranda, where it was cooler. Suzanne remained calmly abstracted. He wanted to *interfere* with her. His young daughter swung her legs under her chair and hummed tunelessly while she devoured an entire cucumber.

Chapter Seven

"It's all right," Suzanne said irritably, "it's absolutely fine and dandy."

A cool Thanksgiving Monday and they were closing the cottage. Emmett handed down to the boat another box of foodstuff that they didn't want to leave in the cupboards for the winter. "It's heavy," he told her, but she ignored him and nearly dropped the box. Her girlhood was especially evident in the way she performed tasks like this, the lake chores that she'd been performing all her life. She slid her jacket off and swung her arms toward him to receive the next load.

Another trade junket had come up for Emmett. He'd been given an assignment, another grease-the-wheel junket with some fellows from Trade and Commerce. This time to Japan.

The trip coincided with Emmett's desire to see his son, James. And it followed closely Robert Morton's unusual disclosure of the "Jones Files," with its casual inclusion of a photograph of the boy. Bill Masters had gurgled with pleasure in giving him the news of the impending trip, pretending that this was exactly what Jones had been asking for, as if it were a foreign posting and not another trade mission. Not another set-up.

Though Emmett didn't know if the Japan trip really was a play by External's Security section, another test of his loyalty. Maybe he was being paranoid. Bill Masters's happy croaking could be real. Two Canadian companies were selling technical knowledge to Kobe Steel Works. Emmett was the only man at External who knew Kobe Japan and could act as interpreter. That's why he'd been chosen to go along. That's how Bill Masters had phrased it.

Now Emmett was saying to Suzanne, "I'd like it better if you and Lennie were coming with me," but he didn't mean it. He didn't know what his real role was going to be in Japan, but he knew it wasn't Husband.

Suzanne said, "I don't want Lennie to know about you and—Japan."

"She's got to know where I am." He had a terror of disappearing from Lennie's life when she didn't know where he was.

"Why?"

"Why? Why would you ask me something like that?"

"It'll upset her."

"It's only business, Suzanne."

"And family. It's your family, Emmett. Yours. Not mine."

"It's Lennie's family too." He heaved a box of leftover liquor toward her.

Suzanne, stricken, let the box drop to the floorboards. A crack. The smell of gin.

He cursed quietly. He'd been thinking this, an angry sentence in his own head: It's my son, as Lenore is my daughter.

Lennie's voice from the lawn, "What are you two fighting about anyways?"

"We're not fighting." Mother and Father in unison. Then he said, "I have to go to Japan."

Suzanne sat down, that gesture: I'm washing my hands of the whole affair.

"Now?" Lennie asked.

"Next week."

"Are you going to go get James?"

"No. I'm not. James lives with his mother in Kobe. And he's going to want to stay there."

"What if he wants to come home with you?"

"He won't want to. He wouldn't want to leave his mother, would he?"

Lenore glanced at her mother, considering. "I don't know. I don't know his mother."

Suzanne asked whether or not Lenore had packed all her Enid Blyton books.

"Can we swim before we go to the city?" Lennie asked, deflecting.

"It'll be cold."

"I know." Lennie stomped down the stairs to the dock, peeling off her clothes, standing shivering in her underwear. "Come on."

She would be a marriage counsellor, he imagined a moment later, treading water in the icy lake with Lennie and Suzanne, exhilarated, the argument on hold.

Her lips were turning blue. Suzanne herded her toward the ladder. "Time to get out."

"Why aren't we coming?" Lennie asked.

"It's too expensive." This was more or less true. "I wish you were coming, you and your mother. But we can't afford it."

"It's around the world," Suzanne said. She was being *helpful*. "It would cost way too much for us to go with Daddy."

Lenore hadn't called him Daddy since she was three so she knew her mother was lying.

"You can send James a letter with Daddy."

"Don't call him Daddy."

Chapter Eight

Before dawn on the morning of his departure for Japan, Emmett descended the stairs of his home in Ottawa. It was cold. He wore pyjama bottoms. His upper body and feet were bare. He went to the kitchen, to the drawer where they kept candles and a flashlight in case of blackouts, and removed the flashlight. Then he went to the hall cupboard and got his coat and went out by the back door to the garage, entering by the crooked wooden door.

They normally squeezed the Alfa Romeo in beside the new Parisienne. A couple of days ago, he'd noticed a scratch in the Alfa's paint and had persuaded Suzanne to take it in for bodywork, arguing that they should get it repaired while he was out of the country. He didn't like for Suzanne to be noticeable when he wasn't here to watch out for her, and the Parisienne would be harder to follow.

In the concrete floor of the old garage, mostly obscured by a patch of oil that had leaked from the old car, was a latch. He bent down and tugged at it. A bit of dirt and oil shifted. He yanked harder and a door lifted, a hatch. He laid the hatch back on the floor of the garage and shone the flashlight down. It was like a root cellar, though it wasn't intended for turnips and potatoes but for liquor; a wine cellar built during Prohibition.

He climbed backward down the narrow wooden stairs to the cellar, his hand groping the damp walls till he found a piece of string wrapped around a nail; he gave the string a pull and a bulb lit up. He laid the flashlight on one of the empty shelves. It smelled of mud in here. The walls of the cellar were made of red brick. On a pallet raised from the floor was a wood barrel stamped with the Seagram's insignia. The lid of the barrel sat askew. He slid the lid aside and set it against the barrel. The top layer was straw. Beneath that was his old tripod, placed over a waterproof satchel. He put the tripod and the satchel aside and leaned into the barrel.

When Robert Morton had put Emmett's files into his hands more than three months ago, Morton had instructed Grey, the rabbity little man who cried in the sun, to take Emmett home. Morton had stayed behind, as had the two plainclothes officers there to witness the delivery of the subject's files. A rare event, such generous disclosure; quite out of the ordinary. En route from the reclusive old house with its groundskeeper's cottage where this last interview had taken place, Grey had engaged Emmett in an odd conversation.

As they drove the several miles, Grey, his face squeezed against the sunlight, sweating in his oversized wool suit, had grown increasingly agitated. He kept looking in the rear-view mirror at Emmett in the backseat. He removed his hat, ran his hand over sparse blond hair, and finally said, "He's just letting you go."

Emmett said that yes, he was going home. He didn't feel confident in Grey's driving, being so blinded by light. He asked him, "You remember the way?"

Grey didn't answer. After several minutes Grey repeated in a tone of incredulity, "Just like that. He fucking lets you go."

Now it was Emmett's turn to be unresponsive. The leather briefcase was heavy on his lap, and he embraced it even while he knew it was meaningless; there would be duplicates with the RCMP, triplicates with the FBI. The files were merely mementos. Grey was muttering, "He lets you go, he fucking lets you go."

When the black Buick finally rolled onto Emmett's street, he instructed Grey not to pull up at the front door of his house but to take him around, down the lane, and drop him off at the back gate. But Grey ignored him and pulled up out front, and then, as if this would further injure Emmett, he pulled into the driveway, braking with a sudden lurch.

Emmett couldn't get out of the car without Grey's assistance because there was no door handle. Grey turned in his seat to look at him. "You make me sick," he said.

"Open the door and we'll part ways."

"I want to puke when I look at you."

"Open the door."

"I fought for my country," Grey said. "I nearly got killed. Buddies of mine, they got killed."

"Yeah, well, it was a war."

Now Grey's tears seemed caused by grief. He said, "I nearly lost my balls in the fight for freedom."

Emmett smiled a little. "Open the door."

"Faggot."

"Sticks and stones."

"Commie faggot."

"Lieutenant Morton will be expecting you to report that you got me here safely. Are you sure you can find your way back?"

"Morton?" Grey scoffed. "I got a more important boss than that dumb fuck."

"Sure you do."

"What do you know about it?"

"Nothing. Only, you have ambitions." Grey began to listen with that greed to be known by another. Emmett said, "You go way beyond this town. You're even working with men outside the country. The RCMP don't know about all the work you're doing. Important work. For freedom."

"How do you know?"

"Morton told me."

"He doesn't know!"

Emmett smiled.

Grey wiped the tears from the side of his face. "I should shoot you. Not right now. When the time is right."

"Open the door."

"I should shoot your whole family."

"Open the door. I'll take my souvenirs and you'll never see me again."

"Oh. Don't worry. I'll see you again." Grey got out of the car. He was coming around, sullen and frustrated to have to let Jones go free, when the door to the house opened and Suzanne rushed out. Lenore tried to follow her and Suzanne shrieked at her to go back, pushing her inside the house and then stumbling down the front steps. She was weeping. She stopped cold when she saw Grey standing between her and the car and cried, "Give me back my husband!"

Inside the car, Emmett was calling her to go back inside. He could sense Grey's thrill, Grey's pleasure. Suzanne made a movement toward the car and Grey stepped toward her, Emmett shouting, "Leave it!" Suzanne finally looked at him, then at Grey, and backed up toward the house.

Grey opened the car door, shaking; he actually reeked, a sharp burnt stink came from him. Grey's voice, trembling, "I seen her," he said triumphantly, "I seen her in lots of ways." Emmett got out of the car, carrying the heavy briefcase. Grey's face was pink and wet. "Your lady friend."

"My wife."

"Sick fuck," Grey said. "I tailed her for years 'n years." He put his hand in the shape of a gun, aimed at where Suzanne stood, and said, "Pow."

Emmett walked quickly to his house and propelled Suzanne inside. Suzanne was still crying, but Lenore was seated primly on the couch wearing a grey cotton dress, her birthday dress, with white bobby socks and her new shiny black shoes; she sat gravely but dry-eyed, like Alice in Wonderland, beyond surprise. Emmett slid the briefcase into the hall closet behind the coats and then he watched the street from behind the drapes until the Buick had cruised slowly out of sight.

Later that night he'd take the briefcase out to the garage and put it into the trunk of the Alfa, to leave it there till he could hide it in the vault under the garage. The encounter with the Rabbit had so frightened Suzanne, she hadn't noticed the briefcase. He'd managed to calm her down, getting lunch on the table for her and Lennie, pouring wine for Suzanne, telling her that the meeting had been a formality, just a formality to mark the end of the investigation, it was really good news, the true end of the investigation, and yes, wasn't that driver a bizarre little man, poor guy, really you have to feel sorry for him in a way, still shell-shocked, a war vet who never got over it, we'll never see him again.

Emmett hadn't destroyed any of the files, though the transcripts and many of the photographs were painful to look at. But air travel, especially of the kind afforded by the Canadian government, was a risky affair. He had to try to see it all through Suzanne's eyes, should anything happen to him on this trip to Japan.

He leaned and dug deep into the barrel till he got a grip on the heavy leather briefcase so generously donated to him by the RCMP, clutching it to his chest, bringing up his cold bare feet with their traces of motor oil till he was sitting cross-legged on the bare wooden bench. Then he began his own, personal analysis of the Jones files.

It took forty minutes because he lingered over the almost-forgotten moments. Suzanne, and then Aoi, each of them photographed in the snow. He would not destroy much of it, but he did make certain selections for disposal. Morton had given him the originals of the photographs, he knew, because they'd not excised the logo of the RCMP's film shop. This meant exactly nothing.

Chapter Nine

Emmett said goodbye to his family at Ottawa's Uplands airport. Dr. Kimura had insisted on driving them. Emmett had to ask him, "How can you take a Tuesday morning away from your practice?"

Kimura said, "I left by the back door."

"Your patients don't know you're gone?"

"They're accustomed to waiting." Kimura winked at Lennie. He was being very merry.

Emmett could see the apertures in Kimura's eyes open and shut as he switched from true to feigned merriment. The doctor had kept in contact only by mail with the sister he'd left behind in Kobe; he had not returned to Japan since the night when he and Emmett had got into the brawl that ended with the death of a Japanese policeman. He said that he preferred to let sleeping dogs lie, and refused to leave Canada; this trip to Japan that Emmett was undertaking filled him with misgivings. Emmett had told him that it was irrational to worry about a bar fight so many years ago. Obviously the crime was never to be solved; no one would now be able to connect them with the policeman's death. Kimura agreed, this was rational, but "I believe that some lives must move in one direction only; I will never go back."

Emmett flew to Kobe, the city of his birth, in the company

of some fellows from Trade and Commerce. It caught the imagination of the civil service that Canada would deal in *know-how*, pure as sunlight. He was appointed as a translator, though he would soon discover that the Kobe Steel men spoke perfect English.

Aoi said that he could meet her at the seaside and that she would bring James. He arrived to find her on the pier. An onshore wind was blowing. Her uncommon beauty was more austere than it had been nearly ten years ago. She was self-possessed, a totem, her face like carved cypress while her skirt tussled in the wind. Her clothing was modern, but it was the same black and ochre of the Manchurian cloak she'd been wearing the last time he'd seen her. She seemed taller, more statuesque than he remembered. She gave a dignified bow, establishing that Emmett would not be permitted to come close. He felt ashamed at the way he'd left her, and embarrassed that he'd imagined she might thank him for the money he sent.

Far from shore a flock of children swam with strong expert strokes past the surf, out to the green roll of the waves, their cries carried on the wind.

"That one," said Aoi, proudly pointing. Emmett's eyes followed the fastest swimmer. She pointed insistently, "That one," toward the pack of swimmers; with their dark heads in the water, they could be seals. And there was his son. One among them, strongly swimming but not the strongest.

"They swim so far out!" He wanted to say, Please call him back! How can she so calmly watch the boy risk his life?

The children rose and fell with the waves, their naked

shoulders gleaming. The sea swells lifted them together to let them fall together. Even from this distance he could see their joy. The sight of his son pierced him with love and pride, an elation that also brought a spasm of grief for his own father, and he dimly understood why, understanding perhaps for the first time just how much his father must have loved him.

But he had a meeting that same afternoon with the men involved in the Kobe Steel agreement. And this evening there was a dinner-party arranged by the ambassador. Aoi sensed his distraction, turned full to face him, and in English she said, "You have things to do." Now he was convinced, it was the old Manchurian cloak stylishly remade, the wind rippling its rich black fabrics, its ochre braid, all of Aoi's magnificent physique given to motion but for the lacquered hair. Her moon face, her big mouth, sensuous and unapproachable.

Speech between them in any language was impossible; there was too much to say. What has it been like for you, raising a boy alone? A boy fathered by a *gaijin*. He could not touch her, but he was desperate to touch his son. He asked Aoi, "Can you call him?"

He had forgotten her vocal training with the *biwa*, the masculine, glottal Japanese by which she called over the windy waves. A boy in the surf stopped, hearing her voice. Emmett could see his excitement, see him shout to his friends and start swimming toward the beach, the other boys following, half a dozen boys racing to their towels to dry their faces, running up the steps to the pier.

The boys crowded around James, who presented himself before this western man. He was nine years old, no longer childish. He did not look like Aoi very much; his features were more proportionate, his beauty more conventional. He was tall and boldly shy; the victory Emmett liked so much in his mother shone in his eyes. Again speaking English, Aoi said, "This is your father."

The other boys pushed James's shoulders, but he held his place, his upright posture. He did not act like a fatherless child; he showed confidence. With a steady voice, Emmett told him that he was very glad to see him. James thanked him in Japanese, his eyes darting to Aoi for a prompt.

Emmett's hands started to shake, and he thrust them into his pockets, but somehow this gesture seemed offhand or disrespectful, so he brought them out again, visibly shaking, and tentatively touched James's shoulder. The boy responded with a guileless smile.

Aoi made a sound Emmett couldn't quite decipher, and James, with all the boys flying around him, shot off, back toward the beach, James with special consciousness, as if crowned with laurel.

"Can I possibly see him again?"

The slightest flinch in Aoi, a tremor. He didn't dare consider how much he might have hurt her.

"You don't have to," he told her. "You don't have to let me see him." He couldn't bring himself to say that he was sorry; it was impossible to apologize for the shame he must have incurred by not returning to her before he left Japan, the difficulties she must have encountered. He'd convinced himself that Aoi was cold toward him, that she was sublimely self-sufficient. That she conveniently would not love him, so he could love Suzanne pleasurably. He'd ridden another wave of illusion. But now he was again awake.

He said, "The money I send doesn't give me the right to see James." He wished it did, and he wished that James would think so one day.

Aoi looked at him. She wasn't cold, she was lucid, and her lucidity made her generous — he remembered the small portion of rice she'd offered to him the night they first met. He remembered her with his blind body.

Chapter Ten

There was a man present at every turn at the American ambassador's dinner party who introduced himself as Jim Smith and claimed he was from an insurance outfit in New Jersey, but Emmett couldn't guess his function. When he tried to find out, the man waved his hands in front of Emmett's face and said, "Ho, friendly Canadian, I'm strictly an observer." At dinner, Jim Smith was seated beside the ambassador, who was seated to the right of Ikeda Hayato, minister of trade and industry.

Emmett took his seat at Ikeda's left. Ikeda was stern, greying, with thin, peevish lips. Emmett politely observed, "I understand Kobe Steel will open offices in New York next year. That's a lot of growth." Ikeda merely grunted without turning his head.

He was rebuked, though the Kobe men had boasted of their developments in America and in Germany, rebelliously intent to show off their internationalism. Emmett looked down the table past Ikeda's blunt grey face and caught the eye of Jim Smith—a lanky man, fair-skinned with light pinfeather hair and sharp, friendly eyes. Jim Smith's tuxedo bagged a little as if he'd recently lost weight; he put his elbow on the table to rest his chin on his fist, and winked—or it was that kind of blinking smile that makes winks inevitable.

A voice came from his left. "Try the duck."

Emmett turned to look at his neighbour, a genial Japanese man with a full head of white hair and a broad flat nose. He looked to be in his late fifties and in excellent health. Unlike most of the men at the table, he didn't wear glasses. He had moist red lips and a wide cheerful smile that revealed a set of false teeth. Emmett had seen him before but couldn't yet place him.

A waiter stationed behind them bent forward to insert a tray of duck prepared in the Chinese fashion, and his neighbour repeated, "Try it. It's good." He introduced himself, "I am Kazuo Takiji," looking Jones over.

Emmett remembered Kazuo now. Kazuo had been senior in the Yakuza hierarchy in 1950, when Emmett had used his position of policy analyst to look into the influence of the Japanese gangsters on Japan's Liberal Party. Kazuo was then running several gangs in the Kobe region, as a rising member of the Yamaguchi-gumi, the biggest Yakuza family. Apparently he'd been successful.

"We have many outsiders coming to Japan now," Kazuo was saying. "'The post-war is over!'" He began to laugh. "Have you heard that expression, Mr. Jones?" Emmett was aware of the minister of trade and industry to his right, of Ikeda's base rate of disapproval. "It is the genius of Mr. Ikeda to coin that phrase, is it not? 'The post-war is over!'"

Ikeda said nothing, did not even look.

"And now my old friend Kishi is playing golf with President Eisenhower," Kazuo continued.

Kishi Nobusuke. Kishi was a Class-A war criminal, discharged after more than two years in jail, driven away from Sugamo Prison in an American army jeep. Now Kishi was prime minister of Japan, playing golf with Eisenhower.

"We are all friendly here." Kazuo Takiji wore a dinner jacket rather than a tuxedo, a rich fabric with satin lapels. The French cuffs of his white shirt extended below the sleeves of his jacket so as to cover his wrists almost to the base of his thumb. It would look comical if it weren't so deliberate. His shirt collar recalled the regency style, rising high around his neck.

Emmett asked about Kazuo's involvement in Kobe Steel.

Kazuo's smile hung in the air while Kazuo himself withdrew from such intemperate curiosity. "I am a philanthropist," he said.

Emmett indicated with a nod, That's nice, retreating into the mask of Canadian civil servant. "I'm sure you do much good work."

Kazuo gave a broad smile with his false teeth. A wet smile that hid nothing of its own cynicism, it struck Emmett as vulgar. Kazuo reached to the centre of the table for a carafe of sake, a gesture that tugged at the long sleeves of his dress shirt, revealing a tattoo swirling around his wrist. He was aware that Emmett had noticed, and when he resumed his seat, he tipped his head and Emmett saw what he was intended to see: a swirl of coloured ink on Kazuo's neck. It was a custom of the Yakuza, the Japanese mafia, to tattoo their entire bodies. He felt the strangeness of Kazuo's dragon skin beneath the expensive suit.

While Kazuo drank and ate, he talked, ostensibly to Emmett but loudly enough so Ikeda could hear. The subject was "philanthropy," Kazuo making much use of the English word, which—as Emmett began to drink with him—took on mongrel shapes. Emmett mildly observed that it had never occurred to him that motorboat racing could be conceived as philanthropic.

The smile vanished. In a deep loud voice, Kazuo said, "You are a socialist." This was intended as an insult. "Communist," Kazuo insisted.

At the end of the table, Jim Smith in his oversized tuxedo broke into laughter and called, "Mr. Kazuo! Are you tormenting our friendly Canadian?" Jim Smith stood.

Kazuo looked at Jim Smith and, after a short pause, switched to English. "Who is this twig? He does not approve of boat-racing!"

"Well hang him for a prude," said Jim Smith.

Emmett said, "I'm with External Affairs, Mr. Kazuo. The Canadian government."

Contempt swept quickly over Kazuo's face. "Does this mean you have no ideas of your own? Maybe you are a good subject of your emperor!" Then he smiled again. His wet red mouth.

Kazuo and Jim Smith laughed. Emmett looked across the table to his counterpart in Trade and Commerce, Clark Haywood. Haywood gave him a wary look and addressed himself to the Kobe Steel man seated beside him, putting his hand around his face to block his view of Jones squirming between the paws of the Japanese mafia.

Kazuo loudly addressed the table, "Such sentiment! The kokutai has been punished! Not to the liking of President Truman! *Punished by fire! Burnt to ash by the inhuman bombs!* Now what do you do? You mimic us."

Ikeda muttered in Japanese, "This will wait for another occasion."

"But life is fleeting!" Kazuo persisted, then mockingly to Emmett, "like cherry blossoms." And laughed with what Emmett hoped was greater goodwill. "I am an ambassador, just as our host is an ambassador!"

The Canadian ambassador turned grimly to Emmett and then was startled when he felt something touch his back. It was the hand of Jim Smith touching the ambassador while he walked past, coming toward Emmett now, his black dress shoes gleaming. Smith leaned down to say in Emmett's ear, "How about we go somewhere we can talk quietly about our divine differences?" He firmly pulled Emmett's chair away from the table.

Emmett was aware of Clark Haywood's pale face and the silence that had overtaken the place. The ambassador began to get out of his chair, Ikeda preventing him with a light touch to the arm while he murmured reassurance.

Jim Smith made an elaborate show of thanking his host. "I'm borrowing your guest for a couple of hours, Mr. Ambassador. I promise to get him back to his hotel a healthy man."

The ambassador nodded curtly. "I have your word on that, Jim."

Emmett, flanked by Kazuo Takiji and Jim Smith from New Jersey, considered his options. He didn't think that Smith and Kazuo would actually hurt him; nobody wanted an international incident. This was the clue he'd been waiting for: what *is* his role on this trade mission? He was curious and invigorated with sake-courage. He bowed to Ikeda and to the ambassador and said good night.

Chapter Eleven

Emmett, who at eleven years of age had twice tried to join a kendo club and twice a karate club and had been rejected every time because he was a westerner, soon was watching karate at one of Kazuo's special nightclubs. He responded with warm admiration. It was wise to show respect to the don. He hadn't had any contact with Japanese gangsters since his time with the Liaison Mission in Tokyo. And he'd never had an evening on the town as the guest of one. Some of Kazuo's mannerisms reminded him of a man he'd dealt with briefly in Ottawa, a devout French Catholic making a fortune building bridges and highways, the same bull-chested, powerful build, the generosity with money, the physical affection for the men in his employ. Kazuo's staff at the club obviously loved and respected him.

At his karate club, the old gangster was surrounded by younger men of extraordinary refinement and sincerity. Emmett watched for excess, bravado, bullying, and saw instead a keen, clear balance, finely pitched. He'd almost forgotten the particularly pure intensity of young Japanese men.

At this late hour the matches were for the masters, while the acolytes watched. The place was lit like a theatre or a nightclub, with white-hot footlights and stark spots on a low stage. The white uniforms blurred with movement. Each engagement lasted no more than a minute, a brief flurry to the deathblow, then withdrawal. Mesmerizing variations of *kihon*, feints and kicks, the hoarse shout, disengagement.

Kazuo lit a cigar and strolled off into the darkness that surrounded the stage, leaving Emmett alone with Jim from the New Jersey insurance company. Jim pulled a flask from his pocket and poured whisky into Emmett's tea before adding some to his own. "These places were illegal after the war," he said. "We weren't too keen on Japs doing martial arts."

"Yes. I remember."

"Our ban was lifted in '52. You were gone by then."

Emmett's face didn't reveal any surprise at Jim's knowledge of his history. He said, "That's right. I was back in Canada." He was thinking, Jim probably knows that the Canadian government has sold me off, given my personal files to the FBI. That would be what had brought me to Jim's attention, whoever Jim really is.

Jim was watching the match. Emmett added, "I think I'll hit the road."

"Not yet."

"I'll say goodnight to Mr. Kazuo." He finished his spiked tea and stood to go. "Thanks for the nightcap."

"Sit down."

Emmett sat down again, and Jim poured more whisky into his cup. "You were on your way to a pretty good position on the Southeast Asia desk when they pulled you. Why'd they do that?"

"How do you know about this?"

Jim shrugged. "It's my job."

"You're not with Prudential."

"Nope." Jim smiled boyishly. He didn't apply that all-knowing irony, the smirking one-upmanship Emmett had come to associate with snoops. "So?" Jim said. "What happened in 1951, made you fall down the ladder?"

"Sounds like you already know the whole story."

"There's never a whole story, is there."

"My name came up. You know that part, I imagine."

"Sure. But why? You a communist?"

"No."

"Just when we need men with some real understanding over here, my government fires everybody who knows anything about Southeast Asia. So now what are we going to do? Let 'em have their goddamn war in peace?"

Jim was talking about Vietnam. But the war wasn't yet official. Emmett said nothing. He had a fleeting impulse to point out that it wasn't Jim's government that had "fired" him.

Jim grumbled, "We wouldn't be backing Diem if we had anybody with any brains making policy. But" — shrugging good naturedly — "who listens?"

Jim's manner was expansive; he appeared to be worldly and disinterested. He asked Emmett if he'd like to work in Asia, in South Vietnam, saying, "It's a nice place if you can stay out of trouble." When Emmett didn't answer, Jim went on, "They're keeping you out. Aren't they? But you know, there are other ways to skin a cat."

"I don't think I'm interested in cutting loose from External."

"Why not?" Jim emptied the flask into Emmett's cup. "You don't like risk?"

"Are you suggesting some kind of — consultancy?"

"That's one word for it," Jim said, smiling. "Hasn't anybody ever approached you till now? Seems hard to believe. Not even when you were stationed in Tokyo? Before you got tangled up in the McCarthy circus?"

"I like working as an analyst." Emmett was watching the match when he said this. All Jim could see of his eyes was the light from the stage glancing off his glasses.

Jim leaned back in his chair to view Emmett better. He said, "You have a talent for finding the little pieces, putting them together so they make sense. You're a rare bird, Mr. Jones." He was exaggerating. Emmett knew he was intended to understand that he had a reputation extending further than anyone had ever let him know. He wondered just how much Jim knew about him. "Tell me," Jim went on, "what do you think's going to happen in Vietnam?"

Here was a test. Emmett said, "I think the Lao Dong party is going to step up an insurgency." It was a relief to use his mind, a cold relief from the heat of his frustrations. But he was sure now that he was being played, and he told himself not to fuck it up by getting angry.

Jim was nodding thoughtfully.

Emmett went on, calmly analytic, a policy analyst. "Hanoi waited a long time for a political solution. It never came. It could have. But the moment passed. President Diem is a dictator. Something like" — he glanced around the club looking for Kazuo — "not far off from our friend here, but more dangerous. Maybe even crazy. Now the Vietcong have been pushed to the extreme. They'll get backing from the Politburo. They'll go to war. And it'll be like a bushfire, impossible to put out." He was reiterating the observations he'd made in his memorandum to Prime Minister Diefenbaker, but here in the gangster's karate club the information felt more powerful.

Jim whistled. "Are you sure you're not already working for us?"

Emmett caught the bait, *us*, ignored it, and said, "I'm talking too much." He had used bait of his own; he wanted to know who Jim Smith worked for.

"How'd you come to such dire conclusions, Mr. Jones?"

"Osmosis."

"You sure are a puzzle."

Emmett didn't respond. A match had ended with a shout. Now a man in his twenties faced his much older opponent. They circled and engaged.

For a while Jim seemed intent on watching the white blur of action. Then he clicked his tongue wistfully and said, "Here, you find what remains of the old Samurai ways. The Bushido. Perfect raw material for evil bastards like Kishi. Like Ikeda. Like our good friend Kazuo. If there was one, if there was *one* first crime in the war, it was in corrupting a fine old tradition." Jim returned his attention to Emmett. "You ever noticed, how one thing always contains its opposite?"

"As a matter of fact, I have."

Jim put his elbows on the table, his hands pressed together so his chin rested on his thumbs. "A man's strength is also his weakness. Same with a system. The greatest systems on earth carry the germ of their own destruction.

"Let me ask you something," Jim went on. "It's pure speculation and it won't cost you a cent."

"Go ahead." Emmett took a drink.

"I happen to know you for a specialist when it comes to Japan. You know more than most civilians about the whole Asia problem."

Emmett was about to demur, but Jim cut him off, "You know a lot about Bushido."

"I've read about it," Emmett said and laughed.

But Jim remained serious, slightly ponderous, as if he'd had too much to drink. "The principles these karate masters live by. Makoto and all that."

"Yes." Emmett felt that he was more sober than Jim was. He corrected Jim's pronunciation. "Makoto," he said, "yes."

"Say you had to choose one principle, one virtue out of all the virtues. What would it be?" Jim asked.

Emmett thought about it. *Makoto* is admirable. Truthfulness, sincerity. In a child. Sincerity can make you a fool; it can make you delusional. Duplicity, compassionate duplicity, is a more natural skill in a man with real integrity. He recalled several of the other Japanese words associated with Bushido. *Yuki*, for one: bravery, heroism. With a quiet surge of love he thought about Suzanne, he thought about Lenore, and James, his son. He thought about the abiding love and stubborn hope that had driven him, and the loneliness of his position. His private life was an endurance test. His heroism, if he dared call it that, existed in his loves.

He let Jim wait a moment and then he said, "Chugi. It means loyalty. Devotion. But in Japanese terms. It doesn't quite translate. But yes, I would say, chugi. That is what I live by."

Jim was watching him with bleary, unfocused eyes. He seemed quite drunk; he showed the drunk's tendency to hear too much in what is being simply expressed. He slurringly repeated, "Chugi."

"Yes. I think so."

"Loyalty."

"That's right."

"Devotion."

"Yes."

Jim sat back in his chair, vaguely astonished. "I would've thought, given the cards that've been dealt you, you'd've come to quite a different conclusion."

"And what would that be?"

"Oh. I don't know. Your country accuses you of being a traitor. You stand up to them. You stand up and clear your name. You retain your honour. You don't cave."

"Yes."

Jim said, "Don't you ever want to break away? I mean, even in your own mind? You have been *betrayed*. And you play loyal public servant?" Jim hit the table with the palm of his hand and repeated, "*Betrayed*."

"That's my own affair."

"I don't dispute it. What I don't get is why you haven't struck out on your own. With what you know, your languages, your background. With what you've learned the hard way, how things work, how things can swing against you, easy as a blade to the heart. Why not break for it? Chugi," he added contemptuously, "it's for amateurs. Inferiors."

"I don't think you understand how the principles of Bushido work."

"Meiyo," Jim said. His accent was alarming but was close enough. Now it was Emmett's turn to feel contemptuous. "Meiyo," Jim repeated more loudly.

"I understand."

"Glory!" Jim said loudly. "Glory! What else is worth fighting for? What else but glory drives great men? Civilization might dissolve into a puddle of piss, but there will still be the few, the few men strong enough to abide by the principle of meiyo!"

The expression was so baldly hyperbolic, he wondered if Jim was joking. Jim's eyes slid sideways to look at him. He now appeared to be entirely sober. "Like I said. You are a puzzle, Emmett Jones."

"A boring sort of puzzle then."

"Boring." Jim snorted. "That's quite clever."

"I assure you, what you see is a loyal civil servant."

Jim snorted. "Okay."

"Do I present anything other than the well-mannered profile of a devoted subject of the Dominion?"

"Not for a minute."

"There." Emmett finished the whisky in his cup. "You promised the ambassador you'd see me safely back to my hotel."

Jim stood. "I'll tell our host that you're leaving."

"Thank you."

Jim left him alone at the table. Ten minutes passed and Jim reappeared and said, "A driver's outside."

He thanked Jim without further question, and was making his way to the door when he heard Jim say, "I suggest you stay home tonight."

He turned.

"I'm suggesting you call it a night. No wandering around all on your lonesome." Jim's winking smile insinuated ownership, domination.

"Yes," Emmett waved vaguely. "Good night, Jim."

Chapter Twelve

Emmett held his hat in his hands while Aoi ushered him into her suite and guided him to a western-style living room with a plush white carpet, white leather furniture, and a glass coffee table. He'd always associated her with the old house on the estate, and now he was disoriented to see her here, in this chic apartment that looked like outer space. He was her guest for lunch. He had come as a modest saviour, prepared to reassess his contributions to her household. He'd brought his chequebook.

He was careful not to cut his shins on the glass while he navigated, dizzy with light, toward the sofa. Aoi kneeled at the table. He was fascinated by her eyes, the winged black eyeliner, the false eyelashes. She wore narrow black pants and a white blouse with a scarf at her throat, maybe playing the part of an Italian moll. A cigarette case sat beside a matching lighter on the glass table, as if suspended in mid-air. She opened it and offered him a cigarette. He declined and she took one for herself. He'd never seen her smoke before. She gave him one of her frank looks, a candid mockery of her own poses.

"Are you hungry?" she asked him.

"Is James going to join us?"

"My cook has prepared your favourite meal."

"Thank you." You have a cook? he wondered. The suite was spare of ornament, except for a fine woodblock print, and the dining room table set with Chinese porcelain. And a beautiful

Kakejiku, a silk scroll, herons in reeds with snow, trembling slightly as if with age.

Aoi saw him admiring the scroll and said, "Meiji-era." Then she said, "Mackerel. Miso. Stewed cherries. I remember what you like."

The fan whirred soothingly. The apartment block was on a busy street but soundproof. He said, "You look beautiful." She laughed. "And James," he persisted, leaning toward her. He liked the smell of cigarettes. "He's happy?"

"You saw him." She smiled to indicate that yes, he's obviously happy.

"When will he be joining us?"

"In a moment. I told him I want to speak with you alone first."

"All right." He waited.

She dragged on her cigarette and then stamped it out carefully with her polished hands. Quietly she asked, "Do you wonder how I manage so well?"

"Yes," he admitted. "But you don't owe me an explanation. I still want to contribute to his care."

She acknowledged this with a slight bow of the head. "It's not necessary. Your money."

"It's necessary to me," he said.

And she nodded again, declining to press him on the measure of his guilt in abandoning her. "I have a profession," Aoi said.

"Yes, I thought you must."

"I work for the Americans. Since the war, I've worked for the Americans.'"

He remembered a blue kimono passing in near darkness on the road past Sachiko's house.

"At first I had nothing and needed their protection," she said. "They trained me in financial services. Now I'm useful to them. They want the government to go a certain way, I help them."

Emmett thought of New Jersey, the craggy head with its light pinfeathers, and observed, "The Americans are involved with the deal we're arranging with Kobe Steel."

"They're involved with everything. Everything is an American deal with Kishi. The Americans want the LDP to run the country forever."

The Liberal Democratic Party. America's choice of Japanese governments. Prime Minister Kishi playing golf with President Eisenhower.

"I invest the Americans' money in various companies that I create," she said. "They pay me a good commission!" She laughed quietly, frowning. "I'm being very candid with you, Emmett."

He said, "It sounds like money laundering."

She lifted her face to him, inhaling the smoke rising from her lips. "It is very much like money laundering."

He looked around the apartment. "Lucrative," he said.

"You and Mrs. Jones don't need to send me money. I provide for James very well."

"Please," he said.

She shrugged.

"When will James be joining us?" he asked again.

A door opened and the boy approached almost silently across the white carpet. He was classically dressed, as if from pre-war Showa, in belted white trousers and white shoes.

Emmett stood up, undecided as to whether he should offer

to shake his son's hand. He searched for himself in James's face. James blushed and tried not to smile, just the way Lennie would do, repressing a grin. It was eerie, an improbable constellation of influence. Emmett had never doubted that he had fathered this boy. He thought of him often, his ghost son, loved him instinctively, compulsively. Now here he was, James, tall for his age, well mannered, self-possessed despite the heat that had risen to his face.

Emmett said hello. "Thank you for seeing me." Then he regretted saying that; the boy was only nine, too young to judge his father.

If a cook had prepared lunch, she wasn't there now to serve it. Aoi brought the meal on a tray from the kitchen. It was good food, but the soup was cold; it had been left ready to serve some time ago. He realized that he'd seen the cook clamber down the front stoop as he arrived; he'd held the door for her and she had looked at him closely, with a glimmer of malice.

Aoi encouraged James at lunch, "Go ahead. Ask him."

The boy began to speak in Japanese. Aoi reprimanded him, "In English." He began again. Did he live in a house in Canada? Did it have a big yard? Is the ocean nearby? Then he asked, "Does my sister look like me?"

Aoi rose and gathered the plates on the tray and took them to the kitchen.

Emmett, glad to be alone with him, said, "No. Except she's tall like you."

"Will I ever meet her?"

"Would you like to?"

"My mother refuses to go to Canada."

"Well, she has work to do here."

"She says they would never give her permission."

Emmett wondered what the boy knew. "Who?" he asked tentatively. "Who are they?"

James shrugged, kicked the legs of his chair, and said, "Mr. Smith."

"Who is Mr. Smith?"

"He said."

"What?"

"We must not go away."

"Did he say why?"

James darkened. Emmett thought, Children are so unerringly averse to deception. James looked toward the swinging door leading to the kitchen and said, "I don't know."

Aoi returned. "You may leave the table now." She ran her hand through her boy's hair and nudged him gently off his chair. "Go, darling."

James wiped his hands on the back of his white trousers as he stood stubbornly beside his chair.

Aoi straightened. Emmett sensed that she was surprised at this small show of defiance; she had strong discipline over him.

James walked around till he was standing close to Emmett. Emmett lightly put his hand under the boy's chin. "I'm very happy to see you."

"Thank you," James said.

"You're a good boy. Your mother is lucky."

James smiled, his pride restored. "If we could go to Canada—"

"That's enough," said Aoi firmly.

James blushed and quietly left the room. When he was gone and had closed the door behind him, Emmett turned to Aoi. "Who is Mr. Smith?"

"There are many. You met one last night."

"Mr. Smith is CIA."

Aoi didn't respond. She lit a cigarette, blew out the smoke, and looked at him. He was beginning to see just how far Gembey and External's Security branch would go in their cooperation with US security interests. He'd been sent here to meet Mr. Smith.

"It's dangerous, isn't it?" he asked. "Money laundering for the CIA."

She shook her head. "No, no," she said mildly. "It's how the government works."

Chapter Thirteen

Lennie was peering up at him as if she'd never seen him before in her life. He was aware of Clark Haywood of Trade and Commerce studying this airport reunion. Haywood had been nervously friendly for the last five days, making a lot of small talk. Now he shook Emmett's hand with great friendliness, "Nice work, Emmett. Glad to have you on board," tipping his hat to Suzanne and stumbling over Lennie in his haste to get away. If Emmett knew more than Haywood did about the money for the Kobe Steel Works deal, Haywood wanted to keep it that way.

Emmett stood in his wrinkled coat with his briefcase at his feet. Dr. Kimura had driven Suzanne and Lenore here to collect him. Suzanne, Lenore, and Kimura now stood to receive what had been sent off at the other end by Aoi, James, and Mr. Smith. Emmett had been awake for most of the past seventy-two hours. He imagined these people as six clay figures he'd take to his tomb. Suzanne laughed nervously. "Emmett? Hello?"

He explained that he hadn't been able to sleep, that he was half-crazed by the din of flying in the North Star. He bent to kiss Lenore and had the disconcerting experience of coming inches from her impersonal grey eyes.

"Where is my brother?" she asked.

"With his mother, in Japan."

"Will he come?"

"Maybe."

"When?"

"Sometime, someday."

Lennie slid her hand into his. It was like being given a white dove. Her cool, impossibly soft skin. She wanted to know, "Did he ask about me?"

"Yes."

"He wants to come, doesn't he."

"Yes."

"So," Lennie persisted, "why didn't he?"

"He has to go to school."

"He can go to school here."

They were walking. Lennie tried to swing his hand and he told her to stop it. Then he apologized. "I'm tired, Lennie."

Lenore was wearing a wide skirt with a crinoline that fell below her knees and she looked gawky and frumpish. She self-consciously collected the fabric and swung it like a country dancer. He felt the lingering presence of his son. As if he'd had a love affair while he was away. Suzanne at his side dropped back to walk with Kimura, and Lenore skipped awkwardly ahead so Emmett was walking alone.

In Kobe, Mr. Smith had arrived at Aoi's apartment and insisted on driving him to the train station. Emmett had his suitcase with him when he went to see James once more before leaving the country. During this visit, again Aoi had left him alone with James for a few minutes.

The boy delighted him with his refinement, his perfect face lifted trustingly. They talked about baseball. James knew all about the New York Yankees. He'd run out of the room and returned with his baseball glove and softball. Emmett was looking at his watch, calculating how he could squeeze in some time to play catch with his son, when Mr. Smith walked in.

He didn't knock, but he didn't enter like one who was coming home either. There was no evidence that he lived here. Aoi rushed in from the kitchen at the sound of his voice. Her nervousness, the entry without knocking, all made Emmett realize that Aoi had no real ownership of this place, and he pulled the boy to himself.

"Well, friendly Canadian, all packed?"

"Hello, Jim."

Jim clicked his heels, "Came to give you a lift to the station."

"That's all right. No need."

"Nonsense." Jim picked up Emmett's suitcase. He gave one of his winking smiles at James and asked him, "Want to come?"

James said that he would like to. He spoke formally to Jim, Mr. Smith, but Emmett couldn't detect any fear.

"Right! Tell your mother, she looks fine, or we'll be waiting an hour while she changes her clothes."

Aoi didn't banter but calmly took her handbag and put on lipstick, saying to James, "We will ask Mr. Smith to drop us at the market on the way back."

Jim drove to the station, and all three of them accompanied Emmett inside. Jim steered him ahead of Aoi and James. "Consider my proposal?" he asked.

"Yes. And no thank you."

"Going to stay on the farm, are you?" Jim said.

"I've got a family to support."

"Pays well. Better'n what you're getting now. By a long shot."

"I'm doing all right."

Jim shook his head in good-natured disappointment. "You don't understand." He stopped, and Emmett had to stop too. Jim told Aoi, "Go away for a while, will you?" The boy hesitated. Jim winked at him. "Get your mother to buy you an ice cream. Go on. There's still time to say goodbye." Aoi gave Emmett a solemn look and ushered the boy away. Jim said, "You send Aoi what? A couple hundred bucks a month? Back home, you have a wife who's been — compromised. That's tough, puts you in a vulnerable position."

Emmett expressed nothing; nothing in his body revealed that he'd heard the slur against his wife.

Jim, as if setting up a joke, resumed, "Hey, Emmett, what's the difference between a prophet and a scribe?" Emmett didn't answer. Jim said, "The prophet isn't just *in* the game. The prophet *is* the game. The prophet doesn't describe things. He sees things before they happen. Maybe — maybe the prophet makes things happen. Now, the scribe, he just copies, he just duplicates what the prophet sees. That stuff you said last night? Your take on Hanoi and the Russians? I don't know how you come to know that, but —"

Emmett interrupted him, "*I.F. Stone's Weekly.*"

"What?"

"The newspaper. *I.F. Stone's Weekly.* I subscribe."

"Oh. The commie rag." Jim laughed. "Scribe."

"I don't pretend otherwise."

"I don't give a rat's ass what you pretend to be, you timid little shit," Jim said lightly. "Chugi. Virtue of the husband drone. But you work for us, understand? You think your two hundred a month sends your son to private school? You think a bastard son of a gaijin will last long without a hell of a lot of money backing him? I'm his father. The American government is his father."

Emmett winced at Jim's hyperbole and asked, "What do you want?"

"Why do you think we let you into the Caribbean when you were barely dry from an investigation into your loyalty? You scuttled around Cuba like a dumbass tourist. Now, it's time for you to do some real work. Your government is going to do trade with Cuba. You're going to keep us informed. Make copies for us. Duplicate."

"Who am I keeping informed?" But he knew, it was the CIA. External had set him up in Japan to meet Jim Smith, and now Jim was requiring him to turn around and spy on Canada, to report to the Americans on Canada's trade with Cuba. He almost felt satisfaction that Gembey, too, was being played. The CIA had requested that Gembey first send him to Cuba so soon after the investigation in '53, to test him in the field. Their suspicion that he was a spy had led them now to require him to actually become one. The farcical reiterations in his life.

"Photographs, pictures, you know, airports, railways, that kind of thing. Union lists, who's in jail, who's not. What kind of cigars does Castro smoke, who he's fucking."

"I said I have to know who I'm talking to."

"Me. You're talking to me. And if you fuck up" — he nodded toward Aoi and James with his ice cream cone — "she goes to jail for doing business with the Yakuza, and the little prince becomes a pauper."

"I'll think about it."

"Very tough on young James. Tough on your whole family."

Emmett found it hard to speak. But he said, "Leave my family alone."

"You work for us now," said Jim Smith. He took Emmett's elbow and guided him to the booth, collected his ticket, and handed it to him.

"Be a hero. Or you and your family can become another casualty in the war against communism. Along with Aoi there, and young James."

Emmett saw Clark Haywood seated, waiting for the train. Haywood saw him too and pretended to be reading the train schedule, keeping his nose clean.

They were rejoined by Aoi, with James, who suddenly slipped his sticky hand into Emmett's and held it until Emmett had to board. He kissed James's cheek, his fine thin face, and said goodbye, James looking at him trustingly, saying, "I will come?"

"You will come."

Aoi said goodbye to him, calmly meeting his eyes; he guessed that she knew that Jim Smith was bullying him, and he had the impression that she considered this a normal condition.

On the train, Emmett was seated across from Clark Haywood. Haywood glanced out the window to where Aoi and James stood watching. "Family connection," Emmett said.

Haywood, searching for something pleasant, said, "Beautiful woman." Then hurriedly put *The Japan Times* between them.

Now, in Canada, in the Ottawa airport, Lenore turned around and was striding backward, taking big backward steps. "I'm glad you came home, Dad," she said. "Even if you didn't bring me my brother."

He caught up to her and they walked together to claim his suitcase, his hand on her neck, stroking her silky hair.

Emmett was too tired to protest when Kimura put his luggage in the trunk of his car and announced that they would go directly to the gallery so Emmett could see his wife's new work. "You missed the opening," Kimura said, "when your wife was beautiful and alone. You'd better make up for it or you will lose her."

"That's nonsense," said Suzanne, flattered. "Are you too tired, Emmett?" She sounded hopeful. "You want to see it?" she asked. He could only say yes.

Entering the gallery, Emmett was confused at first by the photographs of flowers, sunsets, and puppies adorning the walls. But Suzanne led the way to another room, and he saw what could only be hers. Lenore leaned against the wall near the entrance and slowly slumped till she was sitting on the floor, her legs stretched straight and covered by the unwieldy skirt, mistrustfully regarding her mother's "art."

The faces masked by a hat, the distance and restraint of the poses, the depersonalized actions of the subject, the bizarre makeup and the artifice of her treatment in developing the film, none of this did anything to disguise the fact that they were all photographs of John Norfield.

Emmett took his time in the silent room, making the rounds, Suzanne watching him, waiting, and when he came around full circle and stood before her, she was trembling. "Do you like them?" she asked. He could hear Lenore rustle her crinoline. He nodded yes. Suzanne seized on him, "Are you sure?"

"Yes. Yes, they're good."

She looked into one eye, then the other, as if she couldn't reconcile each view of him. "I want you to like them."

"Well. I do." He felt the pounding from the airplane against his skull. Suzanne's eyes filled with tears. "Come on," he said and put his arm around her, "home."

PART FIVE

Chapter One

1961

Lennie smelled perfume and looked up at her mother floating down the stairs, her feet in satin pumps placed sideways, bending her knees like she was waltzing. As her mother grew closer, the scent of her perfume got richer and so did the swishing sound of her evening gown. Suzanne said, "Watch out, darling," and Lennie had to move aside while her mother swept past. Lennie's hand darted out to feel the silk chiffon. "Don't touch!" Suzanne said.

"My hands are clean." Lennie held up her clean palms, ten clean fingers, then turned her hands to look at them. "Clean as starfish."

Suzanne laughed. Emmett was helping her with her cream linen shawl, throwing it around her shoulders. She wore pearl-buttoned kid leather gloves that came up to her elbows.

Lennie repeated, "Clean as starfish."

Suzanne bent down to kiss the side of her mouth, then wiped away the lipstick she'd left there. "Be good."

The babysitter, Marcie, a dork, was watching from the living room. "You look like Jackie Kennedy, Mrs. Jones," she said.

"Oh, I hope not," Suzanne said. "She'll think I'm just a copycat."

Lenore sat on the stairs while her father escorted her mother out of the house. She was glad to have a beautiful mother, but she wondered if all mothers were so fake. She heard the Alfa Romeo back out of the driveway and went to kneel on the couch to watch them leave. The car was blue as a raincloud and the top was down and her mother's head was wrapped up in the linen shawl, looking back at Lennie in the picture window.

Suzanne waved a gloved hand to her. "Do you think she's all right?" she asked Emmett. She felt a thrill at going out into the lightening dusk of May, nestled in the leather seats as she once had done when her father drove this car. She loved the Alfa and was glad Emmett loved it too, kept it repaired; he'd even rebuilt the engine a couple of years ago and had it repainted the same gunmetal blue.

"Which?" Emmett asked. He was distracted, shifting gears. They didn't have far to go but they were late.

Suzanne looked back again and saw the lonely half-shell of Lennie's face in the window. They rounded the bend and there was only the night ahead. Dinner at the home of the American ambassador. The Kennedys were in town. How marvellous it was to hold sway like this, a woman and a man, good people. She glanced at Emmett, handsome in black tie, any match for Jack Kennedy. Emmett turned on the headlamps. They hurtled forward, rounding the curves of Sussex and following the river, lights from the little houses on the Gatineau shore rippling snakily.

"Who will be there?" she asked.

Without taking his eyes from the road, Emmett leaned sideways to hear her better, his voice smooth against the rumbling engine. "Who will be there? State Department, a fellow named Armstrong, a good man, actually. Merchant, the ambassador, he's all right too. Mike Pearson is invited. It's going to drive poor Dief mad with envy."

"Poor Dief," she said, excitement and pleasure rising in her throat. She loved to see Diefenbaker humiliated. Pearson was always gallant toward her. "Poor, poor Dief," she repeated tenderly, loving them all.

At the reception before dinner, she got stuck with Olive Diefenbaker, who didn't bother to make small talk but glared banefully at the guests and gave Suzanne such a bold look of disapproval when she accepted a daiquiri just like the president's, Suzanne put it down and then lost it to a zealous waiter. Olive muttered to her, "I'm sorry, my dear, but I've forgotten your name." Suzanne told her, using her maiden name too, "Suzanne McCallum Jones." Olive pursed her Baptist lips and forgot her name again. It made Suzanne wish that Ethel Masters were here. Ethel was cut from the same cambric cloth as Olive, but for some reason she had decided to like Suzanne and treated her with a mother's forbearance; or, at least she always remembered to ask about Lenore. But Ethel was with Bill at the hospital; Bill had had a heart attack.

The ladies were excused after the raspberry tart, and Olive quite suddenly disappeared. Word went round the salon where the women were politely ensconced that Prime Minister Diefenbaker and his wife had left early. Jackie Kennedy, speaking French with a beautiful young woman married to somebody Suzanne didn't know, stopped and turned and, into the quiet room, said, "Quel dommage." It was the first time that Suzanne had clearly heard Jackie's voice. A kittenish, breathy voice, it shocked Suzanne a little, so utterly sexy, so pink, so creamed.

When the ambassador's man reopened the doors to the salon and announced that the gentlemen had finished their cigars, Suzanne swept ahead of the others in search of Emmett. Entering the dining room in a flurry, she then had to drift and study the paintings when she realized that Emmett wasn't here. A waiter came so close as to brush her arm, inquiring, "Would madame like something more?" The answer was most obviously no. Suzanne said, "I would like a cup of coffee," and sent him off. She saw a coattail she knew instinctively was Emmett's and pursued it, just as it disappeared around a corner.

It was Emmett, Emmett as he was when he wanted something more than he wanted her. She hurried to follow, and when he stopped before the doorway to another room, she stopped too and could see a wall of books, a masculine leather-bound library in the rosy, darting light from a fireplace.

Emmett didn't go into the library but stood his distance. She saw he was like a hunting dog, perked, listening, and she stayed, fascinated to see her husband, where his glasses wrapped about his ears, and his long, muscular back that she knew with her bare hands, in a tuxedo, poised to absorb whatever went on in that room.

They stood like that for several minutes. But why doesn't he go in? If it's a private conversation, why is he eavesdropping on them? She didn't like for Emmett to behave strangely as he was now, almost skulking, and she felt suddenly queasy. Then Emmett turned to retreat. When he saw Suzanne standing there, he approached her without greeting and took her arm to lead her quickly back to the company who were gradually dispersing, bidding the ambassador and his wife goodnight. Jackie was there, momentarily alone, and Suzanne saw her youthfulness, her brief show of disappointment, seeing Emmett and Suzanne emerge around the corner, then her smile returning and coming toward them and gliding past because the president was behind them now in the company of a man whom Suzanne knew to be the minister of defence, both of them smiling too.

They left then, and on the street, Suzanne waited while Emmett pulled up the convertible top on the car, for it had grown cool. When they were driving, in the leathery warmth lit by the low dash and streetlights showing new small leaves on the trees and hedges, she asked him, "What were they talking about?"

"What were who talking about when?"

"What were the president and Harkness talking about in the library?"

"You're a curious one, aren't you."

"Why didn't you let them know you were there?"

He didn't answer. As they neared their home and she realized that he wasn't going to tell her anything, she felt foolish and angry but didn't wish to spoil the night. Remembering Jackie's breathy purr, she softly asked again, "Tell me. I'm your wife. You know it doesn't go any further than this car."

He turned onto their street, the cambered road tilting her toward him, and she kissed his ear and whispered, "Tell."

He pulled irritably away. They were at the driveway now, their headlamps sweeping the dark house. She said, "Why on earth wouldn't Marcie leave a light on?"

Emmett was out of the car, running into the house. He rushed into the living room and turned on a lamp. When she arrived a second afterward, she found Emmett strangely frozen, and Lenore sitting on the couch with her bare feet tucked under her dressing gown. Suzanne thought Lennie had been left home all alone, but then a man stepped out of the shadows at the far end of the room.

Chapter Two

"I let the babysitter go," said John Norfield.

Suzanne went to Lenore, "Are you all right?"

"We were sitting in the dark," Lennie observed.

"She doesn't mind the dark," John said. "Do you."

"No." Lennie seemed unafraid but far too alert; it might have been noon. Suzanne thought, She should be afraid, why isn't she afraid?

Emmett went back outside to the car on the driveway and closed its doors. When he returned to the house, he was carrying Suzanne's evening bag. He gave it to her, then went to check the rest of the house. They heard him go out the back door.

"What's going on?" Suzanne asked John. She heard herself sounding as if she were afraid of him, afraid of John, it surprised her.

"I'm sorry," he said. "I don't wish to be dramatic. Ill judgment on my part. It's become a habit, I guess, preferring the dark."

He wore a jacket she thought she recognized from years ago and he did look seriously ill. Lennie was sitting very still, quivering. He said, "Lenore has been wonderful, keeping me company while we waited. Perhaps you'd better go up and put her to bed now."

Suzanne was about to protest when she saw Lennie give her a look of relief, and she guessed that Lennie was tired of playacting, that she needed to let down her guard. When Suzanne went to her, Lennie even raised her arms as if her mother could carry her, then they both realized, she's too big now, and they walked clumsily up the stairs, Lennie leaning on her step by step.

After several minutes, Emmett returned through the back door. He entered the living room. "What are you doing here?" he asked angrily.

"I'm losing my touch." John stood as if he needed support, as if he'd lost reference to everything,

"Sorry," Emmett said. "I guess we both panicked when we saw Lennie like that." He went to get them both a drink.

"She's going to be beautiful. Like her mother," John said, accepting the drink. "And how was dinner?"

Emmett realized that it was obvious they'd been at a formal dinner, both of them wearing evening clothes. "It was fine."

"Are they glamorous in person?" John sat down, putting his drink aside and lighting a cigarette. "Jack and Jackie."

Emmett went to the window, pulled the drapes aside and carefully looked out. "John?"

"Yes, Emmett?"

"Are you alone?"

"Yes."

"No one followed you here?" A small figure was walking away between the houses across the street.

"No. I was careful. And I believe that the dandy, our old friend Robert Morton, has kept his word and left you and your family in peace."

John's bargain with Robert Morton, his sacrifice, giving himself up on Morton's promise that the RCMP would leave Emmett and his wife alone, returned to Emmett in all its humiliation. John continued, speaking gently, as if he understood Emmett's embarrassment but had further news. "I think Morton was more interested in Suzanne. He sure thought she was one hot ticket."

Emmett said, "I know about that."

"Bob Morton's infatuation? You know?"

"He's probably still watching her."

"Then you should protest." John looked yet more abandoned. "He gave me his word," he said softly. Emmett hesitated. Then John knew, "Oh. You're bluffing. Well, let's hope he's not. She hasn't turned into a ban-the-bomb lady, has she?"

"Look. You know that we can't talk here."

"I came to give you a message. Once I've given you the message, I'll leave. I won't be back. Not even to see Lenore."

"Why would you want to see Lenore?"

"Shall I tell you?"

Emmett sat down.

"Good," said John. Now that he had Emmett's attention, he put his head back against his chair and rested.

"I've been travelling," he began. "It's rather difficult to find work. The RCMP track me, you see? Not as they used to, not the excitement of surveillance, though there's that too, in a dreary, everyday sort of way, my mail and so on, not that there is any. They follow me to my jobs if I'm lucky enough to get one, and tell my new employers I'm a Red. And I'm let go. So I travel."

"I'm sorry," Emmett said again.

"Not your fault."

Morton had botched John's arrest years ago by using un-authorized police surveillance, but, Emmett saw, Morton didn't need to arrest John; his imprisonment was general.

John saw Emmett's face, his pity, and he repeated, "It isn't your fault." He rested again for a moment. "I saw Winnipeg," he said then, falsely bright. "My home town."

This surprised Emmett. He'd gotten the accent wrong.

John continued. "I haven't had any word from Leonard Fischer. Or his letters don't reach me. I don't know if he's alive." They were quiet for a few moments. "I hope he's all right. But I don't know. His lungs . . . " he trailed off, rested again, and smiled. "Pathetic, isn't it."

It was unlike him to talk so much, and Emmett realized how lonely he must be. Emmett wished he could hold John, he hurt with the yearning to hold him, in his shabby suit, with not much more than his adopted upper Ontario accent intact. John had even lost his old sense of irony. "They contacted me a little while ago," John said.

"Who did?"

"Old friends. They're looking for some information they say only you can supply." John ignored Emmett's tense face; he leaned back in his chair as if indulging in nostalgia, and mused, "Generous of them, really, to make me feel useful again. Don't you think?" Emmett said nothing but listened carefully. After a moment John repeated, "I really do think it's generous, decent, to let me serve in this way, after I've quit the game and all."

Emmett took a drink. "Why would they choose you to be the messenger? They know how risky it is for you to be here. The RCMP would consider it a breach of the contract. You could go to jail."

"They knew I couldn't resist." John shrugged. "I guess they

know I love your wife." He laughed with his cigarette between his lips. "There. I've said it."

"What information could I possibly have that would interest them?" Emmett asked again.

"Actually," John began and paused, staring at Emmett almost like a man with amnesia, as if trying to recall Emmett's identity. Wonderingly, his tone, mystified, "They said I was to warn you."

"Warn me? Warn me of what?"

"That you're not moving fast enough."

Chapter Three

Emmett stared at John. "What does that mean?"

"I don't know. It's what I'm instructed to tell you. That you're not moving fast enough." John rested in his chair as if after some great effort. "I don't know what it means."

Emmett was silent, thinking. Then he said, "The missiles are filled with sand."

John laughed. "Are you talking in code?"

"No. They're actually loaded with sand. The Bomarcs and rockets for NATO are loaded only with sand. I don't know which is crazier, nuclear bombs, possibly aimed at us, or sand in our defence missiles."

"Sand in our defence missiles. Well. That should please them."

Emmett, bitterly, "This country has zero defence. Not even Kennedy can make Diefenbaker load nuclear warheads into the missiles."

John shook his head and said, "Do you ever feel old, Emmett?"

"Sure. Sure I do."

"It occurs to me that we have been set up."

Emmett didn't answer. It was terrible to hear John express what Emmett had dreaded and resented ever since the investigation in '53, ever since being sent to Cuba soon after being "cleared," and later, to Japan, where he so conveniently fell into the sphere of Jim Smith and his special requests from the CIA. The set-up.

"All these years." John smiled a little, and his handsomeness, his beauty was evident. He wearily sat forward. As if to a lost lover, he said, "Remember how it used to be, Emmett? Remember why we got involved so long ago? Think about it. Think back to what inspired us. What led Leonard to Russia. What led you and me to"—he hesitated—"live the way we do."

A stubborn trace of hope in Emmett shifted, gave way. He wanted to let everything go; every remnant of what he wanted to call his private self was like a contraption he could no longer carry. Lowering his voice, intending John to understand that they must not be overheard by Suzanne, Emmett spoke barely above a whisper, "Nothing stays the same."

John went on: "You called it 'redemption.' You claimed you could 'redeem' your life." He shook his head. "Lovely dream. Turned nightmare." John looked too ill to stand; he hadn't touched his whisky. "We imagined we were saving the world. We didn't even save ourselves. Now they're putting pressure on you."

Emmett bent down, picked up his drink, and drained it. "I'll deal with it."

"They're coming after you, my friend. They want more information than you're giving them."

"I don't have anything."

"It's not something you can just quit, Emmett."

"I said, I'll deal with it."

"I suggest—"

But Suzanne came downstairs. She'd changed her clothes, wore a woollen housedress. Cinderella. John stared. Emmett believed that he was trying to memorize her. The excitement between her and John was intolerable. John said, "I must be off."

Suzanne made a helpless gesture, grasping the air involuntarily, making a fist.

John said, "Pardon the cloak-and-dagger stuff, but would you mind closing the light?"

Emmett turned off the lamp, and John said, "Thank you."

Emmett could see him make his way to the front door, Suzanne following. He heard John say goodbye, and when Suzanne returned to the living room, he asked her, "Do you want to go with him?"

She gave a low, nervous laugh. He could see her rubbing at her arm. In a small voice she said, "I hardly think I'm up to it." It was more than she'd intended to say. She gasped a little, he heard her dry mouth, *tsk*, and she came to him and put her hand against his chest as she so often did, saying, "Emmett," calling him.

Chapter Four

Suzanne took Emmett's hand as he steadied her up the last few steps and out, till she was standing on the oily floor. "I never knew!" she kept saying as she emerged to the dank cold of the garage. A cold afternoon. "All this time and I never knew!"

"I only just found it by accident," Emmett told her. "I got down on my knees here," he indicated where the Alfa was normally parked, "to look under the car because I thought there was a leak in the oil pan, and then I thought, What the hell is that?" He'd already told her this story, but it was worth retelling; such an odd bit of luck. "I couldn't believe my eyes."

"Imagine!" She nervously stood clear while Emmett lifted the hatch to let it down into position and stamped it into place. "Just when we need such a thing."

"Dual purpose," he said, a joke he'd kept running in this discussion. "Liquor vault and bomb shelter."

She laughed, her recent weeping surging up in her chest. "Just imagine. It's incredible we're even talking like this."

"I'm sure we won't need it."

"Shall I start getting supplies?"

He said that she should and again, her weeping laughter, "This is completely mad!" They agreed on that, and Emmett guided her out the crooked door of the garage and back to the house. "How will we stay warm in there?" she asked. Then, more shrill laughter, "This is mad!"

Now it was late fall and so bitterly cold even the squirrels had retired. Emmett bought a Geiger counter. He lined the liquor vault with insulation that he stapled tight in sheets of plastic. He purchased a chemical toilet and a carbon air filter. He bought boxes of candles, along with five lanterns and kerosene, thinking that, with their body heat and these light sources, they might stay warm enough. He shopped for batteries and cots and sleeping bags. As he descended the steep stairs into the bomb shelter he had the old sensation of being under surveillance—though now the spy would be a Canadian bureaucrat stumbling out from behind the shrubbery to commend an obedient citizen on preparations for his own annihilation. Emmett was reminded of how the Japanese had behaved, stupefied by obedience, till the atom bombs fell. He was angry all the time, even his dreams were angry.

Suzanne was listing the things she'd pack; there were lists all over the house. One list she'd left in the bathroom included nail polish remover. Since she'd started to make lists it seemed she couldn't remember anything. She got Lenore up early to go to school yesterday. It was Sunday. Lennie didn't bat an eye.

"This is retarded," Lennie had said. "You can try sticking me in school on Sundays now, but I'm not going to 'bomb drill.' I don't feel like burning to death with that bunch of nerds." She hated school. General assembly was sickening, the other children's bodies pressing against her, crammed into the gymnasium to learn about where to hide when the Russians come to kill them with gas and fire.

Monday, Emmett drove Lennie the few blocks to school. A cold, sunless morning, heat blasting in the car. Lennie coltish, a stiff mass of resistance. He pulled up at the red brick building with its chain-link fence just as the bell sounded and the other children filed inside, Lennie not getting out but watching them, dry-eyed with a wan sort of grief. She seemed old, as if she had already lost everything, had accepted an enduring betrayal. He spoke gently, "You're going to be late."

Lennie wearily opened the car door, got out and shut it without saying goodbye, and walked away, struggling with the heavy wooden doors, disappearing inside. Not angry but resigned. Abandoned by the things that had made her a child. Nine years old.

He was late for a meeting with the prime minister. Diefenbaker had taken a shine to him, especially on the subjects of Cuba, China, and Vietnam, and used him as a sounding board, his silent confessor, for Emmett was never asked his opinion, was only invited to agree. Yes, Mr. Prime Minister, we shouldn't isolate the Cuban people. Yes, Mr. Prime Minister, it's a great day for prairie wheat farmers selling $400 million worth of grain to Mao Zedong. No, Mr. Prime Minister, the president of the United States can't push you around. No, Mr. Prime Minister, that callow son of a bitch Kennedy can't turn our ploughshares into swords. Perfectly right, Mr. Prime Minister, we won't use our wheat exports to manipulate the Chinese on Hanoi.

At noon, Emmett crossed Wellington Street to walk down to Sparks Street, to the jewellery store that housed in its upper storey the National Press Club. He told the girl at the front desk the name of the journalist who was expecting him, then passed the men trading jokes at the bar and wove a path through the tables toward one of the booths at the rear of the club. Blue ribbons of smoke were illuminated by small yellow lamps on the tables and by brass fixtures with green shades on the walls. He recognized Wilson by the way he wore his hat, pushed back on his balding head.

Wilson stood up to greet him warmly, shaking his hand and gripping his shoulder, "Here you are, I'm glad to see you."

Emmett sat across from him in the booth. "You look great."

"Bullshit," Wilson said.

"You don't look any worse than you did ten or eleven years ago."

Wilson tipped his glass of whisky. "Guess I've achieved saturation."

When the waiter arrived, Emmett ordered a drink and a sandwich and a refill for his friend. Then he asked Wilson where he'd been since he left Japan. "Last time I knew your whereabouts, you were watching the retreat at Pusan."

"My last and final foreign assignment."

"Korea was?"

"Yup." Wilson noted Emmett's surprise. "Oh, come on. It happened to you too. Didn't it?"

Emmett asked him to explain what he meant.

"You got yourself in hot water, didn't you. Been anywhere since?"

"Jamaica."

Wilson laughed.

"Worked on a deal to take bauxite alumina out of Jamaica. Went to Cuba. Havana. Where I met Ernest Hemingway at lunch at the embassy while arranging a delivery of salt cod from Labrador. I got back to Kobe once too. Aluminum. My career often intersects with aluminum."

"How's life in Ottawa?"

"Unremittingly dull. Is that why you're here?"

"A fellow with the Canadian air force is creating a lot of heat over NORAD." Wilson hesitated while someone walked close by, then resumed. "I met him in Colorado Springs. He's drumming up opposition at NORAD headquarters. Here too. A lot of people are unhappy with your prime minister. Here in Ottawa, and in Washington too. Of course you know all this."

"I know there's some dissatisfaction over the Bomarc missiles. The Voodoo interceptors are sitting useless."

"The Pentagon's getting mad. If this was Central America, there'd be a nasty coup and it'd be all over for your Diefenbaker."

Emmett took a bite of his clubhouse sandwich. "We call it an election up here."

"Guess it doesn't affect you. You're one of those deep-sea fish lying on the bottom while the storms pass over. Insulated by all that bilge."

"That's a good thing, right? Public stability, bottom up."

"Maybe. Your life's dull, though. So's mine."

Emmett ordered another drink for each of them. "I don't know why I'm buying lunch when you're so insulting."

"I like you. I know you're more than you pretend to be."

Emmett looked around the room, seeing familiar faces and some hardy types that suggested American military. The idea of a coup seemed almost plausible. Wilson's green eyes observed him coldly, then quite abruptly, awash with affection, as if he'd turned on a tap. Emmett asked him to fill him in on where he'd been since Korea.

"McCarthy kept me home," Wilson said. "When I finally got a clean passport again, I did some work for *Colliers*, till it went down. Freelanced myself almost sober. Then I did a long piece on the slaughterhouses of Chicago. Won a prize, and got myself a Midwest syndicated column." He laughed. "Serendipity."

Emmett thought that this sounded small compared with Wilson's early career, but he said, "Congratulations."

"I'm not touching Indo China. Not with a ten-foot pole and a nickel-plated condom."

"I understand."

"I'm a tough bird, but I can't stand being considered an enemy of my own country. I can't go through all that again." The watery green eyes observing him. "And I'll bet in that respect, we're birds of a feather."

Emmett finished his second drink and said, "I have a meeting at one o'clock." He stood. "Would you like to come to my home for dinner? Meet my wife."

"I hear there's going to be some kind of rehearsal for Doomsday this evening."

"Christ," Emmett said. "We don't have to pay attention to that."

Wilson said he was tied up for dinner but would meet him later, here at the Press Club, at about nine. It was an odd suggestion. But Emmett agreed, he'd be here.

Chapter Five

At five minutes to one, Emmett walked back outside to a nearly deserted street. A patrol car slowed beside him and the cop looked at him carefully through the window. It was the kind of day that needs snow. Chilled, in his suit jacket, he ran across the street against the light. He took the stairs to his office, passing no one. His secretary was at her desk, and she jumped a little when he walked in. "Oh! Gosh, you startled me, Mr. Jones."

He said, "It's quiet around here."

"Well, it's the exercise day. You know, what's it, the defence day against the Russians."

"Right. How could I forget?" He was passing through to his office, but she was so intently drawn that he stopped and asked her if anything was wrong.

"Oh. No." Her hand went instinctively to her phone. "It's just my husband calling all morning. Honestly, he's such a worrier." Emmett asked what was worrying her husband now. "Oh, I don't know. Just, he thinks it might be hard to come get me at five o'clock. If there's a panic and people start leaving the city? We're renting out in Westboro now, you know. And he's afraid of the traffic if there's a panic."

"Why would there be a panic?"

"Oh. You know. If people start to think it's real? My husband thinks some people might not get that it's only playacting. They might think it's real that the Russians are attacking and start to get into their cars and go who-knows-where. He thinks people are dumb." She looked longingly at her telephone. "I told him not everybody's stupid."

"Would you like to go home?"

"Oh! That would be swell!" She dove under the desk and produced her purse. "You're sure?"

He told her he was sure, and she was pulling on her coat when he asked her, didn't she need to phone her husband to tell him she had the afternoon off?

"I bet he's out back already, Mr. Jones. He left about an hour ago." She tied a yellow scarf around her hair. "He says the Parliament's going to be the first place the Russians bomb."

"But it's just playacting."

She stopped and stood with her hand on the door handle, and in a low voice she said, "I know that. I really do. Anyways. If the Russians bomb us, we won't have time to phone our husbands."

"I don't think you have to worry about that."

"Really?" She looked him in the eye. "Well, of course I defer to your greater knowledge, Mr. Jones. But I also know we don't have more than a candle in the wind if they ever do drop the Bomb. I don't just sit here and type, you know. I read."

She slung the purse over her arm and backed out of the room, pulling the door shut with both hands.

Alone, Emmett had a reflex of secret freedom, a physical rush of pleasure in being alone with state secrets, and now this made him squirm in shame. That love of secrets, a competitive quality, had made him easy to manipulate. His secretary's fear leached into him like a bad dream. Restlessly he shuffled with the papers on his desk. He didn't have a meeting, as he'd told Wilson; he needed some time alone. His phone rang.

"Emmett?" It was Suzanne.

"What's wrong?"

She seemed to be speaking away from the receiver; he could hear her take a step in the kitchen, hear her pulling at the cord the way she always did, wrapping it around her hand. Then he heard the siren through the phone even while it sounded in the room where he stood. A high plaintive wail rising insistently, the authority of fear. "There it goes. I've got to go get Lennie."

It was only one-thirty. He asked her why she was getting her so early and she answered angrily, "Oh for chrissake, Emmett, why do you think?" She slammed the receiver into its cradle.

He walked out into the hall. A dozen people were standing there. The siren shrilled. He said, "It's just an exercise." They stood and listened. It was hypothetical as one's own death is hypothetical, and someone said, "Imagine."

The secretary from across the hall shuddered visibly. "Thank god it's not real."

The siren slowly descended in pitch till it sounded hollow and off-key and then it sputtered out. Several of the people in the hallway chuckled, and someone said, "Fire drill's over, children, back to your desks."

Emmett walked to the stairs and down to the back exit, where he had parked his car. The Alfa embarrassed him today, struck him as frivolous. The police had stopped the car ahead of him to ask the driver for his papers, but they just took a quick look at the Alfa and waved him through.

Suzanne was pulling into the driveway when he arrived,

and he parked behind her. She got out, had started to walk back toward him when she saw that Lenore was still sitting in the car so she turned and went around to open the passenger door, leaning down. When he approached, he heard her trying to coax Lennie out of the car. "It's all right, darling, there's nothing to be afraid of."

He joined her; together they stuck their heads in to croon their words of comfort and persuasion and then a mild threat, "If you don't get out of the car, Lennie, you're not going to see the television."

Lenore wore a dazed, sullen look, but hearing this, her eyes moved to her parents' faces and she viewed them closely and separately. Her skin was milky, shiny with sweat. More than frightened, she looked resentful. She put her legs out of the car as if following her own feet, Emmett and Suzanne backing away, then Suzanne running ahead to unlock the front door.

Lennie went straight to the TV and turned it on. A man was standing in front of a map of Canada. He spoke with a severe, scolding tone. Emmett came and tried to put Lennie on his lap, but her hard, thin body didn't bend.

The man on the television said, "The most common answer is that they'll die. And there's no need for it. Improve your chances of survival. At the sound of the alert, keep calm. Do not use your telephone. Gather your family and check the gas in your car. If you choose to leave the target areas, take a blanket, two quarts of water, baby food, medicines, a battery radio, eating utensils, an axe and rope. Know your destination. Have identification for any lost children. For those who choose to stay, find protection from the blasts and heat effects. Protect yourself with bedsprings. Remove small objects that would fly around. There might be twenty or thirty minutes before fallout comes, perhaps longer. Use a fire extinguisher. Ladies, know how to get rid of radioactive dust. Turn off gas and water and electricity. And wait for further instructions."

Chapter Six

Lennie's parents had the sun behind them. The day that had been sere revealed a radiant November sun unobstructed by leaves, the sky stark blue against the grey branches of the trees. Lennie wasn't used to seeing the sun at that angle, like a yo-yo broken off its string, because normally she was at school at this hour of this month. It made a rainbow through the high window in the dining room and hit her parents so she could see the wrinkles in their clothes and the frizz of her mother's hair, their arms raised to tell her, Wait, wait, you have to make us feel better. She couldn't see their faces, and she didn't want to. Screw them. Screw Screw Screw.

She went up the stairs to her bedroom but hung around on the landing a few minutes to listen to them say, Her Her Her, She She She.

"I had to," her mother said. "They phoned. They told me to come and get her. They said she was disturbing the other children."

Her father said, "What about her? What about her feelings? Didn't they think about that? What's she going to do tomorrow when she has to go back? Now she's a freak."

"Don't you call her that," her mother hissed.

"I'm not. Jesus, Suzanne, of course I'm not calling her a freak."

But Lennie knew, he said it because he thought it. It came out of his head. Communist spies are the real freaks.

Lennie went into her bedroom. To celebrate her ninth birthday because she was "nearly a decade old," her mother "redecorated" her room last June and got floral skirts for her bed. Lennie found them beautiful — skirts for a bed, big blue flowers with yellow tongues. Lennie crawled under her bed. She was protecting herself with bedsprings. From downstairs she heard the distant vibrations of their voices.

Emmett told Suzanne that he had to go back to work. She followed him out to the car, kept him talking in the driveway. He only wanted to be in his office, to close his door.

He hadn't been contacted in some time, not at all since John Norfield was sent as messenger. Emmett had made the decision; he'll make contact with them, he'll tell the Russians that he's finished, he'll tell them to leave him alone.

No one ever did catch him in his work for the Russians, no one at External Affairs, no one in the FBI, no one in the CIA.

The Americans think he's one useful patsy, giving them stuff on his government's plans in Cuba. Information, photographed documents that made the Americans feel in control. He was a success, a great success as a spy. Now the continent might be destroyed by an atom bomb.

Celebrate the end of your brilliant career, he told himself, have a party all by yourself. He'd always had to work alone. There were no Spymasters Clubs, no conventions in Moscow. No professional conversation had ever been possible — that was the nature of the game, and he'd accepted it, even welcomed it, perceiving himself as exclusive, private. But he was merely desolate.

His hand was on the car door. Suzanne was standing before him with her arms wrapped around her shoulders, shivering in the cold while she talked. Emmett felt a tremor of panic. His mind went up—he was in his airplane, his Lancaster, high above a city on fire. He was also, of course, in his driveway. It was daytime. His body was swept into a whirlwind, the wild wind of a firestorm. He shuddered, she didn't notice. She never seemed to notice.

She was talking. She must never know. He'd contact his Russian handler, he'd tell him that he was through, he would retrieve himself. He would be a husband and father, an ordinary civil servant, and if there were another war—if there was another war, it wouldn't matter anymore, they'd all be dead. He needed to gather his son to him; maybe they should all go to Japan, it had already come through fire; it was hard to think clearly, and Suzanne was telling him, "I'm so worried."

"I know."

"I can't protect her. She's strong, but it makes her vulnerable. Do you know what I mean? Am I making any sense?"

"Yes." He'd tell the Americans too, he was through. No more duplicates. His stuff on Cuba had seemed harmless. Even Kennedy had liked Castro in the days after the revolution. The Americans would cut off Aoi, his son would suffer. He had to go to his son; they should all go to Japan.

She was talking about Lennie. "If she wasn't so bright. If she was less, less of everything, and more, more silly, I wish she was silly."

"I have to get back to work."

Suzanne said, "Of course." She stepped back from the car to let him go. "That goddamn siren."

He got into the car and rolled down the window.

She leaned down and said, "Do you think they'd actually drop the Bomb on us?"

"They might. I don't know. We did."

"No we didn't."

"Oh," he said. She believed in countries; didn't she know that there are no countries? There's only power. Mad generals and a sad, crazy prime minister.

"Are you all right?" she asked.

"I'll see you tonight."

"What should I do with Lennie? She's so scared."

"Read to her. Keep her away from the TV and the radio. Tell her she's good. Tell her it's going to be okay."

"I love you," Suzanne said.

Emmett drove back downtown. He thought about how Suzanne loved him.

How? In the light of day with her conscious mind in all its sundry calculations.

One day, when he's clear, when they're all clear, he'll go away alone for a while, till he feels strong enough to ask himself if, in the world as it must be, without that ideal that had once loaned him a secret radiance, without his talent and that private light he'd thought he lived by, her sundry love will be enough.

Chapter Seven

Close to nine o'clock that night in cold, hard rain he parked in his spot near the East Block and walked down to Sparks Street. Wilson was standing under the store's awning, smoking a cigarette. "Thanks for showing up," Wilson said, taking his arm to guide him back out into the rain to where an Edsel Corsair four-door hardtop was parked at the curb. Wilson dropped his cigarette onto the sidewalk and said, "Rental. Shitty car. Jump in."

They were driving. It was raining very hard. Emmett asked where they were going.

"We're off to see the Wizard." Wilson grinned. He was having a good time. Emmett felt his spirits lift. It had been too long since he'd spent time with a happy person. Maybe men are more naturally happy than women are. More foolishly optimistic.

They actually went back to Jones's neck of the woods, about half a mile from his home in Rockcliffe, and pulled into a circular driveway of the kind favoured by Ottawa socialites, replete with a green canvas umbrella funnelling from double front doors to the edge of the boulevard, fortification for hairdos. A large Stars and Stripes drooped in the rain. Wilson parked and tossed the keys cheerfully—"Back entrance"—leading him around to the back of the house, where somebody had built an addition, a modern contraption of sheet metal with steel beams that extruded from a brick facade. Emmett realized he was somewhere official, something subsidized by state money, American state money.

They were greeted by a tall, lanky man with an open, Nordic face, wearing the casual dress uniform of the American air force. "Hello, friends," he said, "Chuck's in here," his voice warmly relaxed, his accent mid-west. "We're winding down, but I know there's still a cold beer with your name on it." They followed him through a chilly, stylish room decorated with a lot of tiger-striped furniture, then down a set of stairs, the smell of wood smoke and cigars reaching up to greet them, and into a rec room with a pool table, football trophies, photographs of college football teams, a padded leather bar at one end, a stone fireplace at the other, where sofas and upholstered chairs were set up around a black bearskin rug. A stocky black maid was stacking dirty dishes with the remains of a late meal of spaghetti while another went around with clean ashtrays. Twenty men or so were sitting in bright contentment, drinking coffee or finishing a beer. Emmett recognized several journalists. Besides the lanky officer, there were others in military uniform, both RCAF and US air force. The American ambassador was here, speaking quietly and earnestly. An athletic forty-something fellow broke away and came to greet them. This was their host, Chuck, the ambassador's assistant.

Emmett was struck by a general atmosphere of gratitude and relief, and he knew that the reporters were getting an unofficial "backgrounder." Chuck spoke in the hushed tone of a church steward. "Glad you could make it. Wilson, good of you go out in the rain to collect him. Emmett, right? Glad to meet you at last. I've heard a lot about you."

Emmett doubted this was true; it would be the kind of

blanket statement Chuck would use often in every posting. Ambassadorial. Chuck murmured, "Come in," and showed them where to sit. To the stocky maid he said, "Leave those a minute and get the gentlemen whatever they'd like."

The ambassador smoothly acknowledged them without pausing in his speech. "The cold and bitter truth is this," he was saying, "if they decide to use the ICBMs, and you fellas don't have the weaponry to meet that challenge, the whole continent will be destroyed."

Chuck took his seat beside the ambassador, leaned his elbows on his knees, and said, "Conventional weapons have gone the way of the dodo bird."

"I'd never tell your prime minister what to do —" the ambassador said, and Chuck interrupted, "Just try it," and everybody laughed.

The ambassador paused, generously acknowledging Chuck's wit before continuing. "Like I said, it's not our goal to interfere in your national affairs. But this, my friends, is international. It calls for a statesmanlike decisiveness —" Again Chuck interrupted and finished for him, "Somewhat lacking in your chief —" The ambassador smiled indulgently at Chuck's undiplomatic candour and resumed, "A decisiveness and, if I might add, a forthrightness in delivering on a promise."

The Ottawa journalists squirmed at this suggestion that their country wasn't playing straight. Somebody grumbled, "It's a damned disgrace."

Chuck scratched his head. "I admit I'm at a loss. The uranium comes from you. Makes more than a billion dollars in Canada, creates a lot of jobs for Mr. Diefenbaker's voters. But when it comes to loading it into the Bomarcs, Diefenbaker is suddenly a virgin." He smiled at them all. "Kind of retroactive."

The officer who'd greeted Wilson and Jones at the door now spoke. "We can't protect you without your full cooperation. That means nuclear, that means we go prepared for maximum war. That's what it means to live in the twentieth century. It's absolute madness to have all these empty cannons sitting up here with the Russians aiming nuclear missiles at you right now as we speak. Don't kid yourselves. Your prime minister is a hypocrite of the first order."

There was a brief shocked pause, and then another of the US air force officers said, "Yeah! Where the hell did you guys get a nerd like that?" He spoke so lightly, the insults bounced off the company, and they all laughed. "He's a big nerd!" the officer repeated indignantly, and everyone laughed harder.

This broke up the party. It was getting late. They began to stand and collect their coats, thanking Chuck for his fine hospitality. "We're not all bad, are we?" Chuck asked. "I often get the impression you Canadians think we're some kind of monstrous, mammoth obliteration of your precious identity. All we want is some help in protecting your north from a nuclear holocaust."

Emmett was wondering exactly why Wilson had brought him here when he saw a familiar face on the other side of the room, obscured by the other men as they were leaving. Then he saw him clearly. Wearing a bomber jacket, and the same, winking smile. A visitor from a bigger place. He caught Emmett looking. Jim Smith, Aoi's employer in Kobe and the man who'd so effectively presented him with his job as "consultant" for the Americans. Mr. Smith was making his way toward him.

Emmett began to speak closely into Wilson's ear, "Nice of you to bring me along. I'd appreciate a lift back to my car in a few minutes." Wilson saw Mr. Smith approach; he stiffened eagerly, but Emmett nudged him to leave. "Wait for me. I'll be along shortly."

"Okey-dokey, I'll be right outside," Wilson said and went.

Jim Smith was reaching for Emmett's hand, introducing himself vigorously, "Emmett, right? We met in Japan, remember? Commerce, right?"

Emmett politely corrected him. "External Affairs."

Smith snapped his fingers. "That's right! Nice to see you again." He took his arm. "Something I've been wanting to ask —" leading him aside.

"I've been wanting to talk to you too," Emmett said. "I didn't expect to see you here tonight. Just seems too lucky."

"Anything to make you happy, Mr. Jones."

"Look. I want you to know. I'm not in the game anymore."

"And I want you to know, the stuff on Cuba is pretty unremarkable."

"I don't care."

"Change of heart, have you?"

"That's right."

"You'd be taking a pretty big risk, trying to wriggle out of this one. Lot of people riding on you."

Emmett could feel the sweat between his shoulder blades. But he said, "Nobody's going to like it when they learn that the CIA is pushing around a Canadian civil servant."

"You won't get a chance to say much, if it comes to that. Besides, we've got a long memory. Some time in the future, when you think it's all blown over, maybe you're even retired with your gold watch for good service to the Canadian government. Maybe you and your wife are on your way to your daughter's wedding, something like that, your lovely daughter in her wedding dress in the backseat. Then, boom, a freak accident."

"You're crazy."

"It's a crazy world."

"I'm through. And if you hurt my family, I'll kill you."

"I do what has to be done."

"If anything happens to me or to my family, they're going to know all about you."

Smith smiled. "Maybe your government will protect you, just like they did the last time."

Emmett backed away, saying more loudly, "Thanks! Glad everything worked out." Smith watched him go, his face set in a small smile.

He took the stairs two at a time, his heart pounding. He would protect his family, he would protect his son. He went outside to find Wilson sitting in the car. Rain was flooding the streets. He got into the car. Wilson took a look at him and asked, "You okay?" Emmett said he was. Wilson said, "They were pretty insistent I get you here tonight. I thought it was because they wanted somebody at External to hear their take on your prime minister."

Emmett looked away. "That's probably it."

Wilson went on, "Somebody sure needed to speak with you." When Emmett didn't respond, Wilson drove awhile, then asked over the drumming rain, "What do you think?"

"About?"

"The coup."

"Kind of an exaggeration to call it that."

"I've seen some nasty situations that started small, like tonight."

"Yeah. But this is Canada."

"Friendly."

"That's right."

"How'd you come to know Jim?"

"I'm not going to tell you."

Wilson gave him a quick look and smiled. "Worth a try. Always a newspaper man."

"That's all right."

They were close to the Sparks Street club. Wilson asked, "Still taking pictures?" Emmett didn't answer. Wilson said, "Okey-dokey." There was a sharp crack of thunder. Emmett told him, "Just drop me off here and I'll walk to my car."

Wilson refused, the streets went stark with sheet lightning. Emmett gave him directions. When he pulled up beside the Alfa, Wilson whistled. "Beautiful. They paying you pretty good?"

"It belonged to my wife's father." He got out of the Edsel and leaned down to thank Wilson for an interesting evening.

Wilson nodded thoughtfully, studying him. "Yup," he said. "You're more than you pretend to be." He gazed around at the empty parking lot. He looked old and rumpled now. "There's something here I can't quite figure out."

Chapter Eight

Emmett made a call. After he'd made the call, he did the usual things: taking a bus to the suburbs then doubling back by a different route, he bought a newspaper, folded it backward, and tucked it under his left arm, he went through the motions spurred by the belief that this was the last time. It was now April 1962. He hadn't had any pushback since telling Jim Smith he was finished working for the Americans. He'd sent a letter to Aoi, asking, Is James well? and received no letter in return, other than a spring term report card from James's private school. He wondered if maybe he was clear of the CIA. Now it was time to rid himself of any expectations from the Soviets.

The meeting didn't go as he'd planned. Sure, it was pleasant enough; his Russian contacts were always pleasant. It came to him over the subsequent days, as the impression of his cheerful contact wore off and his position came more clearly into focus: there were those who believed that the decision to leave the service of the Soviet Union was not his to make.

It was a new contact, yet another replacement. He calculated that this was his fifth since he started, twelve years ago, at the same time he'd joined External Affairs. Each man was as pleasant as his predecessor, sympathetic, admiring of Mr. Jones's commitment to the cause.

"You must understand," Emmett interrupted, "I have ab-solutely no faith in your government. I have no faith in any government on the planet." He was tempted to go further, to explain to the Russian that it was his lack of faith in government that had started him on the path of being a spy. He'd been inspired, lured by the promise, the ideal of a stateless society. He suspected that the Russian would laugh heartily.

The man, whose given name was Oscar, smiled, real amusement in his eyes. He had thick black eyebrows and a generous moustache, like a shorter, chubbier version of Groucho Marx. Emmett reiterated that surely it must be obvious, no man could support a government that planned to obliterate millions of people.

"But there are no such plans, Mr. Jones! This is wild talk!"

Emmett said he could no longer be sure of that.

"Well, if we are pushed—" Oscar shrugged philosophically. "But you will talk sense to your prime minister."

"Yes, but not for you. I don't work for you anymore."

"I understand. When you're alone like you are, it's hard to resist the propaganda. But you must be assured —"

So it went, and then they shook hands, this man Oscar with great warmth and a happy sense of silliness that Emmett had never before seen in a Russian contact. "You're a brave, heroic man," Oscar said, his smile indicating that no such thing exists.

"I quit. Get it?"

Oscar laughed indulgently, wiggling his Groucho Marx eyebrows. "Let the world go to hell in a handbasket!" He'd adopted a New York accent.

Emmett walked across the street, caught a bus, and rode it till it looped and came the other way. The bus driver, watching him in his rear-view mirror, thought it must be a bankrupt, or a man who'd just confirmed his wife's infidelity—the blank face, the shock.

His friend Wilson started to travel up from Duluth to Ottawa often during the federal election campaign that spring, and they'd have a few drinks. Wilson refrained from asking Emmett more questions about his relationship with Jim Smith, though he teased him about how tough it was for a reporter to endure unsatisfied curiosity. Wilson did ask Emmett a lot of questions about Prime Minister Diefenbaker. "I hear he hates Kennedy's guts," Wilson said.

"I hear it's mutual."

"I also hear he's crazy. Actually mad."

Emmett told Wilson unofficially, "The prime minister's just a bit frantic for affection. I think he's secretly, deep down in love with Kennedy. Envious. Jealous. Kennedy's handsomeness and charm suck the joy out of Dief." He trusted Wilson to steal his words and refashion them into his own. Wilson had to keep things pitched sharp for his editors.

The election went badly for Diefenbaker, but he survived with a minority. June 18, Emmett and Suzanne watched the results on television, and invited Dr. Kimura to watch it with them. "Poor Dief," said Suzanne in delight every time his party lost a seat. "Oh! Poor Dief."

When he'd lost fifty seats from his once majority, she brought dinner on a tray into the living room so they could watch TV while they ate. Lennie lay on the carpet and observed her mother's pleasure with narrowed eyes. When the last results were in and the government had held on but Diefenbaker had lost ninety-two seats, Suzanne brought forth champagne. "What a terrible night for Dief!" she said and she even poured Lennie a half-glass.

Kimura was offended that the election had resulted in a

minority government; it would be a weak government; his instincts were to respect power, despite his solitary, peaceful nature. "You are a strange woman," he observed, "who cheers for the bad fortunes of her country."

Lennie stiffened.

Suzanne quickly drained her champagne, poured another, and said, "We'll all be fine. It's always fine." These days, with the bomb shelter stocked and ready, with a generalized sensation that the sky is falling, that the end of their lives would be quick and violent, all this had inspired giddiness in Suzanne — she felt that she was sliding helplessly, a toboggan run, a plummet. She was having dizzy spells, and the liquor would quite likely make her sick to her stomach later, when Kimura had gone home. "You're fine, aren't you, Kim," she declared. "You're becoming a business man! What could be more fine than that?"

"What's this?" Emmett asked.

"Oh, you know, darling, Kim's gone into business."

Emmett asked what this meant.

"I'm still a doctor." Kimura crouched to put his hand on Lenore's forehead. "You're getting drunk!"

"Am I?" Lennie asked. So this is what they're always doing. It felt good.

"I'll always be a doctor. But can't a doctor also be an entrepreneur? I'm investing in a company. We're going to import medical equipment from Ohio. Very good machines for anaesthetics." His voice had quickened with excitement.

Emmett and Suzanne agreed; that's a good business for a doctor to be in.

"I'm always a doctor. But I have a partner who's not. Still, I think he's a very decent man." Kimura slowed, his attention strayed to the window and the green dusk. It was nearly solstice and still light outside. "A smart man," he said quietly. "Someone you know."

Suzanne so wanted to be gay. "How nice! We'll have him over!"

"You might not think it's nice. Someone from your past, Emmett. A man you knew very well. But he's retired now."

Emmett asked who he was. "A tired-out External drone?"

"Not tired. Perhaps disillusioned. Not External. The RCMP." He made himself look Emmett in the eye. "Very high up in Intelligence."

"Morton," Emmett said, "is not retired."

Kimura's face revealed his uneasiness. "Yes, he's retired from the Mounties now. Did you know he has five children? He can't afford such a family on what they pay him. And they frown on any man who tries to do business on the side. So he quit."

"Who's Morton?" Suzanne asked.

Lennie sat up. The Rabbit. "The man with the pink eyes."

Emmett realized that Lennie was thinking of her birthday a few years ago when the little man who hated the sun had arrived to collect him, the day when Morton had pretended to give him all his files. "Another man," he told her.

Kimura said, "His eyes aren't pink, they're brown. Are you mad at me, Emmett? For colluding with your enemy?"

"You mean *Robert* Morton. The spy from the RCMP?" Suzanne paled. "How *dare* you?"

Kimura had felt Suzanne's anger before. "But he's retired. He's started a new life. And a business venture that will make a lot of money. Me. A rich man without children. I'll have to give it away!"

Suzanne was not to be deterred. "Don't you realize what he did?"

Kimura said to Lennie, "Shall I give my money to you?"

"No, thank you," said Lennie. She held her empty glass like an egg and went to take it to the kitchen.

"How did this happen?" Suzanne wanted to know. "I can't believe you'd work with that awful, *awful* man."

"I think it was his job you didn't like," Kimura said. "Not the man."

"He spied on us!" But a tremor ran over her. She had spoken of John, "us," her instincts went first to John. Robert Morton was listening on the phone, it made a clicking sound when he tuned in.

Emmett saw fear in her eyes, and then she crossed her arms and she was uncontrollably angry because she'd cornered herself and it made her righteous. She said, "How can you even *think* of *colluding* with that *snake!*"

"That's enough!" said Emmett.

His scolding, masculine correctness did what it always did to Suzanne: it triggered tears.

Kimura helplessly offered, "I'll cancel the deal." It was apparent by his limp voice that the deal was not to be cancelled.

Emmett asked, "When did he quit the force?"

"I don't know for certain, but it was more than a year ago." Kimura looked miserable. "Two years ago, I think."

Then it was soon after Morton had pretended to return all the Jones files.

Lennie had come from the kitchen. She stood at the doorway to the living room in her stork pose, one socked foot tucked up against her knee. She was ten years old. Once she'd been skinny, but now she'd grown slender; gawky had become graceful; her bony face was striking. She had a beautiful mouth.

Lenore caught her father looking. Emmett had come to

expect a childish reprimand, a rolling of the eyes, but what he saw was forgiveness. Austere and impersonal forgiveness. She turned away and climbed the stairs toward her own room.

Suzanne began to apologize, "I don't know why it hit me like that. It was the shock. I'm sorry, Kim. God, I fight with you, don't I?"

Kimura, bewildered, reassured her, it was all right, it was just passion, "the passion of an artist," he called it, putting it beyond reason. "I wouldn't like you any other way."

"He was such a bogeyman in my mind," she said, adding ruefully, "I'm falling apart."

"Oh, I hope not!"

Emmett listened. Had Robert Morton gotten frustrated with the bureaucracy and decided he'd make some easy money? Five children would be expensive. He was a smart guy, a loner. What better way to fight communism than to make a fortune selling anaesthetic equipment?

One more thing troubled him. "How did you come to know Morton?" he asked Kimura.

Kimura's eyes went to the TV. He hesitated. "A mutual acquaintance. Happenstance." He stared at the television, feeling Emmett study him.

In the silty darkness, the election results were final: Diefenbaker's government had squeezed by with a minority. The summer of 1962. The bomb shelter was stocked with tomato soup, nail polish remover, and a broom for sweeping radioactive dust.

Suzanne sat down beside Kimura on the couch, and with puffy eyes and sisterly persistence she tucked herself under his arm, Kimura looking relieved but baffled. Emmett thought about the leather briefcase with its photographs and transcripts.

He had removed it from the vault beneath the garage; he'd taken it out to a quiet place in the country, wrapped it in a tarpaulin, and buried it in wet, mulchy soil. The tarp would loosen and rain would get in. Surely the rain will get in.

Chapter Nine

Gophers are solitary and they like dry ground, so the prime minister's remote summer retreat in the Gatineau Hills was idyllic for one particular gopher who seized the occasion of a summer's day to burrow the hole into which the prime minister put his foot as he descended from his flagstone terrace, thus breaking his ankle. His wife, Olive, got a doctor from a nearby village who might have set the cast too tight. At any rate, it swelled. Olive had him moved to Ottawa, to his bedroom on the second floor of Sussex Drive, where he was stranded but where she had access to better doctors. Still, blood vessels behind his knee burst, and blood filled his leg, and there was talk of amputation.

Since he'd been laid up, Cabinet meetings were taking place in his bedroom, so it was strange but not entirely abnormal for Emmett to receive a request for a consultation with the prime minister at his home, at bedside.

He was shown to the bedroom by Olive herself. He followed her up the broad carpeted stairs to a closed door, where she turned to give him an unfocused look and say, "Don't keep him too long. I've got his supper waiting." She ushered him in, "The young man you wanted has come, dear," and left him, closing the door behind her.

It was late afternoon and sunny, but the drapes were drawn here. In the gloom Emmett made out a four-poster bed and a figure propped up against a stack of pillows. From under the bedclothes a foot protruded encased in plaster. There were newspapers and several files strewn on the bed. Diefenbaker's freckled hands were knitted on his lap. Emmett saw that the prime minister was wearing yellow flannel pyjamas under a plaid bathrobe. The room smelled of Absorbine Jr.

Diefenbaker's eyes, like plums, set deep in his loose, wan face, followed Emmett as he crossed the room and came to stand uncertainly nearby. Dief nodded in recognition: this was the fellow he wanted, though Emmett had the impression that the prime minister didn't really know what exactly he did in the East Block, only that he was a comparatively friendly man who would agree with him. With no words of greeting, Diefenbaker told him, "Harold Gembey was here this morning."

Emmett went on alert. Gembey, chair of the Security Panel during the early days of Emmett's ordeal, was now head of Intelligence with External. He mumbled something congenial. The prime minister shivered irritably. "Pull up a—", waving with both hands. Emmett saw a row of chairs at the side of the room and pulled one toward the bed, aiming to place it at Dief's waist, avoiding the purple toes where they emerged huge and hairy from the end of the cast.

"He said he'd been down in Washington," Diefenbaker resumed. "At a conference for so-called Intelligence. A meeting of the spooks. He was invited to the British Embassy."

He drifted off, as if his message had been fully imparted. Emmett cleared his throat. The freckled hands plucked at the bedclothes. It appeared the prime minister was having difficulty swallowing. Yet for all his dishevelment, he acted as one who believed himself the only sane man in a madhouse. His over-sized head of curly yellowing hair trembled, his tongue darted out to moisten his lips, his eyes were bruised by exhaustion, but he evinced a prideful fury.

He gave a chuckle. And made a noise to indicate, I've got their number, the jig's up. A glass of water stood at his bedside and Emmett wanted to offer it to him, this man like a felled bird, a battered old falcon.

"Something's going on," Diefenbaker said. "And I'll bet my boots that hothead pup is at the bottom of it." The air whistling in his nose, Diefenbaker went on, "That arrogant son of a bitch is going to get us all blown to smithereens!"

"President Kennedy, sir?"

"President Kennedy, sir! That callow young bastard. That vain cock of the walk! That tinsel, that glamour boy, that prick! Well this is one prime minister he can't push around."

The door opened, a shaft of evening sunlight streaked across the carpet, and Olive came in with a glass of milk and a vial of pills. She told Emmett that it was six o'clock, just as a clock out on the landing struck the hour, tolling. Maybe it was the sunlight or the presence of his wife, but Diefenbaker seemed to shrink into his bed. "A baby boy, eh?" Diefenbaker said. "Dimples!"

Olive put the glass of milk into her husband's shaky hand.

When Emmett stood up to get out of the way, Diefenbaker cried out to Olive, "Don't let him go yet! I'm not finished! Don't let him out!"

Olive didn't appear to be surprised, merely petulant to match her husband's petulance, as if this was a typical bicker, but she turned the argument Emmett's way and said to him, "Oh please just say your piece, it's suppertime!"

He asked what the prime minister would like him to do.

"Get it clear!" Diefenbaker told him. "Find out what's going on!"

"With?"

"With Harold Gembey, with that arrogant bastard Kennedy, with the American security machine right outside my window!"

"You want me to speak to Gembey. And find out what happened in Washington."

"Find out everything! Before it's too late! Kennedy will destroy me, he'll destroy the Conservative Party of Canada! Don't kid yourself for a minute, he'll destroy you too! You! You're chickenfeed compared to the big stuff that little upstart is going after."

The prime minister's fear of personal slights outweighed his fear of nuclear devastation. In the silence following Diefenbaker's outburst, the tinkling of pills in the vial in Olive's hand was a reminder of time's passing. She held it pressed beneath her bosom and sighed and stared at Emmett, who thought how it was kind of funny that neither she nor her husband wore glasses, and how they had similar skin, soft as old peaches.

He left them there and soon found himself walking up Sussex without remembering that he'd left his Alfa parked back near Rideau Hall. The mild evening air was pleasant on his face. Walking, he imagined a nightmarish conversation with Harold Gembey.

— Dief has asked me to speak with you, Harold.

— Has he now?

— Yeah. He wants you to tell me, what went on down there in Washington, at the conference for spooks.

— You spying for him now, Jones? First you spy for the

Russians, then you spy for the Americans, now you spy for the prime minister?

— He didn't think you'd tell him what's going on, so he asked me to ask you.

— Of course I'll tell him what's going on. He's the prime minister of Canada. Even if he's nuttier than a fruitcake, I have to tell him. Even if he's barking mad, I have to tell him anything he wants to know.

Then Emmett imagined himself with his little Minox camera suddenly visible in his hand, and Gembey sitting up, alert. — Say, Jones, what's the game?

What's the game? A Chevrolet Bel Air lurched to a stop, squealing its tires to avoid hitting him as he blindly crossed the street. He stood in front of the car, feeling the heat from its engine, then leaned over to peer through the glare on the windshield. There was Oscar, his fifth Russian contact, his last, grinning back at him, wiggling his Groucho Marx eyebrows. Oscar stuck his head out the driver's window and said, "Get in the car, Mr. Jones! In a hurry! Before somebody bangs me in the rear."

He got into Oscar's Chevrolet.

Chapter Ten

Suzanne was working in her darkroom in the basement. She didn't notice that the sun had set since Lennie had got home from school so the house was in darkness but for a sliver of electric light illuminating the upstairs hall from beneath a closed bedroom door. From outside, Lennie's was the only light shining in the dark house.

Lennie was in her bedroom, standing on her bed. She was in debate with a throng of vile inferiors beneath the precipice where she stood, sword in hand. It was her sacred task to lead them from their weak and evil ways, on the difficult path toward the Good. She felt the fury of righteousness swelling in her heart.

She had almost made it through another week at school—one more day until the weekend. The pain of contact with all those people in the hallways, in the classroom or at bomb drill, inescapable in the washrooms and the change room before gym class, the exposure of her face, the feeling that her body had been cut out with scissors and pasted onto the scene, the long hour when she had to find somewhere to sit in the lunchroom and then outside to huddle in the grass with her back against the brick, making her face hard and blank.

She gave her foes one final thrust with her sword, then leapt off the bed into a freezing river that tumbled her over rocks into a waterfall, swimming even as she fell and so propelling herself into a glassy pool surrounded by ferns where a heron broke from the reeds and she lay on her thick wall-to-wall carpet and heard the shushshush of the heron's wings as he flew away.

Lennie floated in the glassy pool. Fish swam beneath her, gently nudging her body or even swimming over and around her with their cool slithery touch, and she turned and twisted with them. Larry, the boy who sits behind her in Homeroom, told her that she's prettier than Monica, the prettiest girl in the class. Lennie saw that he wasn't being mean. This moment is a rare reprieve, too small, too fragile, too dissimilar; on such fractional lapses in a day, week, month, school-year of pain, Lennie thought, yes, it's actually pain flowing out of the A where her ribs meet, like her soul is leaking from the punctures they make with their eyes, on Larry's surprising minute of kindness you can't build a person who can survive Grade Five.

She went down the dark stairs to the back door, opened it, and looked out across the lawn. There was that figure again, a ghost slinking away. She retreated, closed the back door, locked it. Then she went to the kitchen and turned on a light. She got a bowl and the flour from the cupboard, took the newspaper from the kitchen table and went back upstairs to the bathroom, and ran the tap till the water was warm. She stirred flour into the warm water with the end of her toothbrush. Then she took the bowl of glue to her bedroom.

She cut the newspaper into narrow strips, slipped the strips of newspaper through the glue, and lay them across her forehead, shocked by the first slimy chill, then liking it, and liking the smell of wet newspaper, she laid more strips across her nose and along her cheekbones, all over the face except of course the eyes and nostrils. She moulded the strips around her lips, smoothing it all around her face until she felt the mask conform to her features. Then she lay down to wait for it to dry.

Suzanne couldn't stop working. She was listening for the Alfa pulling into the driveway, for Emmett clattering in the front door, and she was counting her lucky stars he was late tonight. Lennie was in her bedroom; this yanked her attention, but it was guilt on a hard-mouthed mare; I'm getting good, she thought, too good at ignoring guilt, living with it, letting it get raw and scab over, a wound that's been with me for years. For how long? How long ago did she meet John?

She slid the paper into the developing solution and waited while the image rippled into existence. There he was again. And again. In the actor she once hired, she saw something of his poise, definitive and lonely, diffident, skeptical; in strangers whom she photographed without their permission — their backs turned away, even women sometimes, exciting when it happened, attractive solitaries with that muscle around the mouth. She saw something of him in gestures even if not in the people themselves, as if they participated in the event that was John Norfield. She took a slug of brandy from the bottle on the shelf where she stored her chemicals. One of these days her hand will choose the wrong bottle and she'll poison herself with developing fluid, a possibility that didn't trouble her, her analgesic being so close to her poison.

Gestures that belonged to John, that had been initiated by him in a wave of gestures undulating under the surface for the remainder of her life: his way of turning his back at the very moment of disclosure when something might have been said and felt and made true; his deflection, his solid purpose against the incursions of love, hard and shining as mica in stone, heat-possessing and older than God, yes, she thought of him as ancient, so ancient he'd outlive himself and her. And Lennie.

Out of the chemical bath Suzanne withdrew an image that no one, not Emmett, no gallery owner or journalist, no one would ever recognize as a continuum of her lode, her muse. John would have found it sentimental, he'd turn over in his grave, she thought, for she believed John finally dead; dead and enduring.

The photograph was a landscape, rock and pine trees, an image she'd caught at Blue Sea Lake from her canoe one morning very early when the lake was a mirror misted by the breath of dawn; a long low shore dividing a southeast sky from still water, reflecting dogwood in flower (it being the occasion of dogwood bloom) and the tidy shelf of cedar that cantilevered over the water and above, shrouded in mist, the pine trees. John's spirit was here. No one would know.

Chapter Eleven

Oscar turned his Chevy Bel Air around and drove back down Sussex toward the prime minister's house, passing it without comment, following the river east to the countryside, leaning over the steering wheel, his right hand loosely drumming the dash. The Chevy was a '61, but its shocks were shot and its back end struck pavement when the car hit a bump. It was dark now, and Emmett thought he saw sparks when he looked behind. Oscar must know how much he resembles Groucho Marx, Emmett thought, the nose, the moustache, the voice, the affected accent. The casual irony and a fondness for non sequitur. Emmett's Russian contact, his fifth, his last.

He let Oscar talk. The headlights strafed trees and brush. What Oscar was saying was interesting and he listened carefully, but he was also playing a little game with himself: he was pretending for a few moments that he was unburdened of connection to anyone on earth.

He pretended to himself that he was a person he'd long forgotten, before Suzanne, before Lennie and James, before the war, when he was young and solitary, and his decisions mattered not a damn to anyone but himself. Then it had been easy to be courageous, reckless. Pain, the possibility of death, all had been heroic fantasy. When he was young, without a family, in that lee of memory when his parents were out of the picture and the war was still something you trained for, he wasn't anyone at all, as if he didn't reflect any light. Now he took a moment to pretend to be him, that young man who'd never killed anyone. A line he'd heard from John came to mind, from that night when he first met him, first met Suzanne and fell in love. "There is no Mr. Tragedy."

But Oscar had finished laying the rationale for the broader plan the Party had laid for him — the information that Emmett would pry out of Diefenbaker during their bedroom confabulations at Sussex Drive, the photographs of documents from Diefenbaker's office — and Emmett was forced to return to his present, compromised state.

"Funny, ain't it," Oscar was saying, his fingers tapping the dash. "But not so funny as a man who never figures out that he's got to serve something greater than himself. *That* man doesn't even know he's a joke."

Emmett saw his own face reflected in the passenger window, illuminated by the green glow from the dash. He'd been wearing this face in its slow permutation for forty-two years.

"A selfish man is nothing but a scrap of irony," Oscar went on, "a thumb-sucking baby!" He gleefully slapped the wheel. "Deluded, silly, self-important! A man who does not serve the state is nothing! Not even a cipher. Unless — ah — *unless* he belongs to a system that will give him — on loan — a meaning. A function. You're a lucky man, Mr. Jones. You're not content to feel the sun on your head, you're not self-indulgent, you don't need to think you're some big-time mystery. That's why I like you! That's why I drive you around."

"What do you want, Oscar?"

"You can get access to your prime minister's desk."

"Even if I could, you don't really need it on paper."

"Sure we do! You know that."

Emmett didn't respond, so Oscar pressed, "Whàs'a matter? Your camera got broken?"

"I told you. I told you, and I meant it. I no longer work for you."

"Ah, come on. The cause was worth risking your life and now it's not?"

"That's right." The *cause*, Emmett thought, is exactly the point: it was individual freedom; it was his hatred of being manipulated by whatever power was reigning over him. It was his love of secrets, the ultimate privacy. Funny. It had led him to a lifetime of surveillance.

Oscar leaned toward him without taking his eyes from the road, his smile wryly generous. "Hey. You know what makes the world go round?"

"I don't know, Oscar. Is it love?"

"Foibles."

It was a great word in a New York accent. Emmett repeated it, "Foibles."

"Human foibles. Quirks of character."

"That doesn't sound very communist," Emmett observed.

"Why not? You know, you ought to take a broader view. Don't be so doctrinaire."

Emmett laughed.

"That's right. Laugh and the world laughs with you. What could be more communist?"

"So I should take photographs of the prime minister's papers as a contribution to an international conspiracy of fuck-ups."

Oscar raised his thick eyebrows. "Nasty."

Emmett wondered if the eyebrows and moustache were real. He said, "Take me back to my car, Oscar. I'm going home for dinner."

Oscar drove on for another mile or so without further conversation. Emmett looked past his reflection to the stars. If a man were to jump out of a spacecraft in outer space, he would have no purchase on his movement; if he began to fall with greater weight on his left foot, he'd "fall" in a perpetual spin to the left and would be helpless to change it. He was now helplessly rotating through Oscar's zero gravity just as he'd once felt he was falling through the zero gravity of his own country. Oscar handled the steering wheel with a light touch, his funny face set to an unreadable expression. As the miles passed, Emmett took a quick look at the dash, wondering how fast they were going, and if it would be possible to jump out of the car and try to run. He didn't know where they were, only that they were east of the city. At some point, Oscar had taken a route south of the river. The Chevy almost leapt off the last edge of concrete. Tall yellow weeds scraped at the passenger window as they tore down a gravel road.

"You don't want to get lost, Oscar."

"I'll find my way back. You don't have to worry about me." Oscar wiggled his eyebrows.

He saw that Oscar's levity was self-conscious, wilful. The gravel got sparse and soon they were driving over dried, rutted mud, the car bouncing so hard, Emmett banged his head on the roof.

The car struggled up a hill. When they reached the summit, Oscar braked and turned off the ignition. The sound of crickets. Oscar got out, Emmett quickly following suit. He stood with the car between them, trying to see in the dark whether Oscar had a gun. Oscar said, "I could shoot you. Or I could be humane, and leave you here and make you walk home."

The pulse of crickets, and wind, warm for October.

"Nice night for a walk," Oscar said.

Emmett didn't wait around. He ran into the field and down the hill, tumbling down the incline to a hedge and a barbed wire fence, someone's field. Oscar fired the gun. Just once. The sound went crackling through the air.

He pressed his body down in the grasses that grew up around the fence. He watched the headlights of the car dip and swerve over the landscape as Oscar manoeuvred the car around to drive back from where he'd come.

Chapter Twelve

Emmett arrived at his home at about six a.m. His last ride had dropped him off at Rockcliffe Park, so he'd walked the last few blocks from there. It was still mild weather. When he limped up his driveway he made out, in a milky pre-dawn, his wife sitting on the front steps. Suzanne was wearing a silk bathrobe, wrapped in a mohair blanket. She watched him approach with dull eyes that gradually began to fill with life. Relief, he was pouring relief into her. She watched him wordlessly, closely; even when he'd sat down beside her, she didn't speak but looked at him intently.

"Why are you out here?" he asked.

"Someone phoned last night," she answered hoarsely. "He said he was a friend of yours. He said I should watch for you."

Emmett put his hands on her face and pulled her close. "Where's Lennie?"

"She's all right," Suzanne said. "She doesn't know." She clutched at him. "Where were you?"

Emmett held her but didn't answer. He could sense that she was thinking quickly, contrary to the drag he felt in her body. As the moment lengthened, she became more solid in his arms, more separate from him. He was too exhausted to do more than marvel, feeling a sort of mild horror, thinking about how separate they really were. She had never asked him for anything more intimate than a reassurance that he was all right; it was his role always to be all right, to perform his function. And now, when perhaps it had occurred to her that she might have, that she should have, asked him something more deeply, that she might have asked him, What drives you? What do you believe in? it was too late. Her position seemed so terrible to him then, he didn't want her to be aware of it; even now he wanted to protect her.

She was weeping; he realized she'd been weeping for a long time, her hair was wet at the temples, her face was salty. "I waited at the window all night. Then I came out here." He recognized that type of weeping, deep and low in the throat. She was mourning him. "I didn't know what to do."

She began to cry so hard her back convulsed. He held her and felt her euphoria. He'd died for her that night, and returned, a second chance. The complexities, the guilt, the discrepancies would resume, but for now she was taking refuge in the room that his imagined death had emptied, a zero, indivisible, and absolutely full. Innocent.

He helped her to stand, and they went into the house. In the hallway, she looked up. Lennie was sitting at the top of the stairs.

Lenore saw her father in yesterday's clothes. She saw that he'd torn his pants. Even from here she could smell the sour dirt on him. She wearily pushed herself upright and went into her room, closing the door behind her.

Emmett said, "She gets more like my mother every day."

Suzanne had one slippered foot on the first stair, but she froze when he said this and turned back to look at him. He saw, he understood, that if she said another word, everything in his life would explode. But what she might say, he couldn't guess. In silence, he followed her past Lenore's closed door, to their bedroom.

He watched her kick the slippers from her narrow feet and sit on the bed and let the robe slip from her shoulders. She was wearing a fine white sleeveless nightdress he'd never seen before. He was so tired. He saw three small basins, two made by her clavicle and one formed at her throat, and he imagined them filled with dew.

Chapter Thirteen

Harold Gembey was standing in Emmett's office, looking out the window, when Emmett arrived there two hours later. Gembey was one of the chosen ones, whose smooth steady progress gave the department its shape, like a shoetree, a hat block.

Even after all these years, Harold wouldn't look him in the eye. Emmett did his best to capitalize on that. He'd had only thirty seconds to prepare himself for this encounter, since arriving, sleepless, and his secretary standing nervously to tell him that Mr. Gembey was waiting to see him. "He asked me to let him in," she said. She looked scared and apologetic.

"Hello, Harold," Emmett said. Gembey turned away from the window to say, "Emmett."

Emmett took a moment to hang his coat on a hanger behind his door. Then he went to his desk to look at the messages his secretary had left beside his telephone. Nothing to indicate that Gembey was due to drop in. He asked Gembey what he could do for him. Then he remembered the prime minister's demand that he question the head of Intelligence about "what's going on."

Gembey stood where he was. "We found your car," he began.

"On MacKay Street."

Gembey looked surprised. "Yes."

"Thank god it didn't get towed away." Then mild chagrin. "Suzanne is displeased."

Gembey waited for further explanation, but when he received none, other than Jones rubbing his temples in a semaphore that indicated "hangover," he said, "I see."

"Always sneaks up on you," Emmett said ruefully. With a trace of piety, "As long as it's only myself I'm harming. Anyway, Harold, it's funny to see you here."

Harold was about to explain, the abandoned Alfa Romeo had raised an alarm, but Emmett interrupted. "Just yesterday, Mr. Diefenbaker was asking about you. You've saved me a trip."

Gembey was attentive but not wholly convinced; mention of Diefenbaker's name didn't necessarily command a salute. Gembey, warily, "Oh?"

Emmett smiled. "You know how he is. Circuitous. And his leg's troubling him. Anyway, he's asked me to speak with you about the Intelligence summit in Washington, at the British Embassy, 'the conference for *spooks*,' he called it." He laughed generously, watching Gembey stiffen. "Listen, Harold, I know better than most men how little you can say about these things, even to your prime minister. But can you give me something? Anything to put his mind at rest?"

"I'll speak with him myself."

"Good." Emmett gave him a doubtful look. "And good luck." He touched the pile of messages on his desk: work to do.

Gembey sat down. "I've got some questions for you, Emmett."

"Go ahead." Emmett leafed casually through his messages. He saw among them one from his journalist friend, Wilson, and the phone number from the local hotel Wilson used when he was in Ottawa. He said wryly, "Though it's not exactly music to my ears, Harold."

"I'm sorry."

He shrugged.

Gembey said, "You didn't make it home last night."

"Well, yes. Technically, it was dawn."

"One of our guys picked you up on the parkway. He dropped you off at Rockcliffe Park this morning at 5:25."

"He was one of yours, was he?"

"When we saw your car parked near Sussex Drive at about four this morning, we got worried. We put some officers out to look for you. Perhaps you should tell me what happened."

"A friend of mine is in town. I'm afraid we're quite bad for each other." He added, "An American journalist whom I met in Korea during the war."

"Ah."

"He has a fondness for Canadian whisky. We got talking and a bottle flew by."

"Where did this take place?"

"I wish I knew. It was quite a bar crawl. Then we got it into our fool heads to cab it east. He knows someone out there. A woman. He decided to stay, and I hitchhiked home."

"Who is your journalist friend?"

"Harold, am I under suspicion now? Or have you just got a habit of prying into my private life?"

Gembey pursed his lips and apologized, saying that of course Emmett wasn't "under suspicion," he hadn't intended to pry, adding brusquely, "I'll let the department know that you're fine." He stood to leave. "I'm glad you're all right. But if you could give me the name of your American friend, it might make everybody feel better."

"Let me speak to him first, if you don't mind, Harold. It's not just his reputation at stake, you see? There's his friend. The woman." He got up to walk Gembey to the door. "You'll speak with poor Dief?"

Gembey studied the brim of his hat. "As a matter of fact, I'm on my way to Sussex now."

"Good," he said. "That's fine, then." He thought that Gembey looked tired, strained, on the verge of being overwhelmed. He'd always looked that way. It was partly what made Ottawa trust Harold: he wasn't a tall poppy; he was one among others trying to do an honest day's work in Canadian Intelligence. Funny, Emmett thought, all the funny ways to be a spook.

Chapter Fourteen

Robert Morton parked several houses down and across the street and used the rear-view mirror to watch Suzanne carry narrow boxes from the front door of their house and out to the trunk of her car. The girl was helping her.

He didn't doubt that the boxes contained Suzanne's photographs. He even surmised they were framed in slim black wood, the way she liked: he'd seen her shows before: tasteful, chic.

Morton knew something about kids. He saw that Suzanne and the girl weren't talking while they moved the boxes into the trunk. They worked unconsciously together, without conversation.

The girl had grown tall. The wistful earnestness he'd seen in her childhood had come into its own; she wasn't the kind of girl who'd ask for any favours nor grant any wishes. The independent type. Doesn't yet know she's intimidating. Sure, he knows something about kids, though he has only one daughter among the brood and that one is more regular than this one, and happier. When Morton was sure that there was no one else around, he didn't linger but pulled out and slowly drove ahead. He drove back downtown to the Chateau Laurier to meet Dr. Kimura for lunch.

The doctor was already seated in the dining room when Morton arrived, and he rose to shake Morton's hand, greeting him with his cheerful smile and warmly saying his name, "Robert, Bob, you're not late, I'm early. Overeager to forsake my patients." Kimura took his seat again, smiling. "I cannot express how much fun it is to be a man of the world!" He stared as a clutch of suits walked past to take a nearby table. "So many celebrities!"

Robert Morton looked. Mike Pearson was ordering lunch in the company of three other men. Morton knew them all. One of them was an American pollster, Lou Harris, granted leave by Kennedy to help Pearson's floundering campaign last June.

Dr. Kimura sipped his ice water, searching the other tables with undisguised delight. "You know what, Bob? Most ordinary humans are ugly when they're naked." He picked up the menu. "If we make a lot of money, my friend, I might just hang up my stethoscope forever."

Morton said, "You've given most of your life to other people. It's time you had something for yourself."

"You too! We're having our mid-life crisis together." Kimura studied the menu. "You know, as a doctor, I use the word *crisis* specifically to indicate the turn, the critical stage of an illness. At its crisis, a disease will go one way or the other. But my life is not a disease, it's a gift I cherish. Ever since I agreed to go into business with you, I've felt rejuvenated. I'm a doctor. It's what I am. I awoke to my fate of being a doctor when I was six years old, when I learned that my life was mine to make, like a waking dream, a dream I can guide this way and that. I remember the moment clearly. I was walking home from school. The teacher had told us about a famous physician in ancient Egypt. I felt a jolt of lightning rip though me. Eureka!

I'm a doctor. I walked home from school knowing, I am Takuya Kimura, doctor of medicine, even though I am only six."

The waitress came, and after she'd taken their order, Kimura said, "Is it this way with you? I am a policeman? Maintiens le droit! Right out of the starting gate?"

Robert Morton said yes, that this was true of his own life, in a way, though he hadn't had quite such a clear idea of how it might pan out. "I thought I was going to be a cowboy."

They ate their lunch and spoke about the small difficulties to overcome in importing the anaesthetic equipment from Ohio. Neither of them ordered a drink. They were having dessert when Kimura, in his most gentle, physician's manner, mentioned that he was attending a "small gala" that evening at "a beatnik club." "The wife of our mutual acquaintance," he said with mild chagrin, "Emmett Jones's lovely wife, Suzanne, is a photographer of some repute. But you know this."

"Of course I do. It's how you and me met, remember?" Morton said.

"At the gallery! When I was so angry. Really, I'm ashamed at how angry I was then. I went back alone to see her photographs of poverty. I was trying to make amends."

"You only got mad because you were worried."

"Yes. But it's always shameful to be angry."

"You've more than made up for it, doc."

Kimura grew thoughtful. "Well, it's natural for you to say so. I don't think I'll ever be sure."

"Emmett Jones needed you. I'm telling you, you're a real friend."

"Is it a friend? One who spies, one who tells?"

"Listen." Morton lowered his voice. "That's in the past.

What information you gave me only helped to clear his name. You let us see what kind of man he is. Naive. Loyal. Ambitious. Am I right? He'll never know how lucky he was that we found you. You've been the only real friend the man's ever had."

Kimura said, "This isn't true."

"No? Let me tell you something. Emmett was used by everybody who ever pretended to be on his side. They did nothing but take advantage of him." He hesitated before adding, "Even his wife."

Kimura quickly protested, "That's not true."

"Sure, okay." Morton smiled and lightly shrugged. "Women do." He tucked his tie in at his waist and smoothly continued, "You, on the other hand, understood him. Without your insights into this case, things might've gone very bad for him. You saved his life."

"I wish I could be sure. I'm fond of Emmett. I've known his daughter ever since she was a little baby. And I love his fearsome wife."

Morton said with a sincerity that surprised Kimura, "She's a beauty all right." He caught Kimura studying him. "They're safe now. All of them."

"Have they been unsafe, Bob? From persecution, yes. But is there more?"

"Not everybody is as reasonable as I am. There are some real nuts out there." He took a look around. Kimura had gotten used to Robert Morton's survey of a room, of a street, his quick inspection of cars at the curb with their windows down. "They don't know when to stop. They don't know any boundaries or borders."

"You refer to the fanatics. The enthusiasts."

Morton felt a warm wash of affection for his newfound friend. Briefly, he wished he could touch Kimura, just his shoulder, a small signal of appreciation for his insight. "The enthusiasts. That's right."

"Yes. They are everywhere."

"Sure. But here? In this country?" Morton took a drink of water as if to clear his palate. "I don't know. Maybe in Japan."

"Canada is my country of birth."

"Didn't mean to offend."

"I'm merely clarifying. There are enthusiasts in Japan, we all know this, especially those of us who lived through the war. Canada has them too. Every country does."

Morton scratched his jaw. He looked at the ring on his left hand, made the diamond dance in the light from the chandeliers above their table.

"A different shade of enthusiasm," Kimura added. But he was searching, thinking, this country is not very enthusiastic.

"Red?" Morton offered. Then, embarrassed at having made a poor joke, he pushed it, "Pinko?" He shifted himself uncomfortably in his chair.

"This is a country of 'dear-hearts and gentle people,' like the song by Perry Como. Every person in Canada is at the centre of his own universe."

"Sometimes they're not such dear-hearts. Sometimes they're just fanatics. I hate communists. But hatred is putting us at the brink of nuclear war. Now's the time to drain the acid from our blood. But there are men who like the feel of hate, and they can make a lot of righteous trouble for an odd fellow like your friend Emmett and his beautiful wife." He pushed his heavy chair away from the table. He didn't normally talk so much.

They patted their lips with the linen napkins and stood to leave, Robert Morton in his crisply pleated pants, shaking his knees a little so the cuffs rode over his penny-loafers. Casually, "So — a beatnik gala tonight."

"That's right. Her new photographs will be hanging in a popular café. I hear there'll be music."

"I wish I could come."

Kimura stopped, embarrassed, "I don't think it'd be a good idea, Bob."

"Oh, I know, I know."

As they were leaving the restaurant, Dr. Kimura said, "I find it hard to be middle-aged."

"Why? You're fit. You're in pretty good shape in every way."

"I'm in good shape. Yet I feel heavy with myself."

They said goodbye on the sidewalk outside the Chateau. Morton remarked that it was a mild fall. There was soft sunlight. But Kimura seemed to have snagged a cloud, for he muttered fretfully, "Such a long season with no change in the weather!"

"Don't worry, doc. It'll snow."

Kimura nodded curtly. He'd gotten cranky, unhappy. He turned and stumbled from the curb. Morton caught his arm to pull him back to the sidewalk, but Kimura's knee gave out and he went down at a funny angle. He heard a pop and felt the meniscus cartilage squeezed, pinched and released, bruised, damaged again. An old, recurring injury. "I'm okay," he told Morton and bid him adieu.

As he limped back to his office, Kimura's irritation yielded to anxiety. His injured leg brought back a bad memory. Yes, Bob Morton had found him. It had frightened Kimura very much when the RCMP nosed him out as the travelling companion named in Emmett's report to the Liaison Mission after the brawl in the bar. Robert Morton had "invited" Kimura in for questioning about his friendship with Emmett Jones. It had taken all of Kimura's skills to conceal his fear during this questioning, his terror that Morton would connect him and Emmett with the death of a Japanese policeman. But it never came up. Morton didn't know about the homicide in the Tokyo bar. And Kimura had helped Emmett, he'd helped his friend by drawing a portrait of him for Robert Morton, a portrait of a man innocently snared by the Red hunt.

Kimura thought, I like Bob Morton. It was true, he was excited now to be in business. Did he like being in business with Morton? Or did he want to keep Morton in full view? Yes, it's this way for him. He has always feared the police and always loved them too.

He'd lost his fervour for practising medicine. The flesh presents untransmutable evidence of disease and decay. In these recent months, he'd felt aversion for his patients. A sort of stage fright. His compassion has been exhausted. Yet he must contrive to play against each sickness, play by play till checkmate. When did he get to be disgusted with human beings? They almost always die meanly. Even surrounded by family, they're alone, even the very old, crying out for their mother. If only illness and death were beautiful. His knee hurt so much it made him nauseous. I should have hailed a taxi, he thought. I've really screwed it this time. I'll be on crutches. I'm an imbecile.

He's lived without great achievement. His most original act has been to serve the RCMP. An agent! Helping the police in the name of helping his friend, betraying Emmett's privacy and in this way betraying his own privacy, inevitably, permanently, a light where there should be darkness and peace. I've become unnatural. He pulled at the door to his clinic. How will I live out my life? He greeted the receptionist and limped to his examination room. I should have married.

Chapter Fifteen

Emmett had noticed a sort of slipstream, when time moved more quickly and when he knew, he almost heard, what was going to happen next. For example, he knew that Harold Gembey would leave his office and go directly to see the prime minister because Gembey had told him so. But he also knew that after Gembey had left Sussex Drive, the prime minister would call him.

Emmett hadn't had any sleep. He had a blister on his heel from his long trek home after Oscar had abandoned him on the starlit hill. Even his secretary warily noticed his high spirits, his quickened mind in dictation, felicity that seemed out of keeping in the doleful East Block. He snapped off three memos on matters that yesterday had seemed too complex for individual solution.

Oscar, you old comedian, he said to himself, we're through, *kaput*, go fuck yourself.

He didn't know if Oscar would leave him alone now. Oscar's true motives would be unknown even to Oscar himself, maybe even to Oscar's Soviet handler, to the handler of the handler of the handler of the air marshal of the general of the foreign minister of the Kremlin. Maybe, if Emmett Jones were wiped out by a rogue Bel Air with bad shocks, it would be because of President Kennedy. The original Marx, Herr Karl Marx, wrote that one brilliant passage on the "perversion of human needs," and it had become a sort of mantra for Emmett. *My means of life belong to someone else, my desires are the unattainable possession of someone else, everything is something different from itself, an inhuman power rules over everything.* An inhuman, relentless power — power for its own sake — an inhuman power rules even over Jack Kennedy.

Two hours later, when Emmett entered the boudoir of the prime minister of Canada, he found Diefenbaker dressed in a white shirt with a loosened tie, but with the same plaid flannel bathrobe thrown over his clothes, seated in a cushioned chair with his foot resting on an ottoman. Emmett greeted Dief a little too fondly and then he sobered, expressing the tired willingness of a mediocre civil servant; a necessary focus for the prime minister in tribulation. He blandly informed the prime minister that he'd had a word with Harold Gembey.

Diefenbaker cut him off with a wave of his hand. "Nothing new," he grumbled, "same old vague poppycock."

A vacuum cleaner powered on somewhere in the house. Diefenbaker's bedroom resembled the one he might have had back in Saskatchewan where he'd practised law, where even his favourite painting of John A. Macdonald would represent not a statesman's forefather but simply a common man's ideal. The droning vacuum now made Emmett aware that Dief was not much more than a hotel guest at Sussex Drive, that the man's chronic fury was inspired by his own sensation of being an impostor, a country cousin, a temporary embarrassment to the Establishment.

"I had visitors," Diefenbaker began. "On the hill. Oh yes, I've been out today. I might just as well have been to the moon."

The snoozy drone of the vacuum was now accompanied by the scent of floor wax. There were other odours too, of an apple

454

pie in the oven, fragrances of Prince Albert, Saskatchewan, wafting on the dust motes through the curtained bedroom. Emmett stood still but perhaps because sleeplessness recalled nights with Lennie in infancy, he swayed a little, or it was the sensation of the earth turning round. He sighed.

Diefenbaker heard the sigh and again he said, "Oh, yes. You can be damn sure I've had visitors. Two hours before he tells the entire world that he's taking us to the brink of thermonuclear destruction, he sends his link boy to bring the prime minister of Canada up to speed."

"President Kennedy, sir?"

"President Kennedy, Captain America, that arrogant son of a bootlegger. I look into a mind like that and I see a little boy, desperate to meet the measure of his own farfetched ambition. Playing politics like it's polo. He'd sooner destroy the world than take advice from other world leaders."

"You've heard from President Kennedy *today*, Mr. Diefenbaker?"

Diefenbaker went on, grumbling, "Of course that majordomo de Gaulle will do whatever Kennedy tells him to do. Macmillan too. I'm the only man strong enough to stand up to him. Which is why he shirks me, dodges me like a guilty schoolboy. Two hours! The very day!"

"The very day of what, sir? Two hours till what?" Emmett knew it didn't matter how nonsensical his prompt might be; Dief would unravel his complaint as he wished. Emmett was only a figure swaying in the shadowy room.

"He showed me pictures!"

"Of?"

"Aerial photographs. Which, he *claims*, show a bunch of Soviet missiles. Blow ups. Squiggles and dots. Why should I believe that wild little gangster? His fool ambassador tells me that I'm looking at Soviet missiles thirty times more powerful than the Hiroshima bomb. Shadows and polka dots! It only exists in Kennedy's mind. He fears Cuba, so he has a nightmare, the missile sites are in Cuba. It's the work of a psychosis. It's a terrible joke. The world is threatened by a playboy in Washington."

"Aerial photographs, sir? Of Soviet missile sites in Cuba?"

Diefenbaker chortled. "With enough power to blow up Hudson Bay. Enough nuclear weapons to wipe out Montreal, Toronto, Ottawa, Sudbury, and Lima Peru. Kennedy's trying to hold a gun to our heads."

"Soviet missiles, Mr. Prime Minister?"

"Pictures of what he says are nuclear warheads. He's got nuclear on the brain. We need better proof! We need consultation! If it's real, it should go to the UN! What we need is an independent, on-site inspection by the unaligned members of the disarmament committee. But what we get is the American president showing faked-up pictures taken from an airplane and telling us it's war."

Emmett said, "Soviet nuclear warheads stationed in Cuba and aimed at North America."

"Quite a story, eh? He'll have everybody's attention now! Champion of democracy!"

"What if it's true?"

"Don't be so easily fooled. It's a phoney set-up by the CIA. It's a manufactured crisis. It's horse opera."

"May I ask, what are you planning to do?"

"Nothing!"

"Forgive me, sir, but that might not be possible. Under the circumstances."

"I say do nothing. Call his bluff. If I let my government go along with the Americans now, we'll be their vassals forever." Diefenbaker's hands clutched the arms of his chair. He stared so hard at the wardrobe situated behind Emmett, Emmett turned around to look, as if an attack might spring from it. Diefenbaker asked, "Do you have children?"

"Yes. Yes, I have."

"Go home then."

Chapter Sixteen

He went home. They watched television while they had dinner, Emmett, Suzanne, and Lenore. Emmett and Suzanne would certainly have preferred to shelter their daughter from President Kennedy's dry, raspy presence at the dinner table but couldn't refrain from moving the TV set around so they could watch while they ate. They had meatloaf with creamed corn, a meal that none of them liked but which Suzanne seemed to feel compelled to offer.

While Suzanne was taking away their plates, Lennie asked her father, "Is there really an imprisoned island?"

"Cuba? No," he said. "It's what President Kennedy thinks."

"He's *our* president?"

"No."

"Are the Russians going to take us prisoner?"

"No, baby. That will never happen."

"Will they blow us up?"

"No. Never."

"How do you know?"

"It would be crazy, wouldn't it."

"It's what people do."

Suzanne returned from the kitchen with ice cream and chocolate sauce.

Lennie spooned ice cream, kicking the legs of her chair. Suzanne told her to stop, but Lennie went right on kicking.

They'd turned off the TV. The only sounds were the scraping of their spoons and Lennie's shoes striking the legs of her chair.

Finally, Suzanne said, "You have homework."

"I already did it."

"Then go upstairs and take a bath."

Lennie got down from her chair. "Dad? Come to my room please."

"Sure. Why?"

"I have to talk to you."

He followed Lennie upstairs to her bedroom. She told him to sit, there, on the bed, and then closed the bedroom door. She still had the ballerina lamp she'd had since she was in a crib. He turned it on and touched his finger to the dust on the dancer's pink shoe.

Lennie stood on the chair in front of her white desk to reach into the cupboard above, where once she'd stored her china horses. Now she carefully lifted down what looked at first like a stack of egg cartons but which proved to be a series of masks, one of them still powdery and unpainted, but the others lacquered in white, like egg shell, with black rims around the eyes. The painting was skilful and remotely Asian. One mask was painted in more ordinary watercolours, Emmett marvelling over the brush strokes, the blending of a sage green to make a skin tone, fawn shading at the temples. Lenore held this mask to her face.

She held the mask in place, an inch or two from her face, and in the quirky lamplight the mask threw a shadow on her own features, making a triplicate of Lennies.

He told her, these are very good; he said, he hadn't realized she had such talent.

Lennie removed the mask and laid it down. She gently stacked them again then stood on her chair to replace them in the cupboard above her desk. "Would you like me to make one of you?" she asked.

He said he'd like that. But he hoped she didn't want to do it right now. "I have to go back to the office."

"Late at night?"

"The House of Commons is sitting tonight. I should go and see if there's anything I can do."

She looked at him without saying anything. She was wearing a navy jumper with a white shirt and navy leotards. She had long legs and arms, long hands with long fingers, and she wavered or it appeared that she did; a concentrated searching of her father's face rippled through her body. As had happened so recently in speaking with his wife, Emmett had the sensation that if his daughter were to say what was on her mind at this moment, his world would blow up. He waited in dread. She was trembling, like water trembling at the lip of a glass before it overflows.

"What is it?" His question was barely audible. He heard her swallow. She looked into his eyes, and when she looked away, down at the baby blue carpet, he felt abandoned, irretrievable. More loudly, in a normal voice, he asked, "What's up, Lennie?"

She said, "I'll never tell."

"But why?"

"I'll never tell on you."

"Well," he said, laughing nervously, "thanks." He stood up to leave.

She didn't move but observed him closely. He might have been a well-constructed robot; she seemed mildly impressed by his ability to operate his limbs. Her lovely face, her suddenly beautiful mouth, and her direct gaze softened. Her kindness completely unnerved him. He laughed again and began to hurry out. He was in the hallway, wondering if she wished him to close the door behind him, when she added, "Don't worry."

"Okay," he said. He made himself smile and lightly respond, "I'll try not to, Lennie Penny. And don't you worry either."

"People always laugh when they know they've done something really terrible," she said.

Emmett turned, re-entered her room, and sat down again on her bed. "Have I done something terrible?" he asked.

She gnawed at her lip. He saw her uncertainty. He asked her to tell him, "Do you believe I've done something bad?"

"Sometimes," she said. "When you're not here."

"Maybe I have. But I've tried to be a good man."

A look of revulsion, as if at a foul odour, passed over her face. She patiently waited for him to leave and go back to the office. He was embarrassing her. "It's hard," he said. "In the grown-up world. In the adult world," he corrected himself; he must no longer speak to her as to a child, "we have to make decisions based on what we know at the time. Sometimes we make mistakes."

"Do you make mistakes?"

"I don't know. Yes. Of course I do. I've made many mistakes, I know." He added, disliking himself, "My intentions were good."

"What have you done?"

"Well. Many things. A lifetime of things." He looked to the ballerina lamp for an answer. He thought, Everything is something different from itself. "I hope you have a life, my darling, my love, that lets you be good. Really good. For your entire life. You deserve that. How I wish it for you, baby."

461

Chapter Seventeen

The prime minister was planting tulips. Olive was helping him because he was still using crutches. Emmett walked up the drive and passed a scowling, furious minister of defence on his way out. Harkness would assume that Diefenbaker was being counselled by civil servants just like Jones, in his decision to stall on putting the military on high alert to match the Americans. NORAD and the regular forces were waiting in vain for the prime minister's okay.

Olive was on her knees digging with a trowel while the prime minister sat on a lawn chair, holding a burlap sack filled with bulbs. She didn't stop working when Emmett approached. Diefenbaker gave him a quick, nervous smile. "I told him off," he confessed without preamble. He shook his jowls. "Those photographs are phoney baloney. It's a set-up by the CIA."

Olive said, "Don't talk. Plant."

"It's going to rain," the prime minister explained. "We've got to get these in before the weather goes sour." He dug into the sack and produced a bulb, handing it to his wife and saying, "Harkness would have us go off like sheep to war. He may be a fine fellow, but he's weak, a follower, he's too eager to please the Americans."

Emmett said, "It might not hurt to let the forces go on high alert, Mr. Prime Minister."

"Hurt! Hurt! Of course it'll hurt! Why, we stand to lose—not just a chance to make peace—we lose our credibility with the Cubans! We lose our credibility for nuclear disarmament. Kennedy wants a war? Let him have his war. He's been itching for it since he messed up the Bay of Pigs." He shook his sack of bulbs.

"Actually, Mr. Prime Minister, there's word that the military has already moved on this."

"Eh?"

"I said there are rumours, generally around the Hill, that the navy and RCAF have already moved onto bases in the south, into Florida. I hear the navy's out looking for Soviet fishing boats off the coast of Labrador. And in the North Atlantic. Working with the US navy."

"I know that. You're not telling me anything new."

"I'm sorry."

"I have my finger on the pulse."

"Yes, sir."

"I don't need you to tell me what's going on in my government."

"No."

"What do you mean, no?"

"I understand."

"How did you come by this omnipotence?"

"Sir?"

"You heard me. Loud and clear."

"I don't follow."

"Ha! Could have fooled me!"

Olive was struggling to stand up. Emmett took her arm to help her. "That's all right," she said. "I've been gardening all my life."

"Yes," said Emmett. "It shows."

A siren raced down Sussex. Diefenbaker's crutches were on the grass beside his chair. He picked them up and stood, dropping the sack of bulbs.

Emmett said, "Your garden is beautiful."

"No, it's not," Olive said. "Not now."

"You haven't answered my question," said Diefenbaker.

"The tulips are *his* craze." Olive retrieved the bulbs from the grass.

"Pardon?"

Diefenbaker pointed a crutch at him. "I said, how do you know what the RCAF has done? And who told you this gobble-dygook about the navy?"

"Of course I don't know for certain, sir. I'm merely quoting rumours going around."

"Then you know he telephoned me."

"Sir?"

Diefenbaker chortled unhappily. "I gave him the what-for."

"Are you speaking of President Kennedy?"

"Himself. The warmonger. He wants the Russians on the defensive. And then they'll go and bomb us."

"I hope that's not the case," Emmett said with a dry mouth.

"Oh, you just don't know the trouble we're in."

Olive had set off for the house, saying, "Come on, Daddy." Diefenbaker began to move across the lawn on his crutches, Emmett following, wondering if he'd been dismissed. Diefenbaker stopped to let him catch up and said, "I'm giving you the benefit of the doubt."

Emmett thanked him, vaguely.

"I hear you were a communist."

"No. No sir."

"A real college Marxist."

They were standing close enough for Emmett to see each wiry curl on Diefenbaker's head. He felt an odd surge of love for this crazy old man. He could almost tell him the truth. "I once admired the Soviet Union."

Diefenbaker gave another of his miserable chortles.

"But I was naive, Mr. Prime Minister."

"Be that as it may, you're a nice fellow. I'm not a man to shy from controversy. If you admire the Soviets, say so. Forthright. Loud and clear."

"I think we have to take the threat of nuclear attack from Russian missiles in Cuba very seriously, Mr. Diefenbaker."

"Very seriously," said Diefenbaker, mimicking. "Well, anyway, I like you because you think for yourself. If we're blown to bits in the next twenty-four hours, at least you can say you always spoke your true mind."

Chapter Eighteen

Bill Masters tapped and came in. Emmett caught a quick glimpse of his ashen-faced secretary with her hand on the phone before Bill closed the door.

Bill had gone grey since his second heart attack, and he'd lost about fifty pounds, had become a shrunken little man; he was like a bad impersonator, hardly recognizable. Emmett was always shocked to see him, though he ran into him often enough. Bill crossed the room and went to the window without speaking. From behind, Emmett thought, you wouldn't even know it was Bill; he hadn't seemed to be so short when he was fat.

Bill seemed to like his new svelte self; had taken to wearing herringbone jackets with coloured shirts. The weight loss hadn't done anything for his nerves. He looked down at the centre yard, then stood on his toes to peer out toward Wellington Street. "You know they're talking about an evacuation," he said.

"Yes. I heard."

"More than five hundred people will fit into Diefenbaker's concrete bunker." He turned to face Emmett. "But not you and me."

"No."

"Head of the CBC, for chrissake. He goes." Bill winced, trying to smile. "Bryce went out and bought a whole bunch of booze. On his own dime." Bryce was the clerk of the Privy Council, a very practical man. "He personally told me, he'd cleaned out his own private bank account to buy it all." Bill returned to the window; he was like a dog left behind from a family outing. "Rye. Scotch. Gin."

Emmett told Bill, Diefenbaker's bomb shelter still wouldn't be very much fun, even with Bryce's booze.

"Better'n being fried on the outside!" Bill's voice had changed too, from a frog to a cricket. "Jesus!" He came and plunked himself down in the chair opposite Emmett's desk. "Something I want to ask."

"Okay."

Bill — this strange new Bill — squinted at him. "You ashamed, you feel justified, you feel what?"

Emmett asked him what he meant.

"The Russkies. What do you make of them? Now they're on our doorstep going to blow us all up."

"There have been madmen for as long as there have been men."

"Sure. But destroy the whole world? I want to know. What do you feel?"

"Unreal. I feel unreal."

"Well, it's real, pal," Bill said angrily. "Answer my question for once. Don't give me none of this real-unreal stuff. You were a communist. Now how do you feel?"

"You're bringing this up now? Now you're frightened, you're accusing me?"

"Be straight, Jones. It's the end of the world."

Emmett paused. He and Suzanne and Lenore might be dead tomorrow. Or, worse, they might survive for a few days before succumbing to radiation sickness. He hated Bill's show, this death's door inquisition. If he and his family were going to be extinguished along with another hundred million people, it didn't mean he had to speak to Bill about his real feelings. He said, "I was wrongly accused. You know that."

Bill sniffed. "Where there's smoke, there's fire."

"Yeah. Sure. I gave the Russians information about the layout in Cuba, possible access from the sea. I took photographs so they could formulate better plans, land surveys from British railways. I kept them abreast of Castro's revolution. I was the Who's Who of Cuban unionists. I arranged liaisons between Russian apparatchiki and Che Guevara. I was instrumental in arranging Castro's oil and sugar imports from the Soviet Union." He paused then added, "And tonight, my family and I are escaping by helicopter to safety in the Crimea."

Bill's face, at first almost gratified, soured. "I stood by you."

"Yes. You did. And I'm grateful. So why are you turning against me now?" He spread his fingers on his desk and leaned forward.

Bill, staring at him, blinked and gazed around the room. "I don't know. I guess I wanted somebody to blame."

"You should go home, Bill. Ethel will be worried." Emmett came around the desk to usher Bill out. He touched the skinny shoulder. He felt canny. Alert. He asked Bill, would he be able to get some rest if he just went home to Ethel and trusted that nobody was going to pull the trigger tonight?

"How about you?" Bill asked. He gripped Emmett's arm; he seemed to have swung from anger to love. "How's Suzanne? Is she scared?"

"She's fine. I made her a bomb shelter." He laughed, forcing Bill into a nervous chuckle. With the door open, Bill turned and hugged him. Emmett heard his secretary give a gasp of despair. He would send her home. No doubt, her husband was already waiting in the parking lot.

Chapter Nineteen

Emmett didn't tell his secretary anything just then but again retired behind the closed door. Raw inside, in the pit of his stomach, raw with a suspicion that he'd been emptied forever, that pretending, feigning, living by proxy, this was all that was left to him; he was dry in his soul. What he knew was no secret: Canada's Bomarc missiles were actually filled with sand; there was no nuclear deterrence there or in the Voodoo interceptors — this was what Oscar wanted confirmed, but it was bankrupt information, pretty well public knowledge. The prime minister wanted the missiles in Cuba to vanish into fantasy, wished them to be phoney photographs, fake evidence manufactured by the CIA. Diefenbaker, the prairie lawyer, needed to have faith in objective information, a loving God, unaligned multiples, disinterested confirmation from the UN, and at the same time, he needed to believe that his nemesis, the handsome Jack Kennedy, was working in subterfuge, from a hidden agenda.

The missiles were real, and there were already enough of them in Cuba to blow up North and South America: this is what Emmett believed. He also believed that the Russians would do it; they'd use nuclear missiles if they were forced to prove themselves, to avoid humiliation, forced to prove the success of their revolution. This was how it worked — every system carrying within itself the seed of its own death.

When External first began to send him to Cuba, in the first blush of the revolution there, he'd taken some good pictures for the Russians, he'd done some very handy sleuthing right under the noses of the embassy staff. Even Kennedy in those early days of the Cuban revolution had admired the socialist freedom offered by Castro. *Time* magazine had called Castro "a humanist." Prior to all that, in Emmett's posting to the Liaison Mission in Tokyo, he'd done good work too, he believed even now; the massive UN force against the North Koreans was unjust; he had believed that it was the occasion for communism, imperfect yet inevitable. The photographs he'd taken of the Yalu River had gone to his Russian contact and he'd felt good about that, it had been an honourable risk in the name of freedom, of justice.

Later, when Jim Smith had forced him to work for the CIA, he'd given up; he'd fed the CIA only the most obvious information, stuff they already knew; he'd never tried to achieve any useful espionage for the Americans. Just when it might have been useful. He could almost laugh at himself. But then he thought, I'm not very funny.

He opened his door to tell his secretary that she could go home, but she had already gone. His phone rang. He let it ring. The only person he'd answer to was Suzanne, and he was on his way home now. But something made him change his mind, and he picked up.

"Emmett?" A man's voice.

"Who am I speaking to?"

"It's Harold."

"Pardon me?"

"Harold Gembey," said the voice.

Emmett warily answered, "Hello, Harold. Anything wrong?"

"I just want to talk to you. How about you meet me outside. I'll be parked right on Wellington."

"Okay," slowly.

"It's your wife. It concerns her."

"My wife."

"Your wife and daughter."

"I see."

"Five minutes."

"No," Emmett said. "I've got some things to do first. Twenty minutes."

The person on the other end hesitated, then agreed.

Emmett couldn't go home. Whoever was on the phone would follow him there. He wanted, at this hour, he yearned to be with Suzanne and Lenore. But he would use what little talent he had left to make them feel, if not safe, then completely loved. He thought, if this passes, if this crisis is resolved, if the world survives, I'll get Kimura to help me bring my son here. And Aoi, if she wants to come. He'll look after them. Lennie will be happy.

Twenty minutes. The duration struck him as a gift, a bit of bliss, a reprieve from this headlong rush toward disaster. He thought he would take the time to practise something. In the future, if there were one, he would live a single life, no secrets. The drapes moved, he saw them move, though there was no one in the room with him. The sordidness of the nuclear standoff struck him clear and hard with a wave of sickness.

He considered leaving his office right now, going outside, walking down toward the riverbank, past the public path, farther, down into the bush where the leaves had fallen, in the burnt orange dogwood and crisp, dun oak, to sit and be alone, to avoid meeting whoever was waiting for him in a car on Wellington Street. A stack of papers lay on his desk, the pen he liked to write with, a blue cup he used for paper clips, a pretty thing he'd taken from Suzanne. By the window (where the drapes moved), a softly worn leather chair, black leather softened grey. The carpet too was worn, its dark pattern. Dark oak furniture, forest green walls, the oil painting in its gilt frame above the door, *The Capture of the Halifax*.

The mantel clock on the credenza chimed. He must not go near his house. Whoever was waiting outside would follow him there. He would protect his family by staying away.

Emmett was enthralled by the oak wood, by the worn wool of the carpet, by creased leather, and a shadow that moved in the wake of sunlight through the drapes (that moved, with light, with time's passing). Everything is something different from itself. Life is beyond us all.

He remembered Lennie's totem, her mortal exchange, her childhood apprehension that we become what we kill. Maybe he was so afraid right now, he had fallen in love with fear.

He remembered Lennie's totem and he could see her, standing on one leg, stork, to meet his eye, and he saw that she had become beautiful and that she would forgive him not easily but through an act of will. Her slender body, her impersonal grey eyes, her mouth. Now he let his own world change shape. Now he let in the knowledge he'd forestalled until he was ready. That Lenore was John Norfield's. Norfield fathered her. Norfield's hovering over their lives; Suzanne's obsession, all those posing actors and strangers and gestures, and the haunting, the grief she inscribed in a landscape.

Among the files so generously donated back to him by Robert Morton, there was, he first thought, none of Suzanne with John. Emmett had found this too unlikely to be reassuring, and when he finally had a chance to peruse them in private, he had discovered that this was not the case; there was a photograph of them together: one. Dated 1951. Precise location unknown but not far from home. John had come back without Emmett's knowing.

Was it only a perverse sort of ecstasy at the eleventh hour that made it so easy to see that it didn't matter? A sublime indifference he might have learned from his daughter. Lenore was his daughter too. He loved her out of dutiful fatherhood instilled in a man of ordinary talent. But the love he felt was also instinctive, adoring, pleasurable; he would give his life for the pleasure of saving hers.

Emmett sat down at his desk. He took the pen he liked and wrote three letters: one for Suzanne, one for Lenore, and one for Dr. Kimura, asking Kimura to find his son, asking him to help Aoi and James to safety.

Are the letters to Suzanne and Lenore truthful? he asked himself when he had finished and was sitting back to reread them. They were more than that. It was something to build life on, the everlasting changefulness at the heart of things, the intricate and ever-changing expressions of love. He found he was good at it, love.

Less than an hour later, Emmett Jones stood on the roof of Kimura's apartment building. Below, the smallest branches of the treetops shivered when their last leaves fell. The common garden, seven storeys down, was going to seed, pale yellow pods pinned to dry stalks, and the darkest red ivy twining the spikes of the iron fence. Beyond the iron fence, the broad river turned on its sullen currents.

Emmett took out his cufflinks and slid his watch over his hand, then placed these objects on the ledge that ran the circumference of the roof. In the pocket of his suit jacket he felt the weight of the three handwritten letters. He took off his suit jacket and folded it so that his letters were hidden, and placed the jacket several feet away from his watch and cufflinks. He stepped up onto the ledge.

He loved the trees, their nearly infinitesimal movement when their leaves let go. Deliberately, he removed his glasses and set them down.

Out on the river, a white boat drifted lazily, a white blur. There were nuthatches somewhere, their low whistle, *whi whi whi*. Emmett envied the boat on the river, the nuthatches in the trees, the garden as it collapsed into late autumn. He envied and loved it all.

He realized that not so very many minutes had passed, and quickly he turned to look behind his back, and then again faced the river. He leaned into the air, slowly gave himself until his weight began to lift from his feet, until he learned what it was like to be airborne and then how it was to fall.

◇

Dr. Kimura had stayed home from the medical clinic that day; his meniscus cartilage was torn again. He was sitting in his penthouse, reading the *Ottawa Citizen* while listening to the radio for news of the missile crisis when, out of the corner of his eye, he saw something dropping past. Kimura limped painfully to his large picture window with its beautiful view. The pane of glass radiated heat. He saw a pleasure craft, a wooden cabin cruiser, drifting on the river. The boat suddenly veered toward shore. He saw a woman sitting on the top deck of the boat; she was clutching two children to her side, and she was screaming. With his crutches, Dr. Kimura took the elevator down seven storeys to the doors at the back of his building, yielding to the patio and garden.

The cabin cruiser had already moored to shore, and a man was running from the boat toward the iron fence encircling the garden. Dr. Kimura stood on the other side, and for several moments, the two men stared at the tall spikes of the fence. Suddenly the man fell to his knees, and the doctor could hear him being sick into the grass. On the boat, moored at the shore, the woman was still screaming. Kimura said, "For god's sake, get your family away from here.

"Take the boat to the marina," Kimura said firmly. "Get your wife to take the children into the cafeteria there, give them hot chocolate or something." Kimura manoeuvred his crutches on the soft ground. "I'll phone the police."

Kimura looked up at the roof of his apartment building, yellow brick obelisk, blue sky, cirrus clouds catching the sun.

As he was making his way back to the patio and inside to the elevator, he heard the throaty roar of the boat's engine gunning in reverse. Kimura pressed the button to the elevator, briefly tempted to take the stairs but knowing he'd never make it up seven flights. He felt he was a clearheaded doctor acting in an emergency. The sight of his friend, a friend whom he'd loved and whom perhaps he'd betrayed, this would wait to be understood later. Suicide is a mystery never to be fully unfolded. But why did Emmett come here to die?

The elevator doors opened. There, coming out, was one of the oddest-looking men Dr. Kimura had ever seen.

The sun was low in the sky. Bright light struck off the river and shattered on the tile and chrome of the foyer where Kimura stood while the man scurried out of the elevator. How like a rabbit, Kimura thought. I should follow.

A small man with anaemic skin and pink teary eyes, he almost knocked Kimura off his crutches on his way out. The Rabbit must have thought that the elevator had stopped at the lobby and was confused to find himself at the lower level accessing the underground garage on one side and the patio doors on the other, leading out to the garden built there for the shared enjoyment of the residents. The Rabbit made a fussy movement toward the patio, pivoted, and scuttled toward the doors to the garage.

"Those are locked," Kimura told him, getting into the elevator. He held the door open. "You'll have to exit at L."

So the little man returned and said nothing of thanks or greeting while the elevator rose again, and at the lobby he hustled off blindly into the glaring sun reflecting from the tall glass windows of Dr. Kimura's apartment building.

◇

Dr. Kimura didn't move out of his penthouse, as people expected him to do. He found the view exquisite, eloquent, and secretive. The private Dr. Kimura didn't give up his penthouse. But he seemed to age quickly, and he retired from practising medicine to focus on importing anaesthetic equipment from Ohio with his friend, Robert Morton, who returned to his position with the RCMP, leaving the daily business in Kimura's capable hands.

Kimura found solace in his efforts to help the boy, James, and his elegant mother settle in Ottawa. He felt himself their guardian, their protector, and this was a source of great comfort to him.

The placid, duplicitous scenery intrigued Kimura more than ever before. He loved his winter view of the icy river and the frozen garden, the snowy hyphens of its iron railing. It kept his lost friend Emmett in mind, ever present.

◇

Years later, at Robert Morton's thirty-fifth wedding anniversary, Kimura rose unsteadily (due to drink; his knee had been replaced) to make a toast. "To Robert and his wonderful wife, Maxine, lovelier than ever," he said. "May we never forget all that we can never really understand. May we always honour the Maxine," and here he laughed at himself, "the *maxim* — that the only thing we know is love. And sometimes, my good friends, we must struggle with ourselves to know even that.

"Love is the light by which we discover our way. Love," Dr. Kimura said, "is information." And then, seeing the indulgence in the smiles on Robert Morton's adult children's faces as they stared into the bubbles of their champagne, Dr. Kimura sat down.

◇

Blue Sea Lake, 1964

Lenore slid the canoe down the sloping granite shore, put one long leg in the bow, and shoved off. She sat in the bow because it's easier to steer from there when you're alone. The morning was calm, the water glassy, doubling the shoreline in perfect reflection, the aspen and poplar in full leaf. Late summer, when the season was nearly turning. She paddled out toward the reef. A seagull was sunning itself there while a cormorant drifted nearby. The seagull lifted off when she approached. But the cormorant stayed, undulating its snaky black neck.

Lennie let the canoe drift, the current turning her toward the cottage. She saw her mother come outside, cross the lawn to the shore, and sit on the rocks there. Over the water, they were aware, one of the other. Nearly two years since her father's death.

Her mother laughed the other day. Then covered her mouth with her hand. She didn't want to be happy, but happiness wanted her.

Her father could only tell her about hope. How all his mistakes had been made out of a wish to be good. He was hungry for something, always hungry. People must be crazy, dreaming themselves up. It made them dangerous, even when they didn't think they were. Then they were sorry.

In his letter, given to her by Mr. Morton that day, her father wrote, "To protect you from myself, I have pretended to be an aspect of you."

Lenore has decided that she's going to be an actress. She thinks that this is the kindest way to live, to give people something to believe in for a little while. She would be an actress and an artist and go to Japan with her brother, James, and they would look after each other.

Her mother was leaving the shore now and walking away. Lennie saw that she was carrying her camera. This was the first time she'd touched it since Dad died. It meant that Lennie was freer than she'd been yesterday. Some people have to work so hard even to pretend to be someone.

Everyone already lives inside her. It makes her ache with sorrow, but Lennie will accommodate the whole world. She can do this without even trying very hard. Because she has talent. She knows she does.

You just have to breathe, breathe in the ocean of air. Because higher than air, we're infinite. And to be infinite is to be all the people, those who were here and are now gone, those who are not you, and all the people you are, from the moment you're born till the day you die, all those hungry creations combined into one great white noise. But infinity hurts in the human heart. Her father is nearly two years gone. Lennie knows that, all along, even since the very beginning when light was first invented, time's passing has been our blessing. Time was created to ease our pain. The cormorant suddenly opens and spreads its slate black wings, and lake water sprays like shattered crystals in the sun. Here is perfection.

Notes and Acknowledgements

Thanks to Peter Wakayama and Ken Noma for meeting with me when I was first researching this novel, and similarly Dylan MacNeil and Chris Baker. Many thanks to my friends who read earlier drafts —Dan Diamond, Jacky Sawatzky, Glenn Buhr, and Catherine Hunter. To the people at *Prairie Fire Magazine*, live long and prosper.

I am grateful to the Manitoba Arts Council, the Winnipeg Arts Council, and the Canada Council for the Arts for their support during the writing of *Mr. Jones*. To the University of Winnipeg, my affection and gratitude.

Thank you Goose Lane Editions; you are the best. Thank you Heather Sangster. And I'm so very grateful to the gifted editor, Bethany Gibson, who rode through all the dust storms, corralling the strays. Any errors in these pages are mine alone.

An excerpt of *Mr. Jones* in different form appeared in *Prairie Fire Magazine* Vol. 30, No. 1.

These are some of the writers and their books that have helped me in writing *Mr. Jones*:

Roger Bowen. *Innocence is not Enough: The Life and Death of Herbert Norman*. Vancouver: Douglas & McIntyre, 1986.

Ian Buruma. *Inventing Japan: 1853-1964*. New York: The Modern Library, 2004.

John Hersey. *Hiroshima*. New York: Knopf, 1946. (And my thanks to Steve Rothman, who made his 1997 background essay, "The Publication of 'Hiroshima' in *The New Yorker*," available on the internet.)

William Manchester. *American Caesar: Douglas MacArthur, 1880-1964*. Toronto: Little, Brown and Company, 1978.

Gary Marcuse and Reg Whitaker. *Cold War Canada: The Making of a National Insecurity State, 1945-1957*. Toronto: University of Toronto Press, 1994.

Knowlton Nash. *Kennedy and Diefenbaker: Fear and Loathing Across the Undefended Border*. Toronto: McClelland & Stewart, 1990.

Kim Philby. *My Silent War: The Autobiography of a Spy*. New York: The Modern Library, 1968, 2002.

Charles Taylor. *Snow Job: Canada, the United States and Vietnam (1954 to 1973)*. Toronto: Anansi, 1974.

Specifics

The epigraph is from Bob Dylan's song, "Ballad of a Thin Man." Copyright © 1965 by Warner Bros. Inc.; renewed 1993 by Special Rider Music. All rights reserved. International copyright secured. Reprinted by permission.

Pages 13 and 97: the references are to John Hersey's *Hiroshima*.

Page 35: Leonard is quoting from Walter Benjamin's essay, "The Storyteller: Reflections on the Work of Nikolai Leskov." *Illuminations*. Translated by Harry Zohn. Copyright © 1955 by Suhrkamp Verlag, Frankfurt A.M. English translation copyright © 1968 and renewed 1996 by Houghton Mifflin Harcourt Publishing Company. Reprinted by permission of Houghton Mifflin Publishing Company. All rights reserved.

Page 42: Leonard is quoting from Friedrich Nietzsche's *Thus Spoke Zarathustra*: the "Midnight Song," or "The Intoxicated Song."

Pages 36 and 46: Karl Marx's famous aphorism is from *The Eighteenth Brumaire of Louis Bonaparte*. (1852) New York: International Publishers, 1963. Marx wrote: "Hegel remarks somewhere that all great world-historic facts and personages appear, so to speak, twice.

He forgot to add: the first time as tragedy, the second time as farce." And, "Men make their own history, but they do not make it as they please; they do not make it under self-selected circumstances, but under circumstances existing already, given and transmitted from the past. The tradition of all dead generations weighs like a nightmare on the brains of the living."

Page 42: Rachel quotes (vaguely) from Marx, *The German Ideology*.

The song on page 66 is "The Preacher and the Slave" by Joe Hill, 1911.

On page 89, Suzanne quotes a line from the film *Double Indemnity*, directed by Billy Wilder (with a screenplay by Billy Wilder and Raymond Chandler), 1944.

Pages 106 and 388: In his essay called "The Perversion of Human Needs" Karl Marx wrote:

> Alienation is apparent not only in the fact that *my* means of life belong to *someone else*, that *my* desires are the unattainable possession of *someone else*, but that everything is *something different* from itself, that my activity is *something else*, and finally (and this is also the case for the capitalist) that *an inhuman power* rules over everything. There is a kind of wealth which is inactive, prodigal and devoted to pleasure, the beneficiary of which *behaves* as an *ephemeral*, aimlessly active individual who regards the slave labor of others, human *blood and sweat*, as the prey of his cupidity and sees mankind, and himself, as a sacrificial and superfluous being. Thus he acquires a contempt for mankind, expressed in the form of arrogance and the squandering of resources which would support a hundred human lives, and also in the form of the infamous illusion that his unbridled extravagance and endless unproductive consumption is

a condition for the *labor* and *subsistence* of others. He
regards the realization of the *essential powers* of man only
as the realization of his own disorderly life, his whims
and his capricious bizarre ideas.

(Written in1844. Weird emphasis his.)

Pages 126-127: MacArthur's admiration of Napoleon, Genghis
Khan, Abraham Lincoln and George Washington, and expressions of
fear of "communistic slavery" are variations of William Manchester's
quotations of MacArthur in his biography, *American Caesar: Douglas
MacArthur, 1880-1964*.